THE GREAT MOON LANDING

KNUT HORVEI ESPESETH

INK START MEDIA
5710 W Gate City Blvd Ste K #284
Greensboro, NC 27407

CONTENTS

"And this shall be Our Moon Landing."
—From Prime Minister Stoltenberg's
New Year's Speech, NRK, 2006

But was it rockets and a race to the moon he was thinking about, Prime Minister Stoltenberg?

Join the Third Man in pursuit of the blueprints for what would become the world's most advanced CO2 treatment plant. The drawings the Russians thought were about something completely different, namely establishing a rocket base at the North Pole itself.

COMMENTS FROM THE AUTHOR

For a time, I worked on an export project for the Republic of Azerbaijan.

During this time, I regularly met people who claimed to represent the marketing community in the country. Some likely were just that, supported by the equivalent from Moscow, especially from Vnestorgreklama. But I also met the others, a lieutenant, a major, and even a colonel who were all former KGB, now mainly connected to the FSB, the national Intelligence, and the later Intelligence for foreign countries, the SVR.

Attempts to recruit me to the KGB were made both during stays in Helsinki, Caracas, and at home in Oslo.

I'm sure there's a file on me somewhere. But the Norwegian Intelligence Services received continuous reports from me.

I do not know why I was of interest. Admittedly, in our company, we undertook many assignments for Norwegian industrial giants. In addition, I had previously been a high-ranking officer in the largest Norwegian EEC organisation. Perhaps a case of the slightly worn-out "right man in the right place, at the right time."

I received many invitations to visit the Soviet Union but declined. Simply didn't dare. Afraid the return ticket would be missing.

So it remained a case of being treated, wined, and dined here in Oslo, privately, in the embassy and restaurants in Oslo and Helsinki in connection with work, i.e., on a commercial basis.

When the Azerbaijani mission was completed and our company had received its payment, I made a final report to the Intelligence, and that was that.

But I kept looking over my shoulder for a while afterward.

Had I argued too much for Sakharov or Solzhenitsyn? Or other so-called dissidents? Both were regular "touches" in all our lunches.

Almost thirty years later, it does not seem that one has finished what some call the Treholt era and the idea of allowing a character in a novel relive what happened and not the least what we do not know about happened, but which is fiction, occurred. But anything could have happened. Later as well.

Not least because of the prime minister's speech regarding "Our Moon Landing," which our Eastern European friends also thought was something quite different!

PREFACE

The novel is in large parts fiction. Most of the characters and their actions cannot thus be linked to actual people or activities.

However, the quote from Stoltenberg's speech to the Norwegian people about the moon landing is authentic. The meetings with the KGB and the Intelligence Services in Oslo and the initial contact with the Russian Embassy are also real.

So are parts of the events in Romania.

Some of the experiences in Trondheim are also based on facts.

Apart from this, the novel is pure fiction.

However, the Russians are believed to have planted a flag in the mountains beneath the North Pole ice using a mini submarine. Reference: statements in the Russian media.

Everything taking place in Moscow is fiction. The same applies to the measures undertaken by the former KGB, now FSB/SVR, in the second part of the novel.

The meeting with the US intelligence colonel and his family is based on facts, even though the NATO HQ in Brussels subsequently categorically denies the existence of the person as well as his family.

Perhaps you would not expect anything else?

Unauthorised sources suggest that more than four thousand Norwegians will be involved in surveillance and counterespionage for Norway, in Norway. Some claim the number is several times higher. The police are not part of this number. Foreign countries' agents in Norway are sometimes considered to be about five thousand.

So things are taking place in our tiny country. Something that the media does not touch either, because it does not dare to. Or for the sake of our national security, as it is often referred to. The handsome man on the tram may not be the good Norwegian you think he is. Maybe he's a former policeman hired by a foreign country.

But the author is left asking himself how it is possible that those friendly, pleasant people he has met along the way suddenly are nonexistent. They've just disappeared or changed their identities.

Finally, why involve Treholt? The answer is simple. His mention is almost inevitable. He belongs to the era along with the novel's protagonist Tor and blends in as part of the backdrop and as a concrete example of how Intelligence operated at the time. And how the politicians acted—some of them.

The author's point is that Treholt was caught precisely because he hardly had anything to hide, was harmless. But he was a person on whom issues could easily be pinned, not least to have someone to target, someone you could hang your hat on, upward in our political systems.

This is in sharp contrast to the novel's protagonist Tor, the active type who moved documents and information. As some probably did in real life. And as the author was to be enlisted to do.

In real terms, Moscow was always incredibly well informed about Norwegian conditions. Were the leaks never found? Did channels exist, like the one with Tor, where the real treats were transmitted?

In such a context, the episode with Treholt becomes a slightly exciting James Bond story and nothing else. A pure diversion, experts would say. Although my neighbor, a journalist during the trial, gave me his daily dose of Treholt's alleged spying, I am equally firm in believing that he was not a real spy.

Undoubtedly the discussion around the so-called proof of money has not weakened his case, has it? Give a man a life sentence for something that could be called playing espionage at best. My Russian, Ukrainian, and Romanian friends are shaking their heads, back then, like now. Even the CIA colonel just smiled a "no comment."

The author never met Treholt, other than in the crowd during the EEC campaign in 1972. (But I met his family though.)

What was it with us Norwegians? Did we need someone to hang? Did we? Or was it the Labour Party that needed it? And what became of the real spies or traitors who must have given the KGB and the later SVR complete information about everything worth knowing?

Because the Russians knew "everything," it would turn out, in retrospect.

It's hardly doubtful that "Our Moon Landing" swirled up a lot of dust, at least in the East. And it will probably continue to do so in our domestic arena as well, but then as a metaphor for a facility in Western Norway, a facility with a huge price tag.

And finally, I'm sure the Stay Behind movement was real enough. Maybe I'll have to look over my shoulder again.

DEAR READER

Tor is the novel's protagonist, the advertising man and former courier for the KGB. Always obsessed about his innocence: "Not a spy, just a courier." Married to Astrid, who in turn is the sister of Samuel, the rocket specialist employed by SINTEF. On the Russian side: Igor, KGB lieutenant (later SVR); the Mongolian Khan, who rose to the rank of major at the GRU; and finally Donetski, head of an intelligence cell in the Russian Ministry of Foreign Affairs.

But other characters make an appearance along the way. I specifically mention: the "Cobra," colonel of the KGB (SVR); Omar, agent of the KGB in Transylvania; Oskar, the nationalist from Stay Behind; Theodore, American colonel in charge of Intelligence on the Eastern Hemisphere; Maria, a spy for KGB (SVR) while working for North Korea; Anna, a central part of Omar's network; Bente, the pretty girl who was used as a decoy; Kosin, KGB man and spy for North Korea; Chernikov, embassy secretary in Oslo; and last but not least, Treholt, the former Norwegian civil servant.

ACKNOWLEDGMENTS

A thank you to the doctors Gunnar, Oslo and Pierre, Nice, as well as the specialist nurses, Therese and the others at Aker Urology

Together, they have helped me obtain the strength to carry out this project. And finally, Guillaume Mary, the chiropractor in Antibes.

1

June 1, 2006

"Grandpa, there's a man here who wants to talk to you."

"Where?"

"On the stairs, at the main entrance."

Damn, now that everything was just peace and a cold beer, and he was free to enjoy it all.

A man in a long, dark coat, which appeared comical in this scorching late June day in which virtually the whole world wore shorts or were simply naked. Even the birds had hidden in the foliage of the birch alley. His face was pale, the sun notwithstanding, it was kind of closed, and there was something rough about the features. Hardly more than thirty if he was even that age. Lived a rough life, this guy. Short cut by the ears and almost slightly spiked. It must have gone out of fashion a long time ago, not? Feeling slightly tucked up in the diaphragm.

Could it be? No, it couldn't. The old days were the old days, were behind him, at least ten years behind. He still pushed his granddaughter away from the door and into the house. Closed the door carefully. Not worth taking any chances. The tingling in his stomach wouldn't stop, and he kind of felt a cold breath from the neck down. Cold in this heat, at 32 degrees? This had to be a warning. Tor strode a little with his legs to get a better balance. Automatically lowered the behind to be safer. An old trick that one. Sensation of throat clearing, but did not want to show weakness and so swallowed it. Looked the man into the eyes and with a cold, calm voice said, "All right, what can I do for you?"

"You don't know me, but you're the Third Man, right?"

Was there a faint burr sound? Emigrated from Bergen or Eastern European, Russian? And yet such a good Oslo dialect, almost without an accent? At that moment, Tor knew the past had caught up with him.

2

Moscow, New Year's Day, 2006

It had long since turned to evening in Moscow when the phone rang at Commissioner Donetski's house. He originally hailed from Ukraine and was called Menchkov but had quickly been nicknamed Donetski after the city of Donetsk, his origin.

"An important message from Oslo."

"Who says it's important?"

"I don't know." He could hear the cypher phantom straightening up and banging his heels together. "But it's coded at the highest priority."

"Get the ambassador. And send the car. I'll be there in twenty minutes."

Damn, to be brought in at this hour. The Black Volga arrived within minutes.

The evening with TV and the family around the fireplace was ruined. He had another vodka before making it down the stairs—coat and fur hat on the arm. Minus 25 and then this message encoded to the highest priority?

He was still athletic, had looked after his physique. The past with the elite troops of the Spetznaz had built the foundation. Tall, straight back, narrow around the waist still. Always wore the same suit. If it got worn out, he would just buy another one just like it. The shirts were the same greyish-white, and the tie? Black, of course, suitable for work as well as funerals. Because that's what life was all about now, yes, and then the family.

The blue light alerted him to the importance of the issue at hand, and not more than ten minutes passed, then he was on his way up the lift at the Ministry of Foreign Affairs.

"Ambassador Malekov? Where is he? You have him on a secure line?"

"Yes, but he's in Stalingrad with his family."

"Stalingrad? It's not Russian New Year yet!"

"No, but he's on sick leave."

"What happened, Boris?"

"I don't know more than you, other than that an encrypted message has arrived, marked the highest priority."

"Who's in Oslo?"

"Embassy Secretary Chernikov."

"Get him and the SVR in charge over here on the first plane."

"Our machine won't run until the day after tomorrow, and I don't have powers to do this."

"Don't worry about it. You act on my authority, put them on Finnair or whatever. Just get them here."

Yes, the message. Transcript of the speech of the Norwegian prime minister, Stoltenberg. "And this is going to be our moon landing!" The moon landing and CO2. Could it be a bad translation? Should he sound off a full alarm?

Norway didn't have any rockets that could reach the moon. Admittedly, they had carried out some simple satellite launches at Andøya up in the North, but the moon? And billions were to be invested. CO2? That's not fuel for rockets! What kind of silly message was this?

Was the whole thing a covert thing?

So little Norway was going to start billion-dollar investments in the Arctic? Svalbard was delicate enough, if there was nothing more to come. Were the Americans on their way through missile installations at Andøya? Everything under the guise of a CO2 treatment plant no one really needed.

Perhaps one should analyse the message in the context of the government's declaration of accession and its new offensive foreign minister?

He was in his own spacious office now, just beyond Foreign Minister Lavrov. It was Gromyko who wanted him placed near his own office.

The most recent file on Norway was brought out. Didn't want having things of a sensitive nature on a computer or network. Norway's foreign minister, there he was. Poor imagery, but good enough for the purpose. Way too young for that kind of job. So was the prime minister.

And what about the political platform of this Norwegian foreign minister? Lots of old money and education from France, the very best as such. But still. He remembered there had been a lot of protests at the appointment. Too friendly with the Americans, not much contact with working people.

Donetski scraped his heels under his desk. New times were just that, new times. And the translation from the interview? Who the hell could read Norwegian?

Now, there it was.

"The High North will be our most important priority area. Getting a good dialogue with the Russians will be priority number 1. But we shall be treated as equal partners."

So little Norway? The Minister of the Law of the Sea, Jens Evensen, had been nagging about the same thing more than twenty years ago. The commission with him and then this Treholt in the hallway. But our man, Isjkov, was in control.

He chuckled lightly.

But a moon landing and a billion-dollar project?

Should he call the foreign minister, Lavrov? The time was already 21:30, and this wasn't Gromyko, no. Him he could call 24/7, if it was important enough.

And yet? He should send a vehicle with a personal message and request a meeting whenever the foreign minister wished so. It would take an hour out to the dacha. But he would have to be waiting in case the minister wanted to meet tonight.

3

Moscow, 21:35

"Meeting tomorrow morning? At 8? All right, all right. And who else? Will you book the meeting? All right."

It used to be his job. Not anymore, just over a year until his retirement, so really, he was already out of the game. He was still in charge of Norway, but a young up-and-coming was on his way here as well, total FSB. Fluent in English and German. And quite up to it in Norwegian as well. The cypher secretary hadn't found him since he hadn't been contacted, or could it be that the cypher secretary preferred to deal with the old foxes?

Age, he tasted it. When would he lose his car and the driver?

He didn't go home, but he called and mentioned it was the couch in the office, an early meeting. Norway's new prime minister had to find out something more about him.

Of course, he knew his father, from Belgrade—yes, at least he'd greeted him. But Lavrov and Stoltenberg Sr. were probably well acquainted with each other.

But this Jens who managed to squeeze Jagland out. He did do it in a rather simple fashion with his 36.9, Jagland. Political scientist and probably intelligent enough this, Stoltenberg Jr. But again, young! Very young. Just like the new foreign minister. Could probably swirl up some dust the two youngsters. Because that's what they were. Not even turned fifty.

Somewhat like Kennedy, he chuckled again at the thought of the Bay of Pigs. *We took one on the chin there from young Kennedy, but he didn't live long after that.* Who was really to blame? The FBI and Hoover? Some knew, but the truth would probably die with the few lefts from that time.

Fourteen months to go now and he would be done with it all.

Going to take the wife and move to the dacha as he'd wanted for a long time.

Then the kids and grandchildren would come to visit Grandpa in the countryside. Woke up from the daydreams from hard knocks on the door.

The guard?

He'd forgotten to inform the staff of his stay. New this one. Correctly asked for ID. Corrected the gun holster, clicked his heels, and walked off.

No excuse for waking people up in the middle of the night. New times now.

During Gromyko's era, the guard would have been thrown on the first train heading to Siberia and the Urals.

He dozed off again, fell asleep properly, and was woken up by Lavrov, who entered without knocking.

"Good morning!"

"Of course, good morning!" Donetski's head almost lifted from the rest of his body, which lay twisted on the sofa. "But the time's not more than 6:00 yet."

"That's right, we'll go to my office, I've ordered coffee."

Wow, and he had planned to dig up information about the boys in Oslo. Now he couldn't do it.

"This could be serious, Donetski. What do you think Little Father will think about this?"

"It could be a hoax, and it's really just a bit of circus for the people. You know, New Year's speech, so you must come up with something. Portray yourself as dynamic, right? Or what do you think? Is he driving forward the environmental case to break Little Brother (the left socialist party) or should I say Little Sister?"

"You mean the party the lady in red comes from? She always wears red now, you know, at least when she's appearing on TV."

Lavrov wore a broad grin, as wide as it went early in the morning.

"Clever and experienced this Halvorsen, Lavrov. But to the issue at hand. Since this is his first major speech as prime minister in the new government, he goes all out spending some oil billions on extinguishing political fires. And the thing about a facility no one knows how to build."

"I didn't know you were so well informed, Comrade Donetski."

"It is our neighboring country, and they have influence not least because of oil and gas."

"Can see that and what couldn't have happened to the price level of their petrol, if we had kept our pipe through Ukraine closed for a long, very long time. Or what do you think, Donetski?"

They were interrupted by the night watchman who brought the coffee.

"I, for my part, believe that this is a domestic political matter. Worse with the blowout from their foreign minister about this issue concerning the High North. But surely cleared by the prime minister."

"Maybe so." Lavrov was in a hurry. "But we'll take the meeting for the sake of it. It is just you and I who know anything about this country. Little Nikolayevich has a lot to learn yet."

"Don't forget, him and Little Father have a common history from Germany though."

"Is that a rebuke, Comrade Donetski? Is my memory of our positions at work so unclear?"

"I'm sorry! You know I'm too old to do stuff like that, Comrade Lavrov. But hey, everything would have been more accessible if we had the Norway channel like before."

"You mean Treholt?"

Donetski laughed out loud now. "No, I mean the channel through the Third Man. We just called him that. Together, we monitored Treholt and Colonel Titov."

"How could you monitor the colonel? By the way, I guess he became a general in the end."

"Promote them and fire them," Gromyko would say. Lavrov seemed to ignore the comment. Was this sarcasm directed at him, well camouflaged? Donetski was quite outspoken.

"But does this Third Man still exist or no?"

"Unfortunately, our main contact has retired from the Ministry of Defense, but the operational arm, it can be found in Oslo."

"You are talking in riddles, comrade. Is the Third Man still there, or is he not?"

"He exists!"

"Thank you, that's what I wanted to know. And, Comrade Donetski, in your opinion, we can reopen the channel?"

"Yes, but we have to get back inside the Ministry of Defense, get a new contact there, and it may take some time."

"Do we really have to? Isn't this case directly under the prime minister and the foreign minister? I think so. So what about the Third Man?"

"He was the courier, the one we could trust, always."

"Donetski, I feel like we have something here and not least, we're ahead of Little Father, and it's not often the case, right?"

Easy chuckling now.

"I think we'll skip the whole meeting, cancel for me, and I'll go straight to Little Father at his dacha. I'll call you later today, so stay here."

"What about SVR? Should they not get informed, not just receive an order?"

"Don't stretch this further, Comrade Donetski. I'll call you later. Didn't I say that?"

"Of course, Comrade Foreign Minister."

So it had been said. The SVR was to be kept out of it for now! He chuckled at the thought. But they would probably come running when they found out about the summons of the SVR boss in Oslo.

The foreign minister, yes. Perhaps it was possible to achieve some good cooperation with Lavrov now at the end of his career.

4

Putin

Just over an hour later, the foreign minister arrived. Saw a man on horseback, some ten meters or so away. Dressage seems to be what it is called. Not for him, but he knew his boss loved to sit on horseback, like many heads of state through the ages. Thought of Julius Caesar and Napoleon. Not that Poutinovitch was not tall enough. But he would probably had preferred to be even taller. *Watch out now, Lavrov, imagine if anyone could read your thoughts.*

The cold vapor from the horse brought him back to reality. Maybe he should have made a call in advance, but at this point, it was too late.

"Drive toward that fence and wait."

The driver dropped him off some distance away from the rider. Biting cold, 25 minus at least, and he was happy about the thick boots as he was left standing and feeling some cold in the faint morning light. But the rider had seen him and came in straight gallops. He didn't feel cold, no, even in light workout attire. At least he didn't want it to be obvious. No doubt, it was "the Czar," as some disrespectfully referred to him. Elegantly dismounting from the horse.

"Do you have a blanket, comrade?"

So he did feel cold after all. Lavrov was quick to get a blanket out of the car. Putin patted the horse and stroked him by the throat before placing the blanket over him. So that's the way it was. The valuable horse had to be cared for. Putin gave a brief message on the phone that the horse should be picked up immediately, groomed, and put in the stables.

"So, Comrade Lavrov, what brings you here unannounced? Not just to interfere with my morning workout?" Putin seemed utterly relaxed and unmoved by the cold.

"I'm sorry, Mr. President, but it's probably worse than that."

"Oh, such a formal tone. This has to be important."

They got in the car; the driver was told to go out and have a smoke.

"But stay away from the horse."

Lavrov provided a brief summary and concluded with the proposal to reopen the Oslo/Moscow channel.

"Excellent, Lavrov. So we'll go ahead and have a flag planted at the North Pole, immediately and underwater."

"Underwater?"

"Yes, of course underwater, on solid, mountainous ground! Do you know, Comrade Lavrov, that in five, maybe six years, there will be no ice at the North Pole itself, at least not all year round?"

The facial expression was one of bafflement.

"Climate change, Comrade Lavrov. Climate change."

"But how do we do this?"

"We use submarines, of course! Get the driver inside and take me up to the dacha, and you can take the day off too."

Was the flag under the North Pole more important than Norway's lunar landing? Lavrov didn't understand a lot right now. But he had things well under control, Little Father. Was there anything he wasn't well briefed on? And now this thing about climate change? I'm sure he'd heard the rumors. When others were done for the evening, the boss continued online. Did he never sleep that man?

As he was about to wave goodbye, then came the final confirmation that he and Donetski were waiting for:

"But, Lavrov, start the channel first, and if you could use little Nikolayevich for something, that would be nice. Bright little fellow."

He could have done well without the last part. But it would be nice to have Igor Nikolayevich sent out of the country. It probably suited Donetski well, too. But the boy in all glory. Now he might need his idiotic immersion in Norwegian.

5

July 3, 1980, Utheim

Deep in Dypfjorden Arctic Norway, on the farm Utheim, lives the small family Karoliussen, trying to survive on fish from the fjord and the small things that the farm could provide. The weather-worn houses, the storehouse that lacked a support stone on one corner, and the barn with the semi-sheer bridge—not a paint stain visible anymore. It would probably never have been painted by the previous owners either. It was all decaying.

But perhaps the worst was the farmhouse itself. Painted white a long, long time ago on the side facing the sea. But then money ran out, or perhaps they thought it wouldn't be so bad if the sides and the wall upward were worn out like a house in the slums.

Not too concerned if the occasional timber had begun to rot. The most important thing was that the house looked nice from the fjord.

The last two years had been rough on both siblings, Astrid and Samuel, the youngest of the two, and little Lars as well. The kid who came into the world in early summer two years ago had been demanding, considering the gossiping and the priest's curse. Astrid barely fifteen at the time. But everyone thought of her as being older as she quite rapidly was becoming a woman.

She gave birth at home, her mother and grandmother helped, and a so-called wise old lady, from the neighboring village, cut the string. This thing with the wise kven-lady was enough for the priest to want Astrid to be excommunicated if it had been possible. In the old days, he'd get the sheriff and throw her on the fire. But the sheriff had already been there with Astrid, and had he perhaps tasted the fruits too?

"That girl over there in Utheim is as busty as her mother—and just fifteen. Did you try your luck, I suppose you did," hinted one of the officers.

The sheriff's wife had become totally shrivelled eventually, almost twenty years older than her husband. Still, the office was one that was inherited. The old man had been overjoyed when the spinster became part of the trade, and young Gundersen could achieve the dream, sheriff already at the age of twenty-five.

There was no talk of abortion, then; her mother would have killed her. Astrid herself refused to put the kid away. But the mother should have known, nagging about who the child's father was. Astrid lied, a Swede she had met at a party in the neighboring village was the one. She'd be way too young to get in at the party. But as the booze kicked in on the boys, she was able to sneak in.

She had been spending the night with a half-aunt while preparing for the clergy interrogation. As far as she knew, this Swede, Olof, had long since gone, so she felt safe giving him up as the child's father.

But the truth was different.

It was her stepfather who had forced himself on her time and time again this winter. As if her mother wouldn't know! But why didn't she do anything about it? Was she afraid that he would throw her out or, worse, run away himself, then she would be left there alone, lonely, and destitute on the barren farm?

The last time, Astrid had cried and cried, and finally, he had let her go, wearing torn underpants and linen. They couldn't afford a bra, and their mother's old one was still a little too big. It was night, and she didn't want to risk waking up her mother. She couldn't lie in her room and cry either. The wall was next to her parents.

So why didn't her mother react that night? She must have noticed the noise and the crying, worse than ever. Oh, yes, she knew enough about it, her mother, and yet maybe she loved her husband? But how could she? The sexual abuse of her own child? Did she think it was fine to receive him in their bed just as he came straight from her daughter?

Astrid had to get out, just get out.

She walked over to the barn with a blanket in her hand and lay in the barn, crying and crying. It was like it was never going to end.

Shush, someone was at the door! But luckily, it was just Samuel, her brother.

"Are you sick, or what's wrong with you, Astrid? And why are you lying here? I just had to get out, and then I heard you were sobbing."

Soon he was with her, and thank God, she was clean tonight; her stepfather had given up halfway.

She clung to her brother the way they did in early childhood and eventually let go, and the sobbing came to an end.

He was tender, her brother. Caressed her and stroked her hair and wiped away the tears. Soon they were utterly close to each other.

"It's over now, Astrid. You don't have to tell me what it is, not tonight anyway," he said.

Then they fell asleep in the hay with a blanket covering them.

The dream was intense. The most handsome boy among the confirmands had chosen her as his girl. Not officially, of course. Then his father would have whacked him. And now, it was her turn—she the one from the fjord, her turn to be made out with and kissed by the beautiful son of Per at Verket. Even was his name, the type of boy she dreamt of. She felt his kisses gently against the hollow of the neck. The memories of the stepfather?

No, she didn't remember anything, just felt the boy's mouth move up her chin and then she felt his tongue tip on the lips, and she opened and felt his tongue against her own. Her breasts budged; at least, she had the biggest breasts of the confirmands. Marit and Eva didn't even have a hint of breasts.

There was his hand on her left breast while his tongue caught the nipple on her right, and she knew this was different, different from everything she had read about.

Different from her stepfather's cruel intrusion. She barely remembered it where she was lying, no, it was gone entirely, and she felt Even got hard down there and knew she would greet him with love and have the wounds of her stepfather's violence erased. And it was soft, and it was lovely, and he came, and she came, and she kissed him and cried a little bit and said, "Thank you because you made me clean."

It had been a cold September night, black frost up in the hillside. Soon the snow would push on.

It must have been somewhat later in the morning that Astrid suddenly was half awake from freezing, and at the same time, she heard the cow low in the barn downstairs.

The blanket was gone. She slipped open one eye, felt someone lying next to her. It wasn't Even; it was her brother Samuel. Her little brother!

Before she could react, her stepfather stood over them. He's the one who'd pulled the carpet. "You fucking whore, wasn't it enough to sleep with me without you having to seduce your brother too?"

That's when she grew up, abruptly became a grown-up. Her brother barely moved and kept sleeping. She pulled her curly underwear around her and slammed toward her father.

"You get out, and hey, as much as one word from you about this, and Mommy's going to know the whole truth! And maybe you'll receive punishment for incest!"

"Phew, she won't believe you, you slut!"

"What's happening, Arne, and why are you all here in the barn, yes, and Samuel too?"

"No, nothing. Astrid went to look for her brother, and I heard noises and came to see what it was."

He could tell that his wife didn't believe the explanation without further ado.

"But why are you yelling at Astrid, who's standing there half-naked? Put some clothes on, girl." She threw her the apron.

"That's exactly what I was going to tell you about, that she's running around out here with no clothes on her body. Breasts like an adult. Maybe she's older than I knew. Do you think she's had a suitor here? I wouldn't be damned." He laughed a little to smooth it all over.

The mother seemed content with this explanation, and Astrid ran in and up to her room while the other two were left standing.

I don't think this is completely over, the stepfather thought. He would have to restrain himself now, would he not? Incest? Oh, he wasn't the father. So maybe the charge would be unlawful sexual intercourse with a minor.

Had she dreamed, or had she slept with her brother?

She felt herself down there—she sure was wet.

Oh, Lord, the creator of the heavens, slept with her own brother!

But it had been so peaceful and good. Finally, the wounds from the stepfather had been repaired.

But now? Now what?

Could she live with this?

And what about her brother? Did he know what he'd been a part of?

Maybe he'd wake up and notice he'd gotten wet too? Of course, he would.

But boys could experience ejaculation just by themselves and wake up with it, that is what she had heard. Then let him believe just that. One ruined life was enough—yes, hers. Because her stepfather would hardly let himself be bothered by what he had been involved in, time and time again.

His conscience, if he had any, was indeed long hardened. Quietly, she dressed.

"I'm going to milk Rosalind, Mom."

"Thanks, my child."

My child, she should have known.

It was a great comfort to start working, and after a while, she was singing and stroked the cow across her neck. So that's how it was, sleeping with someone she loved. She still felt something delicious down there. And it wasn't her brother who she'd given it to. It was Even.

Halfway through the milking, she noticed someone was standing at the barn door.

"Where did you sleep last night, sister?"

She felt the blush pressed on but hid her face as best she could under the cow.

"I was lying next to you for a while before I went back inside. Then I went out and placed you on the blanket until this morning. Dad came looking for you and Mom, too. Why were you lying out there by the way?"

"Yes, but are you completely lost?"

"I went out to comfort you, don't you remember?"

"Thank you, Samuel, I guess I'm the one talking nonsense. I just fell asleep a little, I did, before I went in, and you, yes, you slept like a rock, so I didn't have the heart to wake you."

Then all the lies were said, and the four of them settled.

She sifted the milk in the portico, but she knew, and her stepfather knew, and indeed her mother knew that nothing was true. But her brother had been spared and would still be for many years to come.

6

July 23, 1980, Dypfjorden

The boy turned two on this day, the first day of Russian summer heat, the temperature would reach well above 30 degrees.

The Karoliussens, sister and brother, were hiking along the west bank of Dypfjorden.

She was seventeen, and he was barely sixteen. Little Lars was in the back of the boat.

They changed rowing. Right now, it was Samuel rowing, so she had plenty of time to study both him and the landscape, mainly the first, though she made sure to avoid staring too much. Otherwise, Samuel would probably stop and ask why she was staring. But in the corner of her eye, she could see Samuel was waiting for something. Waiting for a problematic question, maybe?

Since that night at the barn, they hadn't talked about what happened at all. It was a topic not to be mentioned.

But it would have been strange if Samuel hadn't noticed that he'd been inside her and that he was there a long time. Why did he never talk about it? Because he thought it was too embarrassing or because he was afraid of the idea that someone would know—that he had slept with his sister and, worst of all, that they both had enjoyed it. He as well! So it was intentional incest and not rape.

Should she bring it up at the right occasion, or should she wait until he brought it up? No, if he had decided never to bring it up, she would help leave it forgotten forever.

But it wasn't just the two of them who were in control of the matter.

Astrid left thoughts of incest and sex between siblings alone. Soon, the two of them were sitting next to each other rowing, and the speed of the boat was increasing. Easy to navigate that Finnmark-type four-oared boat. There was a happy tiny pinch from the little child at the stern, and then the thoughts came flying again. Was it her stepfather or was it her brother? Preferably the last one, she thought again. She felt right there and then that now she had to finish this. Just the fact that her stepfather could be the father made her want the life for her own child. It was spinning around in her head. "It's the Swede Olof who's the father," they said down at the Coop. Thank God he left before anyone could figure it out. Perhaps he would have claimed his right if he had been up here and been charged with paternal responsibility. But now, she wanted it to be her brother to be the child's father and be done with it forever. It was no worse than in many other small areas where it could be a long distance to the neighboring farm. She once again clung to the hope that this would be the truth. Was the truth!

Thanks to the sheriff, she was allowed to be confirmed in spite of her age and her motherhood. The priest had been very unaccommodating, but after a visit from the sheriff, things finally went smoothly. He didn't quite understand why the sheriff put so much into this. Maybe there was a connection with the girl's mother from before?

Yes, who would know? There were tight-knit communities up here in the North. At home in Hamar, in the south of Norway, something like this could never have been accepted.

What he didn't know was that Astrid had been in the sheriff's office for questioning about the child. The sheriff had sent the officer to the house and had threatened her with imprisonment and worse.

And when Astrid started crying, he placed her in his lap. She couldn't help it; the tears just flowed when he penetrated her. But then it was over. This was the cost of getting confirmed and avoid punishment. Because the sheriff knew very well what had been happening in Utvik. It was not just the stepfather. The girl had probably misled others and why should he not get to enjoy the young girl. He the one with the dried-up old bitch!

Astrid managed to suppress the encounter with the sheriff just like she suppressed her stepfather. But she knew it could only happen this one time or she would run away immediately.

But it wasn't just the mother who knew or had her suspicions. But Marte as well, someone from the confirmation hearing.

She knew, because she was the one who had been with the Swede Olof the night Astrid should have fallen pregnant. And if anyone was going to get pregnant with the Swede, it was Marte.

And Marte had actually decided that she should have a chat with Astrid's mother about the issue. In return for some silver spoons that suddenly disappeared, she swore to shut up and the Swede Olof? He never came back to the village.

"I think I have a big one, Astrid. Bring the fish hoof!"

She ran after, into the water, too, thoroughly wet her feet. But with the excitement of the big fish hitting with its tail out there, she got as excited as her brother, and they shouted and screamed at each other. No one else was using otter for fishing in the fjord. Still, Samuel had imagined that they would use it later in the day, now it was just dipping at a reasonable distance from the shore when it all happened, and he had been quick to give out more line.

It had to be big, the fish, maybe a big one of ten kilos or more, and to catch it with an otter. For sure, no one would imagine that was possible.

Samuel was completely crazy, standing in his stepfather's rubber boots a long way from shore. It took an hour for them to get it in the shallows, and Samuel could finish it mercifully with a pebble.

"But where has the kid gone, Lars?"

"He's probably sleeping in the dinghy around the headland."

Samuel tried to calm her down. But she was already running.

"The dinghy's gone," he heard her shouting. Then he set off, too. A fresh breeze dragged across the fjord.

And the dinghy? It wasn't to be seen. On the other hand, they saw the contours of something black that appeared far away in the fjord. Was it a wreck? Of a cargo boat, maybe? Or? Was it a submarine? Yes, that's where the tail-fin appeared, and there were people there. Then it was gone. The periscope also disappeared, and they glimpsed the remains of the white-painted dinghy. They must have collided.

But the kid, where was he?

Had he been on board the dinghy that had drifted off into the fjord? They walked along the shore and shouted and shouted, but no answers.

Could he be in the waters further out? Either way, it was too far to swim out there, at least five hundred meters, and the water was cold. And when the dinghy was crushed, the kid would probably have drowned long ago.

No, they couldn't find him. His toys were not to be seen, nor the wooden horse that an uncle had whittled.

Lars must have been on the dinghy when it slammed.

Why had the submarine stopped?

Was it to pick up the kid?

Was it Norwegian, the submarine?

They quickly realised that they had to get to people and make a call to the armed forces.

But it was going to be a long way to go.

Astrid wanted to leave the fish behind, but Samuel insisted. Knew it was too late anyway. He recalled the conversation with his stepfather before they left.

"God knows who is the father of this child, Samuel. What happened between you two before I came out that night? The priest would have placed her on the fire in the old days. And you, what do you think would happen to you, Samuel?"

He hadn't been able to take any more from his stepfather, but he'd just left, not sure if Astrid had eavesdropped.

His conscience was hard at work now. Had he remembered mooring the dinghy, or had he just left it in the hope that it would be gone? But Astrid wouldn't let it drift off, would she? The dinghy was in a bay by itself, and perhaps Astrid hadn't paid particular attention either. Would a mother want the life of her own child? No, he didn't really think so, but still. It was convenient for the dinghy to disappear. So it must have been him, Samuel, who had deliberately or unconsciously not moored it. Goodbye to the shame and let everyone begin a new life. But Lars? Had he sent him to his death? Yes, maybe so, but then again there was likely a meaning to everything.

"What is on your mind, Samuel?" She was hoisting her breath going up the treeless mountain.

"I am thinking about what people will say and the priest and not to forget the sheriff."

"What do you mean? Say it then?"

"That we deliberately let the dinghy with the kid drift off and disappear."

"We're not child killers, are we, Samuel?"

"No, of course, we're not."

He would have to support his sister as best he could. But he didn't have his peace of mind. It was probably his fault, and if he had put a child on his sister that night, this was the best thing that could happen—that the kid just disappeared. Time heals all wounds, Grandma always said. She was wise. He dribbled himself into a bit of a smile for himself. Had to watch out for Astrid. She would never forgive him if he let it somehow be known that he might have let the dinghy loose, knowingly. By the way, it wasn't his kid. If it wasn't the Swede "Olof," it was indeed his stepfather's changeling.

Only in the morning did they arrive at the outermost farm after passing the mountain, taking the shortcut to the village.

Their strength almost gone, and the salmon was heavy, but they had to reach people with a phone.

It had to be the co-operative, but they were not open yet, so they had to wait until the manager showed up. But the police couldn't promise anything.

They first had to talk to the right agency in the military and then call back.

"We'll wait here," Samuel said. "At least I'll wait."

Just as well if Astrid didn't get more involved than necessary. What if they found the kid alive? But she didn't want to give way.

"No, go home and let me know. I'm going to stay here."

She got a couple of buns and a cup of coffee from the manager, and soon, half the village knew what had happened.

"Astrid, there's a phone call for you."

Hope came. Was it a Norwegian submarine, and had they rescued Lars?

"Commander Henriksen here. Am I talking to the child's mother?"

There was barely a yes across the lips.

"We had no military vessels in Dypfjorden at the time."

"What about a submarine?"

The voice was groggy.

"The answer is negative, nor are we allowed to refer to the positions of vessels."

"But it's about my child's life. Maybe it was an allied country's submarine?"

"I'm afraid I'm going to have to disappoint you again. If so, we'd have received a report a long time ago. And by the way, as a private individual, I can tell you that if, for example, there was a Russian submarine, they would never have admitted to having been within our borders."

The stepfather drew a sigh of relief, as did their mother. Finally, they could both have peace. They knew very well who the father was, although the mother sometimes doubted that it had to be Samuel. His whole face was like a copy of Samuel's from when he was a little boy. The first time she thought it clearly, she was almost shocked. Ran into the living room and taking out the drawer at the bottom of the old skillet. There were those pictures from the two, from their childhoods. The stepfather did not want them displayed, and thank God for that today.

She quickly picked out the few pictures of Samuel as a toddler and then carried them straight into the oven. Not all of them, one she kept. She started crying when she hid it in a shopping bag and then carried it out in the barn. Up under a beam, there was a space, and there it could fit, invisible to those who did not know. It was better that way, and of course, she could have been entirely wrong.

The similarity between Samuel and little Lars could have its simple explanation, in herself that is.

The memorial was simple.

Just the two neighbors and the priest and then the sheriff. Could it be murder? His officer had said candidly what others were thinking. But the sheriff had silenced him.

And kidnapping, from a submarine? The things people say! The credibility of the siblings was wearing thin as time passed. They'd probably killed him, the changeling. But would it be helpful to investigate?

The stepfather was a bit drunk one night. It was good telling Samuel that he got to get rid of him, the kid.

"Did you say that?" Astrid was upon him.

"No, are you crazy, that was just wishful thinking on my part."

He didn't have to say any more. She'd figured out what had happened. So it was murder. But if she pushed Samuel away, she had no one left.

It had to be the way it was. At least the kid was gone, maybe, no, for sure forever? But being a mother, there was hope deep in her that once far away in what was called the future, there would be a Lars. Her Lars.

Some nomadic Sami came across the wreck of a rowboat on a fine July day, on the east side of the fjord. A storm should not have built this time of year. But the waves were tall, and the boat sent to pick them had not been able to come. Perhaps it went down? Perhaps the wreck belonged to the person who was supposed to have picked them up? Had they drowned? There was an ugly mark in the bow as if it had been hit by an iron boat. Should they notify the sheriff?

"No," said the older one. "The sheriff, that means trouble for us. Maybe they think we killed someone, and then we will be receiving punishment. No, we'll pull it ashore and hide it inside the scrub here, and we can use it during the next spring."

"Shouldn't we be looking for survivors either?"

It was the fifteen-year-old girl who was brave enough to ask.

"And what will you do if we find someone? Then we'll be blamed for killing them."

"Yes, but what if we find someone alive?" She wouldn't back down.

The older man looked at the girl's father, and they started walking east, inland, towards the mountains. A few stone's throws behind followed the girl and her dog.

7

The Russian Heat

It came, continued, and thus they could salvage a lot of hay for winter feed. But finally, one day in August, it was over, and Astrid got a day to herself. Enjoyed being able to run away under the hazel, run and throw herself in the sun on dry ground.

She buttoned up some of her dress and pulled her skirt up to her knees. She had been left alone for a long time now and finally felt a longing for something in the heat from the sun to her half-naked body. But Even was probably completely unattainable by now.

She felt great and dozed off into delicious dreamland. Then she suddenly woke up as someone was lying heavily on top of her. It was her stepfather who had found her.

He put his hand over her mouth and held her down, the knee in her crotch and the other hand over her breasts. Was this the end? Was she going to get assaulted here again and be pushed down the hill?

"If you keep your mouth shut about this, Astrid, then it will be just this one time. And hey, as the sheriff got something for free, I guess I can too."

It wasn't a question; it was just a statement of fact. The sliver from his mouth ran down toward her breasts. Maybe he'd been drooling for a while. How did he find out about the sheriff? Then her right hand was loose, and she scratched him with whatever strength she had across his face. Where did the strength come from? Blood was pouring from his face, and in dismissive anger, he had both of her hands pressed on her back, drove his knee even harder into her crotch, almost through her, before he tore the dress off, from the chest down.

She closed her eyes and let the tears just flow. She wanted to live.

But then, suddenly, the weight of the stepfather disappeared. Was he done already? But through tears, she glimpsed her brother. He was still holding the cane in his hand. The blood was dripping from it.

"Did you kill him?" She had stood up and seen her stepfather lying still right next to them.

"No, I'm sorry, but it'll probably be a while before he wakes up."

Samuel went for a bucket of water, and Astrid got up to her room and got to change. To all good fortune, the mother was at the neighbors. I guess that's why her stepfather had felt safe enough to attack her.

Samuel emptied the bucket over his stepfather. "So get up and keep your peace, and I won't say anything to anyone. But the next time you try, I'll kill you!"

Astrid went south permanently a few weeks later; her brother followed. But her brother returned, even though he had also said never again Finnmark. This return journey would have consequences for both Astrid and for her brother.

The village up north, the impoverished village, yes, it was left alone for a while. However, after a couple of years, their stepfather and mother also said their goodbyes and moved to Vadsø. The neighbor received the cow and the grazing rights. No one thought the kids would come back to take care of the house.

Finally, after a few years, all traces were gone. Nature had taken the small holding back. The child? Nobody talked about him anymore. And the picture of Samuel as a kid? When the barn collapsed, it disappeared as well.

8

July 23, 1980, Dypfjorden

U5 of the Delta class was heading into Dypfjorden at periscope depth. Lieutenant Volganov was concerned about reflexes against the periscope in the bright sunlight, and there was a pointed exchange of words with Captain Tsjubolk about safety concerning patrolling U-II aircraft.

"Then dive, Lieutenant, if you're afraid. A Soviet officer doesn't know what fear is!"

The lieutenant, all white in the face, shrinks and commands, "Dive!"

"Captain, a small vessel is on a collision course," the petty officer in charge of the periscope management exclaimed.

"Cancel dive! Ten degrees starboard. Prepare to ascend."

It was the captain who was in charge again. The moment had passed for Lieutenant Volganov. Back in the machine, and the large vessel stopped.

"Surface position, okay, Captain."

"It's just some kind of a dinghy, Lieutenant. Let's see what this is before we wave Norway goodbye. Our mission has been accomplished. Let's go home. We'll dive in two minutes."

The hatch is opened, and Lieutenant Volganov, the petty officer, and two able seamen follow on the heels of the captain up the ladder.

"A little kid is in the dinghy. Seems to be sleeping."

"We can't just run away from him," the petty officer says.

"What are we going to do with a baby on board?"

Lieutenant Volganov is trying to win the hand.

"We won't be home for another eighteen hours anyway, and what are we going to do with him in the meantime. And the admiral?"

But the petty officer won't back down. Has children of his own. Twins just under two years old. The captain cuts through with a "Ready to dive in thirty seconds!"

The seamen get the boy on board. He wakes up screaming, and then he's below deck, and the diving maneuver is underway.

"We'll just ram the dinghy, so that it sinks." The hatch was already in place. "Periscope up, again." They tilt fifty meters and then full power forward. "Twenty degrees."

They don't even notice the bang. But see that the dinghy has been hit.

"Dive to a hundred meters." Then they're submerged and can head home. "You can retake command now, Volganov."

The kid screams until he gets the wooden horse and a cup of milk from a galley boy. But he stinks from a full diaper, and no one wants to do the job until the petty officer asks for relief and does the job.

"What should we call the boy, and what does the admiral say?" The nervous lieutenant was even more worried now.

"What does it say on our pennant, Lieutenant?"

The lieutenant looks at his boss.

What was this? I can't put him in charge of the vessel, the captain thinks. *He should never have been an officer.* The captain looked at him.

"Now, Lieutenant?"

"Yes, Igor, of course."

"Igor he shall be named."

"You mean the boy?"

The captain turned his back on him and left. They approach the mouth of the fjord, where there is a ridge up to fifty meters.

They noticed the sinking mines as they go over the threshold. Gradually, they go with the bow down to four hundred meters and reach the seabed. The big diesel engines are switched off, and they lie still. They hear Igor crying.

"Get the kid to shut up," the captain hissed.

On the destroyer above, stable echo is reported on the listening device, heading 180 degrees and 400 meters depth.

The officer asks the skipper if they should turn back. They're heading into the fjord. Again, they get echoes, but weaker now, and suddenly child cries cuts through. Then it turns quiet again, completely quiet.

"Stay the course into the fjord. We can't steer by cries of a child that mixes in our listening gear. Time to get rid of these old boats. We do not log this, otherwise, we will be put on land the whole bunch. But drop several depth charges just in case. Cries from a child or not."

They noticed less of the depth charges at this point, and after a short while, the signal diminishes completely, the danger passes, and they can restart and go full speed.

It never gets dark at this time of year, so it's not a question of doing periscope depth. But after a few long hours, with a whining kid, it's Murmansk, and a report is to be written.

This was the lieutenant's job.

"What do we do with the baby, uh, I mean Igor? We can't just smuggle him ashore."

"Just tell it like it is. We found him at sea and prayed for him to be sent by a nurse to the KGB's orphanage."

The lieutenant was looking forward to reporting to the admiral. But to his surprise, crews and officers were praised for the salvage operation. Not least the captain who had named the boy after the pride of the fleet.

9

Igor

Igor quickly settled in. He cried little and eventually turned into a sturdy boy. Orphanage Number 113 was the orphanage of the KGB in Murmansk.

For five year olds already, the systematic training began that would lay the foundations for the later elite school. Young Igor was baptised Lars, but no one knew that.

He wasn't so unique among all the other orphans at the orphanage. A few others also had parents just lost. Or been separated from.

Igor's story or parts of it were buried in an archive in Murmansk, in the log of the submarine Igor that was about to be chopped up or perhaps used for potato transport like the other Delta Class submarines.[1]

But eventually, someone would take an interest in this log. Someone who came from far away.

---

[1] A regular joke in the mess in the US Navy.

10

The Christmas Party

Astrid was never going to come back to her childhood home.

After a brilliant matriculation certificate and four years as secretary at the Ministry of Defense, she met the advertising man Tor. It was a yes, and there were children. New children. Did she think of her firstborn that fate took away from her?

Or maybe it wasn't fate; it was some kind of rotten interaction between her stepfather and her brother. Samuel ended up at NTNU (University Trondheim) with rocket research as his specialty. After several visits to the US, a PhD and a research position in Trondheim was waiting.

He returned home for his stepfather's funeral. Then he received an envelope that he had to swear would not be opened until after his mother's death. The mother sent one to Astrid, too. Samuel forgot the whole thing, but Astrid couldn't wait. She knew what was in the envelope, the accusation of having shamed the entire family with her loose behaviour, first her stepfather and then her brother. Did her mother know anything about the sheriff too? She burned the envelope and its contents, unread, right away, and vowed that she would never see her mother again.

A few years later, when everyone was gathered at Tor and Astrid's for a Christmas party, Samuel led his sister out to the kitchen. Wanted a sibling talk as he laughingly put it.

Astrid realised that something special was coming but was still totally unprepared when it came.

"What is it, Samuel? What happened?"

For the first time in a very long time, she spoke Finnmarking, i.e., the northernmost dialect.

"I see you get nervous and maybe for a good reason. Perhaps I should have waited and not risk putting a damper on this Christmas celebration. But I couldn't wait."

"Yes, okay, spit it out, Samuel."

"The envelope is gone."

"What envelope?" But she knew very well which one. "Mine is gone too. I burned it without looking at its contents. I knew what she'd written. God, why couldn't she let the past and forgotten stay in the past, forgotten, our mother!"

"You want to tell me what was in the letter? You probably knew, even without having read it."

"No, Samuel. And let this be buried now, please."

She cried out loud now, and the crying came and the tears and Tor stood in the door.

"What are you guys doing? Do you cry like that because of childhood memories from Finnmark?"

He tried to joke it off. But for Astrid, this wasn't a joke.

I must; I must be able to make a joke about this. Otherwise, our whole lives will fall apart. And not just ours, but Samuel's and his family's—yes, everyone. She managed to turn it into a laughing type of crying. "Leave, Tor, we'll be done with this soon."

Samuel had stood completely still. Terrified of the thought of what might come if Astrid cracked. Now he moved to keep Astrid close to him.

"We'll be with you right away."

"Tell me, Samuel, how did it get lost?"

"I helped Tor with some old papers, something about some drilling platforms."

"Now watch it, Samuel. Drilling platforms? What was Tor to do with drilling platforms?"

"You know he worked with Aker. But forget it. The only thing I can think of is that the envelope joined this jumble. I'd stowed all this away and thought no more of that damned envelope."

"Could Tor have it then, you mean?"

"I don't know. I just got panicky when it wasn't there anymore. I thought it wouldn't be good if it got into the wrong hands and old shit popped up."

But Samuel probably knew what could have happened. The envelope could only have ended up in one place, in between drawings for the drilling platforms; yes, it was probably correct. But not Aker drawings, but Condeep 2 that went to the contact in the Russian Embassy.

"But, Astrid, if it had come to Tor, he would have talked about it with you or me."

"What did you do with all your other clutter then?"

"No, once I'd picked this out for Tor, I set the rest on fire. Just old shit. Collecting too much. I'm sure you do too."

"But nothing from our mother, no."

She went quiet as time went on.

"I'm going to ask Tor tomorrow or later tonight, and if he knows nothing, it's probably gone through the burning."

"Why don't you ask Tor right away, so that you'll let me know after dinner."

Samuel went in to the others. Waved to Tor that he was going to come out to the kitchen.

"So many cooks, then there must be food soon," the little statement came from her daughter. But Tor was quickly back.

"Let's go to the table."

"Nothing in this house, so you should probably check the ashes in Trondheim," he whispered in her ear now. I guess the others were wondering what was going on.

Astrid laughed. Finally. A happy laugh this time, and Samuel laughed along, and soon everyone laughed.

But Samuel's laughter was hollow. He probably had an idea about the envelope's contents. Still, he feared that the envelope had been sent to Moscow by pure accident. And if so, someone had a gun pointed at the two families. A weapon that could be used for something, anytime. The mother would not have held back.

Would an accusation of incest be statute-barred after so many years?

It had happened while asleep, all of it.

Ask for the envelope in Moscow?

He bit his thumb for his mind to be clear. At least someone would be interested.

Forget the whole thing, Samuel.

But someone had a job to secure tracks and evidence like this. They also had a job of not to forget.

11

Farewell to Orphanage 113

The move from the orphanage in Murmansk to the KGB's boarding school in the Caucasus was the end of a safe and sound life. Now the great unknown awaited. They were two six-year-olds from Orphanage Number 113 who were about to take off on the long journey.

One was a boy who occupied the bed next to Igor. Thin and already at six years old, one could see that he was going to be tall. Igor was tall himself but much better built. If there was a fight in the yard, Igor became the rescue for the thin Andreyev.

"Why is your name Igor by the way? Not common name. Not very common in any case?"

Igor fell silent. It wasn't the first time anyone had asked him. But never Andreyev. It was kind of a personal threshold that his friend hadn't wanted to step over. But now, they were on the train from Murmansk and were travelling far.

Boris from the orphanage was to accompany them to Moscow, where they would change trains. There would be more children and a new officer to accompany them on the journey.

"I don't know, Andreyev. I was just called Igor as far back as I can remember. Maybe we're the only ones who don't have parents that are alive anymore? To me, they said mine had perished."

"But maybe it wasn't true, perhaps I've never had parents? Or if I had, maybe they gave me away. Even more unforgivable."

"Idiot, of course, everyone's got parents, you're born right, all children are."

Igor had to laugh.

"Yes, I'm standing here. But hey, why are you and I going to this school in the mountains?"

"I asked Galina several times before the train departed, but she just cried and wouldn't answer. Did you ask as well?"

"Yes, and she replied that it had been decided far south, in Moscow, and that she had nothing to do with it."

"I thought it was sad to leave her and Murmansk."

There were a few tears, but Boris enticed them with tea and cakes at the next station, and soon, Murmansk was despairing yet weaker memories. Boris had been to Moscow before and could talk about the most impressive buildings and how pretty people were. The ladies wore long dresses and wore fur. But the boys were more interested in shops.

A new station awaited and then the night slowly came on to them. Boris put blankets over them. At six o'clock the following day, the train came into Moscow's main railway station. Now the stores were waiting.

But there would not be a long stay in the capital. As early as 8:00, the new train was supposed to go west. Two days it would take, and eventually, they would be picked up by a separate bus going toward the mountains. But there were shops inside the train station as well.

"Do you have any money, Andreyev?"

"No, do you?"

Head shaking and brave smiles at each other. So then looking in the windows only. But it wasn't that exciting, just newspapers, tobacco, and stuff like that. But they saw soda, and they really wanted that, but no money.

They couldn't get inside either. At the kiosk, there was only room for the fat man. He'd probably gotten fat eating candy.

They got their own big carriage now, and there were six new children and two officers. Both wore uniforms with medals.

Only two of the other children knew each other. Otherwise, they came from different places. One was a little strange. Didn't look quite like the others. Was relatively small, but yet big build and had stinging eyes. Igor stuck out his tongue at him. But he probably should not have done so.

He who came from the same orphanage whispered to Igor, "Watch out for him. They called him the Mongol at the orphanage we come from."

Igor didn't understand much of it but wondered with Andreyev that everyone except the Mongol was thin and that the clothes were kind of slanging on them.

But they shouldn't have to freeze. They would get thick boots, a coat, and a hat. That's what the officers said. Because even though Moscow was in the midst of spring, the late winter waited in the mountains. Igor had repeatedly asked Boris why they should travel so far and to a particular school.

But there was never an answer.

Should he dare to ask one of the two new officers?

But then the train started, and they were on their way.

Wonder how far does this train travels?

It was massive with a lot of wagons. But Andreyev wanted to know.

"Why are we going way up to the mountains, Comrade Alexis, and what is it waiting for us there, and when do we get food?"

"You are a curious guy." He looked at the name tag on Andreyev's coat. "Oh, you're Andreyev."

The boy blushed and later turned pale. A little appalled by his own boldness. In Murmansk, they were trained not to speak to officers but to wait until someone eventually talked to them. But he just forgot now.

The question probably came on a little abruptly for Alexis as well.

"Hasn't anyone told you where you're going and why?"

"No, nobody knew anything," Igor says. He felt he had to help his friend a little bit now.

Alexis conferred with his colleague.

"My name is Mikhailov, and I'm your boss on this trip. Alexis and I are responsible for making sure you get there safely, so we don't want any issues. Nobody leaves the carriage without one of us. Not even to the bathroom. Is that clear, boys?"

Because they were just boys. Everyone looked up now.

"Yes, officer!"

Mikhailov was smiling now.

"Good boys. First, you might be wondering who your parents are. We don't know, but we ask you to remember that you should be grateful that the orphanages have taken good care of you.

Many other children live with their destitute parents and starve and freeze. You've got food and clothes and warm beds. I want you to be happy about that."

But the others have moms and dads, Igor thought.

"Now we're going to be together on this train until tomorrow night, and we're going to make sure you get food and drink and a blanket for the evening."

Igor took his chance, raised his hand as he had learned.

"Yes, Igor."

"Why are we going up in the mountains? Shall we live there? And why didn't the other children join us?"

He heard someone who laughed and turned around. It was the Mongol who now stuck out his tongue in his direction. The officer was not making it known that he noticed.

"You eight are chosen. Do you know what that means?"

Silence. No one dared to say anything. Perhaps he wasn't waiting for an answer either.

"You're going to go to a special school where you're going to learn to be the best as some kind of soldier. Yes, Igor?"

"Are we going to war like any other soldier?"

Mikhailov laughed. "Not like regular soldiers, no, and no regular war either."

"But could we die?"

This time he heard the Mongol's raw laughter; the officer heard it too.

"Why are you laughing, Khan?"

"Afraid of dying this Igor or whatever his name is."

Mikhailov ignored him.

"If you're paying attention at the new school and you're learning how to take care of yourself, you don't have to die for a very, very long time. But that's enough. The food is waiting."

Andreyev whispered to Igor, "Did you understand anything? And what's the matter with this Khan?"

"Just that we should become the best, a school to become the best, to fight wars and everything."

"But do we have to kill someone?"

"Hush." Mikhailov didn't like the whispers.

But Igor did not give up, whispering if possibly even lower, "The other boy says there's something about the Mongol's brain. Supposed to have received a blow!"

12

The Chechens

It was night, and it got dark, and then it exploded. Wild shouts were heard from the riders outside. Igor could see the locomotive lying overturned in the bend in front of them. He lay tangled between the seats at the front of the carriage, with his head barely up to the edge of the window. Someone was screaming. He called out to Andreyev, but there was no answer.

The light had gone off, and he just heard Mikhailov whisper, "Be still, everyone."

Then there were bangs again but from firearms this time. The cries eventually died out. The bandits had probably been well prepared since they didn't search all the carriages. Mikhailov mentioned they had brought a load of weapons in the first carriage.

"So they were probably Chechens," the Mongol said.

Igor wondered what Chechens were but didn't dare talk now. Some emergency lights were put up, and Mikhailov began investigating the damage. Alexis was dead, and so was one of the boys. Igor prayed to God that it must not be Andreyev. He didn't see who was being carried out from where he was hiding. He didn't dare ask either. The cries for Andreyev had not been answered.

Eventually, crews arrived to help separate the twisted seats so he could get up. Seemingly unharmed, just chest pains.

"Maybe you've broken some of your fine ribs!" Sarcasm from the Mongol before Mikhailov briefly told him to shut up.

"But what about Andreyev? He wasn't there."

"Do you miss your friend?" It was Khan again.

No one else said anything. Mikhailov once again told him to shut up or be sent back to the orphanage.

So his best friend, the only one, was gone. If he could see him. No, Mikhailov thought it would only make matters worse. His face was smashed in the abrupt stop when the track was blown up.

A new locomotive arrived, and the track was quickly repaired.

It was very dark into the remnants of a wild night. Eventually came a new, grey, sad day as the train drove across vast fields, the steppe they called it. They did not see many houses, just a few small clusters, and occasionally some cows on the pastures.

And it was raining, raining all the time. Igor sat by himself, was not hungry, but Mikhailov forced him to drink. None of the other children did anything to comfort him. They just sat there together, except for Kahn, who sat by himself.

Sometimes, the rain was almost white, and Igor dreaded the encounter with winter again. Well into the afternoon, the sun had barely arrived, but now it was already getting dark. There was finally the end of the train journey. They were at the final stop, and the bus was waiting, as Mikhailov had said.

But the luggage? Yes, he hadn't thought of that.

But Mikhailov was in complete control.

Otherwise, it wasn't much luggage he carried. Just a little brown cardboard case with his favorite toy, the miniature wooden horse that he'd been given by some people a long, long time ago.

Those people were dead by now, Galina had said. And then he had a little pennant where it said Igor and the picture of a strange boat that Galina called a submarine. No one else had been allowed to see it. Worn toothbrush, nightshirt, and underpants, that's all that was in it.

"It's no big deal with your suitcase, Igor. You'll get everything new when you get there."

New, how about the wooden horse and the pennant? Would they take away the only things he owned?

"Where are you going?" Khan shouted at him. "Did you try to run away?"

He had to look in the suitcase. The pennant, it was there. He put it under his shirt. But the wooden horse? He couldn't hide it. It was too big.

Mikhailov is coming after him. "Get on the bus. We're leaving now. By the way, what have you got there?"

He grabbed the wooden horse and threw it away on a pile of garbage. "You won't need this much. You're not a baby anymore. Now you're going to grow up!"

His other arm locked Igor in an iron grip and dragged him aboard.

Igor wanted to cry, but he couldn't. No tears, just a terrible feeling of the loss of that most precious. No parents, Andreyev gone, and now the wooden horse. What would life be now? But he had the pennant.

"What happened?" whispered one of the others.

"He threw away his wooden horse," Igor squealed.

"Quiet, children. Now we're going to drive a bus for two hours and do prepare you directly for a new world until we get there."

New world? What was that?

Without the wooden horse? Without Andreyev. Without parents. He was old enough to realize that he was all alone and in a new and unknown world.

Then, finally, it let loose; he quietly cried inside him. But Andreyev?

Igor was going to be the best soldier of them all and avenge his best friend. Being a child was over.

It was dark outside; they didn't see anything, just lights as they drove past some buildings. And then the snow was there, and they had to go slower, the driver said, because now the road was partially iced and it was steep, but they couldn't see that, the children, sitting far behind in the bus. Igor had his hand inside his shirt, held on to the pennant, the last and only thing he had that was just his. He woke up when Mikhailov clapped his hands.

"Now we have arrived, out all of you, bring your luggage and go straight into the building in front of you!" A little milder. "Thank you, behave appropriately and do not ask any stupid questions. Did you hear that, Igor? Now you're going to be turned into a man, you're no longer a child. And, guys, don't worry about the accident on the train! Soon, you'll have forgotten all the bad."

Easy for you to say, Igor wasn't finished at all. The image of Andreyev did not leave him.

13

The KGB School

On the inside of the door, two men in uniform were standing and greeted them. All the suitcases were thrown into a big box.

"These you don't need anymore. Welcome to our place. Now, shower first, then new clothes, get a bed, and then supper and good night. At 6:00 in the morning, the day begins. So full speed ahead."

He was happy he had removed the pennant. But where would he hide it?

"Can I go to the bathroom first?"

"Same direction as the shower but be quick."

Inside the toilet, there were no hiding places. But there was an old lady in some kind of uniform waiting for the boys. She looked nice. The others disappeared in the shower.

"Now, Igor, aren't you going to hurry up and finish as well?"

So she knew his name.

He was finally standing there naked.

"What is this?"

He just had to cry now.

"It's a gift from those who brought me to the orphanage."

"But you're not a child anymore, and you're not in an orphanage either."

"You look nice. Can you promise to take care of it for me? The wooden horse, Mikhailov took away from me and threw it when we were about to get on the bus. And Andreyev died when the train was attacked by Chechens."

"Yes, I heard about that, poor he and you, but this pennant, is it so important? And why is there a picture of a submarine?"

"I don't know, but it's the only thing I have that's mine."

Anna was smiling now because Anna was the name on her badge.

"Then you must promise me that I will never have any problems with you, that you are obedient and clever. And you have to promise me that you'll work hard to be the best at all times."

He nodded bluntly, and the pennant disappeared under her uniformed shirt. What if she could have been his mother.

He couldn't help but cling to her, and tears ran. She stroked him across his black hair.

"In the shower now, my Igor."

Oh, what did she say? She could be sent away for cuddling with the boys.

14

And Igor was the best.

The best at everything because that is what he had promised. And when he finished the primary part and turned ten, then and only then, was he going to have the pennant returned.

Anna kept her promise, and Igor continued to be the best.

At the age of thirteen, he was transferred to the aspirant school. The others, he didn't see again except for the Mongol. And especially one particular night.

The lights in the dormitory were out, and everyone was asleep, Igor thought, when he had to go to the bathroom. Snuck out and quietly went back.

In the middle of the dormitory, there was a separate cubicle where the officer on duty slept.

Some noises were coming from there, and Igor wondered if he should pull the curtain aside and check if the officer was ill.

But then he heard there was not only one person, but two.

One voice was very, very similar to Khan's, the Mongol?

What was he doing in there with the officer at this time of the night?

Then came a loud moan and, a little later, one who spoke low. Had to be the officer: "If you say anything about this Khan, then you're dead!"

Says something about what, Igor was thinking.

"Go into the bathroom and clean yourself. If anyone should come, I'll tell them you got sick. Don't forget to be ready again in a week. Then I'm on duty again."

Igor stretched himself to be able to see better in the dim darkness.

And so, Khan was getting out of the cubicle, completely naked, and his penis seemed half-erect.

So that's what it was. Khan and the officer had slept with each other. Deadly sin. No one in the KGB could be gay, as it was called.

Igor gently pulled the rug over him. If that's how it was with Khan, Igor sure would have to be careful. Don't let anyone know he knew.

But perhaps this could come in handy sometime. The fact that he had something on Khan.

At the aspirant course, new boys arrived, and the competition got more challenging. The closing day before the trip to Moscow, there was a full inspection, and the captain took out the pennant he had found, taped under Igor's bed. No one laughed; everyone was strictly serious, except the Mongol with the strange grin. Igor didn't think he could stand that yawning on the train years ago. Full line-up.

"Aspirant Igor, step forward. You've been the best of the class, but why have you been keeping this pennant from an old submarine? Give me an explanation before I throw it away!"

"My parents died in an accident at sea, and I was the only one rescued by the submarine crew. Then I received this pennant as a gift."

"But was the submarine really called Igor?"

"Yes, Captain."

"Strange, okay, but keep it. So your name and that of the old submarine is the same."

He had a little bit of a laugh before he stopped himself.

And Igor had suddenly gained an identity. Parents died. He survived.

He was no longer a non-person. He had roots.

But had the parents perished?

That night, as they boarded the train to Moscow, the Mongol came all the way upon him.

"Hey, you, boy clever, how do you know your parents are really dead? Maybe you weren't something to keep and then they just threw you into the sea!"

That was how long the joy of having gained roots lasted. Like the Mongol said, he was just a changeling that they wanted to get rid of, if it was true. But why would they want to get rid of him? Could it be that his parents weren't married, and they had to get rid of him? But throw him into the sea, I guess it would have been the sure death if the submarine hadn't arrived.

"You got something to think about there, Igor. Get a real name and get rid of this pennant, and you will become a man."

"What do you have against me, Khan? Have I ever done anything to you, teased you, or gossiped about you or anything?"

"Aside from that sticking that tongue on the train from Moscow, you've been sucking up to teachers and officers and grabbed my first place."

Is that how it was? So Khan couldn't stand Igor being the best, the best at everything. But did Khan have a point anyway when it came to this thing with his parents? That they had simply dumped him at sea?

What a terrible thought.

If they were still alive, they'd get to taste his revenge.

It was as if the Mongol could read his mind.

"Go back to Murmansk or wherever you come from and shoot them. You were the best at gun shooting, too, Igor. Shooting may not be good enough. Tie the hands and feet together, put them in separate bags, and dump them in the river or at sea. They don't need a mask because if they open their mouths, they'll just die faster."

"Is that how they do it where you come from?"

"I would think so. They tied my hands and feet together, put me in a bag, and left me on the banks of the river in Moscow. But someone must have come and surprised them."

"How do you know all this?"

Was there suddenly something human about this Khan? Should he feel sorry for him?

"I was three years old, and you do remember important things like having survived, for example. But find them and let them have a slow death."

A cold chill went down Igor's back; he ultimately refused to believe that this was how it had happened. That he'd just been thrown into the sea.

"Aren't you going to go to your homeland and get revenge?"

"Russia is my homeland, Igor."

"Yes, but your parents don't come from Russia."

"So you don't like my look? Don't you think I'm a good-enough Russian?

"It's not easy to know where yours came from. Maybe they were Samis or Eskimos!"

His gaze was hateful now.

"And you, Khan, you should know what I know about you and your sexual orientation!"

Khan faded. Igor could see lights of murder in his eyes. The officer who accompanied them on the trip had overheard some of the talk and banned any further discussion. Igor was sent into the neighboring compartment just in case.

There should not be many words exchanged between them until much later during their active service.

But Igor had now really felt the desire for going north to access this archive in Murmansk.

If it was that he'd just been dumped at sea or wherever it was, someone would taste his revenge. He swore to himself. How could a mother do that to her own child?

15

The Recruit School

Igor and the others from the class had arrived by train from the Caucasus, and Igor had been handed his registration form.

The social security number was already printed on the form.

Name, last name, and he started writing.

This was the first time, but did he have the same last name and first name?

Yes, what else would he write?

He handed over the sheet to the inspector, who immediately gave it back.

"Look, no funny stuff. Write your last name."

"Yes, but my name is only Igor."

He turned pale now. Best in class and end up in trouble straight away. Perhaps be rejected and transferred to the training of regular troops.

"Sit over there and wait. I need to talk to the boss!"

A young lieutenant waved him into his office.

"Igor, don't make a fool of yourself. You have excellent papers, but we can't have that kind of nonsense."

The lieutenant was a young fellow around twenty-two years old.

"Are you going to ruin your career with stupidity from day one here in Moscow?"

"Comrade Lieutenant, what's your suggestion?"

"Mine?" The lieutenant was furious. "Listen, Igor, or whatever you call yourself. You have a social security number. You have a first name. Igor, right? Then we must be able to give you a last name. What day is it today?"

The controller jumped up.

"Tuesday, Comrade Lieutenant."

"Idiot, of course, I know! But what name day is it?"

"I don't know, but it's Nikolayev's name day tomorrow Wednesday."

"Then it's all right, your name is Igor Nikolayev from now on. Everyone happy with that? Congratulations on your name, Igor Nikolayevich, and welcome to Moscow."

A dry laugh came from the hallway as the Mongol passed by. It took away some of the joy Igor could feel, the joy of getting another name of honor. But the Mongol should watch out; imagine if the truth about him came to light. The truth about a gay aspirant in the KGB! No, he should have to keep it for future use.

Three Years Later

"Igor Nikolayevich, I hereby have the pleasure of proclaiming you the best graduate of this year's graduation class. After a specialization in English and possibly Norwegian—whatever you are going to do with that, you will be sent to London, to the embassy. With you from the group, the number 2, Khan."

The Mongol again. Should he never get rid of him? And why did Khan have to be after him all the time? Strange guy. He hadn't been able to make any connections to his fellow students here in Moscow either. Maybe he didn't even try. The loner!

Igor had not been able to put aside his interest in Norwegian. Did not even know why this language interested him. Either way, it was a good language as an entrance to Scandinavia. But changes were coming. Berlin suddenly became "hot," and he was sent there. It would prove very useful as several of the latest leaders of the party served in Berlin at the same time as him.

Then came London to refine his English and then, after a short stay at home, New York and the United Nations came next. The idea of the front in Chechnya became increasingly distant. The revenge for Andreyev as well.

Finally, after ten years, he faced the biggest challenge of his career, unveiling the Moon Landing Project alongside the famous Cobra. And best of all, he was picked by Little Father himself, whom he had met in Berlin.

"Who is this Cobra?"

The SVR major just shook his head. "Stupid question, Igor. We all have field names, and yours will now be Ivan—remember that and have an excellent trip to Oslo."

16

Courier Once More

"Why didn't you call?"

"Your phone is probably still bugged, even ten years later, both landline and mobile. And I wouldn't be too sure there are no microphones inside the house. Have you ever checked it?"

Did he hear him correctly?

Ten years had actually passed.

"Go around the house, out into the garden and take off that horrible coat, so that you don't scare Nicoline or the neighbors."

His granddaughter enjoyed her time with him these summer days—got to do what she wanted.

"Hey, an insurance agent has dropped by!" he shouted into the living room. "We'll stay in the garden, so just shout should there be anything."

No, the video was far more interesting. And it was also nice when it was just her and Grandpa. No hassle. As long as he didn't drink that stupid beer.

Maybe she could ask if she could bring her best friend tomorrow. Then they could pretend that they were both Hannah Montana. No, by the way, she wanted it for herself only. But there wasn't going to be a tomorrow morning with Grandpa.

"We need a courier, just like in the old days."

"Just a courier?"

"Yes, and more than that. We need the Third Man."

Did he sense some kind of attempt of a smile?

"You must retrieve the drawings we want to include, and you must use Omar as a contact in the east as before."

So Omar would have survived.

"But why don't you send the parcel or whatever it may be as a courier mail through the embassy?"

"Not going to work, the Foreign Ministry has decided that we cannot risk but must use direct couriers."

"The drawings? Can you let me know more?"

"No, I just know it's about an aerospace project."

Igor actually became solemn for a moment. This was his first big mission. A mission like this would provide him with fame and honor for the rest of his career. He already envisaged stars on his shoulders and a dacha near Moscow. Then it finally came, with pride in his voice: "The Great Moon Landing!"

Tor was thinking, something crackling in the back of his brain. He had surely heard of this before. The great moon landing. It had to be something with the Americans.

"But who's keeping drawings here in little Norway? We are not an aerospace country."

"Scientists in Trondheim, SINTEF, it seems to be called."

"Dear me, NASA would never let Norwegian scientists be part of their projects, would they?"

The other man's face had closed entirely by now, seemingly afraid he had said too much already. His Norwegian was almost perfect. But then he grinned a little, pulled his right hand's index finger over his throat.

"What is it that you refer to in Norwegian: Death secret?"

"But why me and now ten years later? Incidentally, you must have been involved for some time, your young age notwithstanding. And what's your real name?"

"Ivan, that's my agent's name, and that's all you'll know."

He had been about to reveal himself as Igor. This was the first time that he was going to use a pseudonym. There's every reason to sharpen up. He felt the blush coming. Good thing he had the hat shading.

"But if you've been at it for almost eight years, you say, you never met Gromyko or the people who worked with him," Tor said it almost like a statement, but also to smoke out what this Ivan knew about Tor's old network.

"Gromyko was a politician, not a spy!"

"No, of course, you're right about that."

Then he knew nothing about the past; it was clear. But from what archive had he picked Tor? He tried a new variant.

"Why haven't you asked Arne for help?"

"I met him at random in Cyprus. He asked me to leave him alone. He had settled with the past. 'Ask the Third Man' was all he said as he walked away, laughing."

Yes, Arne would have settled, to be sure. Used as a pawn to smear the Minister of the Law of the Sea, his political father? Or were there other agendas as well? Had there been a significant leak, and then they needed a scapegoat? They? The heads of the party and the Foreign Ministry? And maybe Department of Justice too? Better watch out at this point in time. The Russians always knew more than they would reveal.

"Do you know why he laughed?"

"No, but I guess it was because the Third Man was in the clear while Arne got caught. He was just a lay figure, really."

"What do you mean, lay figure?"

Igor grinned now.

"I am not familiar with that type of slang, but he was like a toy spy or whatever you call it. Just total crap, all of it. But someone at your end turned fanatical."

He laughed again.

"We were serious about Arne at first until the new channel appeared, and here we are now and need the Third Man again."

"How much did you pay Arne?"

"You know I can't say that. But you got far more."

"I was only able to cover travel expenses," Tor wanted to say. But Igor had already turned around.

"You know, I have to go now. I reckon I was followed here. You'll probably be followed as well, as before, whether you take this job or not, so you might as well jump into it."

"Me, almost a pensioner, what do I get for this?" Tor's slightly joking tone didn't cover up the seriousness.

"100,000 USD in small unmarked notes on delivery to Omar as before. Then you must also cover your and Omar's costs."

"But doesn't Moscow have to control the item first?"

Igor laughed.

"Even if you're getting a little old, you're going to live a little longer, are you not?"

"But how can I reach you?"

"I'm not the one you have to reach. Your contact will be the Cobra. He is usually stationed in Tokyo, but he's kind of on loan here for this assignment. I guess it says something about its importance and what happens if you get it wrong. The next instructions, you will find behind the Ibsen's family burial site at Our Saviour's Cemetery. There's a little watering can there for flowers and stuff. We change it a couple of times a week. The area is prominent, and it is impossible to be shadowed without you not realizing it. Bring a new water jug in a carrier bag, and you'll just change. Stasi's recipe, as you can see."

"What's your role in all this?"

Igor smiled.

"I can't tell you that, but I'm sure we'll meet again. Stick to the Cobra!"

Was this a trap? Was it something Intelligence had set in motion to get him Tor, finally? He had to be to the point at this time.

"Just one thing before you go. I wasn't a spy. I wasn't paid to hand over secrets. I was simply a courier for a good cause for my country."

So it had been stated.

"But how about the money you received Tor? What about that?"

"Since you're so well informed, you probably also know that I only got a reasonable travel allowance covered."

"How many years would you get? Convicted as a spy for a foreign power? Guaranteed twenty-one years. But you'd survive. You wouldn't do that with us! Dog food in Siberia, best case."

Igor laughed, walking down the road.

Sure, Tor would have been convicted even though he didn't know the contents of what he was carrying. But prison was one thing.

His whole career and social life would have been lost. Probably the marriage, too.

Where did this Igor come from? Not Moscow-Russian. More like some kind of dialect. Well, that was not a matter of importance. The important thing was that they had found him, Tor, again. There must be a shortage of spies, or couriers, or both. Or was his reputation that good?

17

The Insurance

"Oh, it's so boring, can't we go to the store and buy ice cream?"

"I'm coming now, Nicoline."

"Who was the black-clad man, Grandpa? Oversized, wide coat in this heat. Was he a foreigner?"

A sharp little girl.

"No, but maybe he had foreign parents."

"Oh, some kind of immigrant."

"Don't Nicoline, immigrants are as good Norwegians as anyone. He was just a poor insurance agent."

"Why poor?"

"That's the kind of thing you just say. No, nothing derogatory, but I didn't buy anything from him either. We're good enough. We're insured, my girl."

She should have known—how little insurance meant in dealings with the Russians.

"What is insurance, Grandpa?"

"You can insure against everything you know, loss of luggage and all that."

"Can you insure against dying too? Do it. I don't want you to die, Grandpa." She clung to him. "Call the man and say you want such insurance."

Tor felt cold now.

"Sweetheart, my best friend. I'm not going to die, not now anyway."

"But everyone's going to die sometime, Mom says. Is it only the ones who haven't insured themselves who are going to die, or?"

"Your mom is right, almost always, everyone is going to die, and you can't obtain insurance against dying."

As soon as death was mentioned, he felt the excitement in him. Could he say no? Say he was getting too old, enjoyed too much, being almost retired? Would they accept it? Hardly, and they had probably checked up on him thoroughly before this mission was put on him. Maybe they thought he was in better shape than he knew himself?

Sure, he exercised three times a week in the gym. The stomach was still a washboard, but the strength, the mental strength. Never feeling fear—for something, what about it?

"You have nothing to fear but fear itself."

I'm sure Kennedy would have stolen it from someone, but it was just damned good still. Was it fear he felt in his stomach?

The Cobra?

This mission had to be important as they had moved one of the top colonels over from Tokyo to little Norway.

But why would it be him, Tor, who would be responsible for its implementation?

There would have to be other and younger agents or spies. Spy? He sampled the word. He had always grinded away about this, he was a courier and no spy. But it wouldn't let go. Spy?

And what about himself, hadn't he put this part of his life behind him for good? Did he need the money, or did he need his life?

There was no such thing as saying no to the KGB. By the way, I guess it was called SVR now. But the essence was probably unchanged.

But if he were to sacrifice his entire upcoming retirement, it would come at a price. The price should be high, much higher than the lousy 100,000. Lousy? It was much better paid than what he was offered in the old days. So this moon landing had to be important. Extremely important.

What if he got caught? Would the Treholt case set a precedent in some way and give him twenty-one years in prison? If he could live for another twenty-one years? And what about Astrid's job at the Ministry of Defense? Would she also be caught and made an accomplice on circumstantial evidence? Her career would in any case be finished.

So 100,000 would not be enough, the bare minimum had to be 300,000. Preferably 500,000, so they could emigrate to South America or something, just be gone.

So just say no, Tor. Take it or leave it.

But did it help to put pressure on the Russians?

He had no choice. Just had to explain to them why and this thing with Astrid, of course.

The thing was he, Tor, had never been a spy and thus betrayed Norway in any way. He'd only been a courier.

But it was you, Tor, who handed over the goodies to the Russians. If it hadn't been for you, the material wouldn't have come into their hands.

Indeed, someone else would have taken the baton. If he hadn't accepted the job.

But now, you're the one we're talking about. How many jobs have you completed for the Russians? Seven? Ten? I don't know, but I've never been a spy, just a courier. He repeated this to himself time and time again. In the end, he said it out loud to himself to make sure it was put to rest. But how many of the Norwegian population would agree with his distinction? Not his wife anyway. And what about the rest of the family? Very doubtful.

Treholt had been caught allegedly handing over so-called secret documents in return for payment. Cowardly and not in any way proven. But Tor, he'd actually done it—several times. And the money? In a secret account in London. Not payment for information, but only covering travel expenses as it was called.

And this time, he was even going to get the documents himself. Forget about being a courier and possibly a milder sentence on that basis. If he agreed to this job, he was a spy, that's that.

But what if he said no? What would the Russians do?

Did they have any leverage?

How stupid can you be, Tor? The means of pressure, of course, was to reveal his previous work as a courier, ten years back. Would it help to say he did it for Norway?

But so did Treholt. Even for the world, he said. And with great credibility even. Few other politicians in Norway saw the value of dialogue at the time.

But all this belonged to history now, or did it not?

Would he enjoy obsolescence? And what about Astrid? Guaranteed she would be fired on the spot. She must have known or? At least she should have figured it out.

What now?

He was trapped by the past, literally. The only thing he could do now was to push the price and at the same time do anything within his power to not get caught. The decision had been made. He had forty-eight hours to enjoy his summer days. But the Russians were in a hurry.

18

The Ibsen Monument

He knew someone at Haugen who would probably look after Nicoline for the fifteen minutes or so it took to leave a message.

"Shall we go to the movies this afternoon, little girl?"

"Not this afternoon. I want to watch a Donald movie now."

"Can you manage it in the heat?"

"Grandpa, it's not hot in the movie theater."

"So you want to go to the movies anyway?"

"Yes, but to watch a Donald film."

Spoilt?

"Okay then, then we'll drive and have an ice cream at Haugen first."

"Where's Haugen?"

"St. Hanshaugen is right up town."

"Then why is it just called Haugen?"

"Come on now, or we won't make it."

I forgot to say that there was a significant detour with Haugen versus driving straight to Vika and the film.

Randi at Baker Hansen took care of the girl with a triple ice bomb, and Tor was back after just five minutes.

"Okay, with 500,000," the note he left under the water jug said. "But must receive a final approval." Would his wife notice that her watering can had been replaced by a rusty one?

It was quiet the next day. Disturbingly quiet. Excited, he waited for the result. For 500,000, they could move to a country without an extradition treaty with Norway. In addition, the sales of the house and cars. But then they had to sell before he was eventually caught, to avoid that all the assets were confiscated.

But who would take care of the sale, and what about Astrid? Would she understand, and would she accept?

Either way, her job would be gone. But running away with your tail between your legs, so to speak? She wasn't the type for that, and how about children and grandchildren? Never being able to visit them.

He envisaged the scene. "Listen, Astrid, I have to escape forever. Why? I've had too close contact with the Russians. Can't say anything else. And you, I'm sure you'll lose your job at MOD. Yes, you get it, don't you? Divorce, you say. Yes, but your job's going the whistle anyway. Join me now, and you can go back to Norway eventually when the storm has settled. You're innocent after all."

On Monday morning, when his wife picked up the newspaper, there was a blank envelope in the mailbox, except that Tor was written in blue letters. Astrid looked at him.

"Letter from a secret girlfriend?"

"Who knows."

Should he open it so that she would be a part of it? He didn't have any doubts about who the sender was. Maybe she thought it was the past that reappeared.

"Why don't you open it, Astrid, if you suspect me of anything."

She gave him a quick hug. "I must run. Enjoy the envelope, Tor."

Then she was gone, and he tore up the envelope. There was nothing there, i.e., no letter, just a small picture of a watering can.

The message was clear enough, and he put on his clothes quickly.

Then Astrid was back.

"Goodness gracious, you're on the move already! But I can't talk, I'd just forgotten the sunglasses."

Then she was out, and he too. Two minutes later, he was in the car.

This time, he chose to enter by the Russian Orthodox Church and then took the back road down toward the Ibsen monument.

A bag with the rusty jug in his left hand.

He sat on a bench twenty meters away and watched the activity in the place. An old man with a cane came and sat on the bench as well.

A somewhat younger woman took pictures of precisely the Ibsen monument. Then came a whole group of children with two teachers, one of them a man.

Heavy traffic. He stood up and tried not to look at his friend on the bench.

But he knew it. The guy with the cane had stood up, too.

Maybe he wasn't that old; perhaps it was just camouflage, the cane.

Maybe he was from Intelligence?

Then something must have gone wrong—how could anyone know about the agreement between him and Ivan, except for the Cobra?

But Tor had survived by limiting all risk, so he walked straight toward Kaffebrenneriet on Haugen without looking behind.

The man with the cane came behind all the way up to the traffic lights. The he was gone, and Tor abruptly ran over toward Akersbakken, turned back, and found himself back at the cemetery. This time, the trajectory was clear, and he replaced the jug and went back the same way. Got into the car and got home. Oh, they were after him from the very beginning? But who were they? The Norwegian Intelligence or CIA, the co-operating partner?

Then the home must already be under surveillance, wasn't it? Maybe it would have been that all these ten years?

19

The Cobra

"The serious business begins tomorrow. Take bus no. 181 to Slemmestad at 09:55. Get off at Furua, and you will be picked up by a small boat at the pier below, at precisely 10.30. 500 okay. But as I said, I must receive final approval in Moscow. Ivan."

So this had to be Big Time.

It probably was, but he'd wait to talk to Astrid until he had a firmer grasp of it all. Talk to her? About what? The moon landing, rockets? No, keep her out of it if she didn't have to be drawn in because of SINTEF and Samuel, this smart arse, her brother who worked at SINTEF.

But the Cobra had thought of everything, it would turn out.

"I'm going to the fjord today, maybe I get out on the fjord with someone I know."

"Yes, do that and have a nice day." Astrid hugged him. "The job's waiting. Thank God we have aircon at the office."

So he was finally going to meet the Cobra.

The nerves were a little frayed on the way out to the bus. But he had decided to be super professional.

He prayed for the bus to be on schedule. And it was. The nervousness let go a little bit. Why bus and why couldn't he drive his own car, with aircon? The sweat was trickling here on the bus. What would it be like out there in the heat eventually? Twenty-eight degrees even at 10:00 in the morning, and it hadn't rained for fourteen days.

But he was feeling frozen inside even though the thermometer at Furua kiosk showed well over sixty degrees in the sun.

He made his way down quickly, staying under the shade of the oak trees as far as possible, not just because of the sun.

The last hundred meters, there was solid sunshine, no shade, and no coverage.

Hat for the sun, yes, head would get burnt, but too late to turn back to the kiosk now. Then there it was, the boat, with the engine running, two men on board, one looking at the clock. No mooring: the boat just laying ready to take off, some neighboring boats were obviously not too pleased because of the smell from the diesel. Thirty seconds later, they were out of the small harbor that wasn't really a port, just a rupture in the rocks with a few planks on it.

They left an exhaust cloud behind them going at the maximum speed and several people on a sailboat throwing their fists in the air, directed at them. Cursed the motorboat people.

Ivan was in a suit, pretty much out of place. The other man was wearing a marine outfit, a cap, no questions asked. Yes, what could he say?

"It's been ten years, Colonel, and I'm not a kid anymore. I ask again, why me?"

"Cheers, Tor!"

They approached Sandspollen, and Ivan slowed down.

"The answer is simple: we need someone who has done it before. Walked the trail several times. Who knows the risks and avoids foolhardiness."

"As a courier yes, but what about SINTEF or the government area, the Minister of Industry, or maybe even the office of the Minister of Defense? Which of these institutions have the drawings you are looking for?"

"You have many friends, Tor, and probably at least one who owes you a favor or two. What was his name, your wife's brother, wasn't it Samuel?"

"You're crazy, Colonel. Samuel would never ever agree to anything. He doesn't even know anything about my past. My wife hardly knows either, even though she's had her suspicions. I'm sure you know she works as a special adviser at the Ministry of Defense. They kept her under constant supervision for a long time. They rightly suspected that my business was not just so-called commercial. But you know very well that she's worked there all her adult life, even four years before we met, she and me. Except for child and student leave. They couldn't just remove her either, just based on a thin level of suspicion."

He felt his stomach was about to be twisted. But he had agreed, and he had jacked up the price. No more cards to play.

"But Samuel, Tor, the one from Finnmark, he is a senior researcher with full access to all documents. Maybe he's got an insider at Oksebåsen, too."

"What do you mean, Oksebåsen? The launch site for satellites at Andøya?"

"Yes, of course, what else. Satellites and rockets. And your brother-in-law's many stays in Houston, not least."

"Are you still talking about this moon landing project that Ivan mentioned?"

Tor shook his head. The sweat bounced away onto the other two.

"But my God, it has nothing to do with the moon. This is about a fully integrated CO2 treatment plant."

"That, too, but we think there's something more behind it. Conclusion: There are further technological advances that both we and the Americans, not to mention the Chinese, are interested in and that hides under the concept of the moon landing. After all, the Chinese will be interested in the treatment plant. They soon cannot even drive a car during the day in Beijing. We are not uninterested in CO2 purification. Still, Americans need it much more with their new green wave that is sure to come now after President Bush. And what about the Arctic and the new Norwegian foreign minister? Maybe your next prime minister? Is he thinking of moon landing as well? Ice cubes, Ivan. What about you, Tor? Have you forgotten the taste of vodka?"

No, he had to compose himself.

"But this CO2 plant should not be in the North. It will be located in Western Norway."

The Cobra pretended not to hear.

"Good vodka shouldn't have a taste, it's the ice cubes that give the flavour, right? Ivan, you've had enough, you can get caught drunk driving at sea, and we don't want any of that. I'm sure diplomatic immunity doesn't apply here. So there are two sources, the government area and SINTEF or maybe even the Ministry of Defense down at Bankplassen?"

For sure, they'd researched in detail, the Russians. But moon landing, now? The moon was reached decades ago.

Some kids bathed right in front of the bow, and Ivan reversed.

"Drop the grapnel here," it came from the colonel. It was quiet on board.

"Our friend here needs a break to think before we eat. But it's going to be short, so just get the caviar. You could have said no, Tor, but your greed took over, correct? When you increased from 100,000 to 500,000, you gave up your hand so to speak."

"The price is not high. It's low, very low. What if I get caught or you sacrifice me?" He couldn't help it. "Not only is it the end of my professional life, but the end also for Astrid. Surely, they'll take away my pension as well and maybe Astrid's too. And hey, what would happen if I said no?"

"Well, I guess we'd had forgotten about you."

"Would you? Didn't I know too much already? I could have sold their plan to the Norwegian authorities who might have chosen to allow me to operate as a spy for both sides."

"And then?"

"Then your entire network could be revealed, not only here, but all the way to Romania. And why Romania really? Can't I fly straight to Moscow or Helsinki or Kyiv?"

"Romania is old and proven, and nothing can go wrong there. You fly to Stansted, from there to Budapest and then to Brasov. Everyone travels to London, and no one would think about following an old retired spy on a shopping trip to London."

So retired, they were all laughing now. But the laughter was short-lived for Tor.

"What if Samuel at SINTEF says no? By the way, you called him the guy from Finnmark. Is there anything I should know?"

"Not yet, but he's from Finnmark."

"But I know that."

The Cobra laughed it away.

"By the way, what is non-declared work punished with in this country? One year, five years, loss of profession, friends, family, and fines in the millions. Was it 200,000 Norwegian kroner he was paid for the drawing of the Condeep platform at the time?"

Tor faded in the solar heat. Samuel, spy? The magnificent, so arrogant Samuel. Samuel with the lovely place and the expensive journeys?

"This is unknown to me. Samuel has never said a word that he was in contact with you."

The Cobra smiled. "Tor, what do you know about your family? I mean about the two siblings. Your wife and her brother?"

Tor faded.

"What do you mean?"

"To put it simple, I mean Samuel has no choice and maybe neither do you. But let's leave it now and deal with Samuel. We didn't really need his drawings, we saw that later. But by then, he had already been paid. So, Tor, this wasn't about non-declared work, it was about industrial espionage. And Samuel will do it again. Tell him it's the last time, what the consequences of a no would be and put 50,000 US on the table. That's it, not a cent more. And, Tor, leave this with Condeep and his past, at least for now. The embassy clerk who had contact with him has long since gone home. I think they first met in the States."

"What did you mean by consequences? Do you think about the regular ones?"

Tor could see Ivan fading there in the sun. Imagine asking the colonel something like that. At least he wouldn't take his chances, and why ask? The answer was obvious.

But it wasn't, not this time.

The colonel picked out an envelope from the inner pocket. "Here lies the consequence in the first place. And if he and his sister don't come to their senses, you can use this weapon. It is an advantage for you if you do not know the content. Because she's your wife, as we know. Should this not work either, we use the recipe from the seventh floor."

Ivan had been quiet but jumped a little by the word seventh floor. The reference to the well-known building in the Kremlin was obviously as threatening as it was during the Soviet era.

What was in the envelope that could act as a means of threat? And how did Astrid and his brother-in-law fit into the picture?

The colonel had obviously and deliberately told him as little as possible. Just as well so far.

But sooner or later, both Samuel and Astrid had to share their pasts. Or did they have to?

Would he like to know the contents of the envelope?

Would it be like opening Pandora's box? A can of worms?

No, maybe not. But sooner or later, he had to talk to Astrid about this job, and then come what may. Hope for the best.

But Samuel then, a spy? Where there any reason to doubt the Cobra? No, he didn't think so.

It bubbled in Tor's head. SINTEF and CO2 purification, fair enough. But the twisted theory that Norway was involved in a new lunar landing technique?

Admittedly, the Russians had not been to the moon, nor did they want to copy the Americans.

"Why didn't you go to the moon based on US technology? You had everything you needed, didn't you?"

"The truth is that we had problems with the disconnection in space. As we had success with the first Sputnik, then we did not want to weaken our aerospace reputation."

Tor thought about it. Credible? Hardly.

But now, perhaps, little Norway had come up with new technology that could be applied to Mars or other destinations in space. His brother-in-law had said something this Easter that there could really be life on other planets and that one could envision the moon as a first base. Not least because there was ice there. And ice meant water. Lots of water, according to Samuel. But could Norway play a role here? Absurd. But this twisted idea, someone had planted in the heads of the Russians. How to convince them that this was wrong, completely wrong? The moon landing was just a phrase the prime minister had used in a New Year's speech.

"Are you sure that there are concrete project descriptions not only for the CO2 purification but also for aerospace? And that's why the whole thing is referred to as the Great Moon Landing?"

"We wouldn't be sitting here otherwise, and, Tor, can we stop this nonsense!"

"Okay. Okay."

Tor gave up.

"Think Japanese," he said half-loud to himself.

"What did you say?" The colonel leaned forward.

"No, nothing, I was just thinking out loud about a Japanese I met once."

"What did he say? I hope it wasn't hara-kiri!" The colonel pushed another vodka bottle across the table. "You know I came here from Tokyo, don't you?"

"Solve the problems as they are unveiled, that's what he said. It is nicely referred to as sequential problem solving."

Ivan laughed. "Did you hear, Mikhailovich? Welcome to our team, Tor. Again! We know where we're going, and you're going to do your part of the job."

"Let's not get too casual, Ivan. I prefer the use of agent names. Let it become a habit."

Ivan had become somewhat of a boss suddenly. The Cobra wasn't going to have any of it. Neither would Tor, for that matter.

He let it go. Almost ignored what the boy said. Because he was just a puppy compared to the Cobra and himself. It was an insult to think in terms of a comparison.

But he couldn't quite let his mind go: what if the Russians were really on to something big? They had to be. Or? Was it just a metaphor on the part of the prime minister? Or no? Moon landing, as if…

But for him, this could mean life or death. If he committed himself to obtaining spaceflight drawings, and it turned out that these drawings did not exist? That it was all a figment of the imagination? What then? Whose life was on the line then?

And what about that damned envelope?

He turned it around. Indeed two-letter sheets and one picture? Held it up to the light. Looked like they were full-written sheets.

Then the Cobra snatched it back.

"Later, Tor, later."

20

Early Afternoon

And it was the end of the caviar and Tor felt more than clearly the effects of vodka bottle number 2.

"Then we have the arrangement ready then, Tor? First, to get a lady who can charm one of the fifteen selected in the Ministry of Defense, one of those who likely has access to the treats we are looking for."

"Fifteen what?"

"Have you gotten this old? Aren't you paying attention?" the Cobra continued.

"Yes, because we have data on all fifteen, right, Ivan?"

"The complete breakdown, with education, the entire CV, financial status, any sidesteps, relationships with wife/cohabitant, children, etc., speeding fines, tax evasion. Social status, interest in gambling, horseracing, etc. Any gambling debts, closest friends, and their status."

"Easily influenced by women, yes, as they are all men, right, Ivan?" It came again.

"All bosses are men," it came dry from him. *For now*, Tor thought.

"Any problems, Tor? You get paid well, you know?"

"No, I was just going to send a message that I'm home, shall we say in two hours?"

"It's faster with the bus from here, it leaves in thirty-five minutes." Tor had trouble hiding his surprise.

"Just call, Tor, we're in control, aren't we, Ivan?"

"Yes, and you will be notified of the next meeting at Haugen as you say."

Deep down, something told him this was crazy. Imagine detailing the top staff in a Norwegian ministry, hoping to find something to hang someone for.

This belonged to a bygone era. But maybe it was still the case in Eastern Europe. But in Norway?

Anyway, he had to develop a cover story for Astrid, but it wasn't urgent yet.

"Then maybe you have the recipe for where I can find the lady too?"

He couldn't help the certain sarcasm.

"We're not going to have a whore," it came in a dry tone from the Cobra. "We have a cover apartment at Frognerparken. You can use it for interviews, yes, before that, you must not been to a restaurant or coffee shop."

"You, meaning?"

"Yes, wake up now, Tor. We're at it now, don't you get it? You put an advertisement in Aftenposten and online and call for a 100 percent reliable, beautiful woman for special assignments. Full payment, duration up to 6 months. Work in the evening."

Tor was dumbfounded. "Do you think Aftenposten takes in such ads?"

"You get to try, and if it doesn't work out, you'll have to camouflage."

"Is that how you took down Treholt, too?"

The Cobra laughed. "We didn't have to. Arne wanted dialogue, and then he tried to become influential."

"Do you mean that the government's plan to send him to the UN and later the School of War was irrelevant to you?"

"It did not matter to anyone except Arne then. But you can ask your old contact in Moscow. Treholt gave us about zero, but some never stopped hoping for the big deal. He should never have been punished as a spy. Only for contact with foreign powers and perhaps for receiving travel allowance."

"What would the punishment be?"

"It doesn't matter, the attorney general and not least the press got someone to play with. The tabloids. I guess it was a couple of books from the VG man's hand. I don't remember his name, the journalist. But for him and others, the whole Project Treholt, as they called it, became an obsession. And a profitable one!"

They were in by land by now.

"Your bus, Tor!" The Cobra smiled. "It's great to be back at work with you."

What were fantasies, and what was reality?

He was the only passenger on the bus that hot day. No wonder, anyone who could get away was probably on the beach. There he should have been, too, or in the shade in the garden with a cold beer.

Complete overview for all the bosses at MOD (Ministry of Defense)?

Astrid should have heard this. *But I don't think she would have believed it.* Or wasn't she the Astrid he wanted her to be? Had he lived with a woman who kept great, essential things hidden from her husband? Maybe it went back to Finnmark; perhaps something was going on still? Did she have an affair? No, he couldn't believe it. Not his Astrid. But wasn't it the case then that the spouse was the last to know something? Tor forced his thoughts away. But something was left behind. The Cobra had an ace up his sleeve; that was more than evident. And the lists they talked about, what about them?

Did Tor himself believe these lists? He had to, for now.

When they met later, he was given documentation—whatever it may be worth. Could it be the SVR chief at the embassy who had cooked something up?

Taken the chance that there would never be any questions from Moscow? Made fairy tale stories about Norwegian officials?

No, it seemed too risky. If he was exposed, simple execution would not be enough. Hiking in Siberia in midwinter perhaps—naked.

Instead, had SVR paid some sort of sheep in the ministry for something that was a dream and maybe a little reality?

But then they had someone on the inside?

But hardly any of the top-ranking officials, hardly anyone who had access to the really top classified material. But someone on the staff function, or who had access to it? A cruel thought ran like a lightning bolt through the brain.

Could it be his Astrid who had joined the team under pressure to get something revealed from the past?

His Astrid, a collaborator with the Russians? To save Samuel, her brother. Or herself? He tried to put himself in her situation. Pressure of liquidation or pressure of a public scandal. Or? What was in the envelope?

Pull yourself together, Tor! If you move forward with these thoughts, it might be the end of a lot, at least someone you love, the grandmother of your grandchildren, among other things.

21

Astrid

The road to the villa from the bus stop had never before been that long.

And Tor, if possible, made it even longer. Actually, he should have been sprinting, considering for how long he'd been away.

But he just dreaded it, and it took a while before he was finally at the gate. The mailbox?

Another excuse not to enter straight away.

What if he put this with the MOD and her brother and her childhood aside and just told her about this Ivan and the Cobra. Two Russians had asked if he would help them with a job. So where did he meet these guys? Someone he knew from the old days? No, he couldn't involve her, not now, way too soon. And it would be a lying carousel, never to be finished. So he decided right then and there: Let the old days be old days and keep this new stuff to yourself, Tor, until you see where it all is heading. But where had he been all day and the vodka? It was odorless, right?

But, of course, she'd notice.

"I met an old acquaintance and had a couple of beers. Bathing and saltwater, I think I need a shower."

"Have you started smoking again? I think I can smell cigars."

Fucking hell.

"No, it was just Johan steaming away."

"Johan, do I know him?"

"I'm not sure, an old acquaintance through the military."

"Where did you meet him then?"

"Down at the kiosk at Furua, but now I have to get up."

"Don't stay there all day, we'll eat soon, and Nikoline's going home afterwards."

He didn't like this, back into the realm of lies. He had sworn to himself that never ever again should he lie to Astrid.

"I was watching Hannah Montana with my best friend, Grandpa, but where have you been today? By the way, are you not on holiday?"

"Yes, but during the holidays, you have to be allowed to do what suits you, right?"

Apparently, the kid wasn't too keen to know what he had been doing that day. But there was to be more to come.

"The weird man with the giant coat that was here yesterday, did you meet him again maybe?"

He's the one she was interested in.

"Man in black coat? In the middle of summer?"

Astrid got interested now. Very.

"Yes, there was someone who sells insurance. He had called me a few weeks ago and asked to come by, and I had forgotten the whole thing."

"Was he the one who delivered the letter, with only your name on it in the mailbox this morning?" This was getting troublesome. "Or was it a secret girlfriend after all?"

"Do you have a secret girlfriend, Grandpa?"

"Yes, many. I'm just kidding, my friend. I just have a girlfriend, by the way, two, you and your grandmother."

"Aren't you boyfriend and girlfriend?"

"Yes, we are, and we have been for many years, and we will continue to do so. Right, Astrid?"

Tor noticed from her that the topic would be picked up again later.

The evening news was finished, the summer show on TV was done, and he didn't receive any further postponement.

"Are you keeping something hidden from me, Tor?"

"Why would one need a lie detector when one has you, Astrid? Something has emerged from way back in time. I don't know if it's perfect."

"Or not good at all?"

He'd turned pale by now.

"You have to give me time to figure it out."

"Is there anything from your past you haven't told me about? I thought I knew everything."

"Almost everything then, sweetheart. But maybe I don't know everything about yours either. I've never asked and dug so much about what it was like up there in the North. I just know your issues with your mother, and you didn't want to talk about it."

She got quiet, reticent. Quite a long time.

"No, but, dear, it was never my thought to dig into your past, my Astrid."

Was there a tear that crept up on a pale face?

"We'll leave it alone, Tor, and I'll stay out of your past. But I hope we don't have to lie to each other anymore."

It was salty, her tears mixing with mine. "You are good, Astrid—always been good to me."

"You too, my boyfriend."

It was a night of holding each other like the old days. Just hold, feel the security of being close.

But in the middle of the night, at three o'clock, he had to get up. Managed to wake her up and apologized for having to go to the bathroom.

The truth was the nightmare. The nightmare of home in total disintegration and seeing this special relationship between Astrid and her brother-in-law Samuel, something the Cobra knew about and had to do with the past.

But you're strong, Tor, at least you have been. Put it behind you, and it'll just be a bad dream about something you don't need to know anything about.

22

The North Koreans

They had come at night. They had likely come by boat. It could be figured out from their equipment. It was summer, and the roller blinds were drawn to make it possible to sleep. The mosquitos were intense at this time, so everything was closed, even the air vents. There was a smell inside.

Her father woke her up, but she didn't want to get up. Finally, she pulled a t-shirt over her bare breasts and wandered into the living room in just that and panties.

She struggled with her eyes in the light. Three men in camouflage uniforms cast greedy glances at her. Her father had been handcuffed with his arms behind his back, fully dressed already. Another man kept track of his mother so she couldn't get out. It was just the three of them at home; the siblings were at summer camp.

This horror image would haunt her for the rest of her short life, the nightmare that would steal her sleep.

Vladivostok was not a small town. But the suburb where they lived was tiny. The school and the (communist) party house were also a kind of hamlet house, the shop, the police station, and a tired gas station. That's it. Everything was very strict due to the proximity to the border and not least the naval base. The KGB had the real power.

In early summer, they had been allowed to host a local beauty pageant. Her mother didn't want her to participate, but then there was her friend. She nagged and nagged, and even though Vassiliev, her little boyfriend, did not like it, she lined up. He's just jealous her friend felt. And I'm sure he was. Maria was already a sixteen-year-old with perky, beautiful breasts, and she was tall, and her legs were as the ones she'd seen when she was looking at movie stars.

Of course, she won, and of course, she was asked to come to the office of the KGB leader.

"I want to send you to Moscow for our school there. There you can serve your country and have a brilliant career."

But she did not want to, wanted to be here at home with her family and with Vassiliev.

"You have to make up your mind before summer is over, and can I be of help to you with something, just let me know."

She didn't like his gaze when she understood what he meant and got out the door and home to her mother.

"What did I say? You should never have appeared on this show."

But Maria cried and hung around her neck, assuring her that she loved her and was not going anywhere. Least of all to Moscow.

Now she stood in the living room with the hungry soldiers or whoever they were. In any case, they wore uniforms. But they weren't her soldiers. They were Koreans. North Koreans, one of them corrected her with a cold grin.

Then came the boss. He'd been inside with her mother. But she wasn't allowed out.

"Maria, we've been watching you. It's a short distance to the border, you know. That's why we're here, and we want you to work for us. But you need training, and you get it just as well from the KGB in Moscow. So in the morning, you go back to the KGB chief here and say you've changed your mind and want to go to Moscow anyway. Your father is our hostage. We'll take him tonight and send him home again when you've signed up for our contact in Moscow. If he's wanted, he's gone fishing, and he's lost. As long as you follow our orders, your father is safe. The day you fail, he's dead."

Then they were gone except for the boss and the father.

"You might think you can go to the police or to the KGB with this story. Do it, and you won't see your father again."

Then she just heard the entrance door close and her mother screaming "Open the door" from the bedroom. The soldier had twisted the key to the bedroom before he left.

"You're our rescue now, Maria, do as he said, or we'll all die. Go to Moscow!"

So she was the one to be sacrificed! But did she have a choice?

She was approached by a boy of twenty-something on the subway in Moscow five weeks later. It all looked okay. Two young people who took an interest in each other.

"I'm Kosin. That's my code name. I'll follow you when there's anything I want. Or you can come here to this station. I'm always here on the first Thursday of the month at 8:00. Later, we'll get a cell phone arranged."

"And my father?"

"We'll send him home tomorrow. If you have any doubts, try contacting your mother in the afternoon. But remember the time difference. By the way, I hear you're doing well at school."

How could he monitor her in the middle of Moscow without the Russians finding out? Strange, but everything had gone the way the North Koreans told her, and her father had come home safely.

She enjoyed herself at the KGB school, but missed her family and home and Vassiliev. But her mother wrote that he had already found another girl. Maria's best friend. So that's how boys are. She wasn't going to let anyone in anymore.

Caracas was to be her first trip to luxury life.

"But don't imagine you're something special. In this life, you live to serve your country, not for anything else. Now you're going to be Ms. Hernandez, and finally, you're going to use your language skills. Your job is to get on to the Norwegians who stay at Regency Hotels. You fly via New York, and this one guy also takes a flight from New York. Everything is mapped. You only have to follow orders that you get along the way."

23

January 4, 1974, Caracas

The flight coming down from New York was an hour late. Tor got himself another dry martini before landing and the meeting with his old mates from university.

Since September, Harald had been stationed in Venezuela. The embassy had received essential visits from the minister of the sea and the secretary, including his buddy from the economics studies. Who would have thought that the career of the two would accelerate like that? But there were no extreme salaries in the public sector, but it is the status attached, as Harald used to say.

Tor didn't feel much for the status. He had been forced to break off his studies. Pregnant cohabitant and without any wealth as well.

The solution to the problems was to enter as a partner with his friend Rolf in the advertising agency Ellipse.

There were no equity requirements, but then this was no 9–4 job, but exploitation as Astrid called it.

The twins never saw him when they were little, not when awake in any case. But exciting clients both nationally and internationally.

Aker had become a meaningful connection and, in many ways, the entrance to other oil-related companies.

Now he had taken the time off for a detour to Venezuela and the capital Caracas on his way home from an exciting meeting in New York.

Someone was interested in buying the shares in Ellipse. This one wasn't just anybody. The tip had come from a friend in London, and JWT, the world's second-largest chain of advertising agencies, fell for the idea. Think about it, buy little Ellipse. His friend Martin was high up in JWT and thank you for that.

"Fasten your seat belts, we are cleared for landing in ten minutes."

Oh, they were already there, just across the bay and into Caracas, the El Dorado of pickpockets.

Not only pickpocketing but also murder was commonplace in this big city.

"So you have to watch out for which taxi you choose." Harald's warning rang in his ears.

Then they were on the ground; the lady seated next to him had white knuckles after the handgrip.

The panic seemed to have taken her when the plane fell into an air pocket and took the ground with a peel. She finally let go of his hand.

Tor didn't bother for his own sake. Still, the lady smiled warmly with all the rings and jewellery. Wasn't anything for him, almost twenty-two and a little bit on the heavy side already? Chubby, at least. But the eyes, the eyes were like black diamonds and intense. Face? Yes, it was beautiful.

Maybe she'd always been chubby?

"Muchos gracias, Signor," she whispered.

They bumped into each other again by the baggage belt.

Then there was a man in uniform there and another, obviously a portier from the hotel. How had these two managed to get inside customs?

"Will you drive with us into the city center, Signor? Yes, me, Pepe, and my driver?"

He could see a light blush on her neck but thought, *Okay, why not.*

"Miguel will take care of your luggage. Just point to your bags."

She was still whispering, maybe a throat infection? Or was it a soft accent that made the words smoother than high-pitched Spanish?

But for sure her voice was sexy. She was pretty tall for being a Latina, maybe five feet three. And he saw it now; it wasn't just her face that was pretty. Strange that he hadn't become aware of her before on the flight.

She must have switched places along the way. And fell into the neighbor's seat while he slept. What would the boys say when he told them he'd been picked up by that woman? Picked up? She'd only been friendly to a foreigner.

After half an hour, they approached an obviously snobbish area. Embassy district? But Tor didn't think more about it. The chauffeur swung the Daimler into a driveway. Maybe she belonged to the jet-set or just the embassy people?

"I live here, but the chauffeur will take you to the hotels downtown. You stay at the Regency, you said?"

Had he told her that he had a reservation at the Regency? Fuck.

Indeed, how did she know this?

Maybe she'd read the label on the suitcase, but there it was, Plaza, New York, and not Regency, Caracas.

The driver held the door for her, and Tor offered her his hand, but she didn't take it.

"Hasta la vista, Signor," and then she was gone.

When she got out of the car, he clearly saw she wasn't fat, just had a bulky coat. He tipped Pepe with a $10. Pepe didn't even move an eyelid. Just put his hand to his hat, and then he was alone with the driver and on his way to the Regency.

24

Pool Time

The Norwegians all stayed in the same hotel; some were out jogging.

Tor left a message to meet for lunch, quickly changed, and went down to the pool. There were no less than twenty-five meters of Caribbean blue-green water and plenty of model-thin ladies trying to look sophisticated under the umbrellas. Nothing for him. Wife and children at home. A margarita had to be appropriate before lunch, and then he was gone, in deep sleep under the parasol.

Woke up from someone splashing next to him and who else but the lady from the plane. No, she wasn't fat. But what was she doing here? He nodded faintly and let his eyes get used to the bright sunlight.

Three guys were out in the water, and there they had drinks pushed over on floating blocks of polystyrene or something. So lovely, get the drinks served in the midst of the pool.

He immediately recognised the minister who received something like Coke. But the other two, who were they? Was it the neighbor, the journalist at VG, and wasn't it the chief executive, Treholt, who had been out jogging too?

He looked at the clock. Damn it, he'd slept past the lunch with Harald. She splashed again, and then she came up from the water.

The lady under the neighboring umbrella had left for lunch, so the deck chair was almost vacant in a way.

Tor was up before he could think, offered her a dry towel, and took the call to wipe her back almost before she could ask. The gaze was clear enough.

"Gracias. My uncle owns this hotel, and when my own pool is under repair, I go here."

A waiter was all over her with vodka lime or something before she could sit down.

Her hands didn't quite get around with the sunscreen, so what could he do other than offer to apply it on her back.

"My name is Hansen, Tor Hansen, and I come from Norway."

She gently sipped the drink. "I'm Ms. Hernandez, Maria Hernandez. My husband is travelling in Europe, diplomacy."

Did she have any tendency of a weak Eastern European accent, perhaps Russian? But she had a Spanish-sounding name and undeniably did not look Russian. Before he could think of anything else, Harald stood there, and he just had to apologise.

"Slept past lunch and stuff, and I see you've had time to acclimatise already." Harald laughed. "Nothing changes with you, Tor, but have you seen those guys in the pool and then with a journalist in tow!" He laughed a little before the grimaces came.

"I need to talk to this reporter. Make it clear to him that there will be no exclusive interviews if he doesn't shut up about the luxury lifestyle."

Tor turned to Ms. Hernandez. But she was gone! Had she been there?

He looked at Harald. "Did you see where she went, that dark-haired beauty next to us?"

Harald laughed. "Everyone is dark-haired here."

But the chair was empty, except for a towel that lay on the edge. Not hers anyway.

But then she stood there, the lady who owned the towel. Dripping, she had come up from the pool, but Tor felt no urge to dry her. Enough now. He could have sworn that he had greeted Ms. Hernandez, driven with her to town, and sat next to her on the plane.

But gone she was, gone. Would anyone believe this wild story? Where did she come from, what did she want with him?

One more occurrence, and he wouldn't be able to discard it all as just random coincidences.

25

Dreams

"A penny for your thoughts? Heatstroke? You know, in the middle of the day, it's usually close to 40 degrees here, so let's go inside. I'm sure our friend will be here soon. I need to talk to him about this reporter before he screws up. The PR can get out of hand for anyone. Yes, dear Tor, this is what it is like when you entice with stories in Norway's largest tabloid. And how about you? You dropped out from economics, didn't you?"

It was several hours later, and there had been some frozen daiquiris for all three of them.

"I couldn't afford to continue my studies, you know. The student loan disappeared into diapers."

Harald laughed. "Yes, and then twins, really, nothing less."

Tor blushed. "But now, Astrid is in the process of law studies. Working part-time now."

"But I guess you're making enough money for both of you now."

"Right, with dividends, it's going to be another million and free car, etc."

"And representation?"

They were both pushing now.

"Yes, some. But you're the ones building careers. Foreign Ministry and Trade. Short distance to the top for both of you."

"Not for me," Harald said, pausing.

"Hardly any embassy advisory posting in 4–5 years."

"You know there's a lot of competition here. And it's not a big deal to be the first secretary at some distant place and forgotten for a decade."

Arne said nothing.

Harald looked at him." Where are you in your mind? At your beautiful woman's house?"

Arne shook his head. "No, I'm in New York, nothing less. The UN will be a great challenge and then top overseas additions. I could stay with friends in New York."

Harald laughed.

"Yes, you might be able to put up some notes on it. But what matters is building a career."

"When you get high enough, you don't need savings. What do you need them for when you're an ambassador in Stockholm, with a residence, and a driver and long, paid holidays?"

"Short distance home to the grandchildren and friends. No, make your career. And then you can become a minister with a considerable pension. What's bothering you, Arne? Is it the farm boy and the craving for land and goods that drives you?"

Arne turned pale. "We come from different environments—yes, maybe it's the security as in the countryside I'm stressed about. Security with money in the bank. I'd love to have an extra couple of millions."

It was late, really late.

"Watch out for this journalist next to you!"

That was the last thing he heard on the way to the elevator. He had avoided him as best he could. Presumably, the writer didn't want anything to do with him either on this trip.

Tor felt he was shaky on his feet, far too many frozen daiquiris.

Shit, the key card didn't fit. Would they have reversed the code? Have to go back to the front desk now?

Tried again, and there it was. Had there been a visitor in his room. His suitcase was definitely moved, and the lock had been broken. Or had he forgotten to lock the bag? Who would be interested in a single Norwegian here?

The junior suite had its own sleeping section. Did he have a visitor?

Would he find a stark-naked Ms. Hernandez in bed? *Now you are turning mad, Tor.* A quick brush before he dared to open the door to the bed.

Was he disappointed? Or relieved? No one, including Ms. Hernandez, was waiting for him. But it was only the first day in Caracas.

26

Ms. Hernandez

The three of them had arranged a jog the following day, but Harald did not come. Occupied, early meeting, the message read. Arne dropped him too, and then Tor was alone down the beach. Maybe not so smart to go outside the fence? He didn't care about the warning that had been put up.

It was nice to get out and walk along the water before the heat hit. After half an hour, he approached an area with a two-meter-high fence and realized it was wiser to turn around. But the voice crying for help sounded familiar. Three teenage boys did their best to harass a young woman who came out of the water. No one seemed to care. So Tor, the gentleman, was there on the water's edge in an instant.

And there she was, Ms. Hernandez, in a slashed swimsuit. Breasts were what weighed on this lady. There was something eastern about her. Maybe she had surgery on her boobs as well? The Chinese generally had small tits, didn't they?

But Chinese? Then she would have had to have facial surgery. Maybe she was of Mongolian origin?

And eventually, she asked him to call her Maria, there at the porch to her suite.

It had been several hours since they started the first Bollinger bottle. Tor hadn't had any thoughts for those at home or anyone, but now out on the porch came the remorse. Or was it really remorse? Or was it a hangover?

"Where are you from, Maria? And what do you want with me? It can't just be the coincidences that have brought us together four times now, can it?" He more concluded than asked.

She had switched to something light, razor-thin, transparent, of course.

"I will make love to you, Tor."

"Stop it!"

This was too strange. He was no Casanova.

There had to be something more and something entirely different behind it. Was he going to let Harald in on what had happened?

Was Arne the target, and should Tor be the way to him? He felt used—cruelly used.

But had he done something wrong?

There had been no shortage of opportunities for an erotic adventure. But it was something that held back, not just the thought of Astrid.

He intuitively felt that this was something scary, and he would get it right, but it would take time.

27

September 3, 1979

"Hi, Tor, are you going to join the fair at Sjølyst?"

"I don't know if I'll have time. What's going on there?"

"Exhibition of things from Azerbaijan," it came from Rolf.

"My oh, when did you become interested in icons and that sort of thing?"

"It could be something oil-related, too. Aker asked us to be there."

Rolf worked with Aker and the H3 and H4 rigs, so he probably knew what was worth seeing.

The fairgrounds were almost empty; there was also no congestion at the Azerbaijani stand except for four guys and two ladies who were the hosts. Quite overcrowded behind the counter.

Some carved horses and piles of documents in Russian and in some kind of strange English were all that was on the bench. And then the vodka bottles.

Lots of vodka bottles. And Rolf drank, and Tor drank, and some of the guys behind the counter toasted and drank. Not the ladies and not the two most well-dressed.

Then Rolf had to leave, and Tor stayed alone. Why did he stay behind anyway? Why didn't he go with Rolf?

But no, something was holding him back, something about that one guy, one of them who didn't drink. And then there was this lady, Tatjana.

"You like our presentation?"

There was a Mr. Sokolov who had come up to him.

Never had Tor seen any documents or presentations with such poor English, almost incomprehensible, a kind of mix of dictionary English, and he didn't know what. Was he going to put it straight to the man? Yes, why not. Absolutely no one would take an interest in this material the way it looked now.

"Thanks for the vodka. I'd like to go now."

But the Russian—because it turned out that he was Russian—hung over his shoulder and pleaded for a comment on the material in excellent English.

"What do you think yourself then about the language in the brochures?"

"Come over to our trade attaché and tell us what you think, what you might have done differently."

The trade attaché was way down the vodka bottle, while this Sokolov seemed completely dry, and suddenly, Tor realised it: this was the usual set-up with jovial businesspeople and the KGB, according to rumors.

But his judgment was already a little impaired, and maybe there could be a job here? Then the vodka bottle was empty, and a new one arrived on the table.

"No one bothers to read anything in such bad English."

"What did you say now, right now, and could you repeat it, so my colleague understands how bad a job he has done?"

Sokolov was all the way back on him, and Tor felt the cold spreading down his back. But what did he have to lose?

"The English stinks."

Sokolov looked at his colleague Piotr, obviously very pleased.

"Do you hear, Piotr? The English in the brochure is illegible—it stinks."

He laughed happily in the other's face.

No doubt who was in charge.

"Tor, because that's your name, isn't it? That's what you said? Would you like to do a job for Piotr, paid, of course?"

This was getting dangerous but exciting too. Work for the Russians, or would it be for Azerbaijan? And where did they get his name? Could they have listened to the conversation between him and Rolf? Yes, it had to be, or wasn't like that? Did they know most of it about him already?

What about Alex, this well-dressed Russian, no doubt KGB, who probably lurked somewhere, and were Alex Sokolov and his colleague also KGB?

Tatjana had come along eventually. Spotless English, maybe KGB she too? Soon they had the whole story. Tor worked for an advertising agency as a consultant and copywriter and had published a couple of books in Norwegian, spoke fluent English, and had a broad network of contacts within trade and industry.

Much later, during dinner with Tatjana and Alex, he realised that the background was perfect for, precisely, the KGB.

Officially, they both worked for Vnestorgreklama in Moscow and were at the fair to help the trade department and the people of Azerbaijan.

They insisted on taking him to the Grotten restaurant. There was always live music there, and Tatjana loved to dance.

The dinner was nice, but it worried Tor that they knew everything about him, while he knew almost nothing about them.

He was asked to present calculations for new texts until the next afternoon, and then they would meet at Grotten, in the bar, of course, together with Piotr.

Rolf was thrilled, a possible order and cash.

But Tor felt he was getting into something unpleasant.

"Shouldn't we call the Police Department and tell them about my meeting last night and that I'm going to see them again?"

"Nonsense, Tor, this is about money for us and no espionage. Relax, at least until you've met them tonight!"

"Okay, then it'll be like this."

But Tor was worried until they started the calculations.

28

September 4, 1979 at 14:00

Tor had arrived late for work. The vodka was still in there. All morning he'd been working on calculations at home.

Was his English good enough, or did he have to hire expertise? Maybe talk to someone from the Chamber of Commerce?

"But these people then, Tor, what kind of English do they speak?"

Rolf was on him, about the money now, easy-earned money.

"The guys from Azerbaijan spoke very poor English, while the Moscow gang spoke almost perfectly as far as I could judge it."

Then he finally realised. He was absolutely sure now. This whole thing was just a cover.

Of course, the representatives from Vnestorgreklama could speak and write fluent English. So Tor, what about him, what role was intended for him? Enlistment for espionage, of course.

"But what contacts do I have that make me attractive?"

Rolf looked at him. "Do the job, get the money and get out. We need the cash."

"But the police, don't we have to talk to the police?"

"Sign the contract and get it signed with payment terms and all, and then you can go to the police."

"You're so right, Rolf, and I shall put an extra 25 percent on top of it. With those guys, you never know."

500,000 was a lot of money, a lot of money for just over a week's work, and then the lady from the Chamber of Commerce should have a couple of notes and a bottle of champ.

What would the police say if they heard about the contract because they had to? He got a twist: work even for a month and then buy external help from the Chamber of Commerce for the finish.

Yes, it could work.

But 500,000, that was the amount they really wanted and then it wasn't a good idea to start there.

"I say 600,000 and let me haggle down to 5. What do you say, Rolf, does that sound wise?"

"Better yes. But no going lower. Under no circumstances."

"You're greedy, perhaps too greedy and maybe they'll check the price somewhere else, at another agency, too."

"Doubtful, I guess they're actually not focusing on the brochures."

It's Tor they want! But the latter he kept to himself.

Rolf laughed, but Tor didn't laugh.

"Don't you think about the risk, Rolf, if that's how you assume the whole thing being espionage?"

Rolf was still laughing, even more strained now. "Sweet Tor, you don't have any contacts worth anything to the Russians, do you? Or do you have a life apart that I know nothing about?"

"But what about our customers then, Rolf. Can't you see that the Russians might be interested in them?"

"You mean industrial espionage?"

"Yes, of course. What about Aker, for example?"

"Why don't we take this job? How about the money? We've got a lot of holes to put half a million into."

"You're in the clear, while I have to take the brunt!"

29

September 4 at 19:30

My nervousness was obvious

"Can't you join me then, Rolf?"

But Rolf was busy and thought it was really best for Tor to go alone.

Busy, what was her name again, the ad assistant across the street? Birte, wasn't it?

Wearing the suit jacket as it should be worn, Alex Sokolov seemed like he was bathing in Armani suits.

Maybe this wasn't such a big deal for him, but for us, it's dead essential, Tor thought. Vacation, new car now. Maybe he could be invited on holiday to Crimea. But what about the police?

He fumbled with the briefcase, so it went to the floor as the door to the restaurant Grotten opened and there stood Tatjana. If he wasn't nervous before, it didn't get any better now.

Wearing black leather trousers and a loose top, black that one too. Flexible enough that the left nipple almost popped up. The hair was the way men want it, long and black, shiny. No jewelry, high heels, high enough.

The contrast with home was striking.

And yet could you live with such a model on a day-to-day basis?

I don't think so. This one was a chosen one to get men into the net of the KGB. No doubt about it. Maybe she was the one with the brains.

But Tor was here to sell, not to be a victim.

"Hold on to what you have Tor," he told himself. Let the babe do it.

Then he was inside, and there was Alex too, respectful as such, and then the person next to him in a bright red leather pantsuit.

"I am Maria. I know Alex from old times. He's a friend of my husband and invited me to join you all for dinner."

So that's how it connected.

He was sorry he hadn't set the price at a million. Now there was 600,000 in the offer, and he couldn't change it.

But Maria, who had obviously caught up with Tor's thoughts, made no mention of the fact that they had met before in Caracas, and then it was a nice dinner. The contract was signed right there and then.

30

The Intelligence

The next day, as early as 08:30, Tor was in line at the Police House at Grønland. It was right upstairs, Intelligence.

"I didn't want to contact you until I knew if this was something to move on with, but now here is the contract with Vnestorgreklama and countersigned of the Azerbaijani trade envoy."

He pulled out the paper.

"And your work here then, Tor, we greatly appreciate you coming to us and not the other way around if you know what I mean."

The assistant, or whatever he was, allowed himself a smile.

"Yes, you mean you'd follow me like I'd be a spy or something?"

"We stop there, it came from Pettersen."

A rough guy at 1.90 could possibly be around 50.

"Tell me what the job is and how you got in touch with Alex Sokolov, not least."

Tor told the whole story, and they agreed to meet on a fourteen-day basis at the start and see how it all developed.

"Then we'll stop contacting you when your mission is complete—if there are no new ones, then. But make sure you get paid on an ongoing basis, and hey, be aware of one thing, but you probably are, already. It's okay that they need help, i.e., Azerbaijan, but there is no doubt what

Moscow wants with you. Do you have any contact with your old college buddies now, by the way?"

The question came over his shoulder on the way out.

"I'm sure you know I haven't, not since Caracas."

Pettersen tried to hide a smile under the back of his hand.

"In fourteen days. Shall we say at the same time then?"

"Where did you go? You didn't answer the phone."

It was a relieved Tor who looked his partner in the eye. "I've been to the police, Intelligence!"

"You didn't save on pace. What about the money? That's 600? Then the cops were happy too?"

"You're taking this too lightly, Rolf. I was being served by four men and two women. They don't do that for just a few leaflets. But maybe you can present the text suggestions, and I'll settle for sending the invoices. Then you can go to the police, every fourteen days that I've agreed. Just to say Tor wasn't for sale, but here I am, Rolf. Just bring me some money, and you'll get me."

Things went quiet after this, and the carton of Camel without filter—the only thing Rolf had in his briefcase—a new one every day, came to light.

"I'm sorry, I'm sincerely sorry. I'll support you all I can."

Nothing more was said, and peace returned to the agency. Temporarily.

31

The Embassy

The invitation to come to the Russian Embassy on Revolution Day, November 9, came at an inconvenient time. He had promised to be home early and, for once, babysit.

But he couldn't say no; the contract and the possibility of new assignments were too important. He had to go home to change into a blue suit, and then a junior employee drove him to the embassy in a BMW. He sat in the back, stature-wise.

Boyish all this, to pretend he had a private driver. But it worked. Two men popped up from chairs at the rotunda on Drammensveien, and then he was bowed in.

But he wasn't alone; more than a hundred guests had already gathered there even though it was only five o'clock. He saw many of the high-ranking people in industry and trade, and merry was the suitable characteristic. Caviar and drinks? Sure, the revolution was celebrated.

But where was the ambassador?

At the far end of the building, he and the Minister of Trade, Haugstvedt, were seated. The latter came from the Christian Democratic Party, and then you couldn't drink with the others, so the two of them had a big Samovar on the table, drank tea, just the two of them, all to themselves.

Tor quickly disappeared back into the great hall and soon spotted a couple he knew and who waved him over.

Almost only men at this event.

He feared that Maria or Tatjana would show up. Not that it would not be lovely as well. But then he might have to explain things to people he knew.

The two men from Kværner, old acquaintances, introduced him to a more senior fellow, Oskar, who immediately sat down with him. Soon after, the two had to leave, and it was just Oskar and himself, who eventually had a little conversation.

Tor felt he had to give a little since the other seemed somewhat reserved. Maybe it was the age difference.

"I am here because I have taken on a mission for Azerbaijan, and then, of course, people came from Moscow as well, from something called Vnestorgreklama. I don't know if they're KGB," he said jokingly. "But I'm just doing my job, and I'm done with it. Of course, I've briefed the Intelligence. And how about you then, Oskar, right?"

"Yes, Oskar Endresen. Guess you're wondering why I'm here? And the answer is not entirely straightforward. Because I really don't know, but sometimes we get some invitations sent from the Foreign Ministry. I guess they've had too many, and then it was my turn to get some air under the wings. Be careful with your KGB review. I have Eastern Europe as my main field in department. Should you need help, yes, without Intelligence, of course, you can call me."

They traded cards on the way out.

Tor didn't look at the card until he got home.

"Ministry of Defense?"

"If you need help, just call..."

Nice contact to have, but he didn't think he'd inform anyone else. And especially not Rolf or Astrid, who was on leave from, just MOD.

"Was it nice, and did they give enough to drink?"

"You can go next time, Rolf."

Said nothing about Oskar.

"I'm sorry, Tor, but I hope we can finish this now. You're the man for this mission. I'm sorry."

He came with his hand this time.

But Astrid wanted to know if there had been many celebrities there or any ministers. He got away with it all by telling her about Haugstvedt, who was in a private tea party. But he couldn't say anything about Oskar. Not yet, maybe never.

32

Intelligence Again

After another week, he was back at the Intelligence with Pettersen.

"Are you okay with the translation, Tor?"

They were in agreement now.

"Sure. The only problem is that it's poorly written, the English, almost incomprehensible. So sometimes, I have doubts about meaning, and I don't know Russian. Maybe I should get myself on to a course."

John Pettersen looked at him. Did he sense there was something more with this Tor?

"Would you really like that? Not just learn to say good day, but to become really good at Russian?"

He was quickly getting intense now.

What was this? Would they enlist him?

"No, I have my job to look after. And this is presumably a one-off mission. First, they have to pay, and then I'll see, if anything else comes up."

"But hey, of course, they've expressed that it's you they're interested in, the brochures they could not care less about."

"Yes, maybe so, but not so fast now, John. We take one thing at a time, right? I also have a partner who would very much like to see the money before we engage in anything else."

"He should cut down on his smoking," John says.

So Rolf is also being kept an eye on? Maybe it's best to get out of this as soon as possible.

"In fourteen days then," he continued as he stood up and reached out with his hand. "Yes, and if something happens in the meantime, you have to call at any time of the day."

I wonder what the two of them will say to each other when I'm gone. This was becoming difficult to carry alone.

Should he call Arne and hear what he thought about the whole thing?

But Arne had long since realised his dream, New York, the UN, and more money and was far above Tor's sphere. He probably had enough with his own issues.

At least Tor couldn't call from the office or from home. For sure he was bugged now, maybe both parties? The translation came along as scheduled.

"Have you sent an invoice?"

Rolf was there again.

"Sure, 200,000, with a deadline of ten days."

"I can guarantee they won't stick to it." Rolf chuckled now.

"No, but then we have a basis for invoicing it in any case."

New customers had come too, and really, they didn't need this Russian job as he had started to call it.

But 600,000! A lot of money there. An awful lot of money! And what would they say if he defected before the job was done?

He had to talk to someone. Someone who was not in the thick of it. Could he call Oskar?

But from where?

If he stopped by Hotel Continental on the way from a meeting he was going to, it would probably be fine to call from there.

Harder to track via a switchboard than from a payphone.

What was about to happen to him? Paranoia?

No answer on the direct line, and he was quick to hang up.

After a glass of dry white wine in the restaurant, he tried again.

A closed voice responded.

"It's Tor from Revolution Day. I'm in need of someone to talk to. I don't know if I'm being followed and by whom, but I'm definitely being bugged on my regular phones from both sides!"

"Today it won't work, but tomorrow."

"Can you be at the landing for the Hovedøya ferry at 15:58? I think the departure is 16 sharpish. Pretend you're going to take one of the other boats. As the ferryman spans the rope and they are ready to go out, you abruptly jump on board this one. I'm sitting there already."

"Dramatic, pure James Bond?"

"No, but you don't know how good they are."

"The Russians?"

"No, both sides. And hey, bring a small backpack with something to bite into and a soda or two. We may not get off at Hovedøya. We'll see."

33

At-Home Tor

"How lovely that you work from home a bit then, Tor!"

"With this translation job, I can work from here for a couple more weeks."

"What about tomorrow? Can I run away from the twins?"

"How about today or the day after tomorrow, please."

"What's wrong with tomorrow?"

"I have a meeting that starts at 16:00, and I don't even know when I'm home."

"So this is how long at-home Tor lasted."

"Don't be too sarcastic. It's all very hectic now as you know."

But she didn't want a hug.

34

The Enlisting 1

"What do you need a backpack for?"

"Everyone carries one now. No need for the dull document folder."

But he left the bag in the car, so Rolf wouldn't come up with the same question as well.

"So a new customer is coming at 15:30 today."

"Today, why couldn't you have told me sooner? You never change, Rolf. But today, it won't work. I'm going to see a translator, and this is something I get for free. There's no possibility of rescheduling."

Tor could see he was getting mad now.

But life was more important.

And Rolf was well to be blamed for the mess Tor now found himself in.

Parked far up by the fortress, bought Coke and baguette with shrimps, and was on his way.

What was he going to tell Oskar?

Had to go with the flow. Just be honest, that was probably the best thing.

Looked neither to the right nor to the left but went straight into the queue to the Langøyene boat. The boats were due to leave a quarter past, but there was always a queue during the summer.

The queue was also long for the Hovedøya boat. He pretended not to look that way at all.

Could he jump the fence there at the last minute?

Yes, he could. They had begun boarding, and the nervousness grabbed him. Would there be room? There was a load of strollers, as usual, but not so late in the day, right? Either way, they were going to wait until the very end.

The departure would likely be a little delayed.

What did it look like behind him, someone suspicious in a black suit? Looks like they didn't have any other uniform. *I'm sure the Intelligence was smarter.* Norwegian standard, jeans and t-shirt with some symbol and foolish text, I love NY or similar.

Impossible to tell if there was anyone in the crowd. No black suit anyway. Perhaps they had switched to summer uniforms, jeans, and I love NY or Paris, to camouflage that they were Russians.

One minute to four, and the last stroller was to be pushed along. Three mothers and girlfriends on a trip. One of them was busy arguing with the ticket agent. Not smart. He heard the skipper tell them that now they would leave regardless of the stroller.

They got it inside, and the ticketer had trouble stretching the strap around. The skipper didn't seem to care.

There was a guy arriving in jeans and a T-shirt, and just right, I love NY, and pushed himself between the strollers.

Now what? But Tor had to be on the boat.

There was a bit of crying and screaming from the queue, but then he was on board. The ticketer cursed, and the skipper shouted and screamed. The man in the t-shirt was gone.

"We let him go ashore first, and then we go to Nakholmen. If he stays on board, we'll land on Hovedøya on schedule. Wait until the last minute. I'm sure he does too. A little cat-and-mouse game this one."

But the man didn't show up, not until the skipper started moving away, and they jumped, and there he was, but now it was too late.

Who was he? From Intelligence or was he Russian? And where was the other one? Always two and maybe more, too, if they were Russians.

"We'll leave separately until we meet outside by the cannons. I go to the shore, and you walk the path. Then we'll have to take it from there."

But Tor, who quickly became aware that he had extra companions, jumped in and out of the woods and down to the shore. Oskar looked at him in amazement.

"Oh yes, there's another one here. Let's go back and go down to the boathouses."

Oskar was clearly surprised. "I didn't know you were so local."

"On the southwest side, there are a couple of sheds, locked, of course. But it is possible to wade around and sit in the opening toward the seaside. Whoever wanted to follow us must also go in, and we will hear the sound in the water. Now you're a marked man as well, Oskar."

"Like if I wasn't already? I'm the only one who worked at Intelligence before I got to the ministry, that alone would be enough for them to keep going, and I don't care."

"Tell me."

"You just have to establish the rules of the game, Tor. You will be overrun with offers, with gifts, and I do not know what. Tell Pettersen at Intelligence everything, but not a word about you and me. Then you don't accept any more jobs for them until the invoices are paid. From that point, we can talk about it further. You focus on your own part, pushing this Rolf in front of you as much as possible. By the way, what do you think of your old classmate from Economics?"

Tor looked at him with a blank stare.

"Arne, must say he's made it."

"Arne was ambitious and for sure is still."

"But what about his dealings with the Russians? Bridge builder somehow?"

"I don't know about that."

"You know, Tor. I'm a nationalist up to my neck. Always has been. Not old NS—"

He saw that Tor had turned pale.

"No, I am for real all through. All for Norway, as in the old king's motto. And me and more people with me, we're afraid of this interaction with the Russians. Check with Youngstorget. Not all floors share today's foreign policy. If you ask me, I think Arne and maybe one more has enlisted. Not only do I fear so, but I feel confident."

"But why would he sacrifice a bright career for some cash?"

"Maybe he thinks he can have his cake and eat it too."

"You mean, I get a sack of rubles and still a one-way visa to a career as a member of the government? Arne is not stupid, wasn't that in the slightest. So this is pulling it far, isn't it?"

"You know, Tor, only the Russians can give us the answer."

"But seriously, you really think they'll give him away if what you're saying is right, and why would they?"

"I don't know if you've heard of the Commission. The border issue between us and the Russians, the Barents Sea, and the fisheries zone."

"Yes, I have some idea about Jens Evensen and some ministry councillors and Arne in the hallway. Some said he was the one who controlled the negotiation from the outside. But the Russian minister Isjkov was the real boss."

"The Russians think they gave up more than they got. But some of us believe Evensen and company were about to give up sovereignty."

"Are you sure it wasn't the other way around? That the Russian wouldn't be accepting our demands?"

"No, and thank God the Russians withdrew. And maybe that's precisely what your Arne is doing now, giving away land and secrets for pieces of silver."

"And the Russians?"

"They think the KGB is in complete control, I would assume."

Oskar shook his head.

"There is still a Gromyko man almost at the very top of the Russian Foreign Ministry. He knows that I trust the KGB little and even less Evensen and co. Donetski's is the name of the man. My age. Intelligence man he too, but from army Intelligence originally, GRU. Hates the KGB."

"Why are you telling me all this, Oskar? I'm not a spy, and I'm not a politician anymore, but an advertising guy. Have a wife that I love and two young children. What do you want from me?"

"I would like to open a channel that monitors both the KGB, the Intelligence here at home, Arne, and the others at Youngstorget."

There was silence. Tor listened for feet moving in the water but heard nothing. He looked at Oskar. What kind of maniac had he ended up with? And how could this man at all be allowed to set foot in the

Ministry of Defense of all places? It must all have gone bad for him at a late stage in his career. He looked at Oskar.

"And that man you found here? Have a Coke and a baguette, Oskar. Call the screenwriter for James Bond, not me. But thank you for listening to me. It was good to talk, but now we're even, right? And by the way, we'll take separate boats back home. Maybe one day I'll call you, if I may."

"Yes, just contact me Tor. But think about what we've been talking about. I love this country, and I don't want it to be sliced up or given away by fools from the western part of Oslo."

"None of the people you mentioned were born in the western part of Oslo, and what do you really mean?"

"I think of the High North, the so-called grey area, the dividing line towards Russia and the Commission. I was born in Porsanger somewhere, you know, and we're not going to give our country away. Not to anyone."

"But are you a better negotiator than the ones we have in Trade, Sea, and the Foreign Ministry?"

"The roots Tor, the roots. It's easy to give away a piece of ocean or land when you've never been there. Think of Nansen and Amundsen, they built new territory for Norway, didn't they!"

"With all due respect, Oskar, do you think the Russian commission leadership bothers to listen to this?"

"No, not them, but maybe Gromyko. It's at the top we have to start. And the grey area and fisheries, not to mention petroleum, are something you spend years on. Don't negotiate while the taxi and bar await."

"But then we must have control about what our civil servants and the colonel over there, Titov, are doing."

"I have respect for Evensen, the newspapers also write that he is an abstentionist. But who is this we are referring to?"

"I hope for you still, Tor, yes and myself."

"Oskar, you're a little crazy, maybe a lot of crazy. I'm leaving now."

Imagine something that crazy. Try to enlist him, Tor, as some kind of agent or courier or whatever he was looking for. Had the whole world gone mad?

At least half of Oslo with spies and Intelligence and what else all around you. Tor, married to a great woman, lovely children, and a good job. Stay away, Oskar and everyone else.

Stupid that he'd gotten entangled in this whole thing with Azerbaijan and the Russians at all. Throughout the evening, he was still doing the translation; by chance, he came across "Stay" in some kind of an encyclopedia. And there was something that made a bell ring: Stay Behind, it said.

But no, it was just a whim, something he'd heard about. But curiosity was aroused.

Wanted to check out the encyclopedias in the office tomorrow.

35

Nittedal

Tor chose to forget both Oscar and Stay Behind. But a bicycle messenger came a week later. What was it now that the happy Oskar had come up with? Checked an encyclopedia as well at the same time, but did not find anything. Brought the envelope from the courier, went around the block and over to Fredrik Stangs Street. Sat down on the bench by the old hospital.

Was he being followed now? Saw no one, so could read the letter from Oskar—handwritten, of course—undisturbed.

"I have spoken to the right person in Moscow, and they are interested, and you will be reimbursed for your costs. So you can inform your business partner that a special mission has been agreed, but you are not allowed to talk about it."

Talk? Did Oskar have his own line to top people in the Russian Foreign Ministry? Now this really was James Bond.

Costs? Were they to send him on journey somewhere?

Perhaps Moscow, and what about the Intelligence which certainly followed every step now? And what about the KGB and little Andreyev, the major from Vnestorgreklama? Sooner or later, he had to admit that he did not have a clue about advertising, but that he was a major or similar in the KGB.

"On Saturday, you take the train to Movatn station and then you take the path up to Sinober, well-marked, takes you an hour. I will come from the Nittedal side, have a car far up, so we go down together. But first, we get to spend the weekend together. Then we can make a battle plan."

But Tor had never said yes to anything. Nor did he ever made any decision to join by himself. *So figure this out, Tor. It has never been harmful to meet new people. Maybe this Oskar is not crazy, maybe he is gay and trying? That's allowed. Or does he have something to do with this "Stay"?* The thought went away.

"Meet you west for the kiosk, by the barbed wire fence. Sinober."

Wow, the man had to be familiar with the area.

Was it Oskar's cabin or one he had borrowed?

What would Astrid say?

Trip to a cabin at Nittedal?

Some old song about the guys at a party.

She had probably never heard it.

But he had to come up with something that was credible and preferably true.

Not pleasant to think that perhaps someone monitored their home, bugged the phone.

What if he said yes to this approach with Oskar, as of now it sounded up in the air.

Crime story for boys with a nationalist from Finnmark.

The whole thing was so strange that no one would have believed it, if it got into the public eye. Except for the Intelligence and of course the Russians.

But how about Astrid?

Say it as it was, surveilled from several angles and she with partial leave from the sensitive Ministry of Defense.

Quite unthinkable. So it had to be a lie and not just any lie. Bad enough that he was doing a job for the communist country of Azerbaijan while she was at work at MOD. Imagine if she got to know everything!

36

The Pursuit

"What do you think about buying a cabin in Nittedal?" He put it on to her at the dinner table.

"Nittedal? And where would we get the money from?"

"The job I do for Azerbaijan, we get paid very well for."

"There is a lot we could need the money for."

"In any case, I was called by this guy from Aker. Cousin of his, he's considering selling a nice little cottage in the middle of the forest and wondered if I knew someone possibly interested."

"My god, have you mentioned to someone that we could be interested?"

"Astrid, you are from the countryside and would it not be nice to have a cabin with pigs and chickens and the like?"

"Yes, and maybe a little fox. Do not try it, Tor. If you want to look at the cabin, you do that. It is this weekend then, right? Do not try to come home in the evening Saturday either, because then I will have a girl's night here. Just travel, my boy."

That hurt. Complete trust and complete deception.

But the whole thing was a little exciting to say no before he knew more.

No way back: the train from Grefsen station? Well, better that than to be shadowed at the East Station.

Did he have someone following him today, early Saturday morning?

To be safe, he parked beyond the Technical Museum and took the path along with the river and came up on the lower side of the railway line.

He could see that he had to jump over the steel fence and the track, but he doubted anyone would care about it. Had another fifteen minutes left for train departure after the car was parked.

Did he have anyone behind him?

Now he must not become completely paranoid, but he could not stop himself from turning around several times, going up the hill.

Finally, there was the fence, and it went well.

Almost empty station and he felt safe when he boarded. Ticket? Wow, that had slipped his mind.

"I'm going to Hakadal."

"Yes, well, but you should have bought a ticket at the station."

Fairly grumpy conductor. So he was gone, and Tor saw no more of him before Movatn Station appeared. And he jumped and ran before the train had stopped.

But he was not alone!

A man dressed in sports gear following. *We'll see then who is in the best shape.* Maybe just someone who was going on a walk, but he had no bag.

Okay, so it would be a battle.

Who could have guessed something about where Tor was going?

Could they have called home and got to know that he was on his way to Nittedal?

Probably so. Astrid had no idea who was hunting him and why. But who had called? The Russians or Oskar or the Intelligence? Not Oskar.

He knew that the path split further up. He deliberately chose the winter trail. Pushed a little extra and went into a thicket and waited.

But no one followed, so he felt safe after that. Did not matter if he got wet from wading in marshy terrain occasionally.

Oskar laughed when he saw him.

"Have you taken a bath?"

"No, but I had to get rid of someone who was definitely not the KGB. Solid Norwegian that I tricked into taking the summer trail."

"And you then?"

"Yes, it was the winter trail for me as you can see."

"Since there are people looking for you, we do not stop here. Sorry, not a coffee break even."

After roughly fifteen minutes, he could see Oskar's car where the timber road from Nittedal became manageable for a passenger car.

"What do we do then?"

"You take the car, drive to Halden, and from there, Blågulan into Sweden. A seaplane picks you up on the south side of Strømstad. Then you meet my Russian contact. Everything is in the instructions that you get here. Pity you do not get to take a bath and change. But drive directly and be careful in Halden. A little cumbersome to find Blågulan. What do I do? I am going back to Sinober and the cabin. Do not think of me. Park the car at the Castle when you come back. I have an extra key. There's 20,000 in Norwegian currency in the envelope. Good luck."

"Well, thank you for that and so what?"

"Read the contents of the envelope when you are in Sweden."

Should he quit now? To Sweden and own plane and stuff. No, he had to carry it out. Enjoy it. Enjoy the excitement. But why could he not have met Oskar in the city and let go of this whole trip through the forest?

Oskar probably had his reasons, and it was clear that all of Tor's movements were carefully guarded.

The common Opel 1978 was in good condition, and after barely two hours, the sign for Halden appeared.

It was challenging, but there he was across the river and past the church, and after a ten minutes' drive, he was in Sweden.

He chose a small exit on the left into the forest and sat down with the envelope.

"The plane is waiting for you at a small pier, and you are the only passenger. Private parking at the pier. Do not talk to anyone, not even the pilot, more than necessary. The flight takes another 1.5 hours. You will land at Vaksholm, middle of Stockholm's archipelago. There you find a cozy restaurant. Look for a well-grown man with yellow and red tie. He is our man in Moscow if I can say it that way. Just call him Mr. D. You're Tor. He speaks good English. He would like to get to know you before he agrees to cooperate with the two of us, so far, everything is at my expense and risk. The plane is paid for. The pilot takes you back to Strømstad now in the evening. But wait to show up at home until the morning sun. Take the same road home, Blågulan. And do not get caught for smuggling. Borrowed a car from a high-ranking official at MOD and everything. Maybe they think you stole it, and I may have to confirm it. You hear from me through a courier like last week. Burn this letter now, but take the money first. Have a good trip."

37

Vaksholm

So Oskar assumed that Tor would not be able to turn down the trip. Overnight in Strømstad. Party town now in the summer. Would not look good if Astrid was told that he was seen at a restaurant in the middle of Strømstad. No, it would have to be a small cottage or something on the way. Perhaps just as well to sleep in the car.

The pilot looked at him. "Have you been lying in the ditch?"

"Sorry, but I had to cross unknown terrain."

He looked disapprovingly at Tor. "Here, you have an extra pillow to sit on." Was probably afraid for his leather seat. "Cleaning is not included in the price."

But he said it with a smile and was okay. Offered Norwegian Marie biscuits made in Sweden and Coke.

"When you exit, you need to try to wash away the worst, or you will not be allowed to enter the restaurant in Stockholm, yes, because it is Vaksholm restaurant you are going to, as we are docking at the pier there?"

"Yes, yes. Thank you for that." Tor said no more.

"Hey, I'm waiting a maximum of three hours. That was the deal."

"Okay," said Tor, "maybe I will come long before that."

"If the bride is nice enough, then you will stay the time."

It came with a smile. So that was what he thought. Just as well. But he should have known.

So they found themselves by the beautiful Vaksholm, where Tor had enjoyed lunch with seafood one summer. Was in Stockholm to inspect a Swan 46, best yacht ever!

The scheduled boat had just left now, in the direction of Stockholm. Climbed out on the wing and "Goodbye!" Got a little water in the face and off with the worst dirt. It was summer and the shirt went in the trash in favor of the clean t-shirt.

"Are you Tor, the Norwegian?" The excessively dressed head waiter, penguin outfit in the middle of the bright summer day, looked disapprovingly at his pants. "Do you have an ID?"

"Eh, do you need an ID to get in here suddenly and how do you know my name?"

"Were you the one who came by private plane here now?"

"Yes, of course and how?"

"But can you prove that you are Tor?"

The irritation could probably be seen on Tor when he pulled out his driver's license.

The butler sighed contentedly. "Well, I have an envelope for you here, and you do not get into the actual restaurant."

"So no food or a beer or something?"

"Sorry, but we cannot bring you into the dining area with the white tablecloths, I am sure you understand."

Tor swore out the door and ripped open the envelope. Then he ran down to the plane and crawled on board.

"Hey, I have new messages. I must catch a Finnair from Arlanda at 17:00 and then I have to return to Strømstad tomorrow. Arriving at Arlanda 11:30. How do we do it?"

"No problem, but you know it will be extra, extra that one! There is a lake right by Arlanda." He looked at the map. "Do not know how we get you onshore there. But I will call a taxi over the radio and then we do the same procedure in the morning. You call when there is a departure from Helsinki? Guaranteed?"

"Yes, of course."

"Then I arrange with a car, and you swim out again."

The laughter was loose now.

"Is it a fucking bride who's making all this fuss to you? Yes, because there is no smuggling of drugs, is there?"

"Just stay calm, you may search me before you fly home in the morning. Today, you see for yourself, I do not have any additional luggage!"

"OK, bring 5,000 with you, and we'll be done with it."

"Then it's Norwegian." There was only Norwegian money in the envelope.

"Then there will be an extra thousand. Our money just drops in value as you know."

"Not there is so big difference on currencies yet. But let us get going, or rather flying."

Obviously, the pilot had a completely distorted view of the exchange rate differences, but when Tor tried to protest, he quickly realized that this would be a complete waste. The pilot was Oskar's issue, and it just had to be the way it was.

There was no jetty to taxi to. Tor had to go in the mud, and the taxi driver got fucking mad.

"What the hell, I did not get a message that I would carry a refugee to Arlanda. And hey, no fucking airline will let you board the way you look! And how the hell do you think my car will look! Here you have a blanket to sit on, and please, sit completely still and keep your feet on the mat literally. Otherwise, I will throw you out of the car!"

It helped with 500 extras, and he promised a pick-up in the morning against an extra payment then too.

"Yes, but then I'm clean."

"Do as you please. Should I come or not?"

"You must come."

He dropped off Tor at International Departures.

Tor managed a shirt and a pair of clean socks and trousers at Arlanda. Lucky with the summer heat and lightly dressed. But they did not have shoes and so the solution was to wash the ones he had and walk barefoot in the shoes until they dried.

He figured that Mister D had been notified about a muddy Norwegian arriving at Helsinki airport.

38

Donetski, the Man from Moscow

No problem finding the contact. A well-grown man, probably sixty years old and quite a teddy bear figure in a black suit, with a yellow and red tie and a large bag with Ahlen's printed. How obvious did it have to be? Well, well, hope they knew the size somewhat. The man said nothing, just took him in the arm and into the toilet.

"You can change here. Five minutes, that's all."

Tor was done after four.

"Where are we going?"

The taxi driver had obviously not been notified. Was Mr. D in doubt whether Tor would come or not? Or was it just a standard precaution?

"Fiskartorpet." It came from the man with the two-colored tie.

He was just about to pay the taxi bill, not cheap all the way to this location he could see on the meter, then Tor saw a man and a woman on the way out of the restaurant. Obviously, they wanted a taxi and this one would be available. He put himself down.

"Drive like hell," he cried to the driver who panicked and pushed the gas pedal, and they were on the return. "I will explain later."

The driver was told to turn onto a side road, and they went out, waited a quarter of an hour. Mr. D did not say a word.

"You can drive back to Fiskartorpet now."

"Why, Tor?" it finally came.

"The man was Arne, my old classmate. I did not want to reveal myself to him. Did you know the lady by the way?"

Mr. D shook his head.

"I thought there was something familiar about her, but the distance was too long."

So she did not work for Donetski, Maria. If he was not lying. For it was Maria, no doubt about it. Maria from the flight from New York, not least from Caracas and from the meeting in Oslo.

"And what about the two who followed your Arne, ten meters behind? Did you know them?"

"No, but they did not look Finnish or Russian for that matter." Mr. D chuckled a little now. "Maybe it was your countrymen?"

He looked jokingly at Tor. Yes, of course, they were Norwegian. Intelligence were probably part of it. Just luck that he had spotted Arne. And thank God that he had to change in the toilet at the airport.

A few minutes earlier and it had been that party at Fiskartorpet.

39

Fiskartorpet

"We will go in and eat crayfish, Tor. There is none better than here. The Volga is far too dirty, and the plague has long since taken over. Did you know that you can no longer use the Volga for vodka production? Totally polluted."

No, Tor had to admit that this was new to him. Probably something new for the vast majority of people.

Coffee had been served and still there was only small talk.

Perhaps this is how it worked in diplomatic circles.

But then finally, there came the cigar and Tor realized that now he had to sharpen up. Clearly, Mr. D could consume unrestricted quantities of vodka.

"Your Norwegian patriot, Mr. O, would like us to get Treholt, and if someone from our side are caught in the undertow, I would not mind."

"You think you want to get rid of Colonel Titov and his local aides?"

"Yes, they have not achieved anything in particular so far, other than to spend lots of money on payment for completely uninteresting information. But we let them hold on a little longer, then they get caught. Intelligence has good control on your man since far back."

"You mean Treholt?"

"Yes, of course. According to Mr. O, he does not have access to any material that could harm Norway and make us happy."

"But what do you want with me then, you and Mr. O?"

"He wants to get rid of Treholt, it has become a mania for him as for many among the top brass in Norway, and I want to get rid of the colonel and his court. It's not easy to just kick him out with the contacts he has got. So I must take him on that he continues to deliver bad goods to say it brutally. Therefore, we want you to help Mr. O monitor Treholt and preferably your Intelligence, even if they also monitor you. In any case, do not get caught by them. So should I cover our side through my contact?"

"KGB?"

"No, that is the Colonel Titov's domain. Do not ask. It can be GRU, or it can be others."

"So the whole hunt for Treholt is really a Russian affair, to clean up internally? Arne is just an innocent piece? You know we attended Economics together?"

He pretended not to hear the last thing.

"Oh no, it's a game that takes place at your home in Oslo, a game about power and positioning and there, Arne is just a piece. A small piece in the Left's internal battle. Fight between Youngstorget ((HQ, Labour party) as you call it and Victoria Terrace (Foreign Office quarters) not least. And the battle has continued ever since the end of the war. Sooner or later, someone steps in and then the race is over for your old classmate as well."

Apparently Mr. D was very well informed about the Norwegian situation. Should he warn Arne? But then his own cover would be in danger. Arne was probably smart enough to take care of himself. Knowing when to lay low. Hiding away as a special counsellor in Greece for a while? But what if he was not a spy? Imagine if he believed in the bridge building work he had started? To end up being sacrificed in one bloody power struggle at Youngstorget, dismembered by the seniors? He had to notify Arne and convince him of the necessity of withdrawing, for a while at least. So no advancement opportunities for this period. Explain to him that the implication would be dramatically large. But would he be believed, he, a measly consultant in an advertising agency?

"What about my travel expenses then? What will I receive to get involved as you call it?"

"Our friend Mr. O at MOD is an idealist and nationalist. He will hardly take it in his stride that you may be used as a courier for services other than those he believes benefit his cause. But I am very interested in oil and gas and probably you have a lot of expertise in this and which is not released due to American components. The technology is developing rapidly and the fact that we get access to Condeep and the entire H. series from Aker can hardly hurt. We already have a lot, but not everything. I have to deliver something. I also have to put Band-Aid on the wound as the colonel and his follower will be dumped."

"You mean promoted?"

"Sure, put out of the game then."

"What about Mr. O then?"

"You must not think so much about Mr. O. He has only one motive, namely, to remove Treholt and the Minister of the Law of the Sea before they can do more damage, as he says."

"But your motives, Mr. Donetski, they are precious?"

Tor was astonished over that he now dared to use the entire name. Donetski had been careless with some notes in which his full name appeared. Just as well jump into it.

"So you know my name and you have intelligent questions. Mr. O prepared me for that, you do not easily let you yourself be intimidated. So I look forward to seeing you here and experiencing you as a person. Your question? But first," he interrupted Tor who was ready to repeat his question. "Remember that Russia has its history in the same way as the United States has its own, although the latter is very short. Almost does not deserve the name history." The laughter was loose now. "When the threat from outside becomes great, very great, you close the borders and become impregnable, fast. Feel free to call it isolationism if you will. One is preoccupied in one's own business and disregard totally more or less good alliance partners. This is what Stalin forgot in his vengeance and his almost manic cleansing processes. Otherwise, he would never have entered into a pact with Hitler before he was strong enough."

Tor realized that this could be long lasting. But he must not be too impatient either.

"That was a fine speech, Mr. Donetski. But to the point. So you want to crack this colonel, really let him do it himself, but at the same time, you are very interested in knowing what is going on in the industrial sector in Norway and will therefore keep him for a while. I have to admit I get confused. Are there any interesting things coming from Treholt at all?"

Then Tor realized that enough was enough and that he would not get closer to any clarification. He was not interested in any new history teaching either.

"What do you need to do some courier jobs, because that's where you can give value for money."

Mr. Donetski was back in real life. No more Stalin and Moscow trials or what Tor had feared would come. Apparently, he also realized that some monitoring job on Tor's part would not lead anywhere either. It would be too amateurish.

He looked questioningly at the older man. "Courier? And what coverage of expenditures do you have in mind?"

"When we now get the opportunity, we might just as well use it to get some of your secrets about oil and offshore. Things will soon become obsolete with you, but we may be able to use it. We find ourselves way behind in oil technology, in any case, offshore, and as far as I know, the Americans do not have anything to give you anymore?"

"Okay, maybe, but again, what does Mr. O have to say about this?"

"Does he need to know? And you get a good chunk of money for every delivery. What do you say to NOK 50,000?"

Tor chose to overhear the amount for the time being.

"Who provides the material then?"

"You do not have to think about that, you will be contacted."

"And then when?"

"As you travel to London Stansted and from there to Cluj or Brasov in Romania, depending on what suits the project. Here you meet our contact. The Palestinian who pays you and you hand over the goods."

"But listen, why don't these items go by courier, diplomatic mail, or whatever it's called?"

"We cannot chance it. A mistake here, and the opportunities for a dialogue with Norway will be destroyed for decades. All trust destroyed. First, the Treholt case, when it sees the light of day, because it is guaranteed to do so and then the diplomatic mail! No, completely irrelevant. On the other hand, a quiet, efficient channel via Romania and then fly up to Moscow. Super smart and 100% percent safe. Should anything go wrong, it is not us, the Russians, we will not be part of the picture at all."

"So I shall therefore be a spy?"

"Absolutely not. You make a few trips to Romania, when it is appropriate, and then you get covered for your travel expenses."

"And if there is a double trip?"

"What do you mean?"

"That in addition to traveling for Mr. O, other cases will also be delivered to you, from your other network in Norway."

"Double package means double package, i.e., 100,000."

Again, Donetski seemed slightly annoyed. Maybe he thought Tor was a bit slow sometimes.

"You get a minimum of three days' notice."

Obviously, Donetski wanted to end the conversation now. Tor had had a certain relationship with the idealist Oskar and became very doubtful. Was this a trap, an attempt to see if he was up to it?

"What if I say no thank you, but hold me to the deal about to convey documents for Mr. O about Treholt and only that?"

"It's up to you. But think about it. 50,000 NOK in hand, per trip, to hand over any documents that you never get an insight in."

"I'd also like not to do anything that drags Mr. O into some spy sphere."

He had gained a lot of sympathy for the fanatic from Finnmark.

"You have my word on it."

"But what about the Intelligence? We are doing this job for Azerbaijan, and I have an agreement to report every fourteen days?"

"Continue with that until the assignment of Azerbaijan has ended."

"What if Intelligence would like me to work for them on the side as well? They have already hinted."

"A dual role you could well fix, but do not get yourself into the triple or quadruple. Almost no one has the brain capacity for that."

"What should I say to Mr. O?"

"Do not say anything, I will inform him first and then he will contact you to tell you how things are going with Treholt and the colonel."

"When will I hear from you then?"

"About one month's time or so maybe. Was there anything more?"

"Tell me a little about the Palestinian."

"Omar has escaped from his country, tired of war and misery. Tired of leaders who never achieves the goal."

"Tired of an eternal quarrel with Israel instead of sensible dialogue, do you mean?" He saw that Mr. Donetski did not like the development. Best to get in on safe ground again. "But why is he in Romania?"

"He went there with his Norwegian wife and moved to Cluj several years ago. Now he has built up a nice practice as a radiologist MD. Sometimes, he will work in Oslo and Stockholm just to keep in touch with the subject somehow. But he does a lot of other things. His wife is also an X-ray doctor and looks after the shop while he is away. The children attend an international school in Cluj. Here you have a picture of him, and you are told where to meet, and then you just exchange suitcases. We owe Mr. O 20,000. Here you have it and 30,000 for the operation or call it what you will. The taxi is waiting."

Donetski was right, the crayfish was excellent and so was the vodka. Should be lovely to get a night just by himself in Helsinki. Still he had to hope that no one familiar popped up. But safer than Strømstad in any case.

They left Fiskartorpet in separate taxis. Mr. Donetski went to the airport, while Tor directed himself toward Finland's pride, the department store Stockman.

But then, he suddenly woke up.

"Drive straight to the Stora hotel on Mannerheim Street."

Heck, not good to know who was on a weekend trip to Helsinki, the Intelligence maybe? They had already been at Fiskartorpet. And what if he ran into Arne?

Damn, he really did not have a choice. When he had managed to be in the clear at Fiskartorpet and in Lillomarka, there was no reason to take any further chances.

The hotel was large enough to be able to hide away.

Welcome, Mr. Rasmussen. Yes, thank you. No more questions. Just got the key to 533, junior suite. Donetski had arranged this. Then he was probably under surveillance from there. The thought of having to hide became increasingly frustrating.

The distance to the minibar was short, but he quickly changed his mind. No more vodka, but a Coke before room service. Did not take the chance at the restaurant, with both the KGB and Norwegian Intelligence in place.

What now then, Tor, now you find yourself in it with both legs and arms in addition. The spy Tor!

40

Stay Behind

It was a quiet dinner in the hotel room. Just bathrobe, no worries about dressing up. Sometimes, room service was okay.

If you really wanted to feel alone and lonely, the restaurant would be the perfect solution. Book for one person and then look at everyone else who were a couple or more.

Yes, the feeling was familiar, but this evening, it was really lovely to be alone and in the room.

At home, there was a women's group, so no one was waiting for him.

He called on the floor butler to get the empties taken out. After a last glass of wine, the bed waited. But he did not manage to sleep. Knew something was wrong.

How could he live on the accusation against himself having betrayed the country for some paltry money he really did not need.

The next moment, the image of Oskar was on the retina. Do not give away the land, but win new land.

It had been exciting so far, exciting to be asked, exciting to be a part of high living with private jets and ostentatious and smug behaviour.

But this was not him, Tor. He would never be able to look Astrid in the eyes if he went on a paid mission as a spy.

He had to get up, go to the bathroom, and throw up, the big man. He did not remember the last time, could well have been eight to nine years ago or something. The light in the room was dimmed for the night, only the lamp on the nightstand was on. He thought he heard movement outside the door, as if someone had lost something.

Then he saw the envelope that had been pushed under the door. It did not have a name, just the words: "If you've come to the right decision, then you can open this envelope. If not, tear it in half and flush it down."

Right decision? Had he? Yes, he wanted to send a message to Oskar that was not to be misunderstood, just one simple word: "Positive!" And then, a message to Donetski: "Only Mr." O. He opened the envelope. "Welcome to us. Regards Stay Behind. PS: You will be contacted by us in Oslo. Our common goal is to get rid of the spy."

That was what he was to contribute to the old nationalist from Finnmark. But he had thoughts about Arne then. Shouldn't he get a warning? Ask him to retire immediately, flee, not to Greece, but even further, to Chile, where he also had friends? That would be as far as he could go and hide.

No, if Arne had allowed himself to be bought, then it was doomed.
Remember that you almost let yourself be bought too, Tor.
Yes, he was aware of that, but he had not crossed the Rubicon.
But you were close, weren't you?
Yes, he had been close, very close.
But sleep would not come.
What do you do with Arne was a thought running through his head. Find him in Oslo?
It was a restless night, and he was just as confused every time he woke up. Because what about his own safety? Sacrificed to Colonel Titov at the KGB?
Yes, maybe that?
And Astrid and her job. Married to a defector, so-called courier?
He was up early the next morning. No, the bill was paid. Room service too, but maybe he had taken something in the minibar?
Yes, a Coke and that was it. But there was an envelope for him.
He put it in his pocket. Got to read it in the taxi.

But his curiosity was elevated, and he broke the seal on his way into the taxi.

Pure PC font, nothing else. Two brief lines.

"Of course, we must respect your decision, even if it would have been practical to use one and the same courier. But we do have others already operating, so don't worry. You aid Mr. O."

So the traffic went as before, completely independent of Arne?

Would he know anything about this? The fact that there were other Norwegians who, perhaps at this moment, betrayed their country. Would it help his old classmate if he went public now?

But what about evidence and what about Astrid?

No, he had to put the lid on. Curled up the nameless envelope.

Then tore the little sheet to pieces, swallowed it all. The driver looked at him several times in the mirror, but kept his mouth shut, wisely.

It took half an hour to the airport. After check-in, it was time for three calls, i.e., two SMS and one telephone to the pilot.

"So you're ready this early? There was no good bride? I will come as agreed."

Tor heard laughter at the other end as he hung up.

41

The Moscow Channel

"Now, Tor, what do you say after the meeting with Mr. D? Oskar had chosen Sundvollen this time."

"I'm probably with you, but you already know that don't you."

It came with a smile. Tor had dreamed of this meeting. He wondered if Oskar had understood anything about the fight that had taken place inside him there at the hotel in Helsinki. But how close he had come, let the money be in control. Was that why he had played the Stay Behind card? What had happened if no envelope had come under the door?

Be honest with yourself now, Tor. Well then, the thought had been up many times the first few nights. Perhaps had he fallen for the temptation to say yes to Donetski?

Dropped with the rational grounds that there was no difference being courier or a spy, in the least from a criminal point of view, not to talk about media-wise.

But now it was over, and it was good to meet Oskar with a clear mind. Only courier for a good cause and then it may take whatever route from there.

He had been enchanted by this grey guy from Finnmark with super noble motifs. Porsanger, he had said. Astrid was from Finnmark as well. Did they ever talk about it at MOD? Oh no, surely the hierarchy was an obstacle to that.

Maybe Oskar did not know that Astrid came from the same region.

Let it lie, Tor. He looked at Oskar. No one should think that he worked at a high level. Comb-over and an old hat, worn jacket and trousers that did not fit well together. But the shoes, shiny polished.

Was today's outfit a pure disguise? Did he have other clothes hanging there at the workplace? He had come in a nice suit to the embassy.

"You will have quite a job teaching me the ropes, Oskar."

"You shall not do anything that requires training, Tor. Every time Arne has sent something to Moscow or handed over material to his contact in Norway, so I get to know."

"You mean that this colonel sends things to you?"

"No, of course not, but most of the material he will hand over goes further to the top guys in the Russian Foreign Ministry and of course also to our man."

"What happens then?"

"They need to consider it, whether the content has any value and whether they must react to it—either directly through diplomacy, or to the United Nations, and in the worst case, militarily."

Tor was scared now. "Militarily, you say?"

"Yes, but relax. It's not about attacks on Norway, but possible, and I repeat possible relocation of more troops or equipment up against our lines etc. Warning shot to highlight that, beware, otherwise…'"

"And your task then?"

"As best I can tone down the content, make it harmless. In doing so, I also weaken the colonel's position. I suspect that he and Arne shares the cake, if at all there is a cake, that is. Mr. D is of the same opinion. But it is not easy to prove."

"But my god, Oskar. What credibility do you have then? It must be huge?"

"Maybe so, but everything here in life is based on coincidences. Mr. D, as we call him, and I met by chance many years ago. And it is not forbidden to have contacts in the East. Moreover, as I have gone through one pretty tough security clearance both at Intelligence and later by the military intelligence here, I'm the one cleared by the CIA because of my special background from the end of the war and the post-war period."

Tor became curious now. "So this Stay Behind is your alias somehow."

Oskar laughed. "Feel free to call it that, but not mine alone. Some other time, but today, we are running out of time. By the way, what is your explanation to your companion when you're gone like now?"

"He thinks I'm messing with ladies and let him believe it. I probably work my share as it is, so there's no problem."

"Be vigilant anyway, so you do not reveal yourself. Back to your mission."

"Yes, but first, what happens when you discover truly sensitive material?"

"As the Russians have got you mean? There has not been too much of it. Some notes and some minutes. It has been mostly guesses, so I've considered it. Of course, I have had to comment on it and justify why I think the value has been questionable. If something came that really can provoke action from the Russians, apart from to increase their focus on industrial espionage, then I have to go to the Defense minister. But for now, I only report to an old reliable person from the Youngstorget-era. But we are also a small group from the post-war period who talk informally about things. But they are not aware of my direct contact. The most important thing is that we stay prepared."

Tor wanted to ask more directly about things but realized that now there was a stop to it.

"But, Oskar, then we have agreed that I am useless as a spy."

"Those were your words. But you can leave the espionage field to me.

What is important now is that we, together with Mr. D, lay the net, and for that, I need you as a courier. Remember, this applies to our country's security."

"What then when the case is closed?"

"Then I shall be retired and this whole chapter will be closed. Have a good trip back to Oslo."

Then he was gone. He had almost become like a father figure to Tor.

They had arranged a new meeting, the same place in a month. Then he must probably tell Oskar that they tried to recruit him as a regular spy for a huge payment. But Tor had said no thanks to it, he would not sell his country for any silver coins. Should he mention it now, and what would Oskar say to the fact that he had held this back? The answer was simple, he would not weaken trust in the dialogue between Oskar and

Russian. Maybe he should never mention it either. It was completely without practical significance.

"Most of it I can discard on the fly as uninteresting. But not always and then there must be an exchange of documents."

But Oskar had not said anything about how often.

"Your task will be that of the courier's, and that's that. You will find a cover story for your constant travels to London. No one will be thinking that you travel further, but do have some potential projects as backup for your trips to Cluj."

He turned off E16 and into Sandvika. Had to calm down a bit.

Even though the conversation with Oskar had been straightforward enough, thoughts he did not like would disrupt his every day. What was it he had embarked on?

What would Astrid say if this came up? That he was de facto a kind of spy.

But he was not bought, did not receive any fees, only travel allowance. And then, the attorney or journalist would not have grounds for making this a case of espionage. Of course, he was a spy in the eyes of the public, but without payment then.

No, he was not. Was not a spy. Did this for his country. But then, Tor had to admit that it was exciting. Yes, it was, of course, exciting. But he did not want a penny or a ruble for that matter. Other than to cover expenses.

Much of what had been said by Oskar out on the island, Hovedøya, was just empty talk.

Should he, the advertising man Tor, monitor Treholt and the colonel if he came to Norway? What kind of background did he have for that?

Those on the opposite side had years of education and training on the subject. So why had they tried to recruit him then?

Double-dealing each other?

Wasn't Oskar just the ardent nationalist from Finnmark with an ingrained desire to nail Treholt, and thereby Evensen, something from the old days? Or was it the money that controlled him too, Oskar? No, he refused to believe that.

But when the night came and the clock had turned almost three without closing his eyes, then came the clairvoyance: there was, in practice, no difference between Tor's courier business and Arne's espionage.

He just had to swallow it, and strangely enough, then came the sleep, the good, deep sleep.

42

The Grip Is Fastened

There had been some trips to Cluj via London.

Officially, he visited his friend at the JWT advertising agency in London.

But as a rule, he had to do trips during the weekend and then there were no questions from work. Except for Rolf who wondered if he had found a lady in London and if it was not expensive. But then there was Astrid.

Pettersen at Intelligence was informed about the London trips and that he also visited a friend in Romania from time to time.

But there were no more questions about this, and around Christmas time, the job was done for Azerbaijan and he could send his thank you, if only the last invoice was paid.

But it was difficult to get the last money, and he actually had to go to Commercial Attaché on Drammensveien to receive the last payment.

He was quite happy not to have any more trips down to Intelligence at Grønland. He wondered if Pettersen understood what had been going on. That someone monitored the Intelligence in the same way it monitored Treholt and that the same person also monitored the Russians?

He was happy that Oskar had found someone else, people who were trained in the profession. Guess they were Americans.

Hardly, more likely people who had retired, but who wanted something more to do in their profession. Maybe it was extra exciting to monitor once former employer. They hardly did it for money, but because they simply loved their country.

In any case, that was how Oskar presented it.

But soon this was to end, and he could tell Astrid everything and that it was over now. Maybe she did not want to hear about everything and his part in it, maybe she would be content just to hear that now it was all over.

There was one small, big job now that he had promised to be part of, namely ending the axis Titov/Treholt.

Wondered if the Intelligence monitored him, Tor?

They had probably checked out some of his London trips, but hardly joined in on all the trips to Romania.

Omar had been careful to choose different venues every time. Last time was at the toilet in Cluj's biggest disco, Disco Borsa.

All the students had stared at the two with their respective suitcases, he remembered. But now it was over. He did not quite understand why he should join at the end, but Oskar had insisted.

"What if the police and the Intelligence fail? We cannot allow that."

It was the Chief who spoke now. One might think that the Viking Age had returned to Northern Norway, Oscar the Chief. Tor had been told to follow closely the police radio.

Strange that one could not settle for the police obtaining the evidence.

However, it was Donetski who wanted as much photographic material as possible about this Colonel Titov. Again, Arne was just a piece in the game, for the Russians as well.

43

The Trap Closes

The clock ticked infinitely slowly for Tor. It had been an hour now since he got the message: "the Candidate has ordered a taxi to Fornebu airport, and we will be following him closely."

"Candidate" had been the code name for quite some time now. Tor sat right by the toilet in the corner of the departure hall. Then he could use it as a hiding place when the Candidate and his entourage appeared.

It was clammy down there in the boiler room in Kongensgt. 23.

The technician Sverre wore headphones; in addition, the police radio buzzed from the extra speaker box.

It was best not to risk any chance of misconception, Tor had said. So far, only the usual messages were buzzing and going. Decent job this one, over in an hour for sure. Then he had to endure the heat, and ten big ones were ten big ones.

Tor had been a little unsecure if he could trust this Sverre even as the recommendation came from a reliable source.

Best radio operator you can find. Expert on police radio. And he always keeps quiet if you pay him what he should have—up front.

Tor had picked him up by agreement at the pawn shop at Trondhjemsveien 8. Would be reasonably sure of not being shadowed and this place was straightforward enough. In addition, they could come out the back door toward Heimdalsgata.

Quite a place by the way.

But this was where they had agreed to meet. Sverre was in there to pledge some medals. That was how they had agreed. Then Tor should show up completely by chance and be interested in the medals. The end of the story was that they disappeared out the back door together, and the pawnbroker would be standing there, with no business this time. But on the desk, an envelope with a small gift to the owner of the pawnshop from his old friend Tor was left.

At the cafe further up in Tofte's gate, they agreed on the equipment.

It probably irritated Tor a lot that Sverre was some kind of a know-it-all. Knew it all somehow.

"This works out to ten big ones right in the hand right now. Where are we going to meet?"

"Kongensgt. 23."

"When?"

"12:30."

"But when are we going to be on air?" He laughed a little.

"Not us but the police."

"13:30."

"But should we not test the equipment then?"

He looked at Tor, shook his head. "If you pay, I guarantee the result."

The arrogance! But did he have a choice? The guys had given him a 100 percent guarantee.

But what was such a guarantee worth. It was now or never.

"I do not like it, Sverre. I'm used to double check and double test everything I touch."

Sverre looked at him disapprovingly.

"Do you really think I have survived in this game without delivering? You may want to withdraw, if that is what you feel like, and then have I never met you. You are completely safe."

Tor pushed five bills across the table. You will have the last five when you arrive, and the equipment works."

"That's not how I work, Tor. Take the money or add five more and we have a deal."

There was blush in Tor's face now.

"You do not give me much choice."

"No, but I know what I do, and I am the best. So take it or leave it."

The lips of Tor curled up almost, but then he realized that this man he should just trust.

"Okay, Sverre, I like you, but I am not that familiar with this pay up front, but here, you got your ten."

"So are we on the network from 13:00? I will be at the Fornebu check-in. Do we need to test that connection then?"

Sverre looked at him and laughed.

"Do you have more questions?"

"Suspicious person, may look as if he is carrying a weapon, reported from Uelandsgt. 5, at the kiosk. Patrol 24 confirm."

"Damn, a white Volvo has squeezed in between the Candidate and us!"

It was the patrol in a civilian car from Drammensveien.

"Absolutely right, you drop back, let another car in between. The man in the Volvo, is he alone?"

"Yes, but there is no male, it is a woman, blonde, approximately thirty-five, smokes while driving."

Slightly nervous now.

"Fuck her, keep your eye on the Candidate in the taxi. And hey, no blue lights or you are finished here. Then there will be foot patrol. Follow the instructions further, you will soon be at the airport now."

How could Arne be so crazy? Believe that he could get out of the country without being shadowed. No luggage, just a suitcase. Traveling light?

Yes, there were many benefits to it, but still. Most people on the Paris plane travelled with luggage.

"Paris, what did I say about Paris?"

Tor was upstairs and could hear Sverre falling off the chair.

"What do you mean, man?"

"Oh, sorry, Sverre. Stay tuned, stay tuned, don't lose the connection."

"He has paid and is on his way out of the taxi. Jens is hanging on."

It was patrol 5 again. "Make sure, Jens, do not lose him. You go to the gate and wait there."

"Which gate then?"

"Paris damn it."

"Cut it out now!"

It was quiet for a few minutes, and then Sverre is on: "This must be one big one."

"Maybe you got him too cheap?"

Tor said nothing but Sverre just laughed. "Hey, I always stick to agreements."

This Jens was on again. "He is not coming here."

"Yes, but where are you now?"

"I showed the badge and have gone through and am now waiting for check-in at Air France."

"But they should have been there by the gate a quarter of an hour ago. Are you sure you're at check-in for Air France?"

"Yes of course, do you want to talk to the lady at check-in or not?"

"Then Paris is not the destination for the Candidate. Which other aircrafts have boarding in about half an hour?"

"SAS to Vienna and Lufthansa to Düsseldorf, yes, all via Copenhagen then."

"Are you sure about this?"

"Sure, I just checked with the lady."

"Yes, but are you sure they are going to Düsseldorf and Vienna?"

"Sure."

"Okay, Jens, you hang on and patrol 24 will report as soon as you have control."

"You will go flying, Jens, we will call back our man in Paris and then get to shadow the Candidate all the way. First to Copenhagen. Call me as soon as you have cleared the destination at Copenhagen, and I will alarm the people on the spot. But no shooting. I want pictures and nothing else from the meeting with the Russians. I bet it will be Düsseldorf. Over and out."

"We as well, Sverre, we will end here, and thank you for your help."

44

Copenhagen

Oskar had provided him with tickets for Dusseldorf, Paris, and Copenhagen, so Tor did not have any problems getting through the gate. Just wanted to wait until the Candidate was on board.

Would have been strange if he would have had to greet him, his old classmate.

"Do not forget that you are doing it for your country." The sentence from Oskar rang in his head all the time.

Then he was on board. Had a seat at the very front, right by Business. Saw nothing of the Candidate. Probably seated far back in the heavy machine.

Tor felt he could relax by now. Stretched himself out with his legs under the curtain. Lovely with space for the long legs and shoes.

Bought at Store sko ("Big shoes"), size 49. What was it they said about shoe size in the canteen? Damn, he only woke up when half the passengers had disembarked.

Candidate gone. So not Düsseldorf.

All passengers for Dusseldorf remained in the transit hall. But the Candidate, he had disappeared into thin air.

Damn it, what would they say now?

Months of hunting and then gone through a miss by Tor.

But where had the policeman and the Candidate gone?

Was it intuition or something supernatural that pulled Tor out of transit and over to check-in for Vienna?

He did not know, but there he saw the Candidate already on his way to the exit for boarding SAS to Vienna.

"SAS route 615 for Vienna, Austria, departure in thirty minutes. Final boarding," the speaker rang in English-Danish.

Damn the ticket, yes, there it was. But it was for Düsseldorf with Lufthansa. The policeman had to have it as well or? How the hell could they have been so sure that it was Düsseldorf and not Paris or other places, like Vienna for example? And why had Oskar offered to double up with Vienna? There was nothing to say about Grandpa's intuition. Stupid of Tor to say no.

Perhaps would this be the final farewell for the Candidate. Finished on Norwegian soil. They just had to get him and get final evidence, photographic evidence.

A redcoat came with a wheelchair, looking around for a passenger.

"He should have been here for the first check in a long time ago. Have you seen him?"

The lady at the gate shook her head.

"Perhaps it is 'no show,' but try the toilet before you give up."

"The toilet? How come he would be in the toilet when he should be in a wheelchair, and I am standing with one right here?"

"Maybe he got help to get to the bathroom and is sitting there now and is helpless?"

Well then, the idea made sense to him, and he strolled toward the toilet with the wheelchair that forced its way through the queue.

Now good advice was for the better, and Tor had a plan. He was inside the compartment for the handicapped before the redcoat managed to get in.

Sitting there and pretending to be desperate. Then the man stands there in the door with the wheelchair.

"Oh, as I had expected. Finally, you are here."

The redcoat was one of the Danes' new compatriots and may not have understood Tor's lightly broken speech.

"I have to get home to Vienna and see my doctors and the plane will leave soon."

"Papers, you must find papers, yes, can we arrange that at the gate? Hurry now, otherwise we will not make it in time."

Then he is into the wheelchair and is waved out into the waiting car to be driven to the flight of stairs. There was no paper check.

"You're Fritz Strobel, are you?"

Well then, he nods and grimaces.

The flight of stairs is hopeless, and he is carried on board, waving goodbye to the redcoat with a thank you for your kind assistance.

The flight attendant fades when she notices the gun in the jacket pocket. Now he knows that the Candidate sits five rows further back. And the policeman probably further back there again. Praise to him for boarding the flight.

Should have more tickets anyway, this Jens.

"Ask the captain to take a round through the plane after take-off and then he can randomly stop by me at the end of the round. He will receive a written message from me right there and then. I work in Intelligence."

She regained her color and disappeared with narrow lips and a strained smile.

"Good afternoon, ladies and gentlemen. This is your captain speaking. I hope you all have found yourselves comfortable. After the presentation of our security procedures, I will make a round and ensure that we are all comfortable."

He was Swedish and probably someone always sticking to the rules.

The same "gospel" was delivered in German. Then he appeared in the doorway. Tor pretended he did not see him.

But after a few minutes, the captain was back at the first row of seats.

Lifted a little on the legs of the disabled Tor and sat for a moment in the vacant seat next to him.

"What is this about?"

"This is a dangerous mission. We have a spy on board, and I will meet my contacts in Austria and get final evidence against him before we bring him down. Here you have an extremely confidential note about the case. You can keep it."

Tor had wisely obtained a letterhead from MOD. Could come in handy.

"I have no jurisdiction here, or I might have since it is a SAS plane, but if in doubt, call this number in Oslo."

Oskar would certainly not be so happy for the phone, but Tor calculated that the captain was not going to call.

"But wait to alert SAS until we have landed, and we both have left the plane."

He looks earnestly at the captain.

"But Fritz Strobel, who is he and where is he?"

"Oh damn, he's back at Kastrup. You need only call Kastrup and get hold of the man. Get him into the airport hotel and send the bill to Oslo."

45

Vienna

Tor was expected and a man with Tyrolean headgear and leather knickers picked him up based on appearance and got him through the arrival hall.

"I have received information about taking you to Hotel Metropol. From there, you can fend for yourself. Do not ask who I am. Here, you have the police radio. I have double-checked that it works. Leave it again at the airport marked Herbert Kaufert."

"Are you Herbert?"

"No, and you should not ask."

Did not seem completely true this. Maybe Fritz was his name. But half of Austria was probably called Fritz.

Then he was on to the radio. German was not Tor's specialty, but he coped somehow.

"We have two men who shadows him and know quite for certain that this is his destination."

Austria's Sonderabteilung was online with the Norwegian policeman, Jens.

"The Russians are staying at Metropol, and we have emergency service both in front and rear. We follow Titov's smallest movements. So if you want you can just as well take the first flight back. Pictures of their meeting will be at home with your bosses before you are. I assume then that they meet already today. But go to the SAS counter first and check the return for the Candidate. Strange nickname you have for him."

The queue grew at the Austrian Airlines counter. The company also had the ground service for SAS. Tor had no ticket going home either. He tuned the police radio on silent for safety.

There, at the top of the queue was the Norwegian policeman, Jens. Still in contact with Sonderabteilung while he tried to get to know when the Candidate was going home. He was obviously confused, did not know how much he could say. "My instructions are clear. Do not let go of our man. Get home with him to Oslo. Over and out." A freshman this Jens.

The SAS representative behind the one-and-a-half-meter counter stood firm: "And the name was?"

Jens looked around. Obviously anxious for someone to overhear the conversation.

"We must have his full name to obtain information about the planned return. Unless he has a one-way ticket then."

Jens stated more easily, "We know he bought a return trip Copenhagen-Oslo. That we know from home. But the journey to Vienna and not Düsseldorf came at the last minute."

"We cannot disclose information about our passengers and at least not to foreign police."

Then he had his moment and could use the trump card. He laughed as he presented a power of attorney signed personally by the head of Intelligence, national seal and the whole thing.

"Alles gut? Ja?"

It did not help. The lady from Austrian Airlines did not give up. Showing up like this and threatening us!

"I have to call the boss."

A moment and then she was gone.

The "No Operation" sign came up on the counter. The irritation was noticeable backward in the queue, but Tor, who was next, did not appear impatient at all.

It took time, yes, many minutes, then she came out from the office.

"Everything okay now?" Jens smiled at her.

"Aber klar, Herr Somsen. Sorry, but we have our routines to follow."

The lips were so tight that the words barely got through.

"What did you say the name of the Norwegian passenger was again?"

"Did I say any name?"

He was still smiling, Jens.

"No, I did not, and we do not talk about it out loud."

Tightened his grin now as well. *Professional in the end*, thought Tor. Jens wrote something down on a piece of paper and gave it to Frau Jancke who immediately started with the passenger lists. Was it the Candidate's name he had written? Tor had stretched out too possibly see the name but did not manage.

"Not today, but the last departure to Copenhagen, at 19:15 tomorrow, there he is. You wanted the same flight? I will check if there is anything available."

"I only travel when the job is done, that is my instruction. That means I travel when he travels. He does not know who I am, so the risk of being exposed is minimal, but a plane ticket can be changed, and yes, then mine must also be changed to the same flight as his. It is of the utmost importance to be able to see him safely home to Oslo. Literally. In other words, the same flight departure."

"Unfortunately, that plane is full."

But Jens was in a good mood, apparently.

"Yes, now it is full, Frau Jancke. Right now. Who do you want to reject, because Jens is here, he is with you!"

Tor did not have a return ticket either, but it was settled elegantly by Herbert at the counter.

Departure the next day, 19:15.

Someone owed Fritz Strobel for the ticket home to Austria. He had to ask Oskar to arrange this immediately.

46

The Hunt for Pictures and then, Homeward Bound

Herbert was gone. But where did he really come from?

It had to be an extra secret network. Oskar had seemed a little strange when he asked about Stay Behind. Would not talk about it, not then in any case. And it was not a name to be mentioned.

But anyway, it was a Norwegian network. Or was it not?

Was Herbert with the Tyrolean hat perhaps Norwegian or married to a Norwegian woman? If his name was Herbert? Stay Behind?

Tor pulled out the picture of Titov and sat down in the restaurant and waited.

He made sure to have a good view of the reception so he could follow the movement in and out. To him, Arne was not the most important thing now. The police probably took care of that. The important thing now, according to Oskar, was to expose Titov in an open street, exchanging papers and money. Then someone should count what Arne had gotten and how much Titov had kept to himself.

And the chance should come before he even knew it.

But Titov was not alone. They were two and went down quickly from the hotel. Tor had no training in shadowing anyone, and what when Arne had to show up? Best testing the camera and be ready.

The sun had come up and made it difficult for the amateur with the camera, backlight, and stuff, but there he got it. Removed the cover on the lens, good idea, and tried again. But now, there were three in focus. Arne had arrived. Elegant as he remembered him from Caracas. They talked and gestured and exchanged some papers without him seeing what it could be. So now it was finally over. Imagine being so careless. Or was this what Arne wanted? To let the world see that he had nothing to hide? That he did what he did for world peace. Not for your own gain and honor. But would they believe it, all those who thirsted for someone to hang? Tor changed film and took a new roll of thirty-two photos.

Finally, he could go and wave goodbye to the whole scheme with Stay Behind and you name it. Free man.

"Astrid, my love," he had to call. "Do not ask where I am. Now it's over and I'm coming home now. Yes, late tonight."

The films were to be sent to Oskar tomorrow. From here and forever, an amateur, how wonderful!

"Nice to see you at work then!" Slightly sarcastic tone from Rolf.

"Sure, you will soon be tired of me now."

"Do you want to talk about it?"

"No, it was just something I had to be finished, privately."

"Are you going to divorce?"

"No, no."

"So there was nothing more with the lady in London?"

Thank God—so that was what he and the others thought.

"No, it turned sour. Nothing is like Norwegian ladies, you know."

"Ahuh" came from Rolf and that was it. "Will we have a beer afterward then?"

"Yes, of course, will gladly have two. But remember your pack of cigarettes."

There was a hint of peace in the office.

May it just last,

And it did, for a few years. For a long time, he looked over his shoulder also on the Hovedøya boat.

"What are you looking for?" Astrid asked.

"Oh, I am just loosening up on a bad shoulder."

47

Goodbye, Moscow?

"You are cleared now, no more mission, and you can tell Pettersen that you want peace and concentrate on your job. No more mysterious wiretapping of the phone. No shadowing of your wife or yourself. But should there be an emergency, then I will have permission to contact you?"

He had called Donetski from a telephone booth. Wasn't sure if it was safe there either. But he was truly bored now.

"Mr. D, what do you mean by crisis?"

"Something really serious that puts security between our two countries at stake."

"Have you informed Mr. O as well?"

"Yes, and he is more than happy with the fact that the era with Treholt and Titov is over and the old one at Youngstorget expresses the same sentiments. But then again, he was officially out of it long time ago."

The conversation on the kiosk phone was almost over and goodbye, Mr. D and Mr. O and Stay Behind and all.

"Yes, the last money to cover the Vienna trip will be in your London account tomorrow."

How was he to spend the days now, no more James Bond? The job, of course.

"Shall we do some travelling now, my friend?" Astrid looked at him hopefully.

No, he did not want to travel anymore, not for long.

"We should build a cabin far in to the mountains. There we can be for ourselves, just the two of us."

"Will you tell me a little about what lies behind now, Tor? You promised it!"

"Someday, I will do it."

It would take another ten years!

48

The Hunt for Ladies

"Where should we send the return answers then, and what is the billing address? Or do you want to pay in advance?"

The lady at Aftenposten was a little too curious, Tor thought.

"Give me one account number, so I pay over the net."

Then he could be as anonymous as possible. Did not have to meet up with anyone who might know him.

"But the answers then?"

"Picking up from you."

The lady at the other end reeked of scepticism.

What was this? Tor could notice that she was on the verge to say: "I need to confer with my boss about this."

Then it was done, paid and set up, and now just wait. The conversation with Astrid from last night kicked in the spinal cord.

No more letters from Ivan in the mailbox, he had to find one other solution. Then it had to be the old pattern.

Put messages in a tree, under a certain stone, etc.

But maybe it could be a solution to put messages in the mailbox at a certain time? No, no more chances with Astrid now.

This Ivan who had worked in Berlin must have picked up some smart ways of doing it from STASI? Strange guy by the way. Quite different from previous agents he had met. And then this interest in learning Norwegian. Obviously, he was not a Moscovite.

Arrived safely from far north in Russia. Got to ask him about things once they got to know each other better.

On the road to Ica at Vettre, he noticed the car following behind.

It came closer now and flashed the high beam. He turned into the bus stop. It was Ivan.

"Drive on to the football field at Vollen. I'm coming there."

Well, they had a rental car now, newspaper and stuff. Wondered what fake names they had used for Avis rental cars? The Cobra from Tokyo? Hardly, it really looked quite harmless though. Ivan seemed to be alone in the car.

He was driving behind the clubhouse. Quiet there now during the holiday season.

"We have to start immediately. Also, do try some websites. But they must not look too shady, the ladies. Here you have the key to one apartment in Halfdan Svartes gt. Right above us."

He drove off, obviously happy to be able to mill around in a western car. So brothel host or culprit or pimp or? He did not know what. And Astrid then? Now he had to come up with an explanation that would stand.

49

The Past

"Astrid, I have been asked to take a job for the sake of old days."

So there was the ghost she had feared. In all these years had she waited for Tor to talk about London and Romania and what had been happening at the time. But no and she would not bother anymore. Their marriage had been a good one, very good, and she so desperately wanted it to last, all that good.

"You fell quiet now."

They sat there, just the two of them on the terrace after dinner. Never tired of barbecued lamb. Neither was she.

They had shared a bottle of red wine, and he felt the time was right. Could not hold back any longer. Knew Ivan expected that he was in place in the morning.

"Can it be dangerous, this job?"

"Hardly, but it can take a few months, so I have to take leave."

"Our summer vacation to the States then?"

"Am afraid I will not manage. But if you want to travel with a girlfriend, no problem."

"You know it's you I want to go with. But perhaps I could go with Randi, Samuel's wife, for one week's trip to Madrid. See the Prado and all that. It's best you do not tell me anything before the job is done, is it not like that, Tor?" Her voice thin now.

"Yes, my girl, it's best that way. Well, I get sufficiently paid, so we can perhaps take one-year leave, just you and I and be gone."

"Do not say anything else, Tor, I can hear the risk between the lines. And by the way, don't do anything you will regret. Money is not that important."

Was there something more behind it? What had she done that she regretted? Did it have something to do with Samuel and the outburst in the kitchen during the Christmas party? He could feel that he was close to catching up now. There must have been something from Finnmark that bothered them both. Could there be something in this damn envelope that the Cobra had shown him, let him hold, touch, and wonder at the contents?

But to have it, no, not yet. Not until it became necessary. Thus, something must have happened, something in Finnmark before they left from there the two of them. The father had died at sea and the stepfather was never mentioned.

Mother, she died too. Any family? Not up north that he knew about, but two uncles at Kolbotn. Brothers of her first husband. They had not been excited for marriage number two and the fact that they just left the farm, so they were not particularly friendly.

Nothing to pick up from there.

But if Astrid went to Madrid, maybe he could do some private research? Ugh, Tor! He did not like himself now. Digging into her past? Poor character trait. But should it be necessary, he did know where the clue to her restlessness was.

Dypfjorden? Yes, if everyone hadn't moved from the little place, but some trace had to be left, right?

"You were far away now, Tor. No, do not say anything. I could see in your eyes that you were on a long journey. Do not go further down that alley, wherever it may lead to. Let go of it."

Could she really read his mind?

"You are right, Astrid. Go and call Randi, if you feel like it, then I will I make coffee, and we will have a brandy for once."

50

Bente

"Any envelopes/messages for me?"

"Which reference number do you have then?"

"What do you mean?"

"Reference number for those who respond to your ad."

She understood that this was not a sport he participated much in.

"Eh, 1333."

"Then there are twelve tickets for you here. Shall we send those to your address?"

"No, no, I will pick them up later in the day, I am in town in any case."

Did he sound nervous? Yes, for sure. He was not in town. Just a lie of necessity. But imagine if the lady had sent the answers home and Astrid had picked up the mail.

Did anyone see him, yes, who knew him or Astrid? No, he saw no one, got the letters, and left.

At a rather shoddy café far away in the old town, he began his process. Those without a picture went straight into the trash. Could not begin to respond, could he really? So this left him with one single, useful response.

She was photographed from behind, did not want to show her face in the first phase, she wrote. Easy to be recognized when you are pretty, she wrote. Stayed at Kolbotn, separated, and broke. Former model and manager of a perfumery owned by her husband. Now fired of course. No children. Very curious about what the job was about. Absolutely perfect, not from the city itself, would certainly do a lot for money. But no whore she wrote. Very clear on that. Should he call from here? The man behind was preoccupied, and the two guys at the table beyond had come a long way in the morning game already. Just grab the opportunity and then dump the rest of the answers in the garbage there.

"Hi, it's Tor. Talking to Bente?"

He had done it. Ready to talk on the phone with a professional. Because she had to be, right? The first obstacle was thus overcome.

"Sure, Bente here."

"Well, not easy this. I do not have any training in personal ads and such, but very nice that you answered. Could we meet in the afternoon tomorrow, you think?"

"Yes, of course, maybe after 19:00 sometime."

"We could have dinner first and then we get to know each other a little better."

He felt quite up to it now.

Well then, she was going to come to town and where would he recommend then.

"Teaterka," but he swallowed the *t* in itself, maniac, think of all known people.

"There is a small Moroccan restaurant at the City Hall, Tordenskioldsgate, not quite sure at what number, but at the very bottom of the street."

"All right, how do I know it's you? How old are you?"

"Tall and dark, no, sorry, not so tall, sitting alone, there are probably not that many of us at that time." He chose intentionally not to respond to age.

"Okay, I have long blonde hair and you will notice me for sure."

Sounded exciting. But then, had he not mixed the cards? Was he not on to an affair with a beautiful blonde? He pushed it away. This was work.

"Astrid, I'm going to meet some people tonight, so I won't be home until 21:00. Dinner in town."

"So now are we are on to it, Tor!" She stated more than she asked.

"Did we not agree about not digging into this?"

"Well then." It came quietly.

He rang and booked a table, arrived even half an hour before the set time.

"Will there be something to drink while you wait?"

"Yes, maybe a glass of white wine will be fine."

There were not many guests, and the restaurant was small.

There was a table in the center of the floor. Not the best, but what could he do now?

Then five ladies hurdled through the doors. My God, anyone he knew? No, not as he could see. What if? He thought he could hear it: "Hi, Tor, are you waiting for Astrid, or is it a secret date?"

"Would you perhaps like to wait with your order?"

He shrugged. The waiter was there again.

"Yes, I'm waiting."

Then his cell phone rang. Maybe she did not come, got other thoughts. Too bad since she was the only one of the twelve. Should he lose her, he would have to go over to the escort girls. But no. "Did not catch the bus, approx. half past seven."

It was not seven yet, but anyway, he was not that bothered about waiting. The most important thing was that she came. He was so excited that he ordered a dry martini.

"The table behind in the corner becomes vacant soon, would you like that one?"

He looked gratefully at the waiter, nodded, and sipped the drink. Best to take it nicely, now on an empty stomach and all.

A quarter later, four men, three of them French speaking, entered the restaurant and sat almost on top of him. Damn, should he pay and go? Unusual with the place crowded this early

No, better sitting with those whom he did not know. Could have been worse.

At 19:35, a young woman came through the door. It was the French guy who saw her first. He noticed that the conversation fell silent and that they stretched their necks like raven cubs. He himself could hardly see her from where he was sitting.

Low-cut white boots, light meshy pantyhose under a fairly short skirt. But very nice top. Old-fashioned piece of jewellery that so far appeared in the throat pit. Pretty, very pretty, but very young looking. Guessed twenty-three plus.

Could she not have put on a longer skirt then or even less challenging tights!

"Hi, I'm Bente."

Very calm and confident, but in an okay way.

It was still completely quiet at the table with the French. Also, the group of ladies turned their heads in sequence. One stared quite openly.

"I am not sure what my daughter would want for starters, but what about les fruits de mer?"

But he did not say it, no one would believe it anyway.

Eventually, he managed to relax, and they could engage in a regular conversation about the job and the weather and traffic and food. But then he noticed her impatience.

"Tor, what does this job include? You seem like a nice guy, but we should not be beating around the bush anymore, right?"

"No, the job is very special. My contact needs a lady who can pick up a guy for him. One who works in a ministry. Yes, do not misunderstand now."

"The bill please."

Beautiful Bente was gone, and he sat there with a rather miserable sense of himself.

He could feel pity from everyone in the restaurant. So not getting any? He heard someone from the group of ladies laughing on the way out the door.

"No, seems she was too pretty, and he was too old."

Who was he? A fucking pimp?

"You come home early, were you not supposed to eat in town?"

"Yes, and I did, but have to take the rest of the work on the PC."

He went into his home office. "I'll stay here for a while, Astrid."

Where should he look?

Time was running out. The Cobra, not to mention this Ivan that surely began to get rather impatient.

Escort girls?

Could it be something?

As long as they were not common whores.

"Hi, Tor, are you busy?"

It was Bente, amazingly enough. He blushed where he sat.

"I have only one question, namely, what do I get paid?"

It came very sudden, but he gathered his thoughts.

"This must be something we talk about, but—"

"No but. I shall have 20,000 upfront and then 20,000 for clothes and so, another 10,000 for operations and then 50,000 if I succeed with the mission. You can answer yes or no, nothing else. If your response is yes, we meet in the morning at a convenient time for your contact. If you answer no, then we have never met."

"Yes," he uttered. "Halfdan Svartes gate number 7 and I am waiting outside at 12:00."

He heard only a click.

"I have to have a cognac."

"Are you starting to become a drunkard?"

"Yes, maybe. Would you share one together with me?"

"When you say it that way, I say yes."

She crept up into his arms there on the couch.

He never stopped being in love with this lady.

51

Whore?

At 11:00, already, he was there.

Down with the blinds, then down to the kiosk and buy mineral water and some snacks. They were sitting on the couch when he returned.

"Does she speak English?"

God, he had forgotten to ask about it—so unprofessional, imagine.

"Yes, because surely you checked it, Tor?"

"Everyone here speaks English, Ivan, so do not think about it."

"Do you have a picture?"

"Sure."

"Very young."

"Old enough, we usually say." He tried with a laugh. But he began to feel the nervousness in the room. He had never encountered anything like it. Hoped it was to be the first and certainly the last time.

"Can't you wait until you meet her? She's outside in ten minutes."

Why did he not ask her to ring the doorbell, it said Kruse on the bell. Completely harmless.

But there she was and, this time, five minutes ahead of time. The skirt was long enough this time. Lace around the neck now.

"You are very expensive, but Tor says you're worth it."

He put a pile of banknotes on the table.

"I have a list here of people in the ministry, fifteen in total. We want you to, what you call it, Tor, get on good terms with one of these. How, we can talk in more detail about later."

"Espionage then and you are?" She looked at Ivan. "You must be Russian."

"And me?" The Cobra smiled? "Indeterminate, maybe something with France or something. So, you want me to spy?"

"No, not at all, take it easy. We just need to get a very good relationship with one of these fifteen."

"So then, you will have me fuck him and get pictures taken and stuff?"

"It is in no way certain. Can we not take one step at a time, Bente?"

"OK, but if I have to sleep with him—once only—no more, then I want 50,000 extra."

Ivan rolled his eyes, and his own desire for the lady froze away, literally speaking. But the Cobra was completely cold.

"What if you like each other and fancy each other?"

"Then you will know it, but professionally speaking, the numbers are as I told you."

"But will you get him to divulge anything, if you get turned on by each other, and will you then reveal it to us, what we are looking for?"

"So it's espionage then. Think about the risk I take if the case ever ends up with the police."

"Then you deny everything, and we will pay for a good lawyer."

"This I want in writing. That's just how it is. Call me tonight."

"No problem, we draft an agreement, in writing and call you."

Then she was out the door.

"If she falls for the guy and refuses to cooperate, we will expedite her. It's your job to make it clear, Ivan. And, Tor, I am not very pleased with the development. You and Ivan must come up with an alternative B, but she must be substantially cheaper!" The Cobra got up. "I'll be back in two hours."

Tor felt the pressure even more now. It was he who was trapped, not Bente.

"Can we not find a common whore instead, Tor?"

"I printed out twenty escorts from the screen yesterday evening, so it is only a matter of choosing. I do not think they will be very expensive. But then it is the issue of ensuring success."

He pushed the sheet over and Ivan threw himself over it. This game was dirty. But he had no choice. Did he?

He wished for Ivan to follow it through alone

Maybe it was possible?

Should he call Bente about it?

Ivan was there in the door on the way out but turned around sharply.

"Let us two examine these fifteen now, Tor. We do it alone, so we can speak Norwegian."

He was incredibly good at it. Did Ivan start to sweat too?

"But the girl then?"

"Do you mean Bente? She is okay and the money too, but an insane amount. What do you think the Cobra thinks, he who is used to picking small geishas for 100 kroner each?"

"Keep in mind that she even wants a minimum of 40 grand upfront."

"Sure, I have that money already. As for clothing, she will have to bring the bills."

"I have to call home, Ivan. Mention I will not make dinner this evening neither. And we were to have the neighbor over for dinner!"

"This is how it is to work with us, Tor. Thought you knew. The day has no hours for the Cobra." He laughed amicably. "And hey, will you order some pizza at the same time? And Coke, not Pepsi. We get enough of it in Moscow. And I'm tired of tuna and mozzarella."

"I should have understood that, Tor, but good luck."

Then she hung up.

The list of the fifteen selected from the ministry came on the table.

Two of the fifteen had played on horse racing, two had been stationed in Brussels and was certainly accustomed to this and that. Ivan laughed happily.

"You spoke with Astrid?"

"Yes, you did hear it." Tor looked questioningly at him. "But Bente, you do not forget about her?"

"No, but everything was fine now, was it not?"

"Call her and get her here in the evening."

"In the evening?"

"She may come in taxi if she wants, just bring the receipt."

At 20:00, she was supposed to be there.

"Arrive a little more anonymous now."

"What about the money and the agreement in writing?"

"You get the 40 here."

"And the agreement?"

"I do not have it, but you will get it next time. Can we not get started?"

"Can I trust this then Tor?"

"I think so. You will receive the agreement at the next meeting."

"Then we will sign the agreement next time, the Cobra and you and me. Ivan as well would be fine with me, but in any case, the Cobra will sign with his full name."

Tor just nodded. The others arrived in ten minutes.

Bente had arrived a quarter of an hour before the agreed time. She looked grown up now, pantsuit and arranged hair. Hardly any makeup. Flat shoes. They almost did not recognize her.

The Cobra smiled wide. "This is how you should appear, not as a Norwegian whore!"

It hurt, but she maintained her composure.

The dining table barely had room for all the papers and pictures.

"We agree to go for these two."

It was Ivan who presented the conclusion. One man was blond, forty-two-plus and medium tall, the other had just turned fifty, stocky.

"I go for the blond first and then I get to have the fifty-year-old as a backup. Can I bring the papers on both? You have copies, don't you?"

Bente was ready to put the things in her bag.

"No, no documents. You can write down addresses and telephone numbers. Then the rest is up to you. Maybe you will hook up one in a week?"

Ivan's face shone with expectations. Break in at the Ministry of Defense. What a coup and something to put in his career folder.

52

SINTEF, the Brother-in-Law

After fourteen days, Bente was finally back.

"These people know nothing about any moon landing. They only remember that the prime minister used the term in a New Year's speech."

"How sure are you that they are telling the truth? And why do you say this, is it because you do not want to sleep with them?"

"Relax, Ivan, I do not say no to 50,000, but why compromise someone who does not know anything, who cannot obtain information?"

"I believe what you say, but think you are wrong. Both of these have full access to classified documents, so clearly, they know something about the missile sector."

The pleasant tone from the start of the collaboration was gone now. Ivan called the Cobra who would come immediately, five minutes max.

"Tor, go for a walk in the city!" Bente turned pale, but the Cobra was determined. "Come back in an hour. We would like to talk to Bente alone."

Not that he had any choice, Ivan pulled him toward the door and out. Did this mean torture? When would the madness end? When would it become clear to them and Moscow that drawings of this moon landing did not exist?

Donetski should never have involved these SVR people. But Putin had probably not given him a choice.

It was not pretty, the sight that met him. Bente sat down at a corner on a stick chair completely tied up. Her hands in her lap and her hair ruffled in front of her face. He could see that she was crying. But he could not see any marks on her face, but supposedly, this is not how it was done anymore.

"The girl will make one more effort and then we will make sure we get good photos. But there will be no more payments unless we get what we are after."

That was how it should be, and Tor felt very bad for having gotten her mixed up in this. But she had got 60,000 despite everything, and if she survived, she should endure it as she was completely broke.

But this was prostitution and nothing else. The accusation shone from her when she dared to look up.

"We are going ahead according to plan. Bente will contact us when she is ready for us." Ivan laughed a little and sent her out with a "max one week."

"Then it is us, Tor. I am starting to doubt that we will get anything through Bente, so we must use another channel."

Tor looked bewildered.

"Your brother-in-law at SINTEF."

"Never in your life will you get something from Samuel, that is if he knows anything or has opportunities to find out."

"We hope he will put in the work for you, Tor. But if the threat of having sold us the Condeep drawings does not work, yes, we have been told that from the highest ranks in the Kreml, then we have to use other means. Here I have," he waved with the envelope, "good indications that Samuel has been involved in attempts of murder long ago. If it is criminally speaking statute-barred, such case is not obsolete when it comes to media and family, not to talk about the job."

The Cobra looked a little sad. "You're an okay guy, Tor, even if you fooled Titov and the rest of us, but do not make it necessary for me to use this envelope. There's more to it than you might think. So speed up on Samuel."

"My god, but it's not a moon landing, but a CO2 treatment plant."

"This you have said before, but we think it is not only CO2, but also rocket material. Information about stationing in the High North etc. We will have these documents, Tor. At any cost. And it's urgent now. Tell me, does your wife not work at the Ministry of Defense?"

As if he did not know. Do not let it get to you, Tor.

"Yes, but that's old news."

"Good, we would rather not have to think of her. Good that we have Samuel, he is probably much closer to the source."

Even in the middle of the hot summer's day, Tor could feel the cold that flowed through. Astrid? Never if they were to pressure her.

"Tor, you need not say more than once that all this moon landing project is only nonsense, and hey, forget this with your wife. Samuel is the one we should concentrate on. You travel to Trondheim tomorrow and report back to me before the weekend."

The Cobra was very determined now.

"Ivan gets to take care of the case with little Bente and the lover. Nice for you, Ivan, to be able to experience a little floorshow. But make sure the images are sharp enough. Tell Bente that we are finished with her after we get the report, but that she will hear from us later."

53

Trondheim

"In the morning?"

"Yes, I'm going to Trondheim for a trip, and now that Astrid and Randi have left, that should be fine. I mean, we can go out on the town?"

"Yes, but he had to clear some meetings first."

"Are you going to spend the night?"

"Yes, but I have an appointment early the next morning, so the most convenient thing is to stay down at Thon Budget. Have a Thon deal. Otherwise, thank you very much."

Samuel lived at the very top of Byåsen. Marka actually. How he had been able to afford the property was something many people wondered about.

"So we meet at the bar in Britannia then? The long one, it is somewhat more peaceful in that place."

Now he was completely pondering on how to present this matter to Samuel. And how about the threat if Samuel refused to participate?

Then next, it would be Astrid's turn and perhaps full liquidation of himself as well. He felt he had to inform Samuel quite a bit, but not give him more than necessary.

Tor had no concrete knowledge of what was in the envelope.

With a little luck, they would perhaps get something on this guy at MOD and could push him. Push him to what?

For what was there to tell about a project that did not exist, a project that was a pure figment of Russian minds.

Or did the Russians know something that Tor knew nothing about? But soon, they had to realise that it was a mere metaphor from the prime minister and that it was not a moon landing project? But if it existed and under Norwegian auspices, Samuel was the only one who could answer any questions. Except for those who had written the speech for the prime minister. But they were just big wordsmiths really.

"You look good, Samuel, very good. Is it all the exercise in the field that does it?"

"Thank you for your kind words, Tor, but that's not why you came here, is it?"

They were in for the second drink now.

"Shall we not eat first then?"

"Are you going to keep me on the seat being tortured a little longer?"

"No, you can get a key word while we order because it may take some time."

"Oh well."

"The key word is the Moon Landing."

Tor watched Samuel's face closely. But no reaction.

"You said the moon landing, didn't you? It's been thirty-five years at least since the Americans landed there."

"Correct, but the prime minister let his hair out in the New Year's speech, remember? I'm having anglerfish. No appetizer and preferably a bottle of white wine to share."

"I am going with what is easy, Tor. Will join you."

They were sitting in the basement at Britannia now, not many people this early.

"But I do not quite understand what this has to do with me."

"The Russians said that you had helped them with some Condeep drawings long ago. And that they had paid you well. Is this correct, Samuel, and does anyone else know?"

Samuel had turned completely red in his face now.

"If Astrid had known about it, she would have told me!"

Samuel was back again. "Did she?"

What the heck did he mean by sowing doubt about Astrid's loyalty?

"I do not like that you remind me of this matter, Tor. All the material was horribly outdated, and I said that clearly. I think it was more about a test with my client. It was never used. They also had no preconditions for it. But why have they come to you?"

"As you may know, us in the agency did a big job for Azerbaijan. One thing brought the other, and both the Intelligence and the KGB were in the picture. Both parties wanted to recruit me. I've hardly talked to anyone about this until now. This about the recruitment attempt, that is. The Intelligence asked me to shut up. But after all these years, people stood at the door and demanded to get drawings of the rocket program for the new moon landing, perhaps also details from our assumed missile bases under planning in the Arctic, perhaps Svalbard or Bjørnøya."

"Hey, Tor," he spoke with the Finnmark accent now, "I have never regarded you as some dreamer, rather very realist. And you look relatively sober, yes, quite, I must say. But those Finn shoes, have you smoked them now?"

"Unfortunately, Samuel. This is bloody serious and several of us stand with both legs up, up to our knees in water, but worse than that, maybe to the shoulders."

"What do you mean?"

"These people think that the case is as I have presented it to you, and they have told me to get all the drawings and plans otherwise…"

"That's why you wanted to talk to me, not to just have a chat?"

Samuel had turned red in the face now again. The first bottle was empty, and they had started on the second.

"The Russians have done thorough research on where they could find the material and seen three possibilities: MOD, with the prime minister, or with SINTEF. They have tried MOD but have not reached the finish line. The prime minister, I am sure you can figure it, is unlikely to get something from him and then its SINTEF where you are with your missile expertise."

"And how about you then, Tor? Are you a spy or something?"

"Me, I'm just a stupid middleman who lent myself to an idiotic project fifteen years ago. It was even a guy from Finnmark at MOD who hated both Treholt and Evensen and everything concerning their contact with the Russians. He was keen to get a channel that monitored the others and got a top-level contact with old Gromyko, the foreign minister. I talked a bit to this guy from Finnmark and did him a couple of favors, among other things in Romania. Now he's gone and so is Gromyko. But his assistant, to call him something, he is still there, albeit on his last legs and Putin himself has given notice to reopen the channel. Since the man who used to be at MOD is gone, it was only me left who they had a name on in Oslo. Believe it or not. But that's why the people came to my door."

This was enough. Had Samuel held back what he was doing, Tor might as well do the same.

"And what should I do for my brother-in-law?"

"Not just for me, but maybe just as much for yourself and for your sister."

Samuel turned pale. "For my sister?"

"Take me first, I risk getting a one-way ticket and cannot do anything either way. As for the two of you, however, they seem to have something on you. In addition to that you helped with Condeep. The boss, who they call Cobra, waving a large envelope which would contain evidence that you and maybe my wife—this last thing I do not know anything about—have been implicated in murder."

Samuel got up, unsteady now.

"I have to go to the toilet."

He jogged the last part. It took time for him to return.

Still pale, but calmer. "Get me a cognac fast, yes, a double."

"Which brand then?"

"Not important as long as it is brought quickly!"

The waiter understood the hint and came with the black one, the most expensive of course. It went down in one go before Samuel sat down. Tor said nothing, just waiting.

"You should not have come with this, Tor."

"Would you rather have the two of them, the Cobra and the other, at your doorstep? The Cobra is even a colonel, so the case has priority."

"No, you are right. What does Astrid know, and was that why you sent her away?"

"Partly that. She knows nothing of the fact that something from the past has emerged and that I have asked for time, time of grace, to settle it. Otherwise, she knows nothing, I hope. Samuel, we do not need to talk about what happened—if it happened—at some point in the past. I said to Astrid that I prefer not to know and the same, I say to you. But the Russians know. What I think about now is that there are probably no papers on any rocket launch in the north, except for Oksebåsen. And of course, there is nothing about a lunar landing. So what then if the Russians get handed over papers on a CO2 purification plant and that's it? Is it always the messenger of the bad news that is killed or how? And will it just be me, or will they take you and Astrid too? Or tarnish you at least?"

"But how will this take place?"

"I will get descriptions, drawings, etc., and hand it all over to the contact person in Eastern Europe, who will bring it to Moscow."

"No courier mail or anything?"

"No, they do not even trust their own. They are three over there, Putin, the foreign minister and his assistant, in addition the two who are now in Oslo and who knows about the matter. The problem is also that I never get to meet Putin. Convince him through two or three intermediaries that the whole thing is just nonsense? Doubtful? He is totally fixed on the idea and will probably also plant a flag on the North Pole under the ice if he has not already done so. I have heard that he and Bush will meet in Romania at some point and discuss possible NATO membership for Russia. Then it's probably okay to have this in his pocket as a trump card."

"Tor, I think we have to be sober when we have to solve this, agree?"

"Yes, and you can just as well assume that we are monitored by the Intelligence and the others. Maybe they have already installed monitoring equipment at your home. That is, the Intelligence. Do you know what we do? We are checking in here at Britannica, I'm paying. Then we take one of the suites at the top. Hard to eavesdrop, I would think. In the morning we take your boat out on the fjord and finalize the plan. What do you say to that? But then, no phones or contact other than with work. Call your boss on a phone from a newsstand and say you just have to take a day off."

"But why should they listen to me?"

"They know that I'm in Trondheim, guaranteed, and I'll probably be checked against the Thon Hotel and your home. Say good night now, there's a guy over there who's been with us for a while. Then you go and call from some kiosk or café, come back via Nordre St. and into the garage on the corner and then the elevator up to the eighth floor. I wait on you by the elevator at exactly 22:00."

Samuel disappeared with a quick "Good night."

The time was 23:00 and still just voicemail on Samuel's mobile phone. He had waited until 22:30, but then he just had to break the self-imposed silence.

Samuel was away and did not answer at his home either. He must have been shadowed and had discovered it. What now?

Without doubt, he himself was also shadowed and by both sides. Because now Intelligence surely would have woken up, if not before?

But perhaps had they not figured out that he stayed at Britannica and under another name?

But Samuel? Should be back at work in the morning. Not sure he would dare. Not until Tor had left Trondheim and he was not going to make it a secret when he left. On the contrary.

But first, he had to find Samuel and solve, literally speaking, the moon landing.

54

Help Is Near

His brother-in-law had once brought him up to Gråkallen, the former radar station. Admittedly, all entrances to tunnels, etc., were closed then, but Samuel had a favorite place, the OBS room inside Gråkallen.

"Here you can hide when there is war again, Tor. Because war will come."

But how to get there without revealing himself and Samuel? The solution was quite simpler than he had thought.

Byåsen Butikksenter (shopping center). Mixing with the crowd. Get out the backdoor by Nille and enter the path to Skistua.

But it required sportswear, even though it might be dry in the forest.

Gresvig on Nordre, change there. Leave the package with clothes and out to the waiting taxi.

No, it was not good enough.

Who did he know in Trondheim? No one now, but from old times?

His mind worked at high pressure now. Bjørn? But Bjørn, did he not live in Spain? But perhaps he was lucky, and Bjørn was at home in Trondheim?

"Hey, Bjørn, it is Tor. What shoe number do you use? 43? Don't you have any really old shoes in size 46, 47, I mean joggers?"

"Oh, it's you, yes. I have to sit down with a cigar when you're on the line. I assume that you cannot say what it is all about?"

"Sorry cannot."

"Did not count on it. I do not know the number you are calling from so it took some time. Sorry about that, Tor."

"I'm standing inside the reception at Britannia, only two minutes away. So, Bjørn, I've been told by those who own the phone to be really quick about it. I need these shoes and a tracksuit, preferably a hat too. I'm not as fat as you, so this is going well. If it arrives at the reception at Britannia by 10:00, I will come and pick it up there. Just say there is a guest coming. His name is Rasmussen. Tell me what about costs in a week and an account number. Send mail to my address in Bærum. Bjørn, I have to hang up, thanks for the help, can talk to you in a week."

"No problem at all, would like to hear how it goes. Does it matter if it says RBK (Rosenborg Fotball Klubb) on the tracksuit?"

He laughed, and Tor laughed and hung up. What did you have friends for? Guessed that Bjørn probably had a double after this.

55

Gråkallen

They surely shadowed the big hotels now. But again, the question gnawed, who were they?

Was it the Cobra who was set on having extra control? Perhaps without even Ivan knowing it? Or was it the competing Russian Intelligence, GRU? Or was it the CIA, guaranteed to have him in their archives from the old days? It could also be Norwegian military Intelligence in combination with the Intelligence at the Police Chamber. In any case, it meant that someone had leaked about this Moon Landing and Putin's interest in it.

Tor got out the back way with his sports clothes in a bag. Up to the Maria church, through a couple of alleys up to the Dome (Nidarosdomen), into the main entrance mixing with wedding guests, then out the side entrance to the waiting taxi.

"Byåsen Butikksenter, thank you and I have not slept, so I will lie down, okay?"

The driver laughed. "Just rest."

There was nothing particular about parading around in a RBK tracksuit at Byåsen mall. Even with an RBK hat, even though it was hot outside.

The girl at Nille got 500 kroner to keep the bag with his clothes until the next day and let him out the back door. Then he was on track.

He caught up with some hikers, greeted, and sprinted on.

A little over an hour later, he got close to Skistua and knew he had to be careful. Got around the little lake and crawled up the hill.

Only a solitary love couple who were fooling around up there. Could they not be done!

After a while, they disappeared laughing down the hill; he did a sprint across the road and the small parking lot.

There was the entrance and the shutters, they were closed. Maybe for the best. He was careful putting them back in place. Found a locked steel door inside, but was prepared for it and had it broken open.

Soon he was inside the old Operations room from military service thirty years back.

From here, they controlled the air traffic at that time.

It was dusty everywhere, so it was easy to see the traces of Samuel up to the Notam room even in the faint glow of the flashlight.

Bjørn had probably wondered what he was going to do with it. Probably thought he was going to the old submarine hall Dora, down in the city.

He adjusted the flashlight so that it shone on the window of the Notam room, and there he could see clearly his brother-in-law.

"You need not pretend that you're searching, Tor. Just come up the stairs, but watch out. The bats sleep on top. I figured that you would come. Did you put the shodders on again and locked the door?"

"Of course."

"Two men shadowed me last night and I freaked out. Nobody finds us here. Drove up into the forest. Had the headlamp in the car and then walked the rest of the way. But it was cold last night. What do we do now?"

"Strategy first, Samuel. I have brought a few beers and some baguettes with cheese and ham, that's all."

56

The Strategy Is Set

"Oksebåsen is completely harmless and open technology, no problem to share, all public."

"But it is not the one that counts. It is the moon landing to the prime minister."

"Someone could be hung, Tor, for bringing the bad news."

"That is always the messenger's fate, Samuel. But at least, you and Astrid will be in the clear. Who has the drawings for the CO2 treatment plant?"

It was quiet in there in the mountains.

"Samuel, I asked you a question."

"I heard it."

"And the answer is?"

"There are no drawings! The whole thing is fiction, something Stoltenberg felt he needed to come up with. Listen up, here I am, head of the ambitious red-green government. This is not Jens."

"What do you mean?"

"I believe that he is an intelligent and balanced person who has been seduced by the concept in a weak moment. A term that may have appeared with the friend in an advertising agency or a late night at the party office. It is all from those close to you that you get it, right, Tor?" The twilight hid the blush. "So what do we do now, Tor?"

"This is a crossroads that has significance far beyond you and me. But can you deliver drawings that at least looks like a CO2 treatment plant? If yes, then I can take them further."

"Who believes in whom? But, dear, no one has ever seen drawings for such a facility. There are hardly enough raw sketches among the top guys in Statoil. That's just the way it is."

Samuel was persistent.

Putin would perhaps have thought of the whole thing as a domestic political statement, but not the others involved. Those who have started the ball there in Moscow.

They are preoccupied by delivering, to show how clever they are.

Get stars from the boss.

And if anyone has said that this is a covert rocket case with a special angle toward the High North, then so be it. No one can afford to be a loser.

"Not the least you and I and Astrid."

"Because of what was in the envelope you were talking about?"

"Listened to us at the Christmas party, did you?"

"No, but I could not help but see Astrid's teary face and heard that it had something to do with the eventually famous envelope. I would rather not know anything about it myself. But if something happens that involves Astrid and exposes something unpleasant from her past, which may also be your past, then I want to know, so that I can take countermeasures if possible."

Samuel was for a brief moment back in the barn up in Finnmark, back in the hay where he had slept with his sister, and they both had enjoyed it. It took him some time to compose himself.

"You love my sister, I understand."

"Would that be news!"

"Since it is you who are the thinker right now, Tor, where is this going?"

"I do not know, but that is why we are sitting here, scared away by two countries' intelligence services. Not only to share a beer or something."

"No, let's be constructive."

Samuel had pulled out an old flipchart.

"As I said, they are welcome to get drawings of the facility at Oksebåsen, they are publicly available, and I do not understand that they do not download them themselves. They are also welcome to get a draft drawing of a CO2 treatment plant. It will take some time but is a completely harmless thing. It is only now when you get to the construction on a mini scale and have variables tested, that this is interesting. As the Statoil guys said in the back room: 'Here you can promise anything, but no one knows anything concrete about the complexity before you start the test.' These Russian super guys, they who have given promises, they will not be satisfied with this. They want something that goes further, to stay in context, which has completely different political implications. They also understand very well that there is no question of going to the moon again. They look at it all as a diversion, a diversion for what it really is all about, namely, to establish a rocket base on the North Pole."

"Fucking hell, Samuel!" Tor got cold on his back. "Of course, this is what it is all about. This puts our foreign minister in focus with the Russians and not the prime minister as much. The High North again, that's the case! Wise one our foreign minister. What do you know specifically about this and how far has it gone?"

"I know only about the foreign minister's interest for just the northern areas, high priority he has claimed. No doubt that he and my American friends have talked."

"The Russians probably believe that it is he who is the brain behind this. But what may we have up the sleeve to try to fool the Russians. Blame it on the fact that we have been tricked ourselves? I could perhaps survive on that basis. But what about you, Samuel? You have the competence to say if something is questionable or reality. I am thinking of drawings, formulas, etc. I cannot stand by and look while you are tossed on the fire. Let us say that we go for point 1 and 2. How far have you come with feasibility studies on the CO2 facility? And what about Statoil?"

"They have taken a distant approach all the time, i.e., the president, Mr. Lund has been twisting on TV, but the guys that stands for the technical-operational features have been shaking their heads from day one. Literally! And especially on New Year's Day. Not that it may not be feasible from a purely technical point of view. It probably would. But it must be run as a test facility, and it will take time. A mini wastewater treatment plant must be built and tested, yes, you have no idea and neither do I either, because on this, I do not have the competence. Just know that there is a long, long way to go."

"But is SINTEF in the picture?"

"Yes, I would think so. Some idiot has probably insisted. But I do not know how tight relations are to Statoil who actually have the expertise, if anyone at all. One other thing: everyone is now aware of that this will be enormously expensive, not only to build the full scale after the test period. But the operation itself. This will be miles away from profitable operations. It will be a monster, consuming billions from the very first day, Tor."

"But you can take the proven variant." Tor smiled now. "Which one?"

"Take the investment over the state budget and let the operation become a profitable thing by itself, ref. Gardermobanen."

"Well yes, I can see that, Samuel. And the prime minister says that we can sell the technology!"

"First it has to be developed, then test-run on mini plants, then full scale and maybe after ten years, you can present data for operational reliability, gains from an environmental perspective, etc. In other words, a minimum of twelve years. There might be hundreds of innovative ideas at that time span, right? I am just asking."

Samuel put a cross over point two on the flip.

"But the Russians, Samuel, what about them? Don't pay attention to the prime minister. Can you get drawings of a similar test project? And how fast?"

"Give me a week and I'll answer it. But still, we cannot get drawings of what is literally the core, the very innermost part to put it this way, where success or failure is decided. Building a plant can be done by anyone, but what about the technology that makes this profitable on a full scale. It can only be tested in a slow process. It's not something you buy at the store. Astute brains will perform continuous experiments, and it is only when they are finished, you may have full-scale operations. Success then will be able to impose requirements on all industrialized countries to acquire the technology—at a price."

"What will Norway charge for this then?"

The calculator in Tor's head ran wild in the billions.

"Say, China alone has to build/buy 100 plants. But calculate with 1 billion in royalties per plant and some discounts for large purchases, then you can safely talk about amounts equivalent to a quarter of today's Oil Fund."

"Yes, unless Norway is foreseeing itself as a world environmental savior and will give away the whole thing, totally free. Think about it, Samuel. Just wait until our Minister of the Environment gets the idea served on a platter. There can be a lot of honor and glory from that."

"I think he is genuinely concerned about the environment and then take any honors as they may come, afterward."

"Have you changed your political position and party, brother-in-law? But hey, let us take away the philosophy: one week for basic material and then we take it from there. Let's now move on to what interests these guys: the rocket base at the North Pole, Norway's Cape Canaveral."

"You talk as if this base already exists, Tor."

"Yes, but it does in someone's brain, Vladimir Putin's."

"Why don't you call it America's new Cape North Pole or CNP? Norway has no prerequisites for this by itself and would not get access to the American missile technology to do this alone."

"All right then, Samuel. Do you know anything about whether this project is ongoing or is it just a rough draft?"

"I don't know, but it would not be strange if some lunatic at the CIA planted the idea in the head of the boss. From there, the road is short to the Bushes. But I do not know how much time he would have spent on it. It is the missile shield that's in his head. But perhaps he learned something from old George?" Samuel was smiling now.

"Do you mean Father George, the president?"

Tor tried to see if he was joking or serious. But the light was in the process of dying out.

"Yes, who else?"

"And what should he have taught, brother-in-law?"

"Translated to our case: I sacrificed the North Pole for the missile shield, or vice versa: I retain the North Pole and drop the missile shield."

"This is not chess, Samuel."

"No? Then what is it?" Samuel seemed offended.

"Okay, then. But do not give old Bush all the credit for this. The thinking is 100 percent Russian. Therefore, we will be able to sell it to Putin. But we must do it before he applies for membership in NATO."

"Big thoughts now, Tor?"

"Not that big. There have been talks going on for at least two years. But there are many camels to swallow for the Russian generals, before this becomes a reality. Let's sum up what we have now, Samuel."

"Have and do not have."

Samuel laughed.

"It is okay with a little gallows humour, but see it this way: the Oksebåsen can be ready in a couple of weeks. CO2 principal sketch as well, if the Statoil guys dare. Otherwise, it will it take me a month. Project North Pole, six months. There is a lot of work to be done here and outside of office hours. How can I explain this time lag then, Samuel?"

"They think you have it all in your drawer?"

"That it takes such a long time! Listen to me now," he leaned forward towards Tor, wanted to make sure the arguments were clearly understood. "People will have to be bribed, etc. Some also do not allow themselves to be bribed."

"But, Samuel, all this is stuff they know well from before, very well. They know all this. It's their everyday life damn it."

"Don't get angry now, it's cold and I'm freezing."

"But give me a date anyway."

"Cannot, it's just a guess. Rather set a date for the absolute latest deadline you can see for yourself, Tor. It is you who know these guys. And like me, you know there are pros who will see this material, Tor. Then it is not enough with fake solutions. Everything has to look real. Preferably be genuine. I must also make at least one trip to the States, and I should have good reasons for it. Remember, I have a boss."

"Okay, I understand you're having a hard time. But let us say that it's all in the box then, Samuel. What happens then? What happens when the Russians tell the Americans and Norwegians what they know about Norway's and the USA's plans?"

"By the way, Tor, where are you and I then. Have we got paid, and are we guaranteed out of this game, forever? What do you think yourself? You think we can get some guarantees and what would they be worth?"

"No, but the option, for all three to be sacrificed now is much worse. Would you talk about what might be in the envelope, Samuel?"

"No, not now, but I promise you to tell at some later point. But, Tor, even though we manage to be smart, perhaps come out of the spider's web, what do you pay me, or what do they give you for the risk?"

"I do not know exactly. Well then, of course, I have received a suggested amount, but that was for the moon landing. Now they do not get what they asked for, because the question was wrong. But they get something else that they had not even dreamed of getting, apart from that No. 2 man or what his position is in the Russian Foreign Ministry, yes, and Putin of course. So I have to go back and give some hints and then find out what the payment will be."

"You know, Tor, that if they ever find out about this with the rocket base at the North Pole and that it's fake, then all three of us will go straight into the furnaces, maybe not Astrid, but the two of us will not be pardoned."

"Okay, but what's the choice? Sacrifice ourselves now or survive for a bit longer?"

"Starting a new world war, what about it then?"

"Within that time, Russia is with NATO and you, deposit your money, so they can be paid back, if the claim comes."

It started to get chilly in the old OPS hall. No more than 4–5 degrees, patting teeth now, and he wanted out in the heat.

"We leave separately, Tor, you go first. But how do we keep in touch?"

"I use Bjørn's postal address and, in case of need, his telephone number. I'll explain to him what he needs to know. Otherwise, we start by meeting here at 15:00 in ten days. I will bring a thick sleeping bag and wait if I must, even overnight. But hey, who writes the strategic note about the North Pole?"

"I do this on the MOD's letterhead as a letter to the prime minister with a copy to the Minister of Foreign Affairs."

"How can you get hold of it, will you deceive Astrid?"

"This is comparatively innocent for her, Samuel. And that applies to her life as well. So let's take one step at a time now, Samuel. I send you a draft and then you call me from kiosk and say okay or not. If there might be changes or additions, then we take it here at Gråkallen in ten days."

The mosquitoes were fierce now in the evening. He would hardly reach Nille at the mall before it closed, if he were to walk down through Marka.

Maybe he was so lucky that Trude at Nille lived downtown and could take the carrier bag? Hardly. He could take a taxi down from Lian, an hour's jog.

Trude wanted to wait until he came and then he was on his way to Værnes. Airline ticket would have to be bought there.

"Can you stop at Hell station, so I can change? It will only take five minutes."

Hell station. He chuckled a little.

He should not be alone on the trip south; someone dressed in black and another in a leisure outfit were quick to follow at the ticket counter.

57

Crisis

They had started to get persistent now, both the Cobra and Ivan.

The Cobra probably because he was going to move back to Tokyo as soon as this mission was over, Ivan to show strength.

"Where are the drawings?"

They sat together in Halfdan Svartes gate.

"Maybe they'll come this week."

"But you said that last week too. Perhaps we should travel to Trondheim together!"

It was more a kind of order than a question.

"No, let me take the trip first and then see we what we have before we nag Samuel more. I know that he is having a hard time and that he is dependent on others to reach the finish line."

Tor could see from the Cobra that this was not the answer they wanted.

"Tor, this is starting to affect our trust. Not between you and me, but between Moscow and me. I must simply begin to deliver!"

They separated there in Halfdan Svartes gate in a dreary atmosphere.

"When will we meet then, Tor, in the evening or in the morning?"

"I don't know, but no doubt it will be in the evening. Can we agree that Ivan and I will meet at 11:00 tomorrow? If I do not come, it is because I am in Trondheim. I'm waiting for feedback from Samuel."

"Bad enough, Tor, but call from a newsstand at 10:00 in the morning so that we know status."

Tor had received the draft with the note to the prime minister from MOD.

Samuel was not sure if it was good enough. It seemed perhaps somewhat amateurish.

Tor sent just one mail: "See you at N-office at 12:00 in the morning."

It was far outside the agreed time schedule, but Tor felt he had no choice. Just had to move on.

Perhaps would it appease the two a little if they received a copy of the letter to the prime minister. There must have been some stamps left behind at Gråkallen. Something forgotten with NATO Top Secret, from the operational period.

The N-office was Tor's own old office from the '60s and stood for Notice to Airmen, i.e., NOTAM.

Well experienced from earlier days, he packed his one sleeping bag and warm exercise clothes.

"Coming back the day after tomorrow," he called his son. Fortunately, Astrid was still on the long US trip.

Backpack? Not smart. It meant the forest, and no one should know.

It got to be the same round as last time, Trude at Nille, and then into the field. But where could he get a backpack?

Got to get it from Intersport while the taxi was waiting.

"Are you at work in the morning, Trude?"

It was the lady at Nille, Byåsen Butikksenter.

"Who is calling? Do I know you?"

"It is the guy who put in a bag with clothes with you a couple of weeks ago, or perhaps it was further back in time. Fredrik is my name, and can we do the same again tomorrow afternoon? You will of course be paid like last time. I'm calling from a booth downtown."

"Oh, are you in Trondheim?"

"No, Oslo."

She was okay with it. Should rather not have any money. But she got something. Strange that he never got used to this with the word city. In his world, there was only one city, Oslo.

What about the Intelligence now?

No strange people to be seen outside the house, no strange noises on the phone.

The mail did not look like it had been opened. Ivan and the Cobra he knew where they were or at least thought so. But they had certainly put someone in control of him, the man in the black suit at the check-in at Værnes. No one else travelled in black suits anymore. Maybe priests, but the man did not look like a priest. Not so Norwegian-looking either.

But still, should he book a ticket online or buy at the last minute at Gardermoen?

But then it would be full price.

Oh well, Ivan would have to pay.

Then he dropped the sleeping bag as well, brought only a small office bag, of the old-fashioned brown type one. Shaving tools, toothpaste, and toothbrush and copy of the note from MOD. Some stationery. And of course, the joggers and the training suit with RBK. It was his now. Could not fit everything in the office bag, had to take a Spar plastic bag as well.

SK 376 to Trondheim, departure in forty minutes. No queue at the security checkpoint.

"You're late!"

The lady at the SAS counter was not very cheerful. Full price and open return. Paid in cash. Looked like she was going to ask, "Don't you not have a credit card then?"

"You cannot bring that shaving foam on board."

Now again, "Then discard it then, be my guest, just throw it."

"Yes, it is above the maximum dimensions."

"Dear, you just throw it."

"Do not be angry with us then, it was between 2 and 4 millilitres above the maximum size."

Tor shut up and was through. No one known, no one in a black suit.

But there was probably someone there. The tingling in the spine was evident. In other words, they had Gardermoen under constant surveillance.

Could just as well have purchased on the web. At half the price the day before.

It was a lady this time. But now they sharpen up. She looked all Russian. But where was the Intelligence? Maybe they did not bother anymore?

"Olga" put herself furthest back in the shuttle bus.

He pretended that if he was like getting off at Lade, and then, she was there like a rocket. But just her, no one else was getting off. Finally, he got off at Britannia. Went right through and came out the emergency exit on the company side, over to Gresvig. Could not see anyone. Bought backpack and sleeping bag. Went to the bathroom and changed. Rushed up the street and around the corner to the transport to Lian. No other passengers.

Left the bag at Lian, with a thank you for the help to the waiter from Nordmøre and then he was off. Started to get a little tired of this now. He was just too old. Five hundred bucks in sandwiches and borrowed thermos, but no shaving cream.

"How is it with RBK (Fotball klubb) now? Are you satisfied with new manager?"

"What?"

"Excuse me, yes, are you not at the HQ then?"

Flash of lightning through the head.

"Was walking around in complete RBK equipment. Yes, but you know, it's new for all of us. The manager? He has just been in charge for two matches then." Emphasized a slightly broad dialect. "Oh yes, that is right, yes, but say hi to that Eggen then."

"Will do.

"Nils Arne was gone already, was he not?"

But would that man actually ever be gone? Could the very soul of RBK ever leave the club?

58

Toy Spies

It was soft now, but cloudberry marsh was tempting, and he was seated in the end of the marsh for a good while. The hot sun was warming up everything.

God, the time!

The agreement with Samuel!

He had certainly arrived now, hurried going up.

Took one detour on to Vintervann. Stopped in the bushes and waited. But did not hear a thing and continued.

There were a couple of cars at Skistua. It was under renovation.

Looked like they've been standing there for quite a while, the cars. He snuck across the road and felt the hoods, completely cold. Took to the trail, and there was one man in leisure outfit like himself, but not RBK.

On the contrary, it was printed Skeid (Fotball club Oslo) on the training clothing.

This had to be a complete idiot if he came from the Russians or the Intelligence. Skeid up here in the farthest regions of Trøndelag? In the middle of RBK land?

But he could not let him go, so he had to take the bull by the horns. "Hey, got lost did you?"

The guy seemed nice to him. "No, I am not sure."

"But Skeid does not belong here exactly?"

He laughed now. "Antonsen, Karl. That's me."

"Nils Frederiksen."

Tor took the first and best name and tried his hand at a slightly skewed Trønder dialect.

"I was going to Storheia, you understand, but I am now quite off course."

Tor drew a map for him in the sand. "You are here now, and as you can see, you have gone completely wrong. You have to get on the road back to Lian and cross the winter trail."

The guy blushed and was extremely thankful. Got the backpack on and sprinted down the road. Completely harmless really. But it should turn out to be a talented actor.

This time, Tor wanted to be safe. Sat down on a pine stump up by one of the entrances to the bunkers and waited.

He caught a glimpse of something black further behind some bushes and just sat still and waited. Had good coverage there and no one could see him until someone came close. The man with Skeid had just been a diversion he now understood. Because there came the tracking dog in Eastern European outfit. Black training outfit.

Did not Ivan and the Cobra trust him more than having him shadowed, or was it the Intelligence anyway?

"Hey, looking for someone since you're searching, perhaps you are looking for me? Propose that you look for me around Storheia."

The guy was completely perplexed, said nothing, but disappeared down the road and was gone below the bend at Skistua. Should he take the chance? He snuck around the first hill and in behind the shodders. Knocked on the steel door and then Samuel was there unlocking.

"Hush, there were two of them, both from the Intelligence, I think, but I do not know. They seemed like amateurs. None of them were from Trøndelag. Maybe the Oslo area based on the dialect. We will go up and into the NOTAM office. The problem is only if they have listening equipment."

Samuel looked closely around.

"I doubt whether it works through soil and concrete and the steel door eventually. But we do not have to scream either. By the way, there is a reserve exit here. I got hold of some old drawings of the plant. But I have no idea how it is outside, whether there are concrete blocks or what."

"But can anyone get in that way then? There are no security doors?"

"Yes, but me and you, we got in." Samuel laughed.

"Good day by the way. Quite eager they are in terms of shadowing you. Or is it me they want through you?"

"In any case. My contacts know that I am in Trondheim."

He told about the episode at Gardermoen, and if the Intelligence spent the night in the rain that was predicted, then good luck. Tor unpacked the bag.

"I have stocked up for the night and bought a sleeping bag as you can see. So perhaps you will leave, while I will stay to the early morning. Let's look at what we have so far."

Samuel began to unfold drawings.

"Oksebåsen. I brought what we have on it, so that you have that one. Have found some rough drawings of the entire plant. Yes, it is publicly available up at Andøya."

"It does not look very interesting this facility, Samuel?"

"It probably isn't either. But this is actually what it looks like up there. So no secrets."

"Then there is the CO2 treatment plant, let's look at it."

A large roll was unfolded.

"Have you received this from Statoil, or is it your own drawings?" Tor was impressed.

"This is not so complicated, not the plant itself. I thought it was best to draw it from scratch, remove all traces. Where does it come from? It is an advantage not to know. Something comes from the textbook." Samuel laughed.

"Moreover, it is not as extensive as it looks. But I thought it was good to have a bunch of drawings, perspectives, and details."

"Foundations and pipelines. This could have been Mongstad or not?"

"Yes, of course, so no big secrets."

"But it is not enough, Samuel. What about the core technology itself?"

"Look, this is a section built in the core as you call it. And this is where I have placed a blue field where I have written test facilities as you can see and with reference to text description in English. This is also not a state secret, per se. It is a summary of all statements about feasibility from different quarters. Also clips from reviews at the oil fairs in Houston and Aberdeen."

"Houston is the one that counts, Samuel. You realize that when you've been there. I was deadly impressed! Have you written anything about the collection of CO2 and storage?"

"Yes, everything is included. But the treatment chamber technology itself is in the testing stage. But, Tor, what is clear, no matter what comes out of this test facility, it will be expensive. Terribly expensive."

"So when SV (Sosialistisk Venstreparti, political party) is talking about a few billions, they are way off base?"

"Completely. At 100 percent cleansing, if it were to be possible, we are talking about a price for a plant in full scale of perhaps 30 billions."

"Does the prime minister know that?" Samuel laughed out loud now and added: "Our dear Statoil director knows it in every case."

"That's probably why he's twisted every time TV has come up with this question."

Tor laughed along.

"But, Tor, there is something positive here too: plant no. 2, half the price or less. Maybe all the way down to 5 billion for multiple deliveries."

"Some billions here and there, Tor, but take Melkøya, it is far from finished. Mannesmann whispers that there the costs will be perhaps 60 billions more than estimated and the delays. So slop, slop what does some billions in overrun on a moon landing matter?"

"But, Samuel, do you now vouch for the technical and cost estimates up to the test chamber?"

"Yes, of course. But these are tried and tested cases, purely in terms of construction. No hocus pocus. But there is no finished CO2 treatment plant and I have explained why. From here, your recipients can research themselves and find as smart solutions as Norway may come up with. Is there any place where the term 'the road is created while you walk' fits in, then it is here."

It was time to taste the food from Lian. Tor had to think a little.

"You have done a great job, Samuel, getting all this and putting it together. So far you agree then that this is not some kind of moon landing, right?"

Samuel laughed. "No, of course, it is not there."

"What do you think the Russians will say?"

"Some engineer will snuggle up with these drawings and then shake the head with the comment: this we do not have resources to, with less we take it from the oligarchs as additional tax."

"A little late out now, isn't he? The richest are sitting in London, but even their fortune is small in context. And there are eight more Russian dollar billionaires, according to the Forbes list. But they are unlikely to throw money into this drain."

"Hardly, Tor, agree on that the only one who can and will raise funds for that is Gazprom, and there Putin is in control."

Samuel rolled up the drawings and they were ready for step 3. And now it was urgent.

59

Rocket Base the North Pole

"And now, Tor, we are in a difficult area. Do you know why? This is where nature itself takes control."

Tor looked at him questioningly.

"Because the ice melts, and even with today's ice thickness of 2.5 meters, it is not enough for the foundation. It also happens that the ice melts completely for shorter periods."

Tor was impressed with his brother-in-law's knowledge, nothing less.

"So then there must be a platform like Condeep."

"Do you mean anchoring in mountains under the ice surface?"

Samuel smiled broadly now. "Well then, anything is possible, and Aker seems to have a plan for this."

"But are you aware of the depth from the ice surface down?"

"No, but since you ask that way, it must be deep, maybe 300 meters?"

"Welcome to reality, Tor. The depth is measured at 4,261 meters."

"That was that. But what about dynamic positioning."

"Ask Aker, you probably get answers. Of course, is it possible. But if you imagine the launchers used at Cape Canaveral, then even small deviations in stability cause disasters. And what do you think your environmental people will say to such a deployment? This in addition to

Russia's objections. This is food for Bellona (environmental activists) and companies for many decades to come. And what about Norway's role as an environmentalist?"

"But perhaps a little trite, Samuel, can there be much pollution from us moving one complete platform up to the pole point?"

"No, okay. And of course, waste can be collected. The combustion in the firing torque may however not be gathered up, and the heat creation will be violent with the effects that it has on the ice. But then there are the Russians, what do they want to say? And is it strategically such large benefit to be on the pole point compared to expand for example Oksebåsen? Last but not least, what is Norway going to do with a rocket base? It is not we who have the technology, it is not we who have the power apparatus. This is all in the first instance about the US and Russia."

"Precisely, Samuel, and here we are at the core point, both politically and defensively. The Russians think of course that one such base with Norwegian flag on the outside has the American flag over the entire inside. Norway gets allowed to build the platform, that's it."

"Fair enough, but what are the Americans going to do with a base at the North Pole, why not Oksebåsen?"

"The next core point, Samuel, Oksebåsen is located on Norwegian territory. While the Pole, it lies in treaty country, literally speaking. But here as otherwise, first come first served if you are big enough."

"Okay, Tor, I'm giving up, even though the whole idea is crazy."

"Of course, the prime minister thought so too, just listen:

"I have read the secret stamped note from MOD to you dated September 14.

"I've scribbled comments directly on the copy, but will deal separately with some of the most important points, see otherwise attachments:

It is of course an interesting idea with a rocket base at the North Pole itself. In a way, it will be to move the activity from Oksebåsen up there.

What about pollution, and will anyone in politics believe that we catch all waste?

What about the heat radiation? Will the ice around the pole point melt completely?

Who will build and operate the platform? It must be us.

The rocket ramp itself and everything connected to it, is it just to move Oksebåsen, so to speak, or is it stupid not to plan further when you first build?

The Americans, who will deliver a lot of equipment, will they demand complicity? (I think so.)

What about the treaty conditions? We are only one of seven countries.

What about the Security Council and China, not to talk about Japan as surely feel themselves challenged. In addition, we have our "friends" in North Korea.

What about the costs? I see that this is big and can have violent repercussions for our industry.

Do we have enough know-how, or are we completely dependent on the Americans?

"Last but not least, what will be the Russians' reaction?"

"I see you mean the Russians have enough with Bush and the rocket shield. But what are we going to do based on the pole point? Is it not enough that we have Amundsen and Nansen and Sverdrup and all these, the world? Envy us because new land was found and won perhaps, for Norway. Moreover, I think we should show a spirit so to help the Russians into NATO."

"Here, the man in the Ministry of Foreign Affairs got something to deal with Tor."

"Yes, it is he who has fronted this with Northern Regions and the remedy. Both they and to a certain extent the Southern Areas, i.e., the shelf around the South Pole will become more and more central. Just think of the mineral deposits. We cannot imagine the values that lie there."

"But what should be the conclusion and are these fake documents you have copies of here?"

"Obviously, they are fake, but it is not inconceivable that this is a discussion. And for Bush, it would of course be a huge prestige issue that his little brother Norway facilitates a US-controlled bridgehead at the North Pole. Because that's how the Russians want to see it, a bridgehead."

"What about the actual note from MOD to the prime minister?"

Samuel had become quite lit up eventually.

"Even though we are amateurs, Samuel, then we are well-skilled amateurs, just listen."

And he read from a document with MOD letterhead and only one stamp:

Top Secret:

We come back to the issue of assessment 3507, Missile Base North Pole.

We in MOD are considering that this project stands and falls with the prime minister and the Foreign Minister, if they will take the political risk both domestic and foreign with the project.

Our task in the MOD is not to give advice on the political issues, we only mention them as an introduction to our assessments and which are of a purely defense, technical nature.

"Samuel, you saw the draft of this before, now I have included in the introduction the political and then I stop here. The rest we agreed on before, didn't we, Samuel?"

"Yes, we let it go. But before we part for now, Tor. What are we doing here and now, apart from buying us time? Are we adding a new confrontation between Russia and the United States?"

"I think the idea never will be realized, look at it as our lifebuoy and that's that, Samuel. But must we not have any drawings/plans? How quickly can you give me something here based on Condeep and Aker technology?"

"Give me a week and then I meet you in Oslo."

"What about Mr. Hong at City Hall?"

"Sounds mysterious."

Tor laughed.

"In that place, we both come with backpacks and then just switch our bags in the queue at the counter. Guaranteed lots of people. Shall we agree the time just now?"

"Why not. Tuesday in a week at 14:00. Who covers my expenses?"

"You can get 5,000 from me in cash next time. Look for the sack. Is that, okay?"

"Sure, but I want to know what the pot will be in the end, Tor."

"The pot is life, Samuel, and if we are lucky, then some money in addition."

"What do we do with the two notes?"

"I take care of them and put copies in your bag. If you agree, burn them as soon as possible or flush them down."

"But we may well talk while we eat, once in the restaurant?"

"Are you crazy? At Mr. Hong, do you mean? Now, listen carefully. I come in with a green Bergan's sack and change with your green on the floor in the queue and then I'm out in 1-2-3, but stay and eat yourself. The food is decent enough. But for safety's sake, go to the toilet as soon as possible, take out the money, and flush the notes down. You risk being stopped by the Intelligence."

"The most interesting will in any case be whatever drawings that I take care of and then get things in place before we meet at Mr. Hong. That was what you called the boat?"

They both laughed.

"Have you really been there, Tor?"

"Sure, been there with a small family."

"Not your own?"

"No."

"Yes, you do not have to say anything more."

"Completely innocent the whole thing, Samuel. But I have been there before, and hey, there were several people with a backpack there, so do not miss it."

60

Back to Værnes

It was getting late. Samuel had one last beer.

"I've made a copy of the key here. Was not easy to get it. This is a secure facility. So lock closely when you go tomorrow. Until then?"

"Until then."

Samuel had done a great job, and maybe the Russians would take the bite.

Samuel had left, and Tor was going to berth at his old workplace, but something pulled him toward the emergency exit. Luckily, he had a spare battery for the flashlight.

The concrete wall was dry and so was the steel door, but the hinges were probably not greased for a long time. Should he try to get out this way?

Yes, why not, now it was dark outside, and he knew the path down to Skistua well enough to walk it in the dark. By using the emergency exit, he also had good cover against any undercover officers who certainly would be focused on the main entrance.

But what would be on the outside?

Maybe there were overturned stones and concrete blocks, possibly also filled with soil. If he went out here—if the steel door opened—he would perhaps be caught in a tunnel. The door had no locking point on the outside.

He picked up the bag, left the sleeping bag, and took the chance. Then he was out, and the door closed.

Now he did not have a choice. Should things go awry, and he could not progress, he would call Samuel. If there was coverage inside the tunnel, that is.

Remains of cracked concrete and rusty reinforcement covered the view for the next few meters. Then, he was through and from there and out there were large stones and soil.

Perhaps best to be careful here if someone was watching.

He shielded the light and moved carefully forward. No one would invite him for a hike the way he looked now. Then he had to go to Lian and wake up the Nordmøringen who lived in the stable house. Finally, he was at the three shodders. Not particularly elaborate from the one who was supposed to secure the place. But they probably trusted that no one tried on the steel door.

But the shodders were tight and there would be a lot of noise if he had to kick himself out. Perhaps did the shodders not fully cover the opening? What if he moved away the soil on the rocks?

He found a rock that could serve as scraper and soon he had a slot.

He stuck his head out through the narrow opening, but here in the bush below the main entrance, it was completely quiet. Should he take a chance on the flashlight? Out with the rucksack first and then the head and shoulders and then he saw the light up at the main entrance. Two lanterns, i.e., a minimum two men.

Someone had figured out that he was in Trondheim and had thought wisely, or was it pure coincidence?

But the two he had sent to Storheia, what about them? It had to be them who had turned back and that now explored the terrain. They probably searched after opening into the facility.

Clearly, they were not particularly knowledgeable about the local area, or perhaps they had seen the shodders at the main entrance.

If not the two, then who could it be, the Intelligence?

Anyway, he had to get out and he had to cover the entrance again without being seen or heard. The two up there were waiting. Clearly confident someone was inside the plant. The lanterns were in the same place the whole time. Maybe there was a third man who had entered the race to the main entrance and who was trying to open the door. It took Tor an hour to get proper coverage at the reserve entrance and then came the job of sliding down to Vintervann.

It was wet and the bush was cutting, but it was not a long distance, maybe a hundred meters as he remembered it and then he was at the water's edge. Did not take the chance of any splashing with washing. One advantage with all the dirt was when he was going to get through the point with all the lights at Skistua. He took one last look, and the lights from the lanterns were there in the same place. Then he was around the bend and could reach out.

Had he left something that could betray him?

No, the sleeping bag was new and not unpacked. The papers? He had everything in his bag and hoped Samuel had brought his as well.

The boy down at Lian wondered if Tor had been assaulted. He could not change into a suit with all that dirt, so the offer of a shower was accepted, and after a quarter of an hour, he was in a taxi on the way to Værnes and the last plane to Oslo.

This time, he did not bother to think of the followers and saw no one he would suspect. Called Astrid from Gardermoen, apologized that he had not able to provide any messages, but would be home in just over an hour.

There were no questions. It had somehow become a tacit agreement not to say anything until it was all over. Would it ever be over?

61

Khan Again

It was his name now, no one used the nickname Mongol any longer. Now he was standing in front of the biggest challenge of his career.

His old friend, the gay man from the KGB school in the Caucasus, had sought him out to a so-called safe place in Moscow.

How safe, one could certainly discuss, for it was quite simply an officer's brothel. Fitted poorly with their orientation, but no problem. The girls could be paid well and placed on the toilet in the meantime.

But it was not just sex it was about this time.

"It has turned out very well for you, Khan, while I have almost been standing still. You are certainly happy that I got you over in GRU, then let you contest with your old friend Ivan."

"You should not put it that way, Victor! We were never friends, on the contrary, and the reason he always came in front of me was the look and the butt kissing. With us, there is no room for types like him, and therefore, I have been paid for my efforts. This was just as strong in the KGB as it was called, but it did not help."

"Khan, may you be kind to forget what I said."

They were naked both of them now, and Viktor nearly lost his erection from fear that Khan just should put his clothes on and go.

"Look here, Khan, I have this one new whip, can I get to use it on you first and then you on me afterward?"

He did not wait for the answer, but let it swing while he spoke, and Khan's butt was in a moment red-striped, and he got a violent erection.

He came in Victor as the whip continued to swing. Now it was Viktor's turn, and Khan screamed, partly in pain, partly in lust, when Victor chased on against the sore ass.

Then it was over.

Fatigue came.

"The girls, Khan, damn, we forgot about the girls."

"Let us arrange with them and then we get into a cubicle at the bar. Via a contact, I have heard that Little Father has put Igor on a mission in Norway. Admittedly under the leadership of a Captain Ivan. Yes, Little Father, he obviously has not spoken to Igor directly even though they were together in Berlin. But he has been recommended."

If this would not arouse Khan's interest, then what?

"What is the mission about? Do you know anything more?"

Khan was switched on immediately.

"No, just that the key word is the Moon Landing."

"And what would that mean? That Norway is planning a lunar mission!"

Khan had a raw laughter.

"This Moon Landing is of course just a code word for something else, and Little Father would not get involved if this is not something big."

"But is Igor and this Ivan alone on this job? And who the hell is this Ivan?"

"Do not know, but hey, even more strange, they have put on the Cobra. The colonel with the most prestige in the entire SVR. He is the boss."

"What else have you heard?"

"Not any more except that the top brass is strongly dissatisfied with the pace. It is progressing too slow in Norway. The Cobra should also be tired of poor progress."

"The latter is the most important thing you have said, Victor. Little Father is not known for waiting too long for results. I must go now. Certainly, best we leave separately."

He put a hundred rubles on the table.

"You probably earn less than me, Victor. Call me as soon as you have something more."

And then he was gone.

Victor was pleased. Now he had found the key to a closer relationship with Khan. He felt it tingle already in the expectation of "next time." Maybe he could get his hands on an even more exciting toy.

It would not take many hours before Khan was ready to travel, but first he had to get approval from the boss.

It was not just anyone that could push to the side the sergeant in the anteroom at 08:00 in the morning. But Khan was not just anyone. He had made a career in a short time and was known for his pace and results.

Colonel Kuznevskov was therefore not particularly surprised that his first meeting had been cancelled and a new one had taken its place.

Probably an illness then. Totally unacceptable. No new audience was to be allowed.

He shouted at the sergeant. "What is wrong with this Kronetsk who does not show up on time?"

"I do not know, Colonel, but I think you might want to be interested in Major Khan in the meantime. He will not say what it is about. Too secret."

"Okay, send him in."

Khan was in a fresh uniform and had his suitcase with him.

"I do not remember that you have any assignments that require a travel bag, Major?"

"Not yet, Colonel. But give me five minutes to explain the project."

"Well, well, we have a project already and you have kept me out of it?"

"The case came up late last night, just listen."

And then he gave the statement in the form of key words.

"It is therefore too slow in Norway and now GRU has chance to tilt the SVR off the stick and serve it all on a silver platter to Comrade Putin. I can travel with the 10 o'clock plane to Oslo via Helsinki if you feel this is something you want to pursue."

There was something with this Khan that he did not find in the majority of second officers. This explosive and absolute willingness to be busy no matter the time, for the service and the Corps.

"Can we trust this information? Who is the source?"

"The case officially falls under Donetski, but actually under the foreign minister directly. Donetski has almost retired. My source is one in a modest liaison position, but with full access to the project, which by the way is not known to more than the three as well as Comrade Putin and the two operatives in Oslo and their contact person in Norway."

Overcome SVR on a project that Putin himself had initiated? Did he get any greater chance than this?

"Go and try to circle in what they are up to. Then, report back to me on the secure line, and from there, we decide if we're going for this or not! "

It was a clumsy journey, Aeroflot to Helsinki and then Finnair to Stockholm and Norwegian to Oslo. Khan had deliberately withheld everything about Igor and his own past with him. It could easily be that the project would be perceived as a vendetta and then he had been taken off immediately. Strange that the boss did not know this Ivan, maybe it was someone that the Cobra had brought with him from Tokyo? Thon Helsfyr Hotel was fairly anonymous. But how was he to proceed? He was going to call the ambassador and come with one good enough explanation on why he was in Oslo and why this should be secret for SVR and the Secretariat, except old boy Chernikov who in all these years had been GRU's man.

The ambassador did not like to have a loose cannon walking around Oslo, so he insisted on daily reporting via telephone, since Khan did not want to avail himself of the embassy facilities.

Six hours after landing, Khan could report back to Colonel Kuznevskov that he had control.

The Cobra and the lackeys were waiting for drawings of a rocket facility, long-range rockets and which were to be launched into the northern areas, unspecified for the time being. Of course, Bush was behind it.

"You have all the powers, Major Khan. I want a report every night. It is we who must come to Little Father with the good stuff, no matter the cost!"

"Even if costs mean accidents for SVR?"

"Do not touch the Cobra. Otherwise, just move forward."

It was all Khan needed to know.

The time had come for the final showdown with Igor and to this unknown Ivan, who would have to be included in the backwash, so what? He had clearance now, Khan.

62

Who Monitors Whom

Tor began to notice the stress. Ivan was constantly on to him. Wanted progress reports at all times. Introduced the old Stasi method of calling at a specific time, one call, do not answer the phone. Just answer the third ring. Of course, he called from phone booths. And then it was all about just to show up in the apartment down in the city.

"How did it go in Trondheim? Did you bring everything down with you?"

"Unfortunately, some drawings are missing, but I will receive those next week."

"The Cobra would like to see the material before you go to Brasov. Have you booked a ticket?"

"Yes, I will travel on Thursday, via London as agreed."

"And the contact?"

"I will meet him in Brasov, Friday afternoon. What can go wrong then?"

Ivan laughed. "Then we agree here on Wednesday morning at 11:00."

"Totally fine, but hey, could you stop breathing down my neck then?"

"Do you say we're spying on you?"

"I do not know, Ivan, but I am constantly monitored. The one party is probably the Intelligence/police, but the other party, who is it. Is it your people, the Cobra, or is it GRU who has got the sense of what we are doing?"

Ivan first turned white and then red.

"Why have you not said anything about this before?"

There was not much kindness left.

"Because I have not bothered, and most of it has been very amateurish. But now, it's starting to annoy me a little because it takes time to take detours, play hide and seek, if you understand me."

"GRU is beyond the control of the Cobra and me. Excuse the outburst, Tor, but on this one, you have been a complete amateur. It is absolute stupidity not to have told us!"

He became thoughtful. "How do these guys look, yes, not Intelligence as you say, but those you assume are from Moscow?"

"I did not say that they were from Moscow, but that I assumed they were your people. Do you think perhaps it is the CIA?"

The thought had not struck him until now. But it was enough to send Ivan into the ceiling.

"Wait here, I will go into in the other room and call the Cobra!"

Should he trust Ivan, that it is not him or the Cobra who were breathing down his neck? He did not have to wait long.

"The Cobra believes the only explanation must be that this is GRU. How they have discovered the project, he could not say, but whoever can put the material at Putin's desk would probably get an extra star."

"Do you think that it is GRU that is trying to coup the whole scheme? Not the CIA?"

"Looks like this. We were told to wait for the Cobra. Do you have something unresolved with someone in the GRU, Tor?"

Tor had to laugh.

"For sure I never met anyone from their side. But, Ivan, think far back now."

"No, really, I cannot think of anyone."

Then the Cobra was there.

"I talked to Moscow and a name came up of a major in GRU who was very interested in Norway. The name is Khan."

So it was him, again! Ivan faded.

"We went to the same school in the Caucasus before he was moved over to just GRU!"

"Friend or foe, or maybe enemy?" the Cobra was very intense now.

"It seemed like he hated me. Could not stand that I was always the best in everything. Went under the nickname the Mongol. He was always no. 2, never worse."

"But not better than that." The Cobra smiled.

"So then it is he who has intercepted this and got the job of following up this operation? But how does he know about you, Tor?" Ivan looked at him curiously. "Is there something you have not told us?"

"Not difficult, far back in time, someone close to Gromyko had his own people watching over you in the KGB."

"Do you think that GRU watched us?" The Cobra leaned forward. "Then I would have known!"

"No, not GRU, but they had their own little unit connected to Gromyko."

"Do you know anything more concrete?"

No, he did not know. Felt he had said too much already.

"I do not like this." Ivan picked up the thread again. "The Intelligence is one thing, and they have no idea about this whole operation. They have probably not just registered that you are moving again. You can never be at peace, you know." He smiled. "Over ten years ago and they're still working on you. Must have a good time those people. But with the Mongol as you call him, there is something completely different. He always wanted to take me down since the time of the orphanage. What now?"

The Cobra looked at them.

"Adding more of our own people now will arise suspicion toward Intelligence and it will increase their efforts. I suggest you and Ivan, Tor, create an advanced reporting system. So you report continuously to each other, up to the time that you have been given the last drawing. After that, we all three meet here as agreed. Do you need to go out at all, or can you stay indoors?"

"No, I can stay put at home. The problem is only that of active listening devices so they can track Astrid's and my calls. And then I am localised."

"Then you have no choice. Call Astrid at work and say that the assignment is nearing its end, but that you must leave for three weeks."

"Then you will be moving into our place!" The Cobra was absolutely determined.

"But can I not live here then?"

"Not now that GRU is in the picture. We have a safe room at the embassy."

"Do you mean a cell?"

"Yes, preferably that if you want."

"Water and bread and a toilet bowl in the corner? Brilliant idea."

The Cobra chose to overhear Tor's comment and continued, "There's only one key and I have it as the SVR responsible."

"Newly appointed then, you are formally stationed in Tokyo?"

"Shut it, Ivan! Otherwise, you will have water and bread too!"

"And no one might have copied the key?" Tor was worried.

"It is possible, but I will put into new lock so have we full control. And hey, my room is right outside."

"But you are aware that this is quite illegal. Breaks the passport law and I do not know which other laws. I will be moved to Russian territory and back again to Norwegian territory without the authorities knowing anything. And I'm not even a diplomat."

The Cobra laughed. "Isn't it great to let go of security checks and all that fuss for once? Now you do not need to get unnerved over the control at Gardermoen. Look at it from the bright side, Tor, so maybe all three of us will survive."

All three? He immediately had Astrid and Samuel in mind.

Tor forced himself to a good smile. "Of course! I will call Astrid immediately and then I will be smuggled into the embassy in a van, then?"

"Yes."

Ivan was completely excited. The thought of cracking down on his old enemy Khan overshadowed everything now.

"But what about clothes and personal effects?"

"Ivan borrows your keys and retrieves what you need. You should have it all promptly, on the day. Set up a list. While you call your Astrid, I will have a TV installed."

Tor gaped! "Russian TV?"

"Are you a complete amateur Tor? No, satellite dish and all channels. The United States if you want it and North Korea."

The gallows humour flourished.

"Ivan comes with the food. Toilet is in the cell."

"Shall this be necessary then?"

"I think so!" Ivan was very determined. "The Mongol spares no means, and we have no opportunity to have him sent back to Moscow. We also do not know what history he has served to Moscow, as a basis for his presence here."

"Then it will be like this."

The Cobra got up relieved to have full control again. His opponents in GRU would get a real slap in the face.

"Hi, Astrid."

Call her at work. It was unusual. And especially now.

"Is something wrong?"

"No. I now see that I will not finish until three weeks from now." He shrugged a little at the expression. "Yes, done with the project."

"Oh!" He heard her express relief, sighing.

"But that means I leave this afternoon and will be gone for three weeks and then that's the end of it."

"Can I depend on it then?"

"Yes, you must. I will in any case do it. Just call Randi and go for a long weekend with her."

"Be careful then."

"Always, love you."

"The car is outside. Put a coat over your head, Ivan is driving."

"But what if the Mongol is at the embassy, then?"

"I cannot imagine that he will reveal his presence, but I will check."

The Cobra got into the back with him.

63

The Cell

Someone had placed a small cactus, probably well-intentioned, but it made the impression even worse. But fresh newspapers and TV with enough channels and Ivan as the waiter. Yes, it worked for a few days.

Short visits from the Cobra.

Mobile turned off from the first moment. Not a tracking device. Otherwise, the embassy was probably fool-proof in that way, but perhaps not safe enough against the Mongol.

The weekend was finally over and there were only three days left until the meeting with Samuel at the Mr. Hong restaurant down in the thick center of town.

He had read Dostoevsky's *Murder and Crime* back and forth and then all the newspapers were read before he left the cage, so to speak.

He had called Astrid on Ivan's phone Saturday night, and she was already in Trondheim. After midnight, Ivan had taken the road to the villa, wanted to wait until darkness came. Parked several meters below and got in the back. He knew where the alarm was, and everything had gone well.

"So you rummaged properly then."

"No, you had explained where things were."

"And no one saw you and you saw no one? Not even the neighbor's dog?"

"No. No trace of anyone. Intelligence must have thought that you have traveled as well. Not just your wife."

"Since they have stopped monitoring me, I should probably call the neighbor and ask him keep an eye on the house, since we both are absent."

"Maybe your wife has told him already?"

"In that case, it's just an extra reminder, and hey, it's not certain it even helps. In any case with the miserable watchdog of theirs. Did you use rubber soles or?"

"Do you have anything lying around at home that can reveal anything?"

No, he did not have anything. Passport and password for London in place in the folder he always had with him. The same applied to drawings and material for Oksebåsen and the CO2 plant, as well as the MOD letters/note. And then the backpack, not least.

"How do I get out of here unseen then, Ivan, now that I'm going to meet Samuel?"

"Just like you came in. I just back the van all the way to the side entrance. Then take your coat over your head, get out with your folder and backpack. The clothes and whatever you have will stay here. We drive straight to Mr. Hong and then back to the apartment where the Cobra meets us."

"Early in the morning, we go directly to Torp and so we are on?"

"No, we do not take it so lightly. The Cobra meets us with a car somewhere in Oslo in the morning. Just as well that you do not know anything about where. From there straight to Torp. So you get a full escort even if it is in the same car." Ivan smiled. "This runs the like clockwork, just as long everything is okay in the afternoon."

"You can rely on Samuel, he keeps his word!"

Coat over the head and lovely to get out, but straight into the car, barely a meter of fresh air and so they were on.

Into Munkedamsveien, across Lapsetorvet, and down by the American embassy. Further across Rådhusplassen and into Tordenskioldsgate. The time was 13:55.

Mr. Hong the sign read.

"We are waiting for another three minutes. Then you enter. Remember the backpack and then I drive around the block. Three minutes past and I'm back. Okay?"

But the folder, that one he could not leave behind. Placed it under the arm and the backpack on shoulder and so was he was down and inside in the queue. Always a queue in that place.

It only took a moment, and Samuel was there with a similar bag. They kicked them past each other on the floor. Tor picked the right one up and left. Soon, the time was two minutes past and then up the stairs and out.

Ivan kept his word. He was in place, and they could go.

None of them noticed a Fiat Panda that had seen better days leave at the same time.

64

The Peace of Grace

Tor began to feel safer now. But what he did not know was that Khan was working in high gear. Had acquired a junior suite at Thon Helsfyr, and from there, he controlled his small apparatus. It had not been easy to recruit local, knowledgeable people in Oslo and Trondheim for the assignment. But he stood firm on the strategy.

If he did not have good enough people to take over the game from Ivan and the Cobra at this time, he would, for the time being, ensure full control of their movements until the time was ripe to strike. The final showdown.

But even gaining control of the opponent's movements had proved difficult and the people he sent after this Third Man had not been worth much. All trails gone.

So he had limited himself to the airports Værnes and Gardermoen. There they were effective, and he knew at all times when this Tor and/or his brother-in-law was on travel and to where.

But Tor had disappeared, and Ivan and the Cobra had apparently stepped down. But Khan was convinced that Tor had not left Oslo yet.

Chernikov had shown himself to be useful. One of his people had been on the weekly fishing trip on the water toward Ås. The space was widely used for the transmission of information. But there had been less in recent years as Intelligence had regular check there to see if they could pick up something.

Chernikov had become happy instead. He was a passionate angler, and the pike was a fully edible fish even though it contained an awful lot of bones.

But it was not pike he had caught on the hook this time, but a beautiful girl who was trying to take her own life.

When she realized that he was Russian, she jumped out and let herself go under. Swallowed water and was gone. Chernikov was not late to plunge after. Could see her down in the mud. Did not get her up on the first try but would not give up.

In the next attempt, it went better, and soon, he had her on land. She seemed completely lifeless. Not a movement. The driver arrived, and together, they started resuscitation attempts. Finally, she spat, but the expression in her eyes was that of terror. She tried desperately to stand up but could not.

Chernikov was an adult, a sheltered father's type, and calmed her by stroking her over her hair.

"You speak English?"

She nodded.

"Okay, I speak very bad. I am ruski from the Embassy."

Again, she tried to get up, but Chernikov managed to keep her down.

"This is Boris, my driver. We are fishing only. Not all Russian very bad."

Boris came with a blanket and one too big overall. Not completely clean either, some oil stains and such. But it worked. Vodka, a bottle of clean water, and a packet of Marie biscuits. It was the inventory from the car.

Boris was ordered to hold up the blanket, with his back to it, and Chernikov pointed to the overall and even went out to the water, not far, just a couple or three meters.

"You take off," he pointed to her clothes, looked at the overall and the blanket and the vodka and the biscuit package. "Now!" And then he turned his back.

The girl was too weak to protest, nor think of trying to escape.

"Okay," it came, and all three laughed at the scarecrow in the big overall.

She herself laughed the most and the field was dry, so she wrapped the blanket around her and lay down again. Chernikov waited for what was to come. But first, he wanted to clarify a number of things.

"Where do you live? And how did you get here? We will drive you home."

She looked terribly skeptical, but eventually thawed up.

"Well then, she lived in Hvitsten and had hitchhiked here."

After a small sip of vodka and a couple of biscuits, the story came. Someone had wanted to use her for a job and then she had failed in their opinion, and they had hurt her. She showed the wounds on her feet.

"They threatened to break any toes of mine and took the little toe first."

Now it was tied to the neighboring toe.

The driver had gone away to the car, so they were alone, the two. Chernikov could afford to be himself.

"Were they police?"

"No, they were Russians, spies."

Oops, here he got it served, on a gold platter.

"Describe them to me," and there was no doubt. "The one was called Ivan and the second Cobra."

So it was these two. This Khan would be excited to know. "What were you going to do for them then?"

Then it just ran out of her also about Samuel's role, she had overheard it all.

"Forget that you have met us and stop this business of trying to kill yourself. The two are going to get their punishment."

"But I got paid for the job and I swore never to reveal them. I would rather die!"

"Your secret is safe with me and Boris then. He has not heard anything. He only knows that we rescued a woman who was drowning, and I will ask him to shut up."

"You trust him then?"

"No, not 100 percent, but I threaten him with being sent home to Moscow. It usually helps," he said with a smile.

"Moscow does not like the methods of this Ivan and has sent over someone to find out what Ivan and Cobra are doing. Can you tell me a little more about their lunar landing nonsense?"

"Sure," she was eager now. "They thought I could get everything about this if I had managed to sleep with one or both of those guys in the Ministry of Defense."

"But listen, if one of our officers at our embassy needs help to get the two, he can talk to you?"

She turned pale. Was clearly scared.

"I cannot testify against the two, then I will be killed or maybe worse!"

"But talking to the officer, will it be, okay? You can meet here, and I will be here and make it safe."

Finally, she nodded.

The next day, they were in place. Chernikov drove the rental car, and Khan wore casual clothing, less intimidating.

He had a tape recorder with him and asked her to read the entire course of events in English.

Then she received 10,000 kroner.

"Forget that you have met us, go to the city center and buy yourself some new clothes, and do not get involved in any more nonsense now."

She thanked them, smiled, and waved to them as they left. She herself was going to be picked up by a friend.

"Was her name Bente?"

"Da."

"Eliminate her when the job is done."

Khan had full control of the whole project now. Colonel Kuznevskov was delighted, knew he could trust his major. Where should they hijack the material? Just as well to wait with it until this Tor had come to Romania.

"But we have no jurisdiction there anymore, Khan."

"Excuse me, Colonel, for being direct, but what about the Leopards and their Romanian branch?"

"Do what you want, Khan, just leave the Cobra in peace."

Who had something on whom? Khan thought.

Ivan was a non-theme, obviously. Then it was just to relax and wait for the courier Tor's next move. He did not know where he had been hiding, but what he did know was that Tor had gone undercover under the direction of the others. The strategy was to continue to follow Ivan and Igor twenty-four hours a day instead of thinking about everyone else's movements. By the way, what was Igor's role in it all? Subordinate and captain? Had to be skilled this Ivan, since Igor with his background ended up completely in the shadows.

Khan did not make sense of it, but decided to forget Igor until further and then concentrate on Ivan.

They were unlikely to release the Norwegian until he was off from Gardermoen or Torp.

When the news of the departure came, he wanted to alert his people in Brasov and Cluj Napocha.

Regarding Igor, he had to wait. Perhaps he would walk directly to Siberia after this blunder. Messed up with the Cobra and that on a project that had the blessing of Little Father.

65

Rocket Base North Pole

"I do not know if it is good for you two to see this." Tor could not hide his nervousness.

"What do you think, have you not got hold of the plans for the Moon Landing Project?"

"Yes, but not what you think it is."

Ivan had turned pale; this was his project.

"What do you have then?"

The Cobra had also become pointed now.

"I thought we could count on you. You have always been sane?"

"But listen please. Let us sit around the table?" He swept away ashtrays and plastic glasses.

"First of all, there has never been any moon landing project. Just a metaphor, that is, that little Norway should create something big. The moon is not interesting anymore, everyone agrees on that. But CO_2 treatment plants, it is interesting, because there is plenty of status and money in it."

"This is not about money Tor, and you know that well, very well, and you've known it all along."

"But status may well also be important?"

"Forget it. This is the loop around the neck for us all! What are the other papers for?"

"But wait a bit, Samuel has really been going out of his way getting everything about the CO2 treatment plant."

"Yes but get to the point."

"This roll contains everything about Oksebåsen."

Ivan looked at the Cobra incomprehensibly.

"Oksebåsen?"

"Sure, the little satellite thing you have up at Andøya."

"Well, that is no moon landing!"

"No, it is not."

Tor picked up roll No. 3. Samuel had surpassed himself. Everything was in English.

"This is definitely NATO Top Secret. You are some of the very first to see it!"

He felt on top of the world now. Thank you, Samuel, you have saved us. They were bending across the table now the two of them.

Basic drawings for the new rocket base North Pole.

Ivan dared not touch the paper, but the Cobra pushed drawings to the side, eager now. Letter from the Ministry of Defense to the prime minister, note from him to the Minister of Foreign Affairs.

"Ivan, translate!" And Ivan started. And it became quiet.

"Is this fantasy or? Where do the drawings come from and where do the notes come from?"

"Samuel has managed to find copies, I do not know from where, and would rather not know. The notes come partly from the Ministry of Foreign Affairs and partly from the prime minister's office."

"But how, Tor? How can we be sure that this is not fake?"

"I do not know enough about the drawings, but the documents otherwise I can vouch for."

"How?"

"When it crashed that arrangement with Bente, something I could have said in advance…"

"How then?"

"No employee in MOD at the level we are talking about here can be blackmailed enough to give away this type of document. No matter how nice the lady is."

"Blue-eyed? What about the Norwegian admiral, or was he not high enough up?"

"Are you thinking of Wennerstrøm?"

"Yes, exactly."

"But he was Swedish."

"Same thing, the culture is hardly that different."

"Okay then, so is it possible."

"Yes, and you had that Treholt?"

"He did not have access to this type of document!"

"No, but spit it out, is your wife in on it?"

"She has made an important contribution, yes, but she thought it was a joke. But note! She has never seen part 2, which is the prime minister's analysis, in which case she would probably have thought completely differently."

"And how have you gotten hold of this, or is it Samuel again?"

Was he being sarcastic now the Cobra? Did he think that none of these documents were authentic?

"That I cannot divulge. Not if you torture me even!"

"Relax, we do not operate like that!"

"Oh, what did you do with Bente then before you dumped her?"

"Forget it, Tor. That is the smartest thing."

"But it was I who tricked her into in this."

"She got paid well for keeping quiet later."

Ivan kicked him in the leg for to clarify that the rubber band was in the process of bursting, so give up now, Tor.

"We have therefore not received any moon landing, but one project for something unique that is called a CO2 purification plant."

The sarcasm continued from the Cobra.

"Then we got something about their satellite stuff up in the North, and then, we got a madness project up in our laps, namely the description of a rocket plant North Pole. And for this you want to be paid, you and Samuel and maybe even Astrid?"

"She knows nothing."

"And Omar should get paid, and so should Moscow decide if this is at all is worth paying for?"

"Is that how it is?"

"Yeah, that's how it is."

"Ivan, can you send my summary in an encrypted message to the foreign minister and get clarification on whether this is something Moscow would have interest in?"

"Now, right away?"

"Yes, now! Now in the afternoon, now immediately!"

"I'm a little disappointed with you, Tor, and especially with Samuel. With his contacts, he should have gotten hold of something more than this."

"But perhaps there is not anything more to get hold of, Colonel. I have checked as far into the government offices as possible, and it was no lunar landing the prime minister was going to present. It was a CO2 treatment plant. But the foreign minister, he has shown a very, very strong interest in the High North."

And finally, the conversation turned to a discussion specifically about Project North Pole, completely independent of this moon landing.

"Personally, I think this is a Bush project initially and that Samuel has become aware of due to his American missile contacts."

"But you can see for yourself from the note that the prime minister has become involved and is extremely concerned. We know from experience that Bush can come up with anything like putting the entire Eastern bloc into NATO at once. Join Putin and Russia into NATO, but at the same time, build their rocket barrage allegedly to stop Iran and North Korea."

"You need not continue."

The sarcasm of the Cobra was gone.

"Answer me honestly on whether you believe in this with the North Pole Rocket Base."

"Yes, technically, there is nothing to prevent it, just looking at the drawings. Samuel vows for that."

"But politically?"

"I do not have the prerequisites to voice an opinion. But some maniac in the States has started this as a project and dragged the Norwegian government along with him."

Tor held his mask now. Knew this was about saving his life.

"That was the answer I wanted. Some maniac and that must be stopped."

Oh, my Lord, my Savior. The Cobra had found the solution. It was a project then and it had just to be stopped before it started. Samuel and Astrid and the Cobra and Ivan, they were all saved.

And not least, he himself. But had they counted on Khan, the Mongol?

"Bet Moscow thinks along the same lines that we do, so get ready for your flight!"

"I am ready. Have everything in the cell, you know." Tor smiled.

"You do not have to go back there. Stay here. Ivan is on guard. When is the flight departure?"

"10:30."

"Then we should be there at 09:00, it is Ryanair, is it not?"

"No, due to some delays at the NATO summit in Bucharest, the flight has been changed. It is Wizz air that flies Budapest and then changes flights to Brasov."

"Why not Cluj Napocha, where Omar lives?"

"Do not ask me, I just follow orders."

The atmosphere was light and pleasant now.

"Good, Tor, here we have Ivan."

"And the answer from Moscow was?"

Ivan handed him the message from the cipher office.

"Short enough!"

"Yes, right?"

Tor looked at him with excitement.

"It was now or never, Tor, at least for now."

"Very briefly, Tor, it is: follow the plan."

Of course, Tor had problems hiding his relief. But he was not alone in that. The road to demotion or Siberia had probably been short for the two.

"It is not certain Moscow and Omar have been notified about the change in flight schedule. Tor flies with Wizz air tomorrow 10:30 from Torp to Budapest and so on to Brasov. Bring the tickets and fix this Ivan. By the way, what name did you use on the tickets?"

"My own, of course. I have to use it as stated in the passport."

"Thought so. Call Wizz air and cancel yourself."

Tor was sitting like a question mark.

"Ivan, you arrange a new passport and new tickets, Oslo, Vienna, Brasov, out of Gardermoen. If it does not work, take him via Bucharest."

"Why not Moscow directly?" Tor smiled a little. "Silly comment, GRU has full control of Moscow airport. Then wipe the grin, Tor. This also does apply to your health. Ivan believes that we still do not have proof. Maybe the Mongol, that's what you called him, has something in his suitcase somewhere along the way. So do not take this lightly now, Tor. Even though Moscow has received the conclusions, they are naturally very excited about all the details. And we cannot afford to lose you on the road or some other place out there. Your trips in the old days were child's play. I take it for granted that you will be stopped some place before this is over. In any case, bring a third passport. We have allowed ourselves to give you a German identity. Assume that you manage yourself well enough also in that language."

Had someone gone totally bonkers now? He looked at the passport. Not bad, Mr Walther Schach, from Hamburg, Donerstrasse, thirty-four, unmarried. Engineer, with patents as a specialty, i.e., patent engineer.

"But who would try to stop me?"

"GRU of course."

"But now Moscow knows what exists."

"Yes, but not the details, the letters, and the note with the prime minister. It is clear that it is convenient for the Mongol to find you dead in a road ditch and then track down the paperwork to some hotel room."

"I know you're trying to scare me now, Ivan. But I've been with you for a while. It is enough now!"

He was back in the driver's seat.

"But, Tor, think of what Ivan has shared. There's probably some sense in that. Was it Bucharest, Ivan? Yes unfortunately, so you get a long ride. We can get someone to deliver you a pistol with silencer when you land there, or any time in Brasov. Do you want it?"

"No, please no. It's enough. And if the intention was to scare me, well then, you've managed. By the way, thanks for the offer. I change my mind here and now. Get me a Walter or a Glock. Add it to pick-up at Lost and Found in Brasov."

The two Russians looked at each other as if to say, "He made sense in the end, the Norwegian."

"Tor, there is vodka and pizza in the freezer. So you do not have to take a chance going out. Ivan will bring your stuff here in the evening. Of course, you do not go out. Need I repeat myself one more time? Slightly milder: We do not play with GRU, do we, Ivan."

It was not a question, rather an order.

"Then you will drive to the same place in Oslo in the early morning. Ivan is informed of the time and place. Presumably we should meet approx. 06:00. Okay with you?"

"Yes, of course. Now I just want to get started. But has Omar been told?"

"Of course."

"And the money?"

"Thought you would ask about it. No change. Careful so Omar does not cheat on you."

"Thank you, I'm safe with you."

The evening was long enough. Both felt that the topics were exhausted.

So only a light nap on the couch for the Cobra, while Tor tried to relax with the TV. This GRU maniac had been the trigger word. Then he would not cause embarrassment neither to the prime minister or others and likely the small shaky confidence was restored. At least to him Tor. Samuel was probably worse off. Samuel was able to fake drawings, Tor was not.

Finally, Ivan arrived and there was a shift change and the papers were packed together for tomorrow.

"Samuel has copies of everything in his private safe. You can choose which sofa you want, Ivan. I will take the widest if it's okay with you."

He went over his case. Passports, cash, medicines, driver's licenses.

Everything was in place.

Who was the most nervous? He or the two Russians? And did anyone think of the GRU major?

But Kahn did not comply by eight hours days. Igor was to be taken out now, and he had Moscow's consent. Use whatever means required.

66

GRU

He did not quite like the development, the GRU general. Everything had looked very fine after Khan's latest report.

But the contact at the Ministry of Foreign Affairs had sniffed out that there had been a cipher message from Oslo from the Cobra, which confirmed that the job was in the bag. The details were to come through courier, lots of drawings as far as he understood.

However, after a few rounds in the park and a couple of phone calls with Khan, he was reassured. He had just been notified that the job in Oslo was completed, that all details of the project existed, and now was on the way to Romania and then Moscow via the "Milk Route." Little Father was informed about the same.

So this was a lost cause for GRU unless Khan got hold of the drawings. The story would be simple enough. GRU had come across the body of a courier down in Romania together with a suitcase containing drawings and various papers relating to a lunar landing project. Even better if they had found a dead CIA man together with the courier.

He already heard the question. Are you sure the CIA man was dead then Kuznevskov? There was always someone who asked about everything, but no answers!

New phone to Khan.

"This is the way it should be. I'll await the report in the course of a few days."

Had it not been for this damn summit in Bucharest, then he would have been able to join in the field as well. But he would be too easily recognizable among all the agents who must be flooding Rumania these days.

67

Gardermoen

It was a restless night on a bad sofa, and already at 05:00, he was up and ready. Had checked the folder with all the drawings and notes and was ready.

"No haste, Tor, but fine that you are done. We meet the colonel at the parking garage at Central Station. We drive up to the sixth floor and change cars. That is, we are catching a ride with the colonel."

There may not have been any reason to make the departure as complicated, but now they were on their way. The E6 was almost empty, and at Gardermoen, there was no congestion either.

The plane was only half full. Tor had looked carefully for the tracking dogs at Gardermoen. But no sign this time.

What about the passport and the tickets? Someone had been skilled, very skilled, and on departure, he was hardly worthy of a glance. No problem getting out of this country. Back home, he had to use his old passport.

Wonder if anyone was waiting in Bucharest or Vienna which was the first stop? No, Air Austria to Vienna or Wien as they said, then Bucharest and he would just reach the departure point for Brasov directly with Wizz air. It was crowded here, probably a lot of press people going east to the Summit.

At last, they were on their way to Brasov.

The airport was a remnant of the war, and a new major airport under construction. *High time, with a rapidly growing traffic,* Tor thought. It took two full hours in the tight passport control. They were probably photographed, all the passengers.

The NATO summit to be in Bucharest, and it was a coincidence, of course, that it was taking place at the same time as Tor's program enrolled. But everything was delayed, and prices doubled. Putin and Bush were not yet in place. They would come later for a mini summit at another place in Romania.

Rumors were endless and so was the queue of all passengers who were going through the foreign police entrance at the airport.

Were they expecting one or more attacks here?

But people took it well, joking that it was because of Bush. No one mentioned Putin.

Where would Khan be located now?

Obviously smart this changing of itinerary. But he was not sure if it would have been as smart to pick up the package with the Glock here at Brasov Airport. Ears were everywhere.

Then he was through. What if the customs should also start examining papers and luggage? Lost and found? No, something like that did not exist. But at last, he heard it.

"We repeat: Ole Rasmussen is asked to come to the Wizz air counter in the arrival hall."

My god, Ole Rasmussen, that was him. At least he was in one of his passports. But should he not really be Walther Schack? Anyway, there was a package for him. She scrutinized the passport, asked him to take off his hat. Looked once more. Pushed a sheet over to the colleague. And then it was okay.

The taxi driver wanted 200 Euro, but after two minutes, he had come down to a fraction, but then in US dollars.

He pondered, what was written on the sheet and why did she hand it over to the male colleague there at the information counter?

He made an abrupt decision.

"Drive back to the airport!"

The driver did not understand much. But Tor went into the airport café and sat there for an hour. Then he took a new taxi into town. If he had seen anything strange? Yes, handling over of the sheet to the colleague was strange. Too special.

The same was the roll call. Anyone must have known?

So it was someone who closely followed his moves all the time. And this someone? Had to be Khan and his friends in GRU? And what would be their next move? Now they knew where Tor was.

68

The Hotel in Brasov

Tor had chosen the small guesthouse with care. Hotel Aro Sport would hardly win the award for outstanding views and standard in general. But it was clean there and the door could be barricaded, and it was possible to jump out of the window on the second floor without risking too many broken bones. The hotel was in itself one of understatement, but the price was also reasonable; eleven Euros was not bad. But it was not the price that was the reason for choosing this abode. Because it was an abode and nothing else.

It lay in the middle of the old town, close to the most heavily trafficked street. On the other side of the alley was a similar guest house, even with a restaurant that turned the other way.

There were several escape routes both toward the main road out of the city and to the bus stop and the train station. And guaranteed there was a back door that would allow free passage to the marina on the riverbank.

If Omar got into trouble, he would be able to reveal that Tor was in Brasov, but hardly anyone would look for this place. The hotel was no doubt at the bottom of any ranking—let alone it would be on such a list at all. But it makes the cut for sleeping and maybe also for tomorrow, depending on when Omar came. Now he just had to meet him and then go home again and hope for the best.

Maybe there would be a meeting in Moscow, and he could finish this forever. There was no message from Omar at the reception. Well, it was only the next morning they were to meet, and they had agreed not to use mobile. So tomorrow at 11.00 it was done and dusted. But it would not turn out quite like that.

69

Pyongyang

On the other side of the great continent, in the palace itself, two gentlemen sat with their tea and enjoyed the view. One probably enjoyed it more than the other, North Korea's UN ambassador.

"Is there any progress for our great peace-thinking ambassador?"

What should he answer?

Messengers of bad news are the first to lose their heads, literally. And just being summoned to the powerful, in the middle of the UN session, was scary enough. His Chinese colleague had jokingly remarked, "Shall we see you again, Comrade?"

The ambassador found it very inappropriate, for it could be only too uncomfortably close to the truth. There had to be something very special coming. But okay, if it had been him personally that mattered, then he would probably have only received a message or been visited by someone. So maybe it was something positive to be called in? But why was he called in alone? Why was not the foreign minister here? Did that mean No. 2 was no longer No. 2? Was there an appointment awaiting there for him, the UN ambassador?

"Well, you hesitate, spit it out then."

"The good news is that Bush is done."

"Yes, but it's old news. He's retiring next year."

The ambassador shrank. What if he told the truth, that the tone between Putin and Bush had never been better? How many minutes would he get before the shots killed him?

"The other is that Obama is coming, but we do not want him, do we?"

"Because? Why do we not want the peace apostle Obama? Would you rather have the warlord McCain?"

"Because Obama could come to get into a long-lasting peace with Russia. And then it is only Iran left to support us."

"Let's talk about something else. Much may still happen until the western part of the former Soviet Union is fully incorporated into NATO. What is your opinion on the forthcoming NATO summit in Bucharest?"

"I think Putin and Bush then will try to find a solution for this with the missile shield as well as the expansion of NATO eastward."

Something moved in the emperor now. The nickname that no one dared to mention out loud. The teacup took the heat in the first place.

"Answer me specifically on one thing, ambassador. Is there any truth to the allegations about Putin wanting NATO membership?"

"Yes. Everything, absolutely everything points in that direction. But some generals hold back."

"Then I think the time has come to talk to our big neighbor in the west. Mention it to your colleagues when you are back in New York. I prefer that it will be an unofficial visit from our side. By the way, what is your relationship with China's ambassador to the UN?"

"He does not want us to be seen too much together."

The great leader laughed. "But you are on speaking terms then." It was more of a statement than a question.

"Yes, absolutely."

"And their brothers on the islet out in the sea?"

"Taiwan is never talked about."

The sun cut into the eyes of the great leader, and after a wave to some invisible servants, the awnings began to move. They still let sunlight in, but not at face height.

"Listen, I have a plan. Bush and Putin will probably meet in advance without the other vassal states. Rumors say that their meeting should be in Brasov and that they both have wanted to visit the Dracula castle there. What if we make a map where we show exactly where we have placed explosive charges that can be triggered with a remote control?"

"But does not the CIA have enough agents in place that can reveal all this?"

"Certainly, but we shoot their leader on the spot, something that will strengthen the belief in that this is a real-time plot."

"Who put the explosives and who has the map?"

"Idiot! Everything should be fake. But perhaps can we get Russian intelligence and CIA to fight each other. And when they finally find the map, they will see that it was all a hoax. But the result of our small operation, it is that Putin and Bush never meet at Dracula!"

He laughed out loud now, and this time the teacup, with the gold insert went to pieces.

"Maybe I should invite them here for the new Dracula!"

And the laughter became even more violent. Only the ambassador kept silent. The emperor clearly annoyed with him.

"Go now and talk with the Chinese."

Who the fuck had recruited this man?

70

Maria Again

She was twisting and turning as she lay in her bed in room 1234 of the ARO Palace.

Another two hours until daybreak.

But she could not sleep more, despite the heavy sleep medication.

It was something she had started with after Caracas and had continued with in Oslo.

Permanently injured by jet lag, said the doctor in Moscow.

But she knew better, it was age and unrest that caught up with her.

As well as the troublesome surveillance and the message that came from Pyongyang that now something was going to happen soon, something big.

Perhaps would it be the last before her father was freed from the curse.

She had served fifteen years for him now, after being abducted for the second time from their home, on the outskirts of the border town of Vladivostok, in the far east of Russia. First released after five weeks, but then, one month later, kidnapped again as an extra insurance for Maria to play for the team. Provide continuous reports to Kosin and be prepared for the "great mission." The mission that never was coming.

And it had not gone completely to plan for her in the Venezuelan capital. The next attempt after Caracas was Oslo and Norway, but there everything went according to plan.

She was put on new assignments, and her commanders in the old KGB eventually became very happy. One more than the others after a night at Hotel Bristol in Oslo. She had been immersed, and she did not know much about what had happened until the next day. From now on, she should take better care of herself.

It had been many years now since the Caracas assignment where she had been asked to seduce the Norwegian. His name was Tor, and she had failed.

So finally, after all these years, the phone had come.

"I'm with you this afternoon. Keep yourself inside and wait. It is the day after tomorrow, it will happen here in Brasov."

And he had come, Kosin. What a name, but it was only a code name then. No one could walk around being called Kosin in real life. Not even North Koreans. But she was not sure if he was North Korean. Maybe he hailed from some village on the border with the Soviet Union.

"Here you have a picture that shows how you will dress, with wig and all and you get a small dog as cover. Then you look completely harmless. You will be in place by the old city gate precisely at 1058 and bring with you a map in one hand and a lapdog in the other."

"What map?"

"Do not worry, it's just a drawing on a plain A4 sheet."

"But SVR then, what about them?"

"Do not bother with them either. We take care of everything."

"We? Who are we?"

"You love your father, don't you!" He grimaced. It was not a question, more a finding and a threat.

But she wanted to know more and this thing about the map made her uneasy, not that she could understand why. She simply needed to know more about her mission

"What am I going to do with the map and what kind of map is it? Just a piece of paper, you say?"

"Bait for Americans. The map is false, but it is only we who know that. The Russians believe that we have mined the entire Dracula castle, and therefore they are looking for the map that shows where the explosive charges are, the fake ones. The Americans have also heard of a map, but they do not know exactly what it is about. Only that it has something to do with the mini summit. Everything is planted obviously to get the two snaps together. The rest you will find out tomorrow."

"Tomorrow? But will something happen?"

"Sorry and enough is enough now. All further instructions are sealed until the morning 08:00."

"And when this job is done, what about me then? You will dump me, back to my bosses in SVR or FSB, or…?" She just left the rest of the sentences hanging there. Gave him the opportunity to fill in.

"Then you are finally free, in any case from us."

"What with father, is he also free then?"

She was in tears just by the thought of her father and the humiliation when she was sixteen.

"Yes, of course. This is an old agreement that must be fulfilled."

Did they lie again now? Or? She was unable to get rid of the unrest. She had been there too long and knew something was wrong. But what? Would they just finish up with her, just like that? Did she not know too much to let her go? And what did Kosin mean by sealed orders? Maybe she should take a run for it now? But then, what about her father? He had been waiting for the final freedom all these years and his mother with him.

And where could she, Maria, escape and be safe. Presumably no place, but the most important thing was that she was not able to sacrifice her family. She was calmer now that the decision had been made. She just had to follow the path fate had decided for her.

A little later, she got up and put on a brown wig before she went out for a jog. Even in her thirties, the figure was still nice. She had saved her breasts and hips from baby births and tears as Kosin called it.

Kosin was waiting for her when she returned.

"I have received an additional order. You're going to kill a man tomorrow afternoon. An American high up in their intelligence system. Here, you have a Derringer that you have to hide in the jacket sleeve until you are close at hand. Sure, just press the trigger if you want to get rid of me. Do you not want to eliminate me and be free until the next person takes over?"

She knew he was teasing her so there was probably something behind it.

"I cannot, have to think about my father." She gave him the revolver back.

Damn, girl, now he had no legitimate reason to throw himself upon her and fuck her. She must have realized that it was not charged.

"What if I refuse to shoot this man tomorrow? I've never shot anyone before?"

"Then you know what happens to your father, and you yourself are revealed to the FSB. Then you will be entertainment for guys in Siberia, first for the guards and then for the prisoners, if you live that long. But you had perhaps seen yourself finish with a modelling career, with your great looks."

She was crying now. This was probably the end and what about her father?

"I have to go to the bathroom and fix myself a bit. I do not think you are naughty, really, Kosin. What is your real name?"

"I cannot tell you that, but if we can have a little fun tonight, the last night before you are free, then I'll tell you later."

Yes, he had wanted the girl many times before, but she had been dismissive. There were rumors about an ugly episode in Oslo with an SVR colleague who drugged her first. But now, she should die, yes, tomorrow, and it was he who should do it.

Thank God he was to stand far away with a special rifle with binoculars. Impossible to miss.

But even he, hardened after many years of training, thought it was special. Especially every time having to take the life of a colleague.

"I open a champagne and celebrate with you," he shouted at the bathroom. Got off his clothes and under the duvet.

She probably understood what was coming, when she found the knife, slipped it into her blouse sleeve and went inside. The one time in Oslo was enough, and now she was prepared. Never again would anyone rape her.

"I do not want to, Kosin or whatever your real name is. I am done with men for ever."

But then he was over her, naked and with an erection already.

The skirt and panties were gone before she had time to react and then she lay on the bed in an iron grip while he tore the blouse open, so her breasts just sprang forward. A moment of greed gave her the chance to bring out the knife. But the lessons learned from the KGB school did not help. She had never killed anyone and could not complete the cut against the carotid artery.

But she would not give in, and even if the knife bent off, it scratched up to the heart. But it must have been a rib that took the blow and then it was over. The grip around her neck eventually made her unconscious. She had almost stopped bouncing with her legs when he relaxed on the rope and tied her hands on her back. Heck, had he held the grip for too long? Slapped her, but it did not help. He sat over her and breathed in air and then she came back.

There was blood everywhere after the shallow wound from the chest. But he did not sense it. Got loose the remains of the blouse, spread her legs, and took her hard till she woke up to life. There was a whimper, and he stuffed the pillowcase in her mouth so that she was quiet.

"I had thought that we could have a good time, but since you put yourself against that, I then give you full package."

She was thrown around on the stomach and then he took her in the anus, brutally, while he used his fingers on the clitoris. She closed her eyes and cried while peeing in fear.

It made him only even more excited and brutal, and she was bleeding already there behind. As if it mattered. She was going to die tomorrow, so he drove on. At last, he came. Turned her around.

"You're pretty, too pretty."

He cut a gash in the cheek under the left eye. Pain? She felt nothing anymore.

"Go see yourself in the mirror now. Any more protests, then I do the other side also. I'll call you in the morning at 08:00. You can keep the knife, so you will cut yourself loose after a while."

She just lay there in a mixture of blood, semen, and urine and then the crying started.

71

Omar

It was a long time ago now, a full ten years since last time Tor and he were together. But the business had flourished, and it was a wonderfully beautiful apartment building he had erected very close to the large hospital in Cluj Napocha. With a great view of the park down to the center. His own villa was within walking distance. But in Eastern Europe, it was nice to drive, even if it was only a few meters to walk. Especially if you owned a car with great status. And Omar just loved the BMW.

Even though the X-ray business was very profitable, life had become even better with the missions for Moscow.

Did he ever had any qualms about serving the Russians? Not at all, if you were born a money nerd, then you were just that, even with a medical degree. Either way, he was glad to be out of the country where he was born. Could hardly be called a country after Israel's devastation and destruction. Over one million people living in the Gaza Strip alone.

Even though he had been in Oslo a few times over the last ten years, all parties had agreed that the smartest thing was to let the past be the past. So Tor had not heard from him in all these years, nor had he made contact himself. He had almost forgotten the meeting before Christmas on Karl Johan Street three years ago. Not particularly cordial. It had been cold. They had been sitting on a sidewalk café and the latte had been as bad as here at home in Cluj. But now, the past had become the present, and Tor had mentioned one last mission. They had talked together from kiosk to kiosk, it had to be the safest, Oslo to Cluj Napocha, the big university city in Transylvania. More than 100,000 students, some from Norway as well. But hardly any risk of meeting celebrities. Then where should they meet?

"You will be contacted by Moscow as in the old days. You will receive a suitcase with agreed contents, one envelope for me and another for you, and I would rather not know what is in it there for you. You should not check what I get, but that I also assume that you will not do. I have others to share with here at home anyway. Then I will give you my briefcase with drawings.

But it will not be Cluj this time. It's going to be Brasov. Something about security I learnt. We meet at the old city walls at the place there at 10:00 sharp on the fourteenth. And hey, you know what I mean about being on time!"

"Sure, boss, what if something goes wrong, that we have to change time and place?"

"Nothing can go wrong according to the leader, who is a colonel."

"It is easy to say when you are not in the center of events. And what if we have to change time and place?"

"Agree, but I dare not rely on giving messages of the operation at the small hotel where I will be staying. I have deliberately chosen a small elusive place. But there it is certainly easy to buy someone's silence for a few US. So stay away. But right at the church, so far within the wall, out toward the old smallest church is a small restaurant where they also serve a simple breakfast.

Horvath, who is an acquaintance from Budapest, works there."

"I thought you just knew ladies and me of course."

Tor chose to overhear the comment. "Horvath you can trust. He is approximately thirty, light hair to be Hungarian really. Slim approximately 70 kg and 185 tall. Do you need more?"

Omar laughed.

"In any case, Horvath will only be a backup if necessary. See you in three days. Ciao."

All right, Italian this time.

Well, Latin was probably still strong in Romania, even in Transylvania.

But Omar had been careless, for the first time.

He was the one who had told Tor about the thirty families that had divided the country between them, on a purely commercial basis, after the fall of communism.

That one of them had taken control of telecom should not have come as a surprise.

On the other hand, it was worse to be prepared for random tapping of kiosk calls, something they had started with after they found out that foreigners agreed on money transactions via, precisely, kiosk telephones.

To carry out these bugs, they used language students from universities. His name was Pavel, the guy who recorded the conversation between the two. Wow, this was a lot of money. He deleted the recording so far and watched while the tape stood still. His girl worked at the Russian consulate.

"What do you think this could be, Anna? If you can pass this tip on and they promise to keep quiet with my boss, then we can get rich, don't you think?"

She did not like this, mixing Pavel into her job; she was after all just a secretary. But she was tempted too. Imagine if they got 1,000 lei for the tip about a lot of money coming from Moscow to a man in Cluj. And this man ran a clinic here in Cluj. Easy to find.

"I think my fiance has some information that you would put a price on, Sajeev." She did not like this with her friend, but Sajeev had insisted. "Something about big money from Moscow."

"Get him here then."

"Now?"

"Yes, now at once!"

Pavel would prefer this not to be so obvious, so this was why they agreed to 18:00, when it would have become dark.

"Where do you get this information from and how secure is it?" He hoped Anna had not said too much, but she did not know anything either. "What do I get if you take the man or both?"

So that is how it was.

"I want 10,000 lei cash if you get the man from Cluj."

Surely a good idea to go high.

"I have to ask my boss about that."

It did not take long.

"You get half now and the rest when the man is caught."

"Now can we buy a new car, my girlfriend, or in any case, a nice used one."

But Anna was no longer happy. She had suddenly realised it could be her uncle Omar. But could he be some kind of spy?

Hardly, but they did not say anything about what kind of clinic it was, if Pavel had not overheard it correctly then. She did not dare to ask either. No one knew that Omar was her uncle. Officially, he was Norwegian, he and his small family. But it was Omar who had helped her out of Gaza on a false passport. Her original name was Fatima, but it was just Omar, her compatriot who knew of her in Romania.

How could she warn him? She felt she had to throw up. Apologized to Pavel and asked for the toilet down the hall.

Was she monitored? She was not certain whether the camera over her head was in order or not. But first, she had to throw up. And it never seemed to end. Betrayed her own family. Her work did not end until about an hour and before that she could not leave. Go? She had completely forgotten about Pavel. Pavel and the car and the money

"We will not get a new car for 1000 Lei, not even a Lada."

She looked seriously at him.

"Look at this pile, Anna! 5,000 lei now and just as much when they have caught him. Is it not fantastic?"

She managed to mobilize some enthusiasm:

"Perhaps we should rather get married then and drop the car? Perhaps I am with children. Maybe this is why I throw up."

He turned pale now.

"Wait now and see first."

He had no thoughts of marriage at this point. Besides, she had become a little fat. Was not like that when they first met during their studies. But she was kind, Anna.

"Maybe they will not even manage to catch him and so I must pay back. No, we'll wait with all this. And I had completely forgotten about a colloquium group I will lead. Call you when I'm done."

Then he was gone. No comments on this with the fact that she may have been with children. But the facial expression was clear enough. It was as if he would have asked, "Are you sure that it's mine?"

She had to go back to the toilet. The tears and crying came again. So she was allowed to go home half an hour before the end of the shift.

But she did not go home. She ran to the X-ray institute. But it was closed for the day. Should she take the chance to go home to him?

Maybe she was shadowed by her strange behaviour. But imagine if it was him and to imagine him being caught and it was her fault?

She had to stop him.

But it was only the maid who was there, and Anna was absolutely stunned. What should she say to her?

White lie came quickly: "I will work as an intern at the institute in the morning and need to ask the doctor about something so that I can prepare myself. Say that Fa…no, Anna has been here and that he must be kind to call me."

"But it may be late before they get home."

"Write a note then."

The maid thought she seemed arrogant, this intern. She "forgot" the whole thing. When Anna could finally get a call the next morning, it was too late.

"Dr. Omar? Yes, who is it who is calling? Are you a patient or is it private?"

"No, I'm his sister-in-law."

That was the best she could do.

"Unfortunately. The doctor is out. Is there any message?"

"No, not really, just say that Anna has called."

She was crying now. So maybe they had taken him? And she, or rather Pavel, had received the silver coins.

72

Judas

He had become an expert in snatching things around the moon landing project now. So when the news came that an Omar was going to receive large sums of money, he put two and two together. So the contact man from Norway was to come to Omar in Brasov with the drawings and then get paid and go home.

What was this worth to the sex friend Khan? A week in a distant hotel suite with a door in between the two bedrooms. Room service all the time. He and Khan.

He felt he got an erection at the mere thought. Had to go to the toilet and help himself. He came fast.

Oh, could they snatch this Omar with the money first, then they could take the Norwegian with the drawings afterward.

Yes, this is how it had to be. Get it done all together, and then only him and Khan…

But he did not want hotels in Russia. Always someone who could leak. Perhaps Khan could contribute so that he got a holiday to Serbia for example. The rapport between the two countries was fine.

And Khan was delighted.

"Take Omar and get him here to Moscow. If there are problems? No problem, take him with a Tupo and straight to me."

Khan could hear the lieutenant slamming his heels together.

73

The Wives Club

Theodore, head of US intelligence in Eastern Europe, remembered very well that evening the trip to Brasov was decided.

"Hey, my dear, sorry that I was late, but I have been at the meeting of the wives club. And finally, they have started accepting me, even though I'm French."

Theodore rubbed the sleep out of his eyes, well, he had dozed off on the couch.

"Of course, I know that you have been at the wives club. What was the topic that occupied you for so long?"

Did she suspect that the mood was not the best? Theodore had been on the road, and when he finally came home, and then it was this wives club.

Sure, it was important enough that the wife to General Storms was a member, but they were travelling steadily, she and her husband. Meetings in Washington and elsewhere and she was with him all the time. Then it was only the wives of lower-ranking officers who made up this whole damn club. But Françoise had seen it as a shortcut into American society. But it had not turned out that way. She was and remained French, and the same was true of their four daughters.

None of them resembled him. But of course, he was the father.

Now she was standing there, his girl, probably a little despairing over the message she was to bring. Did she look American? Did she speak without an accent now after fourteen years? No. She was and would forever remain beautifully French, his Françoise. But maybe he should remember to tell her more often. That there was no American girl he had wanted, nor any American girl he had married. But precisely his own beautiful French Françoise. And no one should dare to call her Franny.

"Maybe it's best we take it tomorrow, I am not sure you will like it."

She had let go of her hair now, the long blackish.

"We do not go to bed with this type of secret. Come on. I can see that you are ready to crack."

She became hesitant now. "Well, first a question then: Could you imagine a holiday with the club, yes, and then all the kids then? Just for a few days, please?"

The hopefulness shone, but he could sense the preparation for the disappointment by a no.

"Together with officers of lower grades? One is even just a second lieutenant, isn't that right?"

"Yes, but his wife is adorable. She chats a lot, but then she does come from Alabama. But it's just for a short week, Theo."

He could not resist her Frenchness, had never been able to.

"But there is something more, is there not?" He had put her on his lap now. "Come with it, my girl."

The top three buttons of the blouse were up, and he kissed her hard on the neck.

"Hm, yes. Everyone wanted to go to Dracula land."

Now it was out. Theodore had come home from there in the afternoon.

"Do you mean Romania?" He released her so that her breasts almost dropped out of her bra.

"Yes, and you have been there several times now over the last three years. Does it not have something to do with the NATO summit?"

"Yes, but I cannot talk about it and that you know well. But do you really mean to go to Brasov?"

She had buttoned up now, and they both sat. He was still in his uniform shirt, had not been able to change after the trip.

"Yes, is that very wrong?"

"Oh no, Bucharest is hermetically closed off due to the summit, so there you can only come transit best case. But let's talk properly about this tomorrow. There are special security rules for the whole of Romania due to the summit, but I will not oppose it if it can be cleared higher up. But I do not like it."

"What is it you like least? That it is Romania, or that it is with the club?"

"Both, my love."

"But, Theo, if we are going, then you promise to be social with the second lieutenant and the lieutenant's wife then, Theo?"

They had gone to bed, and she bit him lightly in the earlobe.

"I love this man so."

"What did you say, Françoise?"

"I did not say a thing, honey. If I did not speak in my sleep then."

But she had to wait to use the strongest weapon until it became necessary.

General Storm had given him a serious look.

"Are you saying that they all are going to Brasov?"

Theodore laughed. "Yes, I only got the message last night."

"You should not laugh, Colonel."

The general, still a vital tall man at fifty-five, got up. Made a blow-out on the floor, with his finger against the upper lip. A pause followed.

"This can be dangerous." He knew about the latest cipher message from Moscow. "There is talk that Dracula Castle in Brasov may be mined. The Russians think it is the CIA that is behind it, but it does not seem to be the case since Bush and Putin may go there in a private meeting before the summit. Probably someone else is completely behind this if it is true. I am waiting for a report from the UN and our contact with the Chinese. Have a cup of coffee in the meantime."

They did not have to wait long before the cypher responsible was at the door.

"From HQ, sir..."

And quite rightly so. The Pentagon denied that it had anything to do with the Chinese, but had, on the contrary, clear indications that

North Korea was involved. But no one knew if it was all a bluff or not, but there should be a map that substantiated the rumors.

"I suggest that you go in depth on this and so I will notify this wives club that the matter will be left until security has been checked, due to the summit. I do not officially know about this. It has to be communicated through my wife."

Theodore saluted and that was it.

He did not like the whole thing, he either. But Françoise had been very enthusiastic and surely the children, not only his, but the others in the club had gotten to know something already. The pressure was going to be enormous.

Luckily, the general was absent due to the meeting of the National Security Council.

Poor Françoise, the others had used her for all it was worth. They could have gone straight to General Storm's wife. She could not be reached, probably busy having to pack. Typical of the others to use Françoise as a lever. Married to "Next in Command." It was cowardly. It would never have come up if she had been a US citizen. It did not make things better that she was beautiful as a celebrity and had dual citizenship. She would never give up her French passport. The daughters also had "dual," which she had taken care of at their births.

It all had started with the trip to last a full week. But Theodore had pushed it down to five days of which two days for compulsory outings, two days to travel, and a day just for themselves, Theodore and family. The reason was of course security for all it was worth and that he had a job to do in Brasov before the others arrived.

But General Storm was not happy.

"Five days is a long time, and I will be absent for a whole week due to the Washington trip. But if we take some action so that the travel time is shorter, then it's okay with four days, don't you think, Theodore?"

"What do you mean, General?"

"Own plane damn it! Straight to Bucharest and the same back!"

Theodore just gasped. This was unusual. Did a salute. Thanking and taking a bow.

"The decision is of course yours and my wife publishes it to the club as usual?"

"Okay just to be 'Second in Command,' Colonel?"

"Yes, sir!" Theodore allowed himself a tiny smile. But Françoise as ethnic French would never have been accepted as the leader of the wife's club regardless of whether he became general or not.

Now it was time to plan the day in Brasov.

Could the castle be mined or was it just a bluff to make trouble out of Pyongyang?

It swarmed with security forces both from the Russian and the American side, even in Brasov. But the Chinese had referred to a map. If he could get hold of it, the bluff would quickly be revealed, because it was a bluff?

The phone rang at three o'clock at night, 21:00 New York time. Did they not have the sense to follow the time zones?

"Sorry, about the time, Theo."

It was John, head of security at the UN delegation. Old classmate from the literature studies.

"There are rumors of a possible defector, a Maria who has been with the SVR for a long time. Also in New York, Caracas, and Oslo. She operated for a period as the Spanish-speaking Ms. Hernandez. I do not know if the tip has credit, but it is rumoured that she is willing to trade a copy of a map in exchange for being allowed to go over to us. She is supposed to have good contacts with North Korea. The person who came up with the tip is a Kosin in Moscow. Obviously North Korean. Well, not tip exactly, but GRU is supposed to have squeezed it out of one of his colleagues before he was knocked off. We also cannot figure out why he let this Maria go but suppose she has made some mistakes, and by doing it this way, they manage to tease the SVR simultaneously. This is a game for the big boys."

Theodore had been light awake.

"Do you think she will go over to our side?"

"Alternatively, she will be revealed to SVR and be finished."

"Go on, John."

"Check out when a handover can take place, and by the way, it is irrelevant without this map, fake or not. But put on a bulletproof vest when you meet her, the whole thing can be a trap."

"I travel up to Brasov a day before you, something with the job."

The daughters screamed and Françoise turned pale.

"Can we not be stay with you at a hotel and wait for you there?"

"Will think about it, my girl."

Old Brasov center was clean and proper enough, but put them in a hotel farther down in the city out of the commotion? Hardly? Anyway, who would know how much time this possible handover would take.

Then came the message from John. "Meet at the old city gate at 14:00 on the fourteenth. You will be contacted. Make sure have backup! John."

The day before the general's departure to New York, Theodore received an emergency summons to his office. He wanted a status report.

"Now, what do you mean, General?

"Do you feel safer now? Being alone, wife and kids in a hotel and solid backup from CIA people."

"I have never trusted these guys and I do not now also. They always manage to mess up the missions. Think of Teheran and Nicaragua, not to mention the Balkans. Who was responsible for Security in Belgrade? I'm just asking?"

"If you send someone other than me, I will take these days as pure vacation myself."

"But they have asked for one high-ranking officer to be sure about authorizations, etc. I can understand them. Maybe we could pick one from the Ramstein base in Germany. Some colonel who is just sitting there."

"What does he know about Romania, and does he have the bare minimum local knowledge? Best case, he has knowledge of Kabul, if he has been on the wings there. But there is surely a medic somewhere there in Ramstein, a stocky one with colonel grade."

"That's enough, Theodore. The job is yours. But bulletproof vest. I do not trust for a second the skewed-eyed guys from Pyongyang nor the CIA."

The job had been easy. The vest was in the luggage in a sealed package. To Françoise, he said it was a gift to a local CIA man and then they were on board, all twenty-six, ten adults and sixteen children.

Theodore, by chance, ended up on the seat next to the beautiful wife of the second lieutenant. And arrived in Bucharest with a broken left ear. Arkansas, that's where she came from. But did everyone have to be as talkative as she and Clinton? It was his home state too. And she just loved Bill. Knew everything about him by heart. The flight was God forbid only three hours. And just that.

Bucharest's inner center had been hermetically sealed. But they were to be escorted to a couple of museums and warm baths, while Theodore and his family were to proceed to Brasov. They chose the night train, mostly to get away, said Francoise. But Theodore had gotten to it first: "Driving the train is exciting, is it not, children?"

"Yes!" it came in a chorus.

"Look forward to a delicious breakfast at the hotel and then we will meet the others out at Dracula's sometime in the afternoon."

At 10:00, the phone rang. It was John again.

"Fine that you are up instead of asleep. Now it is night in New York."

"Stop it, Theo."

"Change of plans. The handover will take place at 11:00, on the fourteenth, that is today your time."

"Okay, okay, relax."

"What about backup, Theo?"

"As long as you shut up and say nothing to the general, this will go like clockwork."

"Thanks, and over and out."

"Say what to the general?"

Françoise was worried but did not want to show too much to the kids as they sat at the breakfast table.

"Just that things are done faster, so we can go to Dracula a lot earlier. Maybe I have it finished already at 12:00."

But what if this was something really scary?

He did not have a firearm or anything. It was the CIA people who were to be responsible for the practicalities.

Would it make a difference to call?

He went out into the vestibule and tried the number of the contact man, but no answer. Deleted, not unusual according to the general.

"Do not have trust in them."

What now and what about the family? Françoise had not received any details, so she insisted that they all would go.

74

May 29, 2008, at 10:05 A.M.

The morning mist lay like a worn corpse cover over the old buildings there at the city gate in the old town of Brasov. The hue below was slightly golden yellow, and the architecture could have been the seventeenth century. Tor felt that this could just as well have been Munich or any southern German city. No trace of communism's Eastern Europe right here in the Transylvanian city.

Even if the clock in the church within the walls had turned their ten strokes already, the square had a deathly silence. Only occasionally a sour gust of wind, but it only lasted a few seconds, then it was quiet again.

The contrast to the rumble of the past and the screams of beggars and others who wanted to enter the city behind the then closed gate was striking.

The worn cobbles rested on that which at one time was mud and swamp with planks on top so people could walk there. Maybe there was some kind of life down there in the earth this early spring morning?

But they hid well, those in the underground, apart from a solitary earthworm who ventured out to sniff the fogged air.

Tor had been standing there for a while, waiting for the bus and Omar, or maybe Omar came in a taxi? A ragged poster on a bulletin board gave timetables in Romanian. Little help in that, no bus in sight, so he strolled the few meters to the taxi rank and waited there. Omar should have been here by now. He was supposed to come by bus, come with the last payment, so Tor could get rid of the delicate documents and drawings not least.

Would the payment be in Lei or Euro this time?

Tor could understand the issues with an alarming exchange rate to switch from Lei to euros or dollars, but okay, had to live with it. Soon he would be out of this country, which was undergoing a violent transition from a totalitarian to a mafia-controlled regime, as Omar put it.

"Money talks," Omar said—all the time.

He looked across the square again. The bus came, but no Omar. But there was one taxi coming. Empty, with a sign indicating it was available.

Should he wait any longer? Something must have happened.

It had been almost an hour past the time of the appointment, so then the agreement was to return twenty-four hours later. Unless a message was with his friend Horvath at the cafe. But of all things, it turned out that Horvath had taken time off and travelled to Budapest last night. And they should only use the mobile phone in an emergency. And Omar had not called.

Apart from the taxi, the place was still just as deserted. No one to be seen behind the windows either. None who waited inanely for the drama that was to come.

Had they all fled to avoid being drawn into something sinister? Because the atmosphere was like that, eerie as in a courtyard where someone was waiting for the execution, the gunfire from the execution platoon or the beheading.

Oh, should he really let such thoughts steal the day? But Omar should have been here, was always on time. Almost at least, but that was in the old days. Maybe he was now lying killed in the river or on the railway lines further down? Could not call him until after 11:00 in the morning. That was the agreement. Tor experienced that he constantly repeated things to himself. But he was tired now, wanted to leave this country and go home and then go up into the mountains far from people, just he and Astrid. He flagged the taxi, went halfway in, one foot outside, kept the door open, and tried to get an answer from the driver about the price to the Dracula Castle. Could just as well spend the day.

"A hundred Euro."

"Not possible. How much in Lei?"

The driver looked at him with an inevitable resignation, shook his head, and pointed to the open door.

Then they both saw it.

A massive bastard of a dog slowly crept across the square, pulled on one leg, and yes, it was a bastard, dirty grey in the shaggy coat. No doubt about it. But far behind him came what was interesting, a beautiful woman, thirty, maybe more, closer to thirty-five, in a short, short miniskirt, red longs, and a short open raincoat, red as well. Just covered the butt. Strange too, that she managed to balance on the high red heels there on the cobblestones.

Imagine if she stuck them in a hole and what was she really doing here? Obviously not comfortable in this outfit on a Sunday morning. Could come straight from the nightclub and perhaps she did just that.

But it was her hair that caught the attention, the long golden hair that almost reached the buttocks. Strange with this hair and the look in general. Was she Chinese or maybe Japanese? Or from the eastern border towns of Russia? Some Asian to her looks, but it did not make sense with the hair.

The puppy that she had on a leash picked the scent of the mixed blood and pushed and pushed.

There they disappeared behind a closed kebab wagon that stood in the middle of the square. But not long after, there she was again. The puppy too. She was close now, and Tor saw a cut across the left cheek, something that could be a cut from a knife. Someone had mutilated this beautiful woman.

Cut her in the face. Had they missed the eye, or was it just a warning? The people of the East do not miss. If it was the East, she came from, so it had to be a warning. Had he seen her before?

Yes, maybe, but not with that scar. But there was something familiar about her. She was carrying something in the left hand, paper, simultaneously as she held back on the dog.

But barely ten meters away, attention was drawn to her right hand. Something blinking in her hand, maybe a Derringer? But why did he think of that? Didn't know exactly, but there was something that triggered him. She pointed to something or someone up there. Shouted and pointed again. Tor? No, he was probably wrong. Or had he heard correctly? She was beautiful, very beautiful, even with the scar when she fell. Was it the heels that got her?

She barely managed to get her arms lifted and the object she was holding in her right hand clinked over the cobblestones almost all the way to the taxi. Her hair, golden even in the drifting fog, whirled rolling around her head when she reached the ground and the puppy, yes, it could not understand anything. She was still holding the paper, but then it went off with a gust of wind. And the puppy?

It just kept walking with the chain and then, then it probably realized anyway that something had happened, paddled around and around the woman and whined. What was she going to do with the dog by the way? Was it some kind of camouflage?

But the hair, what was it with this big hair? Slowly, it changed color from honey blonde and golden to pink and faint red. And so it separated the teams from the head. It was a wig and the hairline that now appeared, it was not blonde, but charcoal black. So Asian? In disguise?

Lord, could it be Maria?

Maria from Caracas and Oslo and now most recently, Fiskartorpet?

Tor had been about to get out of the taxi but had waited and seen the scene halfway through the door.

"You are too expensive," he said to the driver as he twisted and grabbed the door handle.

The driver did not answer. His head leaned against the headrest, and blood trickled out of his forehead, where the bullet had gone in and through and into the headrest. It was pouring rain now, and Tor felt chills, pulled out his raincoat, but did not manage to get it around the faintly sand-colored t-shirt before his eyes were drawn toward the square again. The engine sound was strong, much stronger than the small petrol engine in the taxi. Things happened fast now. A huge garbage truck at high speed chased into the square, directly opposite them, and for a moment blocked the view of the woman lying there. Two guys in black overalls came around with the woman between them. Hard to see where they belonged, no label on their outfit. Could it be a pigtail on one of them? No, maybe a kind of ponytail. Impossible to say, everything happened in a flash. They carried her between them like a sack of flour.

The short skirt had slipped all the way up and with the longs torn off in the fall, it revealed her genitals. But they did not seem to care. The puppy was still hanging on the chain tied around the wrist when they eased both the woman and the puppy into the back of the garbage truck. Then only the sound of the grinder was heard, and the whining of the puppy was no longer there, only a faint scream of death was what was heard as the garbage car disappeared, spinning around the corner and into the gate.

But the bastard, how about it? It was there, the visible proof that something had happened.

Pressed flat in its own pool of blood after the encounter with the front wheel of the garbage vehicle.

Only the face was preserved, except for the eyes that hung outside, as if pushed out by the pressure. The tongue did the same, hanging there faintly grey-pink. Some huge birds were already in the process of finishing what once was.

"Did you see it, did you see the murder, because it surely was a murder?"

But the taxi driver was also dead, and Tor was out of the door in one leap.

Looked around the square. Had anyone seen anything, had others come because of the shots? But no, he had not heard any shots either, so they have had to use mufflers or the shots were fired with incredible precision from long range. It was unfortunate for the driver that he had the window down, but the bullet had of course gone through anyway.

Out of the bus shelter came a family of six, an adult and four children. A man stood at a distance in front. I wonder if they had seen something, yes, they had to. They had been there too. Maybe they had just seen the woman fall, stumble somehow, but heard the shots? And what had really happened? Two murders here at the city gate? Was it real or a dream? Why the taxi driver? Or maybe it was Tor someone was looking for?

And the lady with the hair, or rather the wig, and the garbage truck and the two dressed in black?

The family at the bus shelter seemed stunned, the man not.

A tall, resilient guy, just over forty, in a worn US t-shirt, characteristic with the sand yellow color, almost similar to Tor's, same trousers and worn sneakers. GI in holiday mode? Or a tourist like Tor? The outfit could not have been more similar?

His face was cold, dismissive, almost arrogant, carved in stone somehow—obviously a high-ranking officer.

Four little girls and a beautiful, petite French-looking woman by his side softened the impression—what a contrast! And what was it about French women and their figure? If she was French, then? Even during his school days in France, he could not remember seeing a single fat French woman. Her face, the blue eyes surrounded by the darkness of her skin, and beautiful hair that shone against him. Tor was taken in—again!

She was the bait. And he just could not help it. And he who had received explicit instructions from home many years ago about to keep himself away from everything that could taste of espionage and beautiful women. Forgot everything he had been through. Get rid of the shadow of the Treholt case. Forget that he, Tor, had been the unknown third man.

"Hey, you saw what happened?" The man looked abruptly at Tor. "Excuse me?"

"You're military, maybe Americani as they say here, so you really did not see what happened? Did you not see the woman who fell when she shouted at someone? She and the puppy and the bastard there and the taxi driver?"

Tor turned around and pointed toward the place where the bastard had been run over.

But there was nothing there, just a touch of discoloration of cobbles as by blood or something, for those who knew. By the way, now there were several earthworms there, chasing after food as well. After the remains that the birds had not cared about.

"Be nice to the man, Theodore."

Well, he was Theodore, the woman who was killed had shouted Theodore. Or maybe it was Tor? He felt he was freezing. Well, that's how it was. They were to kill both him and the American. Chance was what made them both be at the same place at the same time and that they, in the least from a distance, looked fairly similar, him and this Theodore.

By the way, who was he and what business did Maria have with him, if it was she at all? The poor taxi driver who took the bullet for Tor.

The bullet that had Khan as the sender. But Khan then had to know that it was too early to shoot Tor if the money mattered. But maybe it was the drawings from Oslo that were the target. Anyway, Khan was too intelligent to shoot before he had both the drawings and the money. Was he not?

Then it suddenly hit him. It may not have been him who was the target, but the American. Yes, that's how it had to be. Tor had just been unlucky to be his double in the wrong place at the wrong time. He felt the confidence come back. But he could not be completely safe until he was out of this country with Omar's money. Safe? The Russians still had at least two hundred agents in Norway, and how many did the Chinese have? And what about the CIA and MI5? He did not dare think of Mossad and Al-Qaeda. What was it the POT boss had said?

"There are groups in Norway that..."

Give it up, Tor, you see ghosts in broad daylight?

Françoise, because that was her name, the wife, grabbed the man's arm.

"Talk to him then, please!"

But there was no sound over this Theodore's lips—only the arrogance shone.

"I'm Norwegian," Tor tried. "I am Norwegian and alone on a trip," he repeated.

"Did you not see the accident where the lady and the two dogs were killed and the two guys who just eased the lady and the puppy into the grinder on the garbage truck? And the taxi driver who was killed too. I sat five centimeters from the shot he got in the head."

The kids were scared now, especially the eldest who got what Tor said and sought refuge with his father.

"Oh my god. Did this really happen here?"

What am I doing, getting involved in a showdown? I had promised myself never again.

He stopped himself. He must have suffered a hallucination—maybe it was the thought of Dracula that had evoked something.

"This is really sceery." It came from the eldest daughter.

"Relax, Madeleine, this Norwegian has only suffered a hallucination."

She looked beggingly at Tor as if to get a confirmation.

"What is hallucination, Mommy?" The daughter did not give up.

"It's a kind of bad dream, my girl. And hey, maybe we should not go out to Dracula after this?"

The twelve-year-old clearly became contemplative. But the other three girls were completely determined.

"We want to go to Dracula," it came in unison.

This Theodore was less icy cold in his face now, so Tor held out his hand.

"I'm Tor from Norway."

Hesitantly he came with his. "Did you stand there, studying us?"

"No, I was just on the way out of the taxi. It became too expensive for me alone, and the driver indeed tried to trick me being a tourist. Then I thought you might be going out to the castle too since you were looking at a map here at the bus stop."

Best to be humble, not provoke this soldier.

"The map, the one she was holding in her left hand, did you see what happened to it?"

"No, I did not know that it was a map. But she had a paper in her hand, and it probably went with the garbage truck."

The man turned silent. And it was quiet for a few minutes.

"I'm Theodore, this is my wife Françoise, and these are our four daughters."

He relaxed now. Looked at Tor as a slightly helpless Norwegian on a trip. Perfect. Thanks to his creator that this Tor had appeared and in almost the same outfit. Then the mix-up, shooting at the wrong guy. But in any case, they had managed to miss Tor with a few centimeters. It had become the bad fate of the poor taxi driver.

"But we will not take a taxi, Tor, we will take the bus down to the exchange and then a new bus on to Dracula castle. You are welcome to join, on the bus, that is since the taxi driver was killed. Is that not what you said? We will meet some friends there," he hurriedly added.

"We are all GIs on vacation." (Holiday whatever, with family as cover).

"Norway, how exotic. Theodore was there only this winter."

She realized that she had said something she should not have said when she saw Theodore's facial expressions, and Tor pretended though he had not heard the slip of her tongue.

It was still completely dead at the square, except for the taxi that was idling with the slow driver. Strange that no one had come. No windows banging, no curious occupants. Should they notify the police? What would happen then?

"The bus will arrive in five minutes," said the American. "See here, take these. He gave him a pair of plastic gloves. "Get rid of your fingerprints in the taxi and forget it all. Do not touch the driver and let the engine continue to run. Hurry up before any other taxis arrive."

Convenient with gloves!

It took less than five minutes and then the bus was there. But no Omar. Where was he? He had never stood him up. And it was about big money this time. Could it have tempted him too much?

The daughters had warmed up, including the oldest, and it got lively on the bus, and they switched to a new bus further down in the center of town. The gloves, he had long before thrown in a trashcan.

And now they were on their way to the Dracula castle together with the Norwegian.

He seemed somewhat naive and quite ingenious. Hardly a member of any plot.

But damned with this lady. Then there was no extradition. Only a garbage truck that disappeared, and he did not dare to think whether the children had understood that the puppy had been grinded alive.

But who had shot her, and did she first try to shoot him? And if so, why? It was him who was to receive her—to freedom. And what about the map? The vital map?

Was this the work of the SVR, or had the CIA messed things up again? Someone must have leaked. Or had "someone" wanted to get rid of her after she had shot him? And who was this someone? But the timing, someone had missed the timing terribly. At least that had saved him. And what about his family. The children and Françoise who would see their father and her husband lying there dead in a pool of blood? But the map, he could not let go of the thought, yes, if it was a map she had in her hand?

He had immediately ordered the CIA via John to screen the castle for bomb installations. It took them an hour, and they reported back negative. But could he trust them? The Russians believed that an agent for North Korea had been seen upstairs by the castle, an old acquaintance, codename Kosin. SVR was therefore, to comb the court once more during the afternoon. Information about this Kosin was scarce. But of course, he was observed in worn sand-colored jeans and a similar t-shirt, similar to Theo's and the Norwegian's. This year's leisure fashion in Romania obviously. So the danger was over? Was it just fake the whole thing? But someone had made a map of explosives installations. And where had this map disappeared to?

And the woman with the wig? What should he say to the general?

How much had Françoise and the children noticed of the whole event?

The children could still believe that the Norwegian had been caught up in Dracula and had experienced a hallucination. But Françoise?

"You are no longer allowed to take such chances, Theo. Otherwise, I will move back to France with the children."

Yes, she was right. He could have been shot. Saved by lousy timing. But the general, he would ask and dig.

"Someone shot her on the way to the meeting, and I never saw a map, General. That's how it had to be."

"And the CIA? They were a little late."

"As usual. Remember I warned you! Then we will not make a further report about this, Theodore. If anything is coming from the CIA after this, we will look at the case again. But I guess they will keep their mouth shut. Messed up again!"

Yes, that's exactly how it would be. He knew the general well enough. But was it really good enough?

75

Securitate

An extra-long Skoda wagon with grimy windows—not so strange really in today's Romania—pulled up in front of the stately building that roomed several doctor's offices as well as the new radiology department to Omar.

Two men in their midthirties stepped out. The driver was sitting with the engine running. The office lady looked up, was a little frightened to see two men in black leather coats. What was this? The time with Ceausescu and Securitate was long gone. Or? Luckily the waiting room was almost empty just before lunch.

"Could we have a few words with Dr. Omar? It only takes two minutes max."

"But he's busy with a patient, I just told you!"

What kind of people were these? Poor hearing or rude or both. Perhaps had it something to do with Omar's past; he was not Romanian by birth. She turned pale, perhaps she had made a mistake. Maybe she would get fired. In an instant, she was up from her chair.

"Yes, sorry, I'm going to ask right away. Who should I say it is from?"

"Ministry of Foreign Affairs."

Oh, she was relieved and disappeared.

"Come on!" She was quickly back, showing them into Omar's private office.

Soon he was standing in the doorway in the white doctor's coat.

"Ministry of Foreign Affairs? But what do you want from me? Come unannounced. Embarrassing for the patients, don't you think?"

Omar had a gut feeling that this visit meant trouble, serious trouble. But it was important to keep your face calm. The suspicion that this was the state police was soon justified.

"Please close the door." One of them was at his back in a split second.

"You have no idea for sure where we come from. It applies to tax transactions, and you need to be with us now! Now on the double!"

The longest of them pulled up a Glock with a muffler and Omar faded.

"The car is waiting outside. Make it easy. We go along and you say to the lady out at the reception that you're back first thing after lunch, ask her to be excused to the patients."

"What about the patient waiting inside?"

"Same message."

The message was given on the intercom and so they were on their way out the back door.

Omar was placed in the middle and the driver pulled down a one-way mirror in front, so they sat there completely isolated.

"If you have any questions, we will deal with them later. We'll go to your house first."

"What do you want in my house? There is no one there except the maid, if she has not gone for lunch."

"We're going to get a suitcase of money. And a map."

"But I have no money and no map. Map of what then? Today's business is taken care of by the office lady and the stock is checked and put in the bank on the same day. Just check with the bank."

"Of course, we have already done that. But it is the map and the suitcase and the money in it that we are looking for."

So had anyone intercepted the conversation from the kiosk with Tor? That was the way it must have been.

"Please do not crush and destroy and frighten the minds of my wife and children. She's to get them for lunch now. All three are Norwegian citizens, so I recommend that you do not use the toughest style. You can do whatever you want with me, even though I also have a Norwegian passport. But I have no suitcase and no money lying around at home, except for small coins. Map? Map of which country? I have no idea what you are talking about!"

"Do you know, Omar, you do not have credibility. We have witnesses who will come forward and tell you that yesterday you should have received a black document case with couriers from Moscow and with a minimum of 700,000 US in small banknotes. Maybe it was the money you were going to use to pay for the map."

My, oh my, was it such a high amount that was going to Oslo. Two hundred to him and then 500,000 to Oslo. But Tor was obviously going to share with others so it might not have been that unfair.

"We can see it is bubbling in your brain now, Omar. But shut up until we find the suitcase. You're done here anyway, and your assets will be confiscated."

"I own nothing. All you think is mine belongs to a trust run by my wife who is also a doctor. You cannot touch anything here without having the Norwegian police on your neck and there is more to it. Norway is a NATO country as well. Remember that there will be a summit in Bucharest in a few days. Bad start for the host country this. Norwegian citizen threatened with life, abused, etc."

The guys looked at each other. This was new, perhaps best to let the Kremlin take the job further. But they had to scour the house, following orders. But this Omar seemed too smart for them. Why hadn't the boss said he was a Norwegian citizen?

"Shut up, Omar, now we are ready for the suitcase. You go first, walk naturally so it does not attract attention. The Glock points towards your spine all the time. Remember there is a muffler on it, so no one will understand anything if you collapse. No one will respond either. Dead like a herring, then it does not help with Norwegian citizenship. And you, you cannot even choose between citizenship in heaven or hell. By the way, all of you Palestinians go straight to Allah and to the one thousand virgins."

The maid had left. But there was one note from his wife, in which she wrote that she did not come home until about two. The maid, she could come back whenever.

"You cannot just destroy our home."

"Of course, we can! So where's the suitcase?"

"Or the money," said the other. "Maybe the suitcase is broken so as not to arouse suspicion?"

"No, I do not think so. He was to exchange with the foreigner who came with a similar suitcase. With drawings and a map. So where is it, the suitcase?"

Omar had been placed on a stick chair, his hands fastened to his back. The classic interrogation position.

"I swear. It is not in the house."

"You know what it is about then?"

"Yes, I have talked with one foreigner about it, but the suitcase never arrived. The foreigner did not show up either."

"We do not believe you. A Scandinavian came by plane to Brasov today. He picked up a package in the arrival hall and then disappeared. We have all possible reason to believe that he was your man. He had a backpack, but the suitcase could well hide in it."

That was the last thing Omar heard. He only noticed the sting in the upper cervical vertebra. Thanks, Allah, he had sent the suitcase with money north to Mares and now he was in dreamland, but not so long. It should not last.

"Nothing more to get out of him. Take a quick search. But do not destroy anything. I'm sure he was telling the truth of one thing: the suitcase is not in the house or on the property."

"And the map then?"

"Idiot, it is certainly along with the money."

The driver backed the car into the door. The newly planted freesias got dirty. But they got him into the trunk and slammed the lid shut. No neighbors in sight.

Freesia bushes were thrown the over the fence and then full pressure to a military airstrip, where one small Tupolev jet was waiting with engines running.

Omar, where was he going to end up?

76

Dracula

Tor and the Americans were all on their way to Dracula Castle now. The colonel and his beautiful French wife and the four children. Pretty unusual, such a super French lady married to an American military. And with a doctorate in philosophy as well? For sure, he was not some ordinary colonel. This was high-level espionage.

Had Tor seen something that he should not have seen? Who had removed the bastard? Yes, because it had been there?

Cold liquidation, a rifle with silencer from distance, before the girl even got to shoot Theodore? Was the Yankee her mission? Or was it Tor they were looking for, now ten years later and then why?

Was it GRU or Asians and was it the CIA that saved this Theodore at the last minute? Who whacked the woman? Where did the shot come from?

Did not Theodore have a weapon himself? GIs on holiday with large family in a former Eastern Bloc country? And last but not least, the Mongol Khan, now a major.

He probably had good private contacts in the FSB since he had gone to their schools before he was transferred to GRU. Who could have made this most extraordinary transition if not for his gay "instructor"? In any case, that's how Ivan thought it had to be.

The bus rolled on while Tor fought with his thoughts and more than suspected that Theodore knew that Tor knew and that the drama on the square was not a dream, but reality. The thought of the gloves that appeared so conveniently would not escape. Easy holiday attire and then gloves like to use at autopsy or by collection of artefacts?

And what would happen now?

Was it his turn again, soon? When?

Had they mistaken him perhaps with another? Who else than Khan could sense something now about his role almost ten years ago?

And what kind of friends could this colonel have out there at Dracula's castle? Could he Tor get away, without any fuzz?

The colonel was also not just an ordinary colonel, but responsible for Intelligence in the Eastern Hemisphere. It was on the business card he had hesitantly exchanged for Tor's. But he himself, soon an ordinary pensioner, was officially only on holiday, even though he was actually going to meet Omar, the Palestinian with a Norwegian passport, living in Romania and then get a settlement for the last job.

But it would be strange to run away from the Americans now, perhaps easier out at the castle?

The cell phone rang, Omar?

No, they had agreed about not using electronic traceable contact.

Then it was Junior in Oslo who wondered what the trip was like, if he had seen anything of Bush or Putin or other greats names.

Luckily, Junior had no idea about the drama at the big square. "Did you hear the latest news then, Dad?"

"About what then? It may have happened a lot in a few days?"

"I know how preoccupied you've been by this Treholt case, and it comes perhaps up again."

"Does it?" Tor tried to seem interested. But it was no longer Treholt that interested him.

"Yes, Attorney Haugestad was on TV, and he believes it has good opportunities to be resumed this Treholt case."

So they were not done yet, and poor Arne, he had suffered enough.

But stupid he had been, anyway, having got in touch with the Russians on a high level and over a long time and without reporting to his bosses.

A little guilty yes, but not in treason.

But it had been convenient for him with Arne there in front, while he Tor had slipped away.

Actors? It was the Russians, with Colonel Titov at the helm.

The picture of him and Arne on the street in Vienna had gone to all the telegram agencies. But Tor, was he himself a traitor too? He had been through this question with himself many times.

The Russians had received and paid for piles of old petroleum information. First and second generation H- rigs from Aker.

That was what he had been told. He really did not want to know anything. Just accept the courier package from Oskar and then go. That was the routine. But sometimes it slipped. He had not been able to ask Oskar.

What were they really going to do with this material?

They did not have operator knowledge that would make it possible to use these drawings. Of course, they could go on with the construction of their own rigs, based precisely on this material. But from there on?

Who should take the operator responsibility and what about the seismic?

The necessary seismic to find oil-bearing layer in relatively shallow areas up in the Barents Sea.

Unthinkable that the Americans had wanted to enter into any Joint Venture back in the seventies. So it had to be the French.

Renowned for finding openings for trade everywhere in the world, no matter block affiliation. He suddenly remembered the Mirage flight contracts. A great example of dealing with obscure regimes, as long as you get paid.

However, it was most likely that the H-rig drawings were well kept in an archive in the Kremlin together with Samuel's Condeep drawings, never to be used. It was a big surprise that the brother-in-law was involved in disseminating this type of know-how to the Russians. Guess if he had been paid properly. And that he had managed to keep quiet about it all this all these years. The villa in Byåsen? Surely, the funding came from the Russians. Samuel was probably smarter in his head than Tor had thought.

But he himself Tor then? He had been an active helper in the Russian industrial espionage. He too. Just like Samuel? No, not really, just been courier. But it gnawed and gnawed.

Who could really claim to be completely innocent?

He thought back on the many receptions in the Russian embassy in Oslo, sometimes with the entire Norwegian industry represented.

Traitor? No, not more than others, yes, maybe a little more than others. After all, he had handed over drawings or something and had been paid for his travel expenses.

But someone at a high level had trusted the contact or the channel and it was not without reason that he had been recruited to continue the good contact with the Russians all these years.

But money then, Tor, you have accepted the payments? Travel allowance, coverage of expenses, and nothing else.

But the risk of being a courier, would he ever get paid for that? And what if he had been taken, would he then have been revealed, exposed in full public disclosure?

Or would he have been shot or offered to shoot himself even?

What was the reward for the effort, there to keep one spy channel open to the Russians? Was it the desire to play agent 007?

Yes, maybe it was like that, but mostly it was the desire to help Oskar in his intention to remove Treholt and Titov.

Then he was back to reality. Forget the money, now it was about life itself. And he knew with himself that one day, he would be too slow on the trigger, literally.

Or would the Russians simply get rid of him, as up at the square today? If it was the Russians, then?

Maybe it was Omar who shot, or he had hired someone to shoot him? Maybe it was the CIA who had pinned down the lady with the hair to protect him Tor? *Perhaps Arne Treholt was the luckiest of us, he thought.*

He was left in peace ever since, while Tor still was in the firing line ten years after. But how could one say no to this last mission. You could, could you not?

Who knows? He, Tor, at least he knew what the consequence of a no would have been. They had the letter to Samuel and which probably dealt with Astrid, his wife and the relationship with his brother from his youth.

Put it behind you, Tor. You were in the right place, at the wrong time.

"Hey, that was a very bad connection, Dad! Can you hear me now?"

And then he was ready, in his own selfishness he had forgotten that his son was in the other end of the line.

"Sorry, but something happened, hope they do not charge you for the time of bad connection."

"Relax, the bill goes to you!" Laughter at the other end.

"But is there something in the media about a Norwegian moon landing?"

"Have you gone nuts, Dad? Armstrong landed there many years ago."

"Sure, I know, but Stoltenberg talked about something he called Our Moon Landing, on TV, yes, in the New Year's speech."

"Probably just preaching, Dad, I have to hang up now. Have a good time and take care of yourself."

But Tor was not finished, preached or not preached. Who had been the target for the sniper, Theo or he Tor? The logic finally prevailed: *It was not you, Tor, who was the target, but the American. So, enjoy the day at the castle and wait for a message from Omar.*

But in the morning, he would be shifting to the civilian attire in place of this paramilitary American leisure outfit.

He hated the very idea of the store round. *But life, Tor, life is the most important thing.* However, there should not be any shopping. Khan had other plans for him.

77

The Americans

They were from Denver, Colorado, and they parted with Tor out at the main gate, where the group was waiting for Theodore and the family. Apparently just like Theodore had said, they were families on a trip, nothing else.

But officers do not go on holiday with private soldiers or officer aspirants, do they? And the five fathers were obviously not all officers, not senior officers. And even if the Cold War was over, so what did five professional military American ones, do on vacation at the same time in secluded Transylvania? With Dracula as cover-up? And what was it this Theodore had said, almost his first sentence there in the square: "What happened to the map?"

Tor had looked at him incomprehensibly, before the American repeated. "The map she was holding in her hand?"

How did Theodore know she was carrying a map? Tor had only seen one paper. But Theodore obviously knew that it was a map, not just any paper. Should he be the recipient? Did they know each other, and was it his name she had called out before she fell? Shot by GRU or SVR? Was she a deserter that Theodore came to assist, take her over to the Americans? Yeah, it had to be like that. And what about the map, was it the payment for coming over and where had it gone now? Blown away by the sour wind?

Maybe lying there in the bushes behind the taxi stand? Map of what? Should he get involved in this too? Obviously, the map was important. And obviously he himself was far too similar to the American colonel in appearance.

But who had shot her and who had missed Tor or Theodore? But was it not a weapon she had had in the other hand? That which flashed? If she worked for SVR, fine, then she would be liquidated as a defector.

But why should the American be killed? Could it be Khan who had come over and become aware of a handover agreement? If she and the map was a part of one barter, what would the CIA be giving back and what was on that map? Was the American a spy for the Russians?

In the morning should Putin and Bush and the rest of the top people in NATO have another reunion in Bucharest, a scanty hour's flight away.

But not security officers. Why would they not be in Bucharest and not her in this remote place? It puzzled Tor a lot.

But rumors had it that the two, Bush and Putin, would meet before the official meeting. Perhaps was it here in secluded Transylvania that this meeting was to take place? Was it because of this that the passport controllers spent more than two hours to let him through yesterday evening at the small airport?

Maybe the two, Bush and Putin, already were here in Transylvania?

The thought was frightening with the murders at the city gate as a back carpet. And then it was guaranteed the American was the target and not him, Tor. But then there had to be a swarm of security officers and other agents in the area. Not just the CIA. Tor gave up. He was not the one to solve the world problems. But the thought of the map would not leave him completely.

Tor took a detour through the small garden with the pond and bridge and past an old guard shed. Thought he had managed to get away from watchful eyes from domestic police, the old Securitate. And he had. But he had seen the others, the black-clad ones.

Admittedly camouflaged as backup to the accompanying armoured weapon Leopards. The leopard tank had long been condemned, but the troops had kept their name. The posture, the flexibility that revealed super-well-trained muscles was enough. The four who searched every nook and cranny at the main entrance, they were not ordinary forces, but elite soldiers, trained and educated together with their Russian colleagues. Maybe some of them were Russians even, deployed here in NATO country Romania?

Yes, for sure they could be Russians. Subjects to GRU or SVR / FSB? And the Mongol? But then it had to be him Tor they were looking for too? It was Igor who the Mongol Khan had laid down for hatred and was to take out. And those around him? And Tor, yes, maybe just Tor! At whatever costs.

But how had Khan arrived at the perception that Tor was to be found in Brasov? Picking up the Glock at Lost and Found at the airport?

The idea of leaks via old FSB colleagues would not completely escape either. Or had Omar been caught and had he cracked? No, he was not the type for that. But serum could have tricked him to reveal the whole scheme. GRU were definitely not amateurs.

The excitement was starting to get annoying now. Maybe they thought he was on to this map, not just the material from Oslo. He had to make every effort to get away. But maybe the map was in the bush at the bus stop?

The group of Americans was already inside the barricades, but Theodore was not among them. Maybe he had gone to the bathroom.

Perhaps was it because he was lacking in the group that Leopards had been panicked. They did not find the main man. Had they once more confused him with Tor?

Then one of them spotted Tor and the alarm signal went and they came chasing him up the steep hill to the entrance by the castle. What if he was caught?

Disguised as a Norwegian on a tourist visa, while his real name was Theodore, and he was an American professional soldier with a colonel's degree.

And why had he slipped away from family and community?

And what if the real father of the family, Theodore, turned up again?

He felt clearly that many years running training: up and down the stands in Midstubakken, then over to the stands in the Holmenkollen, for a final to round off to Frognerseteren and then back to Skistua. Twice a week until the snow settled. Then a first round with the Ski Association and then on his own the next nights.

But the cobblestone was worn down and it had been raining. Tor recognized at last that he soon could take no more, and he felt that the four approached him for each slip step up toward the castle. At the top of the paved path was a small cave to the left and the main entrance to the right.

Tor looked around, relatively few people now, and he made a run to the cave. There had to be an exit from it, at the back of the cave wall.

What if there was not?

But he was done, and if he had run into the castle, he was guaranteed to be taken.

But he was probably not the first to have sought cover at the back of the cave because there was actually a small light opening up there under the roof, at the very back.

Maybe it was thirty centimeters in diameter—too narrow as it looked from below. The rescue came from outside.

A couple in love sought cover for the world, she tall and blonde and he as well. Had to be Nordic, maybe Norwegians?

"Hey, I hide from the rest of the group, may I stand on your shoulders and come out from the top of the cave?"

"How did you know that we are Swedes and you, yes, you must be Norwegian."

Tor smiled broadly. "Just had to take a chance, brothers. But it has to go fast now and not a word if someone comes and asks. When I'm gone, you do what you came in here for."

She blushed and beat awkward with her neck, the long bright hair tossed away.

The boy was athletic and gained unprecedented strength through the girl's admiration.

Tor got his hands through the top, and with the help of the boy's push, he had his upper body through and was able to work his way up.

"Thank you," he whispered.

But there they stood, two of the Leopards, the two others had gone into the cave.

But Tor had covered the light opening in the ceiling with his coat, and there was only a frightened cry from the girl to the two men in the armoured uniforms.

Soon they were out again and the group of four stood together. The arguments were loud. But then one of them took command, pointed down the path, and there he saw it. The five families came in droves toward the entrance with Theodore and his four children first. They must have refrained from entering the castle or the entrance had been closed by the Leopards. But why did Theodore go in peace? He did not show signs of panic either. Could it be that there was a third person? Another who looked like Theodore or Tor?

But who the hell would that person be? Could it be the one who had shot Maria?

And if they were three, then it was not strange that the Leopards were confused.

So far, tussocks hid his head and he emerged as one of the uniformed turned up toward the cave.

What now, had he been seen shouting? Yes, they did not leave room for doubt. Off with the coat and down into the cave with a bang. He put his hand over the woman's mouth and hugged the man. They were literally in the act.

"Keep going," he whispered, hiding behind the woman in a pile of twigs. Poor coverage, but anyway.

He could not think any more until two of the black-clad stood in the cave opening. Then she screamed and the boy with the tool inside her turned his head.

"What the hell, get the fuck out."

The two black-clad laughed and so they were gone.

"Thank you," Tor whispered with his back to the two, "but I have to stay here for a while."

They laughed all three now.

"Thank God you're too old to be a danger for us."

The two young people laughed even louder. They should just think what Tor thought.

"Cover yourselves up in the least, and can you not wait with the absolutely huge part until I am out of here?"

"Wow, free live show and the old man says no! Okay then, we may offer a little decency as you say in Norwegian, not just Swedish sin."

The girl laughed even more, and he took chances to check on the outside.

But the four Leopards were gone, and in seconds, he was out of the cave and inside the castle. There were the two younger American girls, both had Dracula masks. They were on to him now and howled warlike.

But Tor had no choice. To the girl's big disappointment, he had to find a way out for his safety. The party would obviously be kept under surveillance.

But where had Theodore been?

Had he met a contact down at the entrance?

The bus ride back to Brasov was undramatic.

He got off at the station down in the city and took a taxi up to the city wall. No one followed him as he looked for traces of the day's event.

But no, no signs, not even a blood stain. The rain had flushed away whatever was left, and it was still raining quite heavily. He found cover in the bus shed while cursing over his idiotic interference with the Americans.

The wind had slowed down, but in a corner of the shed, it had blown all the worst rubbish, empty cigarette packs, used tickets, and not least a dirty A4 sheet. Could it be? He looked around. A couple came to wait for the next bus. He did not have many seconds to do it. Quickly bent down, stuffed the sheet in his pocket, and triumphantly held up a snippet and asked politely for fire. They just shook their heads and left. Would not have anything to do with the bum.

There was the so-called map and Tor jumped off at the hotel. Did not take the chance of any investigation there and then.

Now they had two reasons for looking after him. Both the map and the drawings. That meant both the CIA and the GRU.

78

Curtain Falls in Pyongyang

Someone was waiting for a report. A report that was to confirm that the Russians and American agents shot each other to pieces and that the visit to Dracula Castle had been a failure. But it took a while.

Finally, a waiter came in with a fax. He was totally alarmed as the great leader's face went pale by the message: Our agent shot by GRU by mistake. The Americans? He missed them.

The case looms as an accident of Securitate chasing the map.

"Bloody idiots, they were going to kill each other, the girl and the American," he shouted.

But no one heard, the waiter had already taken cover behind the heavy curtains.

79

Drama

Tor had come out behind the hotel.

It was still raining heavily. Instead of going straight to the hotel door, he did one round as a precaution. Could not see signs of life. Dark in his window too. Hungry though, and he went on to the neighboring cafe and ordered a simple peasant omelette.

Where the heck was Omar and what about Horvath?

However, it was not Tor's day. The cook had saved on cooking. The rest of the eggs floated in the butter, so most was left on the plate.

Could not see that anyone was interested in him, as he slipped around the corner. Finally, he was in the vestibule, though it hardly deserved that name.

The bed was lovely and soft, and it was clean, no cockroaches as he had feared.

Only noise from young people who were in for a cheap room and partied next door. Giggling girls were heard in the stairway as well.

He tried to order a bottle of beer and was directed to a room further down the hall and that was it. There was a maid sitting there. If that was what she was? Had she turned sixteen? *Did I seem threatening?* thought Tor.

But then he realized the reason for the fear that lay thick outside on her as well as the other two. An elderly woman and one boy sat further inside the room and tried to hide the stove. But the smell revealed them. Goulash stewing in the pot.

Probably it was mother and brother who had come to visit the daughter, the maid. It was almost zero degrees outside, and it was raining and raining. Delicious then to be inside and get hot food. He was hungry himself too, but did not feel like being invited into the small family. Maybe it was for them the only hot meal of the day. So he left them and got out back to the room across the hall with a beer in hand.

They did not want payment. Maybe it was the fear of being exposed with the stove? Tor had left 10 lei, equivalent to 3 Euro, which would give them the opportunity for a cheap breakfast as well.

The local pilsner, Aurora, hardly cost more than a quarter and bread was cheap. The smell of food from the restaurant kitchen across the street became more and more intense and nauseating. Just the way it can be with a frites cooker. But the window had to be ajar, and the radiator could not be turned off.

There was not any table in the room, so it was the bed again. But first he had to have something for his stomach.

He had bought cheese and ham sandwiches at the kiosk at Dracula castle and there were still a few pieces left. With the pilsner, he would have to be content with this till the morning. Where did the shot come from? The bullet shattered the beer bottle in the windowsill, and he was cursing, taking cover as best he could. Then came the second shot. This time, the bullets hit the bed.

The shots must have come from upstairs across the street or higher up in the neighboring building. So, it was only a matter of time before he himself was hit. He had to leave the room. But how? In the hallway there was a strong light, and if he opened the door, he would be a perfect target. It had become very quiet in the room with the partying by young people. Presumably they were lying on the floor too, waiting, waiting for someone to finish the job, find the victim, and then run away.

But who was after him?

Was it the Leopard or the CIA or the SVR/GRU or were there friends of the Asian-looking girl in the square this morning?

And again, what did this have to do with him? Except for the confusion with the American colonel? If it was a confusion. But they must have sorted it out now when they saw them both at the castle at the same time? Or were they still unsure who was who? Bullet number 4 came closer. The hole in his shoe indicated that someone was narrowing him down. This close to the big toe.

But first he had to get out.

And the door was the only option.

Take off your belt and then lasso up around the door handle.

It did not work the first time. Not the second either. The third time the closed in, bullets no. 5 and 6. But now the door was open.

Then there was the backpack. He just had to have it.

The belt would fasten itself in a strap so that he could get the sack. But what about the damn corridor light?

Yeah, what about it?

He tested with threading coat over the chair and push the chair out, looked as if he had curled up together and were on his way out the door.

It had to be an automatic gun. The crackling was unmistakable. Probably an Uzi. The coat stunt was revealed.

A naked girl screamed in the corridor, she probably called for help. One of the two girls on foreplay with neighboring guys?

It must be someone they had picked up from the street, Tor thought. Cursing sounds the same in all languages. Fuck you, the most ingenious.

He waved her away from the doorway, pointed to the light on the ceiling, and well, she understood what it was all about. Or maybe she thought that it was smart to extinguish the light as she was naked.

The snipers must have understood what happened. As the light went out, then began the stutter from the Uzis again.

Why no one called the police. Or maybe were they were on the same team?

The girl was gone, and the shooting ceased. Should he take his chance, or would his shadow be drawn against the light from the stairwell?

It was now or never. If he lay here, he would definitely be shot or picked up by one of those who were after him.

Through the bullet-ripped window, he could hear the sound of a truck that approached in slow speed.

From the loading platform or the roof of the truck, someone would be able to look straight into the room.

So when the noise from the diesel troll was at its highest, he rolled himself up as a ball, out the doorway, and pulled the sack with him.

They could not have followed when he rolled out, but when the rucksack was pulled out, the reaction came quickly, and the bullets slammed into the PC. Fortunately, he had taken backup, now in his jacket pocket. Just hoped that the metal plates in the suitcase inside the backpack protected the drawings.

Then he was down to the first floor. Not a soul to be seen and he plunged for the basement downstairs. But there she was, or was it not her? The girl from the corridor? Her hair was the same, but she was dressed now, very dressed in a khaki uniform almost. "Against nuclear weapons" mark and "women's lib" something on the lapel.

He had seen the outline of her naked in the corridor, so he knew what was hiding under the unbecoming and far too large uniform.

Clearly, it was not her uniform, neither was the pistol she held tight too.

But the finger on the trigger made it clear that she was scared.

"Do not shoot yourself, my girl. That thing can go off any time."

No reaction. Maybe she did not understand English?

Then he tried his hand at German, but no. Still just as expressionless and the gun pointed uncomfortably at the umbilical region. Maybe she was a pro anyway? Seemed as if she could handle firearms.

He held out his hand, but she backed all the way to the wall, without the gun changing direction.

"You are Tor," she uttered in some kind of Russian/Romanian.

"Da," he replied and then she smiled and waved at him, while she gave him five fingers and pointed up the stairs. "Five minutes maximum and pang, pang dead!"

80

The Escape from Brasov

The back exit from the basement was cramped. Hardly a hole that a man could creep out of. Only clay and rubbish.

But first, he barricaded the door at the foot of the stairs. Came across a large oak barrel and some lead weights, for what use—to drown someone with?

He could hear someone slamming the door with an axe or something upstairs at the front desk. Maybe they did not have even five minutes to get away. But the girl was already out whispering impatiently to him, still in a somewhat incomprehensible language.

He hung on to his backpack, got it off, and sent it out first and then himself and then they were both out, running down the alley to Hotel Aro Palace and further past down the main street. From there, the park and there was a jeep parked in the direction of Lunga Strasse toward Sighisoara.

Well then, well planned this. But why to Sighis? Was it where Omar had hidden himself? Had it started to burn under his feet in Cluj?

Someone had followed him and knew he was to stay at Aro Sport. This "someone" obviously knew that it was dangerous and that someone would come after him and had made sure that the escape route was ready. This had to be Omar's network, right? But he could not be sure.

She was a tops driver, the lady, but her English was poor at best. She stuck one note in his hand.

Impossible to read, so he would turn on the light on the dashboard. Her hand just slashed his face. A warning finger came on to his forehead, "stupido." Well then, easy to understand! He was an idiot. Found a small flashlight in the glove compartment.

"I will leave you in five minutes at the next bus stop. There you can hide in the bushes and wait for the bus to Sighisoara. The driver, Rudolf, is one of us. Pay in Lei, no Euro, and shut up. Someone will contact you at Casa Wagner. Ask for room 312. It has been reserved."

"Thank you."

Then it had to be Omar's network?

Who was Omar's agent for? Himself? CIA? Hardly, then he would have known. But why should Omar haul him to Sighişoara? A place he had barely heard of. There was no airstrip there either. Was Omar waiting for him there? If not, then this seemed completely pointless.

Tor waited in the bushes. The bus was to arrive in forty-five minutes. It rained heavily still, he was soaked, hungry, and tired, but he was alive.

Where the hell did the girl come from and who did she or those behind her think he was? It rattled in the backpack. Got to look at it in daylight. Also, it was best to stay hidden from the traffic on the road. He got stiff from lying there in the bushes. There came a big car in slow speed down the road, it seemed as though it could be a Humvee.

He showed himself even more down in the bushes and hoped for the best. A large package was hauled off and then a man in a black suit jumped off and the big car was off.

The bus stop was not great and not particularly well illuminated either.

Tor moved his backpack and heard the clatter of the broken PC again. The man in black seemed to have heard something.

He came closer. Hell, the gun was at the bottom of the backpack. Fucking Omar. What have you gotten me into?

Had Omar been there on time, then they had both been out of Brasov now. He himself on a plane home via Buda.

The man came closer, and he could see it clearly, the Leopards. So it was GRU who was behind it all, and it was Tor they were looking for.

Then the man took off his suit but kept the gun and then suddenly, he was just a regular youth in worn clothes.

But the big package, what about it?

The man dragged it closer, then he threw it into the bushes together with the uniform.

The package landed on Tor and he knew that there was something warm, something soft inside it. Some liquid seeped through the straw. Blood? Yes, it was blood. The soldier went out toward the road again.

Who was he waiting for? The bus, he too?

It hurt to breathe, and Tor had to get rid of the weight of the straw sack. Yes, it was a dead body.

The body was still warm. Maybe it was not completely dead, only unconscious?

He carefully cut up the top of the rucksack. The soldier followed the traffic. Tor prayed for a big truck coming soon and making real noise.

It helped to pray because there was a whole military column coming. Tor got the chance to cut more of the sack. It was a young woman. God help, it was the same woman, the rescuer. The blood came from the carotid artery that was cut all the way.

Suddenly, the soldier was gone, and he could get up, bloody now from the woman's body. Dead? Yes, she was dead.

He felt her. They had removed all ID, no wallet nothing, even the marks on the lapels were gone now. But in the left boot shaft sat the Beretta. In the other sat a magazine. Then they could not have been so skilled anyway. Or maybe they had been short of time.

His eyes were wide open, and he rushed out to close them.

But what could he do with the body? If he was found with it, he would be nailed to the murder and charged with murder, blood all over him. He pulled her out and wanted to wrap her in the Leopard suit. But then he noticed it. She was naked downstairs. It smelled like piss, and obviously, the body had reacted in fear—he had got shit on his fingers. Tried to wipe it off on the backpack. Then got her pants first and then the Leopard jacket. Poor girl probably raped first and then the knife. Why had it always to be like that? Why did women have to get raped? Once they had to die, why couldn't they make it in a more humane way, the assholes. She must have been terrified this girl, despite her training; otherwise, her body would not have reacted like that.

Tor closed the sack again and then showed it all down in the ditch behind the bushes.

But he must not miss the bus and what about the soldier?

Far up toward the center, he saw a bus coming. The street lighting was dim, but the driver saw him. Help, he had not cleared away all the bloodstains from the woman, but the backpack was clean, so he held it out in front of him. Nodded to the driver, "Sighisoara" and offered him 20 Lei.

The driver looked at him wonderingly and said something in Romanian. Tor did not understand any of it but gave him 20 more and the driver nodded contentedly. Gave him the ticket and kept all the money. On the ticket, it was written 25 lei. No wonder he smiled, pointing to the blood dripping. The backpack did not hide everything. Maybe he thought it was Tor's blood. He limped sort of and looked for a seat far behind. The other passengers slept. In the abrupt movement when the bus swung out, he landed in the back seat almost on one tiny woman in a gypsy outfit. Apparently, she had slept and obviously she was annoyed, so Tor made some apologetic movements before she flew up, pointed to the blood, and moved forward. The bus had turned into the roadside again.

81

The Bus Trip

A passenger arrived at the last minute. Then he moved toward the back. Tor hid his head behind the backpack, but the holes after the shooting in the room were certainly clearly visible.

Then he realized who the last passenger was. It was the Leopard soldier. The driver had extinguished the inside light, but Tor knew the face only too well. How far back would he come to take a seat? Tor did not dare to look up but prepared the Beretta. Heck, he should have had his own solid gun in front of him. The Beretta was a women's toy.

Should he wait any longer?

The one who shot first would survive; the other would not. Then he lifted the sack aside and directed the Beretta forward. But the Leopard soldier was not there in the aisle anymore.

He had taken the vacant seat two rows further in front. The man was dark, short haircut, and did not look Romanian at all.

Russian? Maybe. But then they took chances. In the middle of a now NATO country? So maybe this guy wasn't a Russian anyway?

No, the features had been a little too western for that? So maybe he was Ukrainian.

No importance, the man had an aura of authority and self-confidence that could only come from long and solid training.

In other words, the Russians / GRU had infiltrated military forces here in Romania. Or were they perhaps secret guests? The regime was still communist.

But why were they after him Tor?

Now they should be fully aware that Tor was not a colonel in the US intelligence services.

Or had the message not reached out?

Or had simply the American colonel made them believe that he was the Norwegian and that it was Tor they should be chasing?

Could it be that there were two Russian intelligence agencies who worked independently of each other? The girl belonged to SVR; little doubt about it.

But this Leopard and his friends who must have killed the girl and dumped her, what about them? They came from GRU, the military intelligence. The people of Mongol Khan? Of course, they did and the prey they were looking for was both the rocket drawings and the map Khan had come closer to. But again, why Sighisoara? Was it because Brasov had become too dangerous? Was Horvath caught and perhaps he had escaped here?

But again, why had they not sent him straight to Cluj? Sighişoara was a dead end. Maybe it was too dangerous right now in Cluj and therefore they had settled for little, sleepy, and certainly harmless Sighisoara, as a place to wait out each other. Not least give the CIA and GRU time to avert possible assassination in the Dracula castle. But Sighisoara should to turn out to be less sleepy than anyone could have imagined.

A few hours later and the first light was coming, slowly. Tor had not dared to sleep but kept watch over the Leopard all the time. It was a critical moment when he got up to go to the bus toilet. But Tor was prepared and appeared seemingly calm down in deep sleep behind the backpack.

But what if the man comes up again and thinks I'm sleep, will he try then? Check out who the passenger in the back seat might be? He has good control from the forward rows.

As the man is on his way up the small stairs and looks toward the back seat, it happens. Sudden stop, roadblock, and both civilian and uniformed police.

The leopard disappears, like sunk into the ground.

Two in uniforms and one civilian searches through the bus. Obviously, they are not looking for Tor. The civilian stops at all the seats and shows the picture of, yes precisely, Svetlana. The name of Tor's secret helper. He shows the photo of a leopard suit. They all shakes their head, Tor as well, and then are they are gone, and the bus is on the road again.

The next moment, the Leopard is back in his seat. Where had he been hiding?

Obviously, he had crept together in the narrow parcel shelf. And no one seemed to have noticed anything.

Sighisoara, yes, the road sign. Far up there the castle towered and in the small house at the foot, it was said that Dracula was born. The castle looked almost like when it was abandoned by German emigrants three hundred years ago, as stated in the brochure. A Jeep blocked the road and then the Leopard was gone and so was the Jeep.

It all went fast, very fast. Was it in Sighisoara then that it would be showdown? Was this where he was to meet Omar this time?

82

The Kremlin

They are in GRU's headquarters, at the end of the corridor, at the very bottom. No sign on the door indicating whose office it is, just bare numbers, room 791.

The smoke is dense. The two guys and the woman at the table by the window facing the courtyard are drinking and conversing politely as in a sidewalk café, while a fourth man is sitting on a stick chair in the middle of the room.

They talk about him as if he is not present.

"Why do you think Omar tried to fool them this time? It would be his last trip. Could sit with his pension down in Cluj and live fat among all his whores."

"Enough of that Alexis, enough."

The other two laughed, growling rather. One gaping laugh. Khan looked at Omar. No doubt about who was the boss.

Khan drank Pepsi, not Moskovskaia vodka like the other two.

"You know, Omar, no, you do not know, do you?" An icy laugh followed the question. "The fact that you tried to escape from the toilet at the airport was your rescue. Then you came straight to us and miss the washing that is standard for everyone who comes as special luggage. Because that was what you were, a hell of a lot of special luggage. Right, guys?"

Everyone laughed.

"He owes us for this, this fat son of Allah. But you must have tolerated a lot or received too small a dose. You should not have woken up before you lay naked in the bathroom and felt drops on your forehead and your cock. Whenever the tub would be filled, you would be stone dead. Did you know we were standing outside the window waiting? No, how could you know that. But our presence has given you two extra days to live. Think about it, Omar. We have given you an extension of your life by two full days. At this moment, you would have been dead with our GRU comrades. Emptied of information through serum and water torture and then straight into the grinder. Not one line, not one shred would have been left of you.

"And if you are cooperating now, yes, I cannot promise you anything yet, then maybe some CEO will forgive you. Not much, but a little and then you get a one-way ticket to the northeast. You know where it is? A camp on Novaya Zemlya or Siberia! Not bad for a Palestinian dog like you. We have another choice."

Omar was excited now.

"You would not guess this. We can empty you and then send you to Mossad. I have heard rumors that they may have started using the old Native American punishment. In fact, much cleaner than the Mongolian, where you are bundled up and hauled in a sack. Then into the river, where it is deepest. Maybe you're dumped in the mud here in the Volga. Dirty enough from before, is it not?"

It was clear to Omar that Khan was on tops now. Able to play all the cards.

"No, Mossad, they think Native American now. There's a lot of sand in Sinai you know. Some places mixed with a special clay. You get to dig a hole for your body and then you are dumped into the hole, head and part of the neck sticking up. But you stand up straight and you can choose whether you want to wear clothes or be naked. Not bad what? They laugh when they drag the Mossad guys. It is still early in the day and the sun is still below the horizon. If you live until the evening, then come the desert reptiles and maybe a hyena or two. Now, Omar, do we start to talking?

"Why, Omar? How much did the North Koreans pay you to play on their team? Yes, we've talked to Mr. Kosin. But he no longer speaks! Did they threaten to take the lives of your two little girls or your Norwegian wife? Or who came with the money? That may be a better question. Did the money come via Moscow? Could it be that it's the FSB that operates and pays a rat like you to be courier and that Kosin spoke the truth when he swore his innocence?

"If so, where is the suitcase from Oslo? Then there are four things you have to answer for, before we possibly start the treatment, as Irina here likes to call it. Show him the wire cutter, Irina. No, it's not for pinching balls, but wait and see. Thus, the drawings from Oslo, money, where the heck they might have come from, and where you have tucked them away, and then finally, the map."

Omar sensed a crack in their wall now. There was the competition with the FSB and SVR that ultimately could be the key to get out of this alive.

"Yes, and one more thing? What about this Tor and his friend Ivan? You get it now. Omar, there are immediately five cases we want to have you sort out. This can be a long torment for you. Maybe I should consider amnesty after four correct answers?"

"Does all this mean so much to you that you had to pick me up with the Tupo from Cluj? The drawing of the North Pole The platform cannot possibly mean as much to you that you involve yourself at this level. Pure engineering or what? Or maybe it was the money? But what is a couple of hundred thousand dollars in this context?"

"Keep your mouth shut, Omar, we know, and you know that we know, and that you and your people and the American colonel planned in detail to murder Putin and Bush in Brasov. Who placed the explosive charges well-hidden at Dracula castle? Plastic seals everywhere it was said. Don't you think our people had found them anyway? If it wasn't a pure bluff, then? But then, where is the money and where is the map of the assumed explosive charges? And where are Tor and Ivan? Did the North Koreans kill everyone and how come you are alive?"

"Up to now, just now," Alexis growled.

"We intend to keep you alive, so we can present you to our Mr. Putin in the palace. What kind of dead faith do you expect, Omar? What do you think happens to the SVR bosses when we take the rat on both them and the North Koreans? So where is the map and the money and the drawings of the rocket base?"

There was no answer, so Andrej got up and checked the straps that tied his feet and arms to the stick chair. It was an exquisite specimen, screwed to the floor, but with a swing.

"We go now, Omar, and you get two guards who are replaced every six hours, until Putin is back from Bucharest in good condition, or you've decided to tell us what we want to know. You will be well taken care of. Black bread and water three times per day, and we will have a portable toilet installed. The guards are instructed to cut off a part of the body at the slightest form of sabotage. They start with the little finger on the right hand, then it's free ride from there on."

Alexis pointed to the crotch and then came the rumbling laughter. Unbelievable what this teddy bear tolerated of vodka. Then they were on their way out, replaced by two guys with the special force's emblem on the lapel, a third one rolled in the zinc. But Alexis came back pointing at Omar and a roll tape which lay on the table. The next moment, the tape sat over his mouth and eyes. The night had begun, and it was going to be a long one too.

83

Casa Wagner and Dracula

Tor went by bus to the foot of the mountain, backpack over his shoulder, and slowly walked up to the fortress gate. Sighisoara was an ancient fortress town.

Why should they lead him to this remote corner of the world? Omar had a lot to answer for. All Tor wanted was to take care of the suitcase and go home.

But was Omar killed? And who was this girl who was lying dead in the burlap sack and why was he hunted by Leopards? Then it hit him. Of course, it had to be that way. It was GRU and Khan who had engaged the Leopards. And Omar must have messed up in something big. Something about Putin's and Bush's visit and the NATO summit.

First the Asian girl in Brasov, yes, if she was Asian then. Maybe she was North Korean, Maria. But he had her close on many years ago, very close on, but also very many years ago. Still, he was in doubt. And what about the Romanian, or presumably Romanian girl, Svetlana, who had saved him from the hotel and who obviously had to be one in SVR's network?

Both dead now and this adventure with the American colonel, his double so to speak.

Why could he not have had the suitcase handed over in Brasov and, from there, gone straight to the airport and home via Budapest.

A slight drizzle, and he chose to take one light military-like raincoat over himself, backpack on top of that. For sure, he would look like he had hunchback.

Could he now be safe from persecutors?

Up in the square in a kind of courtyard was a beautiful little house. But it was not so small, just not flashy. The style was German, late medieval. Looked like 3.5 floors.

Tor walked through the small front yard, into what was a beautiful little reception area. Time was close to 10.00 according to the big floor clock, and the last breakfast guests forced the door into the dining room.

Why do a lot of guests always come right at closing time for breakfast? They then had to understand that at the buffet there would only be leftovers since 07.00.

"Someone has booked a room for me," he said in his poor Italian.

The man behind the counter, a well-groomed twenty-five-year-old, asked him to fill out a standard form for arrival.

"The name sir?"

"Tor Hansen."

"No, unfortunately, can I see your passport please?"

Tor cursed inside. Of course, they would see the passport.

"Yes, Hansen is my author's name, but my name is Tor Wisting."

The young man seemed to disregard the comments.

"Mr. Wisting. That's right. Your sister called and ordered the room. Yes, of course I remember now. She also asked specifically if room 312 was available as she had stayed in that room and very much enjoyed it. But unfortunately, the room is not ready till after one o'clock. Maybe you will visit some tourist attractions in the meantime. I recommend..."

But Tor was far away. Well, his sister...

"Oh sorry, I'm probably a little distracted. Thanks a lot, may I leave my backpack here and I would like to have my passport back just now please. "

The boy looked at him. "Now, at once? It is quite unusual, border police you know. But I take a copy of the most important pages and then I keep the passport, while you get the copies."

The boy was gone for a while. Once back, he gave Tor the copies and locked the passport down in a drawer. Put the key in his pocket.

"We have a very famous wine cellar here, will you look at it while you wait?"

But Tor did not want that. He wanted to get hold of his passport and the Glock from the bottom of the backpack.

It was obvious, something was fishy. It was Rudolf, the driver, who had arranged with the room and no sister.

He rested himself in the lobby and waited for the opportunity to open the backpack without being noticed.

There he got it and there was the Glock. The next moment, he had both the Beretta and the Glock as well as extra clips in the small carrying case.

"We came to hear that your name is Wisting, right? Should you be related to the polar explorer, perhaps his grandson?"

Middle-age, typical English, Tartan waistcoat, matching Sherlock Holmes hat. The man hardly listened, looked boring, and he probably was. It was she who spoke, he just nodded to Tor.

"No, unfortunately, or thank God, I have never taken any interest in the polar challenges."

What was it with these two? She with the greyish ordinary appearance and he, well what about him? Flannel grey trousers, low, dark brown boots, high-necked sweater, and plaid jacket, red base color. And he as well, with the famous Sherlock Holmes hat with flaps everywhere.

Was it he who was the bad guy if any, of the two? His spectacles had a faint brownish tone that prevented you from seeing his eyes.

Well-planned of course. *No way, give up now, Tor.* This is only a nice English couple on holiday. Probably from Middlesbrough or something like that.

"Do you hunt, Mr. Wisting?"

Finally came a peep from the man. The question took Tor where he sat and tried to turn himself away from the couple.

In all days. What made the middle-aged Englishman to utter such a question? The man pointed to the cartridge that lay at Tor's feet. Obviously a 7 millimeter. No calibre neither for Beretta nor the Glock. How had the cartridge got there? Had it been lying there all the time, or had it been brought over from the raincoat, and if so, who had put it there in the first place?

"No, sir, at least not with that calibre." He kicked the cartridge with the tip of his shoe. "Ask the receptionist instead." Tor pointed to the counter.

Now, maybe this was his chance

The boy came over to the three. Got an eye on the cartridge and faded.

Tor got up, took his carry bag, and walked one small round away, before he threw the bag on the reception desk, waiting a while as the boy and the couple studied the cartridge.

In which drawer would the passport be?

He searched with his left hand, and there was the key, turned it, and pulled the drawer out. The passport, the red passport was on top. He immediately looked across the floor, but it was clear that the cartridge had taken all the attention. Then he had replaced the passport with the copies and closed the drawer. Took the key and went over to the three.

Drawling, humped a little on one leg. "What about you, sir, do you hunt, and to be blunt, if you carry a gun, then it might be yours?"

The man faded and then he turned red. "I do not know if I like your insinuation, sir. I do not think anyone has permit for this weapon, yes, outside of the police and the military. I am definitely not part of the Romanian police, I'm as civilian as I look."

Tor smiled disarmingly. "Of course, I did not mean the regular police." Then he laughed a little. "Let's forget this. I never got your name?"

"I never gave it to you. But if you insist, then it is John Smith. This is my wife, Adele."

Tor smiled kindly. "Have a nice day both of you."

Then he was out. Tossed the key far over the nearest rooftop.

Hell, John Smith! So unprofessional.

Well, they were waiting for him here too. But on which side was this man? Could it be something as clumsy as the CIA?

But what interest did this organization take in him? Small fish as he was. It had to be the branch of Omar or also Theodore and then this with the map. Breakfast was next, and he went across the street to one small internet café. Clearly just opened. The pink color of the façade totally in contrast to the medieval building style that otherwise characterized the courtyard. But the place was nice enough with homemade scones and hot chocolate.

The lady was beautiful, indigo eyes, but a little too skinny for Tor's taste. Half-high heels, three-quarter length dress that hid much of her pretty legs.

But it was snug enough for the dress, so even though the breasts were flattened by an overly narrow bra, the dress gave room for the imagination as it emphasized not least her lovely buttocks. The long black hair was divided into two matching bows, indigo they too. Matching lipstick and high cheekbones. Quite certain, she was beautiful. Could she be twenty-five-ish or something? No, she was not Romanian, but an Italian niece of the owner who came out of the kitchen as soon as she noticed that the niece was too talkative with the guest. Could this be one of Omar's contacts?

A beautiful Italian girl placed in this remote corner?

Tor was the only guest. So why this extra service? Could it be CIA that was located there to follow, and if so, follow for what?

The girl was dragged into the kitchen, and Tor took the chance to check the carrying case with the weapons.

Hardly any doubt about that the 7 millimeter was planted on him. Planted by whom then? There were no more loose cartridges in the bag. He also checked the clips. Both with standard ammunition for the Beretta and the Glock.

He got to be patient and wait till 312 was vacant. Maybe there would be a clue there.

Then they tumbled and howled in the door and stood there the entire family of six, led by the colonel.

"Oh my goodness." It came from Françoise and the kids were a little confused, all four of them. The eldest looked at his father and there was an almost imperceptible nod, and then they were all over him.

"Do not kill the man!" Theodore wanted them to calm down.

"Hi, Tor, we are here just for the morning." But she, she had to go neck out again?

"Oh, are we, Theodore? I thought you said…"

She did not get any further before she blushed under the gaze of his.

"Possible that, Françoise." He looked at me. "But first, shall we have the tour at Dracula's birthplace and then decide from there on? What about you Tor and how did you end up here? I thought you were going home to Oslo?"

"Dracula, Theodore, Dracula, but I go home in the morning."

Françoise and the children had obviously wanted to stay, but Theodore was determined. After a joint lunch, he was clear as to how to spend the afternoon: back to Brasov and then Bucharest and Brussels.

"Good luck to you with your moon landing" was his parting words. Tor was standing with an open mouth while the American laughed, leaving him a question mark

They left in the pouring rain, and Tor hurried into the hotel to change, soaked wet like a drowning cat.

Sheer luck, he still had the sand-colored outfit to put on, while the morning's clothes dried in the bathroom, and he went down to see the alleged famous wine cellar.

Well then, it was extensive, with many well-known brands and vintages. But Tor felt that there was something uncomfortable in the air and where could the jeep with the Leopards and their comrades be hiding?

Since it had stopped raining, he went bareheaded down the little street to the exhibition of Dracula effects.

He chose the torture chamber and then suddenly no light. Not for long, maybe a minute.

Then he heard rapid footsteps on the stairs. He was already lying under the stairwell.

Three or four people came running out onto the street, wearing regular jeans and regular breakers. But the black sweaters and the well-trained bodies could not hide they were Leopards. Had they once more mistaken him and the colonel?

He did not know, did not want to know.

The thought of Theodore's farewell would not go. Where had the American heard about the moon landing, and was it just a joke or was it not just the Russians who had stuck to Stoltenberg's New Year's speech?

When he came back to the hotel, Tor was told that his passport was missing.

"You are certain that it was your passport and that you truly are Mr. Wisting?"

"Your colleague took a copy this morning. So where's the copy?"

"I do not know. The key is gone."

"But how do they know that my passport is missing if the key is gone?"

He just shrugged as if he did not understand what Tor was saying.

The concierge was replaced by a slightly older person who stared at him intensely.

Perhaps had they checked the backpack with all the bullet holes and the bullet-ripped PC. Should he throw it?

No, he would bet that the hard disk would make it.

Upstairs in the room, which was not so remarkable, he checked the rucksack. The PC was gone.

Furious, he stormed down to the front desk and said what he thought about the theft. The man was obviously even more nervous and asked him to take it nicely and have a drink in the bar, then he should promptly get hold of the hotel manager.

Ten minutes later, his patience had reached its breaking point. Then the director stood there in the doorway with all the excuses of the world on his face.

"Sorry so much, Sir Wisting. This is completely unheard of. I came as fast as I could. But can we look at the scene together."

He spoke German and had obviously followed loosely the Derrick series.

"Yes, but how will it help me?"

Tor could not help but show his irritation. "But okay then, come on," and they rushed up the stairs. The door was open, and it was guaranteed he had locked it, or did he not? The bag stood by the side of the bed where he had put it.

"Can we open it please?"

Yes, of course he could. The PC, just lying where it should, in the middle of the bag. Nicely decorated with five bullet holes

Tor turned to the director, who was standing with his face in neat folds.

"Now, Mr. Wisting, is this the PC im Frage?"

"Yes, of course," Tor stammered.

"Can you please check if everything is in order?"

Tor followed the invitation, but noted that the PC was hot, thus must have been used only minutes ago. Most likely someone had recently checked the contents. But what could he do?

"By the way, did you know that my passport is missing?"

Tor turned toward him. The faces were barely ten centimeters from each other. Did he feel mockery in the face of the hotel manager? He was tempted to ask where he had learned German. Tempted to ask if the family had been Nazi sympathizers or worse. But above all, he was cursed because the director so obviously knew that the PC had been in use and probably emptied or copied.

"Mr. Director, I shall crash here for the night and then immediately go back to Bucharest to the embassy to get a new passport. And I am very pleased that the PC has been found. Incidentally shall you not ask me where the bullet holes in the bag and PC come from? And who had a 7-millimeter cartridge lying on the floor in the reception this morning?"

Then the episode was over.

After one early dinner and a boring televised movie, it was time to think about tomorrow. Still nothing new from Omar. Was Sighisoara just a blind alley?

What about the colonel?

Why prolong the journey for themselves and the whole family with eight hours just to see another old castle?

Must be something covert.

Perhaps the colonel also thought that Tor was a dangerous agent.

Maybe he had checked with Brussels, and they had found Tor's folder from the past with the KGB, via the Intelligence in Oslo?

Even though no one would admit it, there had to be a folder on him.

He called the front desk: "Are you completely sure that there is no message for me or that no one has called and asked for me?"

"I will double-check and get back to you. You are Mr. Wisting, are you not?"

"Of course, I'm Mr. Wisting, Tor Wisting." He felt the irritation grow again.

"Mr. Wisting," it was the concierge again: "There was a waitress from the Internet café who came over here this afternoon. She thought you might want your newspaper back, so it's on the shelf downstairs."

Tor was down in seconds. "So nice that she brought it in. I am very happy for Italian newspapers. "

"Omar could not come, has been taken by the Russians. We just had to get you out of Brasov. Sorry for the detour. Anna meets you at Hotel Europa in Cluj. Did not get a chance to say anything since these Americans arrived. There have also been four younger guys here. They got into a jeep and wanted to know everything about the Americans. I knew nothing."

That was it. Then the niece was an agent. But was it necessary to recruit only the most beautiful ladies for such jobs?

Too late to move on now, so it had to be the bed here at Dracula's and hope for a good night's sleep.

Tor burned the message that was well hidden inside the newspaper and went to bed. The last thing he remembered was the poster with the picture of Dracula lying on the bedside table. It was dark when he woke up to a scratching sound. Was it Dracula or Russians or North Koreans who believed that Tor was the colonel in the American Intelligence? He turned off the light again but could not sleep. The sound came from the bathroom. What could he use to fight someone? His bare fists?

He took the wooden chair, but it was little suited.

Quietly, he got hold of the PC. He had to sacrifice it as a weapon. Slowly the bathroom door slid open, maybe five centimeters at first. Was he disappointed when there was no one in the bathroom?

But the image of Dracula who had been lying on the nightstand? What about that?

Gone, yes maybe under the bed, but no, without a trace, gone and the door was the still locked? Yes, absolutely.

He checked the window, someone could have come over the roof. But the window was probably too small or was it not?

Could he have gotten himself through? 20x 30 cm?

Yes, that would be possible. No, by the way, it must have been a slim, very slim person, maybe just a child or a woman, yes, maybe a woman from the East?

He closed the window, made certain the hasp was set on. The wood was darkish, warned down, so maybe someone would be able to take the entire frame off?

Shivering, he crawled back to bed. What about the PC? Best to get it in the bag again and lock it safely.

Did he manage to sleep? No, absolutely not. Thoughts of one little Chinese or Japanese who had been with him that night, or maybe it was Dracula's descendants, or Dracula as a teenager, narrow round the hips, that had slipped through the window.

But he would be gone now, Dracula or whoever it was.

The door, was it still locked and the key on the inside? Yes, everything was fine.

Damn Omar who had messed him up in this, but maybe it was not Omar's fault. Maybe Omar was ditched into another hole and was completely innocent.

And where was the message that was to come to him here in room no. 312?

Had this someone been inside with a piece of paper or a message in some other way? Up again, scoured the room.

It smelled of something strange. Did it not? Maybe there was something under the bed?

He was everywhere now in desperate sloop on what the smell stemmed from.

A kind of dog poop or the smell of excrement from another animal? Perhaps had the previous guest brought with him his dog or cat?

Or was it he himself who had stepped into dog poop on the road away to the castle? But then it should have smelled like this long ago, or maybe the smell only came when the shoe got hot in the bathroom.

He was in there in seconds.

Could dog poop be so impenetrable smelling?

The left shoe was completely clean. For safety's sake, he cleaned it over the toilet bowl.

Dried it thoroughly with the smallest towel. What would the maid say if she discovered what he was doing? Would he have to pay extra? Maybe get thrown out.

Blacklisted here at Casa Wagner for all time? So what!

He looked at his watch. Oh no, only three. Too early to get up. Had it been six or even with quarter to six he would have got up. Settled the bill with the night watchman. They had already taken a copy of his Amex card.

Then he would get straight into the cab with the backpack, his backpack with five bullet holes, and then travelled to the railway station. Rather wait there than in this smelly hotel. But what about the message?

Was it just nonsense that he was going to get closer instructions here in Sighisoara? And why was the messenger killed?

I'll get up, he thought. Skip shower and shave and get going. Half dazed, he put on his clothes and his left shoe.

It smelled just too damn bad in the bathroom. But where was the right shoe?

Obviously where he had left it to dry there inside. He first cracked up the window, the small window, turned on the fan, and wanted to chase the smell out.

But just one shoe.

Then he picked it up, the right one.

It was obvious that the smell came from that shoe.

It was a fat one almost glued into the sole. He was damn sure he had not stepped into something like this unnoticed.

He carefully placed it on the same towel he had used to wipe the other.

Off with the coat and jacket and the left shoe. This was going to be dirty.

Should he sacrifice his toothbrush for to get dirt out of the sole pattern?

No, he tried first without, but it was too late now, everything had dried out in the rough cracks.

It would have to be the toothbrush.

Amazing that dried dog poop could smell so damn horrible.

But it was going to get worse when he got to shower it over the toilet bowl. Too bad with the toothbrush.

It was just as brown in the bristles, even after undergoing torture brushing with the remnants of the bath soaps.

Why were there not real pieces of soap in any hotels anymore, just stupid small containers with liquid?

People steal. Better they steal a mini soap piece than chocolate. Chocolate now, no thanks. The color may have been the same, Freia Melk, but the smell was still different. The little soap bar was soon used up, and he looked around for the liquid soap, and quite correctly, there was one in the rack on the wall.

He tried to press the spout, but nothing happened, and in the end, he had to face the technical challenge and dismantle the entire container.

Now, what if someone had heard all the noise as the holder popped down from the wall?

But he had to get a hole in it. Equally damn as to open a toothbrush casing. Not any tool, should he shoot holes into it?

That would definitely mean trouble. Even the little Derringer would probably make a fuss.

Put on the left shoe and then he placed the container close to the toilet bowl so it would not slip away. But he himself slipped, almost a meter. His hair stroked the ceiling beam. Then he sat on the floor in the middle of the soap.

He had hit with all his weight and the left shoe was now a bit pink, yes, the whole bathroom floor was pink, and his pants and shirt were pink-stained, and it no longer smelled of dog poop, but deliciously perfumed soap, lavender plus.

Yes perhaps, or was it a Tibetan one, or another from the Southeast? Jasmine was it maybe? Of course, it was Jasmine.

He smelled like a whole brothel or something.

Off with pants and shirt, socks, and left shoe and the phone rang several times.

The night watchman: "Has anything happened? Is everything okay?" The only thing he understood was OK.

"Si, okay, okay, okay." The man at the other end said something.

Sounded like it came in a lousy German.

"No, everything's OK, OK. OK! Good night!"

Then it became quiet at the other end, and he could begin the cleaning process.

It took an hour.

Could have been on the road by now. But the toothbrush?

Out the window and then full flushing of the whole bathroom and finally it was his turn. Finally, it was past four and he lay in bed. Shirt, trousers, and socks hung to dry on the radiator.

Maybe he could get a few more hours sleep while things dried. But what about the dog poop? Planted in the course of the night to delay one hasty departure, at dawn?

Perhaps would the message to him come in during the morning hours. Best not to rush.

Thoughts raced around and around. Three murders or executions already and yet he had not met with Omar.

Would he ever get himself out of this damned country alive? Was it him, Tor, they were looking for or had he just been in the right place at the wrong time?

But the link had to be Omar or was it the American with the beautiful family? Did anyone here too think he was American?

But they were gone just after lunch or?

Maybe it was only Françoise and the daughters who had left, while Theodore was back to make a mean streak and why?

His brain had no more capacity, and he was gone into a deep sleep.

He dreamed of the lady with the Derringer and who now probably lay at the bottom of the river in the straw sack. Probably gone into decay already, if not one or more big fishes had eaten her for breakfast or dinner.

84

The Tarantula

The dream was horrible, and he woke halfway as he scratched his chest.

His eyes were first drawn to the bedside table where there was now a picture of just a cruel Dracula face mask, almost a death mask to look at in the dim light from the bathroom door. But it itched. Wow, were there fleas here?

In the next moment, he drew the sheet, and there it was, sitting right in between both nipples. But it was not a flea!

It was something big, something.

Many feet, a little hairy, and two claws. The nipples budded, stood stiff from the fear that cut through him. Was this a poisonous spider or a half-innocent tarantula? Widow spider or dance spider? Why did it not escape from the breast? Was it not frightened when the sheet flew off? Maybe it was dead and if it was of the dangerous kind, why was not he, Tor, dead? And how had this animal gotten in?

Damn, the window was open. Someone may have thrown it in through the window now, while he was sound asleep.

But what now, another movement and the bite would come, if he was not bitten already. But he did not notice anything, only the irritation of the claws and feet that tingled into the tense skin over his chest.

It was as if it was shrinking up now, the breast skin. But he had not trembled. This was torture of the first class. A twitch or a sneeze and madness would bite.

Was he perhaps dead already?

Was this such a post-mortem experience? Tor overpowered by the tarantula. Sparkling name for a short story—something like "From Reality" in the weekly magazines. The seconds dragged off.

Maybe it was just an innocent spider? There should be at least one hundred completely harmless ones, someone had told him, but that was at home. This was Eastern Europe!

The comrade, if one could call him comrade, was probably five centimeters long. Clearly, he had nourished well from egg to full size.

So, perhaps it was poisonous and could kill his spider colleagues

He wasn't dead frightened anymore, brain started to reflect upon the situation, but there the beast moved on, the tarantula. A few millimeters back and forth? No, it did not go back.

Still, it seemed as if it wanted to return to the heat, pointing to the navel and down. Tor knew that his genital already shrunk, but the most important thing was that it was walking away from the heart region.

Were there some marks there where it sat, some track after sting? But no, he could not see anything of it there in the semi-darkness.

Could he just get hold of the image of Dracula from the bedside table, but then he had to stretch out and then what?

Thoughts raced through Tor's head. Did the planner of the assassination stand outside of the door and waited, or was he smart enough to hide in the stairwell?

And who was it this time? CIA or GRU?

Why was the one claw shorter than the others? Was it like with the lobster?

The animal had come to the navel now and the smallest claw just waved a bit. Then it found a small woollen dot that came from the sweater having escaped from the shower. The claw lifted the little woollen dot as in triumph. It was as if it wanted to tell Tor that now the way was open to his inner organs, and Tor felt that it was now or never. He prayed a silent prayer not to Jesus or God, but to the Virgin Mary. "Take care of my children and grandchildren" and then he reached out for the picture on the bedside table.

85

Kremlin at 07:00

Daylight was on its way, cold and misty grey. Not much warmth from the cloudy skies.

Omar hung on to the ropes. Maybe he had dozed off occasionally.

The guards sat motionless. He wanted to go to the bowl, but maybe he could hold on until the replacement came. Maybe the change to day guards would be nicer.

A heavy click-clack sounded and his ears, which had now become accustomed to the slightest sound, caught up a pair of boots that approached him. Soon the guards also heard the clattering and straightened up.

Nobody said anything. There was a kind of chill over the room. The dark oak tree panels gave not much encouragement either.

Worn floorboards were the only bright spot. They bore witness about that people had come and gone; in other words, this was not a death chamber. It would be possible to get out. *But hold it, Omar, no one said anything about you leaving here on your own two feet.* It may not be the prisoners' feet that have worn the floor in an outward direction.

His little hope was quickly shattered, and dreams were replaced by the sound of the key that rumbled in the door and there was the replacement.

But now, there was only one soldier or policeman in boots with iron fittings. It was him they had heard. The woman had not heard any of them, not even this Khan who came in ordinary civilian clothes like yesterday. New shirt for the occasion, so he had been changing somewhere, maybe at home, or the Kremlin guys had an office with a wardrobe, or they lived in a hotel?

No matter. He concentrated on the woman. How would he manage to pee with her sitting in the room? Perhaps was she the type who got turned on from pissing?

Well, he had to hold it in until he really had to go for the bowl.

Piss was one thing, but worse with the other.

Thanks to fate, he had learned a little Russian at the University of Kiev.

"Is it a good morning for you, Omar? Hope that today you shall tell Irina about drawings of Dracula castle with plastic ammunition. We also want to know who has been your contact person with the North Koreans and where is the suitcase you should hand over to the Norwegian, or was it to the Americans, as a thank you for the help? By the way, I said have been. I did, didn't I? The man is no longer with us. Do you hear, Omar, your contact person is no longer alive among us!"

There was something friendly about Khan after all, as if he wanted to say "I am sorry, but we will have all the answers from you before you die."

For there was hardly any doubt about what the end of the interrogation would be.

One is not rushed up on to the seventh floor for survival, only when significant. And Omar knew he was not. Not unless he got them to believe that he belonged to a group of top leaders in the spy world. Some Mafiosi or something

Clearly then, however, they seemed to be of the impression that he was quite well thought of by the North Korean Intelligence. And that could be the rescue he was looking for.

But then he had to produce something they could bite into, but first, he had to go to the bathroom.

The night watchmen had left the room and the policeman and Irina had taken over their roles.

Khan had thrown away his jacket and sat there in his shirt with an English cut, apparently bought at the specialty store for senior officials and people with western currency.

There was a knock on the door, and another policeman came in with drinks for the two, Irina and Khan. Nothing for the third Russian.

"Vodka is good for the stomach, Omar. You can have one you too, just give us the information we want from you."

"It's just shit coming from me and it's coming soon. I have to go to the toilet."

"If shit comes, you have to go to the toilet in the hallway! Irina and Sergei will be with you."

"Irina too?"

"Sure, she's good with the shooter if necessary."

Degrading, but did he have a choice other than alternatively shitting in his own pants?

They were back after a quarter of an hour, and it was delicious, and he was literally relieved. But the attempt to sneak into a sip of water had failed.

"Cheers and welcome back, Omar."

Khan let him not long in peace. The hands were again tied on the back and the ankles fastened to the chair legs.

"We are running out of time, Omar. Irina, start with the fingers of his right hand. When we are finished with them, then off to his right foot. All toes in turn and order before we go further on the left hand and then all the toes on his left foot. Perceived?"

Irina went against him with a pair of gloves and put them on slowly.

"The drawing, Omar!"

What now, should he be credible as North Korean middleman? He had to sacrifice something.

How long time would it take for one fractured little finger to heal? Irina took hold of him with one hand, the wire cutter in the other.

"Well?" Khan looked at him.

"When this drink is down, I give sign to Irina and then we are on track. If you faint, Sergei hits you in the face until you wake up. Or he's pissing on you."

Omar's brain was working in high gear. The finger was allowed to go, but he had to come up with a credible story afterward.

Khan's drink was emptied in one puff, and he lifted his hand as to start a race at the racetrack. Omar closed his eyes and waited.

Was it pain he felt or was it relief because he had now found the code—the code of how to survive at least for a little while longer?

Who was it who screamed? Then he got a cloth in his mouth, and it became quiet.

Slowly, he opened his eyes and was greeted by Khan's gaze. Not hateful, but compassionate in a way.

"Your deal, Omar. Irina is paid for the job, well paid. You get a break of some few minutes now to think, yes, think deep and then she continues. This time, she takes the thumb. Maybe she will have to use this rod here as well."

Omar looked at the rusty instrument on the stool in front of him and knew that he had to be good, credible and good, so they had to shoot him rather than carrying on with this slow torture. The mother of all the meat grinders said nothing, just picked up the tools and approached him again. Where had they found her? Was she a survivor of the Gulag and the Siberian concentration camps? Khan raised his hand, while Omar could smell Irina's body odor as she breathed into his neck. One hundred fifty kilos. Did not fit in any shower booth, seemingly. She smelled. Now she fastened the grip on his right thumb and looked at Khan who had his hand ready.

86

Live or Die

Tor could see twitches in the diaphragm when his hand was almost out on the bedside table. But the spider calmed down. Was lying completely silent a moment. Then it seemed as he was through with the navel and started at a slow pace downward toward the pubic hairs.

Fuck that he lay naked. If he got out of this alive, then he swore to always have a tight boxer short on during the night.

He gradually began to tremble in his upper arm and knew that he had to strike now. The next moment, he had grasped the drawing and was ready to begin the opposite movement back from the table with his arm.

The animal was lying almost still now, perhaps barely two centimeters from the pubic hairs. Had someone cut off his limb at night? There was not much left of the skin fold now, shrunk completely in fear.

Slowly, he pushed his Dracula image down.

Maybe if in some way or another, he would manage to flip the image into the body of the spider, from the side or from behind. It was too late now to attack with the picture in front.

Was it now that he was going to die?

To be found with the image of Dracula on his stomach. Keeping the myths alive? No way!

And who was it who had put the spider into the room? He knew now that he fought against a many-headed troll.

The North Koreans, the Americans, and the Russians. But then their interests had to be conflicting? The Americans?

But what then with Theodore as chief of Intelligence Eastern Hemisphere, according to the business card?

He had been here yesterday, and they had lunch together. Could it be he who wanted to kill Tor?

But would they not all be interested in finding the suitcase first, if they knew about it at all?

Some had to know about it since he was asked to travel to Sighisoara.

Perhaps the Russians had the clue, yes, they must have, and then the others just hang on to them? Why didn't my contact in Moscow answer the phone? Maybe my contact in SVR did not speak to GRU and then all three followed one another. Comedy, yes, but that's what it had to be.

But Theodore's farewell remark, "the moon landing," what about it?

Was this something he had got to know when in Oslo or was Bush crazy enough to have started some project, then Samuel at least could be saved.

Or could Theodore simply be a double agent?

The tarantula was awfully close to the penis root now, and Tor no longer had a choice. Would he die now?

He knew that the poison of the sting would remove him from the livings in the course of seconds.

But then suddenly, it turned around.

Began to move up again.

Was instantly over the diaphragm and approached his heart region before it stopped. Would it jump off the body all by itself?

Slowly he showed the picture of Dracula upward. Two back feet moved to the picture and almost, but only almost, stopped. Then started to crawl further out of the Dracula picture.

Death was on to him again.

Now the animal had bearing on the pit of the neck and the main artery. Yes, well, then death would come even faster.

But Tor would not die, would not die just yet in any case. First, he had to find Omar and the suitcase.

One small stream of sweat ran down the chest. The guest quite obviously did not enjoy the sweat.

Should he try the Dracula picture one more time? What if he failed?

He decided that it would be now or never. He could not hold on to dying several times with this cursed beast.

Perhaps was it not one poisonous spider either.

Maybe someone had just sent it to scare? As a warning? None of the parties wished him dead, not just now or? The positive thoughts jogged through him and then his chest lifted up in sheer joy, lifted tarantula up even higher, and he swept it away with the Dracula picture as weapon.

In the next second, he was in the bathroom, got hold of one wet shoe and then, having the tarantula clearly in focus there on the white sheet, he made his blow.

The mattress took off for the bang, it crashed when the animal met death.

Some fluid came out of the dead body and on to Tor's hand and he was out in a flash and let the shower run for a long time. Finally, he was back in the bedroom. Well then, the remains of the animal lay there in bed. It took him barely three minutes to pack his gear, get into his clothes, and then he was down to the reception.

It was barely six o'clock. The night watchman, the young boy, was gone.

Instead, there now was a heavily built man in his forties.

"My passport and the bill."

The man looked at him incomprehensibly.

"But will you leave today?" Tired voice in a stuttering German? But now was not the time for discussions.

Tor slapped the key on the table. "Travel now! But fast!"

The man did what he could to slow down the process. He must have had some kind of bell under the counter. After five minutes of talking about missing keys and a card machine, the director stood there.

"What can I do for you?"

Tor found the Amex card. He was bored now. Just wanted to move on fast as hell. Who was this gorilla who had taken over for the night watchman? Was it he who had been up with the tarantula?

"We hope you have had a pleasant stay with us. Sorry, no breakfast until 7:00. Yes, will you wait for it?"

"I just want my passport and pay and then I want out."

"Has something happened, you seem a little upset?"

Tor managed to bring out a smile. "No, I just need to move on."

"Your bill and your card."

So that was fine.

"My passport?" Tor did not want to let him off the hook.

"Oh yes! Your passport, it has gone missing. We have unfortunately only a copy, so it must be supplied by the police to get a confirmation, so that the copy is valid. It can take some time."

"Forget it, give me a copy of the copy."

The director looked at him incomprehensibly. "Copy of the copy?"

"Yes, for you do have a Xerox or whatever?"

"Oh yes!" He lit up literally. "Yes, of course, I shall get you one copy. But really, you should not leave from here until the police are notified that the original passport is gone. "

"Who's going to stop me?"

"Okay, sign here please, so we know you will seek contact with the police yourself." The "Gorilla" had followed with interest. Too interested.

"I can drive you to the police or wherever you want to go at once."

Tor said, "No thanks," and walked towards the exit.

The "Gorilla" was clearly disappointed and somewhat in disarray.

The director then gave him the copy of his passport, folded. There was something more there, a small envelope. Both kept the mask. Perhaps it was there now, the message he was promised if he came to Sighisoara.

He gave his hand a light handshake. "Thanks for the copy. I have also something for you. He listened, very interested "The Gorilla" now. Both looked questioningly at Tor.

"There is a dead tarantula on the sheet upstairs. At least I think it's dead."

Then he was out, got the sack on his back and, with rapid steps, walked down toward the town.

He knew that the "gorilla" would come by and heard one car starting. The next second, he was behind the bush by the gate post out of the property. There was not much to do. Then another car. The director banged the door open.

"Jump in. I'm driving you to the railway station."

The "gorilla" was gone but appeared again as he kicked the door open to the battered station.

The monument to a failed communist regime.

Ticket? No, not the hell. Then he would reveal where he was going.

Right now, he knew he rather not tell anyone where he was going. The director had been completely silent, not responding to anything.

It was lifeless on the platform of track no. 1, but there was an underpass to track no. 2. He could see some people there.

The rucksack was heavy to carry now. Maybe he should just as well get rid of the PC? But no, he came down in the underpass that stank of piss. Stools were strewn all over. Then he was up to the platform and there stood the world's most beautiful little family of four, mother and father and two children, a boy and a girl—gypsies. She in a yellow ankle-length coat and beautiful long black hair. It was the lady from the night bus. Smiled gently now. The man, brown long coat and brown hat.

He managed to see that the kids were wearing gypsy costumes with embroidery before heavy steps across the platform confirmed that the "gorilla" was on the rise.

The gypsies should be the rescue.

He dragged the kids on the bench, and Mom and Dad were there immediately. But Tor had a chocolate bar on hand and waved it and saw the smiles. While the four were occupied by the good stuff, he got the Beretta from the bag. Heck, he could not reach the Glock.

The little Beretta snuck into the coat hand, and he waited and waited.

The "gorilla" was clearly uncomfortable with the gypsies. He waved at Tor who pretended as if he did not see him. Then he came closer, and at barely three meters, he made a terrifying impression on the four and the gypsy mother pressed the kids onto her.

Tor could see that he put his hand on the inside of the jacket and knew what was coming. He could not miss at this distance, even with the Beretta.

He let it slide down in the right hand. Poor kids. The hand of the "gorilla" came forward now with the steel.

Tor could not wait any longer, aimed well to the right of the shirt buttons and pulled off. The kids screamed and the mother screamed and the father stood for a moment like a pillar of salt before throwing himself at the kids.

But it was over. The "gorilla's: gun had fallen on the concrete with a clink, and he now lay straight out with open mouth. The shot had been a stroke of luck.

But where would he hide the man? He took the gun and the extra clip and put both parts in his bag.

Had anyone heard the shot? It was early yet.

But soon, there would be more people on the platforms.

He tore off the gorilla's jacket and wiped up the bloodshed with it. Could he manage to drag him over the rails to the thicket on the back? There was a freight train, ore train, or maybe it was coal, in track four.

The man had to be dragged behind and past it. But could he do this alone?

He tried to talk to the gypsy dad, but no. The only thing he had to answer was "Nicht Sprech."

But could he not help?

He took hold of the "gorilla's" hands and pointed at his feet, and then, the gypsy was on board. Over the first rails, it went well, but over to the freight train, it got worse and then he heard someone shouting. It was the gypsy woman who pointed to some passengers walking toward the underpass. Heck, they would be able to see him in a minute.

But gypsy father also sensed trouble. He pointed to the open carriages, and together, they threw the "gorilla" over the edge. Now new passengers were coming.

But obviously, they were not interested in contact with the gypsies, as they hurried up far away on the platform, looked neither to the right or left.

And thank God for that, it had not been possible to keep the gypsy father and himself hidden along the track. The two walked slowly back to the others while they pretended looking for something.

Then the two of them were back and the mother and children huddled up to their father.

Tor found several chocolate bars, cigarettes, and snuff and 500 kroner in Lei.

"Take this."

The man looked at him, but before he could say anything, there was a shaking through the freight train, and happiness on earth, it slammed into connections and then the locomotive was in place, and with a long howl, it left the station.

Tor tried to figure out where the train was going. The man probably understood more than he had expressed.

"Train Bucharest. Romanian hates Rom people. We hate too."

Then he laughed and the half-empty denture shone on Tor.

"You American?"

"Well," Tor denied wildly, "not American but, Norwegian."

The man shook his head. "You Americani." Then he laughed again.

An old rundown train came gradually onto slot 2.

The locomotive that had dragged it forward was disconnected and a modern locomotive was connected. Sibiu was written on the side of the side of the wagons, and Tor was on board as the whistle blew.

Sibiu, obviously the gypsy family was not heading for Sibiu.

He threw himself down on the first vacant bench, and there were a lot of them. In fact, this cart was completely empty, an early Sunday morning.

The envelope. Yes, what could be hidden in the envelope?

And why had the director been so helpful and who did he represent, the North Koreans? GRU? Maybe, or a hitman for the SVR?

"Omar has been taken. The suitcase is hidden behind a blue tombstone. Horvath…" The rest was unreadable. The blood from the "gorilla" had covered the text.

He tried to scrape it off with his fingernail, but the writing disappeared along with the blood. Blue tombstone, the name Horvath?

Where was a cemetery with blue tombstones?

If only he could get on to the internet or ask a priest.

87

Sibiu

Two hours later, he arrived. But that was just the first stop. He knew that he had to get through to Cluj Napocha and Anna.

Had anyone found the body yet?

And what about the lack of feedback on the "gorilla"?

The train to Bucharest took maybe seven hours slow moving as always for a freight train. Moreover, it would hardly be unloaded before Monday morning.

Only then would the "gorilla" be found.

So he had a time advantage now and who, if anyone knew, that Tor had gone to Sibiu? The gypsies hardly gossiped. The hatred was too strong, and moreover, the man had been helping to hide the corpse.

Blue tombstones?

No priest had never heard about it, not here in Sibiu in any case.

What about asking in the restaurant at the church? Tor looked at him, the church. Lots of churches here. The pastor spoke excellent German.

Obviously, he felt a little offended.

"Yes, of course, but for me there is only one, the Evangelical Lutheran Church."

The church was under reconstruction, and there was not a single person there, except for some craftsmen who were setting up a kind of stage.

One pointed to the dial on the clock, so at 19.00, something would happen here. Tor thanked him and walked across the street. The name of the café was in German; this city had also been central during the German immigration in the eighteenth century.

In a separate room, some twenty people had gathered for lunch. Otherwise, it was completely empty.

It was long since dinner last night, so why not coq au vin and one carafe of red wine.

"Blue tombstone?"

The lady looked at him. "Was there anything more you wanted to book? Maybe a dessert?"

She looked at him hopefully. Clearly, they were not very busy here, apart from the group of twenty.

"You can have chocolate pudding or ice cream or Crème Brulé."

"Sure," he waved annoyingly at the menu. "They can serve me a Crème Brulé, but what about the blue tombstones?"

Apparently, she thought something was wrong with him.

She was back as a lightning with the dessert and the bill. Would definitely not listen to any more nonsense on his part.

On the right wall, there was a kind of a window to see into the closed company. Germans all. It was toasted for someone, and they were singing.

"Then see you in church at 7 p.m.," he heard someone say to a man who left the table before the others.

Tor caught up with him in the locker room. "I am Norwegian, and I am looking for a cemetery with blue-painted tombstones."

The man began to laugh.

"Yes, excuse me, but that question was too special. Are you thinking of one particular headstone or all stones at the cemetery? "

Soon the whole group was involved, and they all wanted to help out.

"But maybe someone could answer him in church. These gentlemen come from Sibiu's' town of friendship in Marburg and are all members of the Chamber of Commerce."

The afternoon became long. It rained and he was happy for having gotten room at the church hostel. No one would look for him there.

At 1850, he was in place in the church and there was the man from lunch.

"I will ask the priest for you after the performance."

"The performance?"

"Yes, they will perform Die Auffersteung Kristus, with a large choir."

"Will it be long then?"

"What, how long?"

"How long will the performance last?"

The man looked at him slightly contemptuously. "We are in the church now, dear man. There is no time here."

Tor sat down on a bench at the far left with a clear path out.

After one long hour, the clock went miserable slowly, one small piece of paper fell on to his lap.

"Anna, Hotel Europa, Cluj, takes you further. Keep yourself indoors and not open up for anyone. Bus to Cluj early in the morning, check the time at the hostel."

Grateful for lunch. There was nothing more to eat nor drink this evening, only lukewarm tea. Half-lukewarm, because it had to be made in a shared kitchenette, and suddenly, he heard people coming down the stairs.

The night was cold, and he lay with his clothes on, except for the coat and the hat.

The lady who took the payment meant the bus left around nine, but a quarter past eight, he was there on the platform at the bus station.

But no bus with sign Cluj. When he asked those who drove around the square, they just shook their heads. Finally, an older guy understood a little more.

"Ah microbus!" He pointed to the Volkswagen, which was furthest away, and quite correctly, it was going to Cluj. But it was full.

"And when does the next one go? The nine o'clock bus?"

The guys around him were all laughing.

"This is the nine o'clock bus. Next may go this afternoon."

But he had to be with this Anna before 3 p.m.

Then came the redeeming words from the driver: "Have you reserved?"

"Yes, of course."

"Well then. How have you booked and who have done it, you yourself?

Everyone here says they have reserved."

"They have reserved from Die Evangelische Lutherische Kirche."

"Aber Jawohl."

The man glared at him.

"Are you a priest?"

"No, but I work for the church."

"Ach so, welcome on board!"

"Rafael," he pointed at one man further back in the bus, "get out together with your luggage."

Then they left thirty minutes before the official departure time.

This was Romania.

After two hours, they stopped for fuel.

"Do not go out," whispered the neighbor, "the bus is not waiting. It's just running."

"Yes, but if you have paid then?"

And he had paid. So that's how it worked. Stupid passengers pay up front, get lost along the way, and new ones come on and pay.

It was a long way to Cluj, and in some places, it was not much like a main road, just a cart path. The road into the center went through the old town or the rest of it, with poor housing from the communist era. But it soon became better and quite beautiful.

Five different taxi drivers wanted to take him to Hotel Europa. The price dropped for each call. Then he finally arrived.

The reception was not exactly overcrowded.

Tor took off his backpack and threw himself down in a chair to wait. It was not yet three o'clock.

The uniformed people behind the reception desk did not seem overjoyed at his slightly shabby presence.

An hour went by, and he could almost hear the tummy was screaming. But he would not take the chance of losing contact. So he did not move.

A man in a pinstriped suit approached him. The sign on his chest said that he worked at the hotel.

Why did they all talk to him in German? Maybe it was that simple, German being his only foreign language. Or could he have received tips about a German patent engineer in transit?

"I am the duty manager of this hotel. You have been sitting here for a long time now. Are you waiting for someone? Maybe you have room, I do not know." He looked at Tor's clothes. "It's full. But if you pay in Euros or dollars, I can probably fix something".

Tor let him get a glimpse of his stack of money in Euro and said that he would prefer to wait.

At 1600 exactly, she was standing there.

Short cut, closest to Eastern hairstyle. Dressed in a light sweater. Slightly too tight over the breasts and thick half-length, blue skirt, 1.65 high maybe without the fifteen-centimeter stiletto heels. Discreet lipstick and then these sunglasses sitting well over the hairline. For once no label for Dior or Gucci or something on the sides.

But the smile, the smile was white.

"Soy Anna."

Kind of Italian. Imagine if he had been younger and single.

88

Cluj and Anna

Tor was tired and wanted to go to bed early, but the contact Anna had wanted it differently and it was late, very late, before he was alone in the sofa bed of the new but unknown friend Marek. Thinking through what had happened since he came to Cluj by the micro bus.

Anna, she was not Italian, but Ukrainian, she had taken him to a sightseeing around in Cluj.

"You will not move on today, until we hear from Omar or Horvath. So we might as well have a good time while we wait. Maybe you want to go to nightclub, Tor?"

"No, I do not want that, let's go to the hotel and we will eat there. Wait outside, and I'll check if the coast is clear."

"What do you mean? Are there any problems?"

"Anna, I should have been out of Romania already. I do not know how much Omar has told you. But it worries me that he's gone, and you showed up."

She blushed now and he would gladly have bitten his tongue for the stupid sentence, as he saw her expression. "Do you not like me?"

"But, Anna, I am not looking for any girl and I could have been your father, and this is all about a lot more than hitting one great girl in Cluj. Because you're a great girl! But I must meet Omar and get what I came for. GRU and maybe the North Koreans are everywhere."

She was fading now. But soon the color was back.

"Tor, my people are accustomed to fight, all the time."

"I know, dear. But these people I have been running from, unfortunately they are much tougher. Here they shoot first and skip asking afterward."

Two guys, in the same type of black suits, were waiting in the lobby and he turned sharply out again and into Anna's car.

"Drive as fast as you can, and give a damn to lights and traffic rules. Drive to a place where we are engulfed by the masses!"

Anna just laughed. "Then you will have it coming to you, old man."

He tried to get a glimpse of the hotel entrance in the mirror, but they were already over the first red light when it hit the trunk.

Anna took one 90 degrees, and they were out of the center, but stopped suddenly at a parking garage and looked into it.

"Let's run up the stairs and hijack a taxi."

On the road again. Tor had no idea where to go.

"I have a good friend, Marek, who works in the bar at the Diesel Club. He's hardly home until early in the morning and then you have to go out."

"What do you mean?"

"You sleep there with me, or alone till 5 in the early morning. Then you go right to the train station. Your train is scheduled for 5:30."

"Train to where then?"

"Did not Horvath say where?"

"No, half the message was covered in blood."

She faded. "Is Horvath dead?"

"I do not know, but it was not his blood, but the blood of a 'gorilla' from GRU."

She was visibly relieved.

"You will get to Satu Mare by train and then you find a taxi or micro bus or something, going further up in the mountains almost to the Ukrainian border. There is a cemetery with some old blue tombstones well north of Satu Mare. Horvath is from a border village up there and thought this was the safest way to solve the case, as Omar was taken. Would not take the chance hide something at home with his old parents. Your suitcase lies hidden behind one of the blue tombstones. That is all I know. Horvath has evaporated, probably gone into cover. Maybe Hungary or Ukraine. Do not have a residence permit here either and Omar is taken by GRU, I think. SVR and GRU do not communicate tops. But I know nothing more. I travel to Moscow, morning flight via Kiev and I'll have your suitcase."

"But who do you work for?"

"Omar, and I hope to bring him home."

"Who will you meet in Moscow?"

"I am not allowed to say, but we both know the man."

"We are going to Marek now, then you will see papers that I think will convince you."

"But should you not leave tonight?"

"Sorry Tor, but you are in the country now. No flights for Kyiv until the morning."

Were her papers genuine? However, her reference to the Russian Foreign Ministry was apparently okay. Could of course be forged, such as Tor's papers, he had three passports now. But what choices did he have?

Marek's apartment was not great, not great at all.

Window onto a rather shabby backyard. Not big, the window. But large enough so that someone could come in with a ladder from the landing below.

It had to be barricaded. And the door? It looked as if there had been an intruder earlier. Double security lock was fitted now, the remains of the old lock were still hanging there.

But Tor knew that if those people chasing him really wanted to get in, there would be nothing stopping them.

"Forget the barricade and look at the window as an escape route." Anna obviously read his mind. "If we lie still here, Tor, and make as little noise as possible, then it is not likely that we will be disturbed before you have to get up in any case."

"We?" He looked at her. She just rolled her eyes and then came the smile.

"Tor, I may sleep on the floor. It will not be the first time."

"Let's start with your papers. I reckon we start with the most faked?"

"And yours then, Tor? Which of your passports are genuine? As for our friend, the German patent engineer?"

It was just to realize that Anna was genuine. Still, they had to find some food. But to go out now, when at least one gang was after him and probably after her too?

"Your friend Marek is like every other bird of the night, isn't he?"

"What do you mean?" She was on guard now.

"No, relax then. I thought that if one works at night, the fridge would be empty."

The smile came back quickly. "Experienced, Tor, in all areas?"

The skirt had slipped up, and it was impossible not to see more than he could take. But Anna pretended as nothing.

"Come with me out to the kitchen, then we'll see."

She went ahead. And there was a kitchenette there, behind the curtain.

But Tor was right. The only thing that was in the refrigerator was a half box of tomato paste, opened long ago, and some bone-dry garlic. And then two beers.

Anna laughed. "Is that so in your dormitories too, Tor?"

It was cramped in the kitchen and even tighter when she bowed to pick up a package on the floor. Could she not in the least wear pantyhose, not just a string?

"I found, I found. Package from Marek's mother."

"But can you just open it then?"

"How long do you think it has been lying here unopened?" She looked at the stamp. "Three weeks since it was sent. Let's see." She unwrapped the package carefully, put the letter aside. "Look, dried meat, sausage, cheese, and a pie that soon will be gone. And bread, home-baked bread, hard. We have what we need, Tor, and I know where the vodka is."

Triumphantly, she hauled out an untouched bottle of vodka from the top of the fridge and the "party" could begin.

But Tor wanted to sleep but realized that here he had to stay the distance.

It was three days ago now that the American had left with his "Good luck with the moon landing."

Tor should have been done with that now, but the thoughts still bothered him.

Tor got the sofa bed. There was only a thin blanket for each of them. He set his cell phone to wake up at half past four. Put 50 dollars in the fridge and crawled into bed in just his boxer.

He got to buy a toothbrush and toothpaste in Satu Mare. The last thing he remembered was the sight of an empty vodka bottle and then he was gone.

He sensed neither time nor place when he later felt the warmth of one soft woman's body against his buttocks.

Did not care about that either.

Only let the woman come to him and he to her. It was a long time ago now, and they were friends and probably needed it both. Then he was inside her and she breathed him in the ear, and they both screamed, and everything went black again.

The mobile phone alarm rang at 0430 and he tumbled up. Was about to stumble into Anna who lay naked on the floor, the carpet had slipped by. God, she was beautiful. He should have accepted the invitation.

But what had happened in the course of the night? He had come, and she, or whoever woman had been with him, likewise.

And she then, was there not a smile of happiness that were playing around her mouth?

"Do you not say goodbye, Tor?" She had pulled the blanket around her now.

"Come." He helped her up, and she pressed herself against him as she was ready for another round.

"Careful, my girl. I'm an old man you know. I just wanted to help you onto the couch. I'm leaving now."

"Where is the old man? I cannot see him. Take care of yourself then, Tor!"

Then he was outside and heard the door slam behind him.

89

The Assassination

It was bitterly cold at the train station in Cluj this morning. How could he get himself a coffee?

None spoke but Romanian, perhaps Hungarian, Tor neither of them.

But finally, he found a kiosk that sold both coffee and Marsh chocolate and cheese and ham sandwiches. The day was saved with a bottle of water as well. It was a scant quarter now to the announced departures. At the last minute, he got off the train to Bucharest and onto a more modern version, almost like a tram.

There were not many along with him in the open carriage. Two elderly women, hard to tell if they were old or just worn out in their black cloaks that reached to their feet. Probably, they have fitted quite well the cloaks before the body was lye and bent forward. And then the classic, no surplus on teeth, quite the contrary.

But there was a young one, twenty-five maybe, beautiful, fake blonde in beautiful western European clothes there. Could she be Hungarian?

Budapest was rightly reputed for its many beautiful women and great western shops, something he knew from several visits.

Fake Gucci box, or was it real? She held it with the label side to her, so he could not see the print.

Take the bull by the horns, he got up and sat just opposite her.

Outside, the landscape became more and more grey. They were now on their way across the eastern part of the Hungarian plateau, and it was far, far between the farms.

The train passed a number of small villages with derelict buildings. Remains from the communist era.

But the lady was apparently not interested in contact.

Behind the big fashion glasses, there were no blue eyes that matched the mane. In a careless moment, brown-black eyes were spotted.

Where was this lady going with that look and the fancy clothes? Here on the puszta, on the way to poor land, literally.

It was all too strange. He had to get to the bottom of this before something uncalled for would happen. Surely, it was the others being in control now. He had to take it back.

Finally, he managed to "lose" a few drops of water on her left leg. She was bound to react.

Anatova was her name. At first, she only spoke Russian. Tor's scarce vocabulary did not hold for any conversation. But then suddenly, she spoke Romanian, and Tor found some familiar words and phrases, halfway Italian. But Anatova did not know much.

Should just go to the final stop and be picked up and get to know more in Satu Mare.

So she was going all the way up she too?

And he then? Tor knew that she lied. Satu Mare was only bull, and she was no doubt taken on for shadowing him. Could he take any more of this now? And did she have a weapon? Why not make the settlement here and now?

"It's me you should fit in with, is it not? Make sure that I could not get away? Do you know what happens when they do not have any use for you no more?"

She shook her head. "No comprendere."

So he had to take it slower. But she had probably understood something, he could see it on her face, which had become greyer and sadder. Where had the gleam of her eyes gone? Then she disappeared to the toilet. She had probably realized that she had literally lost some of her charm and face. What was her background? She was no way as trained as Maria had been. Maybe she was a random escort down from

Brasov or Bucharest. Empty in the head, but pretty to look at? *Now you're stupid, Tor. It would be too easy.* But she did not seem particularly alert nor trained in espionage. And he then? Did he have any training? But he had survived, but she would not. Not according to the pattern, he had seen so far. It made him think of this Bente from Hvitsten. Was she still alive or had Ivan dispatched with her?

Then she was back.

She looked better now. Tor chose to continue where he had left off. What if she had a weapon? He drew a gun on the damp window. She froze and then he pointed to her purse. She shook her head violently. Fellow passengers had begun to take interest now. He did not think she was lying. She was too amateurish for that. But he had to find out. So he found the map, pointed to Satu Mare and Sighetu Marmatite. She nodded and then he pulled his finger further up toward Ukraine.

"Yes," she whispered.

He stopped with intent at the small village completely at the foot of the pass.

"Yes."

Come on. She probably understood as much as she wanted to, he thought. But why not try to help her? Up with a sheet of paper and a ballpoint pen. As at school, the difference was that Tor had not become any better in drawing. But match drawings would do the trick.

Anatova, she was now smiling kind of childish. "Anatova brings Tor, me," he tapped his chest, "to the next man. Man has a gun." A little harder to draw it. "Man, first shoots Tor and then Anatova in village. Man take suitcase from Tor who is dead."

She was crying now, disappeared to the toilet again only with a makeup bag. The large Gucci box remained on the seat. Tor covered it with his coat and got his hand into it.

No gun, no knife, but a small brown bottle with text in Russian. Got the cork off and he did not have to keep it close to his nose. The smell of chloroform was penetrating. *That was close, Tor,* but he got the cap on and put it back. Moved his coat back, there she was.

They were almost there. The train had slowed the pace. She knew it now, that she would die right out there in the remote village.

"Goodbye, Anatova. Take the train back." She looked at him in astonishment as he handed over 50 Lei and made a complete turn on the windowpane. "Go back with train and maybe you will live."

He saw her get off the train, maybe to find one that went south again?

But she had no chance. A man in black suit and driver's cap held her already hard in the arm, and Tor could see they disappeared into a black limo.

How had he come on to this crazy idea to try save this woman? Had he started to get soft?

Yes, maybe so, but it was the sight of Svetlana for his inner self that had been the driving force.

Svetlana in the overly large camouflage uniform. Svetlana who had ended her days with a severed throat in a straw sack by the riverbank in Brasov. Shit and urine all over the body.

They were about the same age, the two, and Anatova realized her fate by the grip of the arm to the black-clad chauffeur.

Could he do anything? Hardly.

Provide for your own survival, Tor. Get your bags and go on home to your Astrid!

The huge station building was large enough to accommodate activities for several hundred people simultaneously. Peeled plaster and remnants of a beautiful golden color from the thirties.

But now, the pure decay. Why had they sent him up here and where was the leak in the SVR system that gave GRU full control over him?

He chose to believe that he still had advantages in this race, just had to believe it, not give up so close to the goal. Because now, it had really become a race, given that they knew that Sapânta was the last stop. Yes, they probably knew that, even though the girl did not know it exactly. He suddenly thought of the map that Maria had held in her hand. And what was it that Horvath had written on the sheet in the newspaper before it was covered by the "Gorilla's" blood? "Some people think you have the map." He had not cared about just that. It was Omar he wanted to find. Omar and none other and then get westward and home. But now he was free.

Map of Brasov? He had never bothered himself about it. Perhaps had it been lost on the hotel room in Sighisoara? Or had it been with the drawings and notes between the prime minister and the Minister of Foreign Affairs from Oslo? Then it certainly had gone to Moscow with Anna.

So now, find the suitcase from Omar and home again and then finished with it all. It was too early to call Astrid, too early. He blushed where he stood. Had he had sex with Anna or was it just an insane, delicious dream?

He did not know, would not think more about it there and then.

A drunk almost peed on him. Stench of urine throughout the space.

If this was the railway station for the artist city of Satu Mare, how would it have been in earlier days, at the time of Ceausescu?

He walked over to what might look like a cafe. A beautiful dark-haired lady came and dragged him into a cubicle, speaking fluent French.

"You're from the West somewhere. You cannot sit out there. Then you will get robbed. Sit here, I'm going to lock the door when I leave."

"What was this? Stop please, I'm going north over the pass."

He showed her on the map the neighboring village of Sapånta. Best to be a little careful yet.

"There goes one micro bus over there in about one hour. The road is awful, and it may happen you must out and help push the bus over the pass."

"How do I get a seat?"

"I have to fix it. If you say you're Italian, is it okay?"

"Yes, all right, but I have to have that bus."

He saw the headline in a newspaper. It said something about Dracula and a picture of Bush and Putin. The only thing he realized was that it had been drilled in the Dracula Castle and someone had tried to put explosives there. A map had disappeared, and the mini summit moved to an unknown location. It was not known whether it was Al-Qaeda or the North Koreans who were behind it.

Why was Maria murdered, because someone wanted the map? Got good use for the Italian here.

Now they thought Tor had the map, the Leopards.

What now, what about the French-speaking lady?

But she was hardly French, even though she spoke almost fluently. So where did she come into the picture?

A man who looked like he could be a bus driver came up to the glass door and knocked.

"I've been told you're going north. The ticket is paid. Do you have no more luggage than that?"

He pointed to the backpack. Tor shook his head.

"No? Then you can take it into the bus, with you. We are leaving straight away."

"But the lady then?"

"What lady?"

Tor shook his head again and smiled and the driver smiled and then they were on to the bus.

"The weather forecast is bad, so we need to just get going."

Tor looked at his watch. Thirty minutes to the announced departure, go now at full speed, and no ticket paid? Was this another trap, or was there a guardian angel watching over him? Could it be the angel, Anna? Or the "French" lady?

The minibus was only three-quarters full. He asked the driver in his stuttering Italian if this was normal, especially when the bus only ran once a day.

The driver shook his head and said that many used to come in the last moment, but not today.

No, Tor thought. Last minute and then the bus left thirty minutes ago!

The shock absorbers had been used up several years ago and the holes in the road were many, and then after two hours, the road was covered in snow. But now they were almost at the top of the pass and could begin a very slow drive through the hairpin curves, downward in the direction of the border station against Ukraine.

Then there was an abrupt stop at the next turn. Across the road lay the remains of the black limo. There had been an explosion. The first thing he saw when he came out was the Gucci box. Pretty grimy now, but still. It was real. But the blonde? Metal parts and remains of two people, one of them was Anatova, lay across the road. The explosion must have been violent.

Who had triggered it and why were the lady and the limo up here?

Wasn't the job done anyway? Should Tor be taken at the destination, Sapånta? Fellow passengers flew around and looked for valuables. But Tor went further down the road. Some birds flying around something down there. He seemed to see a foot sticking out of the bush. And quite right, there she lay the French-speaking lady or rather the corpse. Twisted cord stumps in the road indicated that it was she who had triggered the explosion. But now she was dead. What the bullets had not managed, the knife that was left under the left shoulder blade did.

Could not have been long since this. Even though there was almost no traffic up here, it would be strange if one or two cars had not come up and seen the remains of the limo? She was naked from the waist down and was bleeding both front and back down there. The nails were full of hair and leather fibers. It must have been one terrible fight there in the underbrush.

He touched her body. She was not quite cold yet, so it could hardly have been more than a half an hour since it all happened.

Clear footsteps were marked inward in the woods in the snow. Must have been one of the limo guys, not just the blonde and the driver? But how had this man managed to get away before the explosion?

Not good to say, but there was blood on the footsteps. Tor followed into the forest. There was more and more blood, and Tor gave up and turned around, this man would hardly survive in the cold night. Were they finished now, Khan and his aides? How many more did they have to kill? And how many more women to rape and molest?

But it was you they were going to take out, Tor. The limo was supposed to be the roadblock itself and this Anatova, she was the one to make you unconscious with the chloroform, and then off to GRU and Khan? But then it was the French-speaking woman who became the victim, together with the mischievous woman Anatova and the driver.

Where did she come from, the French-speaking woman? Tor did not even know her name. Perhaps was she Hungarian? A girlfriend of Horvath? Sacrificed her life for Tor to live! *Do not think about it, Tor.* She was trained to kill; otherwise, she would not have had the job of blowing up the limo.

They had become silent now the fellow passengers and everyone wanted to get going. Preferably not getting mixed up in anything. Together, they managed to make an opening, so the micro bus got through. The driver had called the police and told them about the accident.

Suddenly, he saw the sign with Sapânta coming up. He shook the driver, perhaps too heavily, because he turned, annoyed.

"I'm leaving here."

"As if I did not know. You have bought a ticket to Sapânta. But I first stop at the church."

But Tor had not bought a ticket. But the one who had bought the ticket to him obviously knew that this was the real destination.

Contact network again and he felt like a piece that was just moved here and there. But now he was hoping to soon have his target in hand: the suitcase.

90

The Rescue

Khan had raised his hand. Irina stood ready with the wire cutter around Omar's thumb. The little finger just hung loose from the earlier blow.

Omar had closed his eyes and got ready for the scream that just had to come. It would be impossible to hold back, and Khan would surely rejoice even worse. He felt the forceps close over the knuckle, and it already hurt in the skin from the rusty iron. Could she not take the joint then, not crush the bone itself! It would never heal. Maybe that was not the intention either.

He was a lost case already. Khan was probably quite certain that he would not crack. Drove the race almost for fun and to gain extra respect as a GRU officer.

But it did not hurt anymore, not violently at least. Was the finger off already? But he had heard the phone ring, and now Khan was talking. He opened his eyes, and Irina stood completely calm with the wire cutter ready. Khan was red in the face, and Omar perceived "Yes, Colonel, Yes, Colonel" several times.

Khan regained his color and confidence and came over to Omar with a contemptuous smile around his mouth.

"The assassination attempt failed. The CIA and GRU have jointly exposed the treacherous North Korean plans. Putin and Bush are in safety in Bucharest, and we don't need you anymore, you little wretch, nor the map! The Ministry of Foreign Affairs has asked for you to be handed over for further questioning about money transactions. You were lucky now, Omar, but we'll probably meet again!"

The policeman was to take him to the Foreign Ministry, with handcuffs on. But Tor, where was he? Had Horvath managed to get posted the message? He was handed over to Donetski's anteroom. A guard received the key, and as soon as the policeman had left, he was freed from handcuffs and taken to Donetski. A nurse was ready with bandage cases and the little finger was closely tied up to the ring finger.

"Six weeks max, then you are okay."

"Now, Omar? Was it worth it? 200,000 US is a lot of money, and you could have lost your life had Anna not appeared with the map in time. We fly you back to Transylvania later in the day, you and Anna. There you meet Tor, completely safe, and he gets on the plane to Kiev, where he lands before our plane flies back to Moscow."

91

The Cemetery

There had been sleet on top of the pass, and now it was raining.

Tor sought refuge at the church while he laid a battle plan. The Leopards were no longer after him, hardly the North Koreans either, if they had been at all?

Of course, not SVR. And GRU had no interest anymore.

The map had no value. The summit was over. The suitcase with the documents was now safe with the Russian Foreign Ministry.

Now there was only Khan and his private vendetta left.

At the cemetery, a charter bus just stopped and a huge crowd of youngsters from Bucharest got out. Obviously, the cemetery was a famous tourist destination.

The description was correct. All the tombstones, and they were in many different sizes, were painted with a special blue color. The motifs were very different but depicted significant aspects of the dead's life on earth. This was what the brochure said and what the guard at the entrance told him. But how would he be able to find the right gravestone, the one with the suitcase?

An almost hopeless task with all the tourists and maybe it was one of them and not Tor who would found the suitcase.

He decided to take break until the bus left with the school youngsters.

On the other hand, what if they find the briefcase, accidentally?

Best to talk to them, get on their mind, so to speak. Were they to return to Bucharest this afternoon? The boy laughed out loud and immediately a whole bunch was on to Tor. Why did they laugh? Tor did not understand much of the talk, other than a word like "idiot." All right then. He tried again, in Italian this time. Apparently, the boys' English skills were in short supply. Well then, things went better with Italian, and the boy could tell that it was at least a fifteen-hour bus ride back to Bucharest, not a trip you did in one afternoon.

"So what planet are you from? You should not fly around the cemetery anymore! Goodbye!"

And Tor could continue the search. In one place, it had been dug only recently and someone had pushed a cactus plant down at the back of a large tombstone.

Strange. It should have been in front, and besides, the cactus was hardly a particular plant to put down outdoors now. But it was there, and the strange thing was that on this statue there was no longer a name. It was overpainted. Could it be a mockery support for Ceausescu and that it was therefore the youths had been standing there laughing? He thought they had said something like that but did not get it all.

Up with cactus, but the watchman stared a little too interested, so Tor fetched a watering can and pretended he was to irrigate the cactus. Then the man disappeared.

"We did not take the chance, go to Sighetu Marmatiei. Check in at Hotel Tissa. We will find you. Burn the note."

He cursed and put the cactus down nicely and watered it. No doubt it would die instantly with the cold of the night.

Out on the road again and started to walk. Could see the Ukrainian border post further away in the valley.

92

Irina

This is where he should have gone on to Kiev.

Irina should have been standing there on the Ukrainian side with the car ready. But yet, he didn't have the suitcase and Irina? Taken out, brought back to Moscow?

Where did she really come from, the blonde beauty?

It had begun with a recommendation whether to find a woman in Kiev which could be of help on his return if everything went wrong. Just get across the border somewhere, no matter where and then be picked up.

But luck had not been with him. Then suddenly, he got a tip just before his departure from Oslo. Check with Uniagency for Ukrainian ladies seeking lovers.

It had to be Ivan who had come with the tip, as a joke more or less, and Tor had only waved him off.

"I have a lover, Ivan, and will continue with her."

"Your wife then?"

"Yes of course, who else!"

But he bored himself in the dungeon at the embassy, and one night, he took Ivan on his word. And there she was, Kiev and thirty-nine, looked a little mournful, but seemed intelligent.

Had a slightly embarrassed smile. Looked as if she was forced into something she was not quite comfortable with.

But she was pretty, and she had an education, so no ordinary blonde. He joked a bit with himself.

Blonde jokes, did they never go out of style?

But what if Astrid came to know that he was on an internet site for girls looking for gents?

But it could not get worse than this with Bente. The credibility was perhaps gone, and now it was all about life.

The letters from Irina got to him though. Romantic and inviting and in an English no Eastern Europeans could have managed, without roots in the UK.

Was she an agent?

He offered to buy her address and make direct contact via private e-mail. Had to. Could not broadcast to the whole world about the plans.

Well then, she was there, and he was quick to get the first e-mail off. The credit card burned a little, but Ivan would get the bill eventually or Donetski had to take it.

No news from Irina, complete silence. Tor e-mailed the provided contact phone to the agency on a Caribbean Island. But received reassuring answers that things take time in Ukraine.

But the e-mail address then? Finally, no, it was Ukrainian good enough, they claimed. Sure, it is not Russia? No. He then knew something was wrong. How much had he revealed about his plans?

There was only one way to stop this. CIA and Langley USA.

But he did not dare to take the chance of contacting them from the Russian embassy, but at the church asylum in Sibiu, he got lucky.

No answer left. Asked the next morning before he left, still no answer. But suddenly she was back on the net, the same Irina in lighter clothes this time and with her breasts pressed together out of the bra.

Now there was barely a smile. Just excessively much naked skin on the blonde. So she was pushed for something, and obviously, the Russians were behind this e-mail address?

Maybe GRU had infiltrated the entire network?

Or perhaps was it one pimp who made big money on her. Just the same. Tor could not afford more chances. Stupid enough to have started this. Now it was time to come up with plan B.

And it came, all by itself.

93

The Mayor

Should he try to hitchhike? Well yes. A lady stopped. Lady, late forties.

"Are there any more buses here or trains and when?"

How to get out of here? Earliest train to Sighetu Marmatiei. She laughed.

"No train in this out-of-the-way place," she said in passable English. But I can drive you there if you wait a quarter of an hour."

"Heavens, I am in luck, how far is it then?"

"Oh, just an hour, not worse than that."

Then she was back and the car, it worked even though it looked somewhat old.

The conversation, if one could call it that, turned to the usual, weather and living conditions and where he came from and going and that was it.

Just before they arrived, he could not help himself, but had to ask why this extensive kindness. She did not want any payment either. Then it came in quite passable English: "I have to help people. I am the mayor of this city."

City? Ten houses and some cats and a stray dog? Yes, and the cemetery, with all its blue tombstones. Should he believe in her or was she part of the network belonging to Omar or Horvath? But did it really matter? He had arrived.

94

Goodbye, Irina

He had waved to the Ukrainian border post as they passed, just two hundred meters away. Perhaps was it for the best to avoid poking themselves away in one woman's history, agent or not. It had to stop with Anna from Cluj.

He could still feel the heat of her sex against his ass. Damn, what happened to Omar? Finally, his phone rang.

"I just landed on a hidden airstrip. Horvath says you're at the hotel. He has the suitcase, and we will come to you."

"You were saved by the bell, one might say."

Omar told about his meeting with GRU.

"So the American colonel and his entourage were cover-up for CIA working behind the scenes! That was the explanation. Smart, that with family trip. And Maria? But she was Russian, wasn't she? Trained by the KGB / FSB. Admittedly from the border with North Korea. But still?"

Omar looked at him incomprehensibly.

"Then someone from the neighboring state must have had something on her or her closest. And when they did not have use for her anymore, just hit her. But then they had missed a few seconds on the timing. The colonel should have been shot first. That's how it was. And then they missed again when they were going to take me! Thought it was the colonel, but then it was me and the poor taxi driver."

"A lot of drama, that, Tor, and I sat in GRU Major Khan's special chamber for torture in Moscow." He pointed to the little finger and the marks on the forceps on his right thumb. "It was at the last minute before the phone rang and they were to start on the toes too. But now, it's over then, Tor."

"Now and forever, Omar. I shall only go home to settle with my partners and then it's the hook on the door and only Astrid, my wife, and me on a trip to an undisclosed location."

"But before we say goodbye, Tor, how did you like my women?"

Tor could not completely hide a blush.

"I was very happy with everyone, especially with the mayor, so I did not have to walk a whole day or night to get here. "

"And Anna then?"

"Yes, greet her and make a wish for her happiness with Marek."

"Marek? I did not know that."

Tor just left and walked toward the train to Brasov and the airport.

Obviously, Omar did not know anything about what had happened at the top of the pass, and Tor could not bear to go yet another round now. He felt he had taken more than he could bear, just wanted to throw up. Got around the corner and let it go. It was a relief literally spoken, and after a sip of fresh drink from the fountain on the square, he could put everything behind and wave atrocities goodbye. Six murders or executions. Call it what you like and he himself had taken one life, the "Gorilla."

But was he not to blame for any of the others as well? *For them all, Tor!*

But was he done with Ivan and the Cobra and what about Samuel and the envelope and this vengeful Mongol?

Maybe the game did not end here in Romania anyway?

And could he hope for protection from the old people in Stay behind in Norway until it was all over. Or was it the E-14 that had taken over? Astrid never revealed anything from her work, not on military secrets in any case. But she had cracked this once. Tor had not asked for more. But it was not at all inconceivable that E-14 had played a role in getting him well out of Romania. Or was it Omar alone who was the hero?

95

The Settlement

"This is the captain from the flight deck. Officer Lillesen will now take us down at Værnes, dot on schedule. Hope…"

He barely listened, Tor, as he sat with his suitcase well placed under the seat. Against the rules, but no one noticed, not even the flight attendant, the lean one with the Malmö dialect. Was probably afraid to get too close, so he could see that it was very much makeup that sustained her face.

Everything had gone straightforward finally.

Even though the trip home had been strenuous and the trip through Romania a little hell, he was still alive.

And he also had added to the account in London a new 400,000 US.

In the suitcase, he had 100,000 for Samuel. Twice as much as agreed, but it had to stand.

They were to meet in the OBS room for the last time in a few hours.

They could only have swapped suitcases down in the city. But it was okay to keep up the routine they had established.

"I need a new backpack," Samuel had parried, laughing. "So buy one for me when you come here. But this time do not think of sleeping bag and provisions."

"Maybe we are overly cautious, Samuel."

He had called him at work from one kiosk in Storgata.

"No, let us run the race, so we will not blame ourselves afterward."

This time, there was nothing mysterious at Gardermoen, although at Værnes, he had seen something that could remind him of a reception committee.

Maybe it was the final now, it's all over? But a little strange was this with Omar who was kidnapped, albeit of GRU, the competing organization.

Strange also with the phone call he had received from the Intelligence yesterday. A guy who introduced himself as Peter Gjengedahl was the one who called.

"Hey, you are Tor Wisting, yes?"

"Yes, then," he was on guard now. "What is it about?" He wanted to cough, but he managed.

"I just had to ask that question. I have taken over from Pettersen. You remember him, you reported to, it was about ten years ago?"

Tor kept his cool, should not let himself be swayed by the stick now. Done was done, for always.

"Yes, of course, I was down there many times."

"It is not for sure you remember me. But I was always present. The routine calls for two of us. I am the one who was tall and thin and sat and took notes."

"Oh yes, it was you, but I must admit that I do not remember your name."

"No matter. I'm not offended, but I have a few questions."

"Come on, you can take them on the phone."

"Best to be on the offensive. Is it okay for you to have the conversation recorded on tape? Routine, you know."

"All right."

What was he up to? Had they gotten hold of something? Maybe a tip from the CIA or MI5? He still had this perception that this Mr. Smith at Casa Wagner, the one who came with the 7 mm cartridge, he could be one of them? And then he just let go of it, but still careful with voice and choice of words.

"We have the not had contact with you in these ten years. How are you? Have you heard anything more from the Russians?"

"No, they did well enough with Treholt."

"But you have travelled a lot, alone, as far as I understand?"

Really, they had followed him closely anyway. What else could he expect?

Maybe it was the American colonel who had asked them to be on guard. The colonel who changed from being a kind of best friend to not wanting to be known by him at all. The colonel who had been to Oslo several times, but who had not been there anyway. The colonel who had welcomed him to Brussels and later Colorado, but his e-mail address was nonexistent in spite of the business card.

Tor saw no reason to lie and be caught with his pants down.

"Well then, I have been to Romania with a friend a few times, but that is several years ago. Yes, and then I was going to meet him this summer, but then something got in the way, so I took a trip to Dracula and the castle over there since my friend did not come."

"What happened to him then?"

"A few questions, you said. Yes. All right. He was kidnapped up at the border to Ukraine and released only after a few days, but then I had gone home already."

"Didn't you know that Wizz air has direct flights between Torp and Cluj Napocha?"

Good grief, the policeman managed to pronounce the name quite correctly.

"No, not until much later, besides, they probably only go once a week, and you have to order months in advance to get a good price. But what do you want with this questioning? Visiting people and having a holiday, that's okay, right?"

"And Trondheim?"

"Please, enough now, Gjengedahl, I have been twice and visited my brother-in-law while his wife and my wife have been on a long vacation in the United States. But you know that, about the United States?"

He did not respond. "Then you have no business going on with the Russians anymore then?"

"No, and besides, it was not formally the Russians, but Azerbaijan."

"One very last question?"

Tor was bored now, shitty tired of the worn-in policeman. Only a few questions he had said. But better by phone than to be summoned to the chamber.

"Come on, you."

"Have you run into an organization called Stay Behind?"

"Funny that you mention it. I've been sitting on a plane to Grand Canary one time. Ordinary large charter aircraft. It flew its last trip at the time and was supposedly owned by a central Stay Behind member. That's it. The flight was absolutely excellent."

"Okay, Tor." *We were on first name now suddenly.* "Will you accept my call if there is anything else I need?"

"Any time, but now must I go. But Pettersen is retired, you said? Or did you say he works for someone else? Well, anyway, greet him if you meet him."

"I probably will not do that, there is some security in an embassy, I think."

Of course, Gjengedahl knew much more. Sooner or later, it would have to crack this with the ultra-secret American group SEAB or something? Tor did not remember the details and did not want to let Gjengedahl know that he knew.

Donetski had talked about the scheme, clearly envious on behalf of the Russians.

"It will be expensive for us this Tor, we have to monitor the monitors. On the other hand, glad we let go of the scandal Americans had made for themselves even there in Oslo."

As usual, the police knew a lot more.

But now it was too late.

The job was done and the money, it was not in Norway, apart from those that Samuel was going to get in the morning or later in the day.

Should it end well then for his millionaire brother-in-law?

96

The Review

He did not have many weeks left, Donetski. What could have been a scandal and given a one-way ticket to Siberia had calmed down now. Even Lavrov had gradually realized that they might have bought and paid for something that might not have the greatest value. But in the end, Donetski wanted to stand his ground. Some had to sacrifice and some dollars too much had disappeared from the account. But now, he had drawings from one or another lunatic in the Bush system, and best of all, Americans knew he had it, all of it. So now it was double worthless, except from the negotiations about the missile shield. Only Khan would not give up. He knew that with a bit of success now, General Kuznevskov's job was his as soon as his GRU chief retired. His immediate superior, the colonel, was no threat, soon to be seventy he too.

This Bente they killed; she had said something about all the drawings being fake. The thought strikes him a late afternoon, and not long after, he has General Kuznevskov, the very head of GRU on the thread. If they could meet early in the morning tomorrow? Before office hours? The general was not that pleased about it.

"Why do not you go the formal way? Where is the colonel you are reporting to? Well, in the Middle East. But this case can wait, right? No?"

At 06.00 he was in place. Then Khan had waited half an hour already with the coffee ready.

"It must be important this, Major Khan? I have not long service time left and have thought to live me through it without a stroke or heart attack."

"Sorry, General, but we have to take Lavrov before he has time to plan countermeasures."

"What do you mean? Speak clearly then, man."

"More coffee?"

Khan pours up plenty.

"What did you say, taking out the foreign minister?"

"Lavrov arrives early at the office today, already at seven thirty. I know, he must prepare himself for meeting the president at 09:00 a.m., and he's probably going to get ready."

"Have you checked this, so we do not waste time? And what does this have to do with us?"

"We need an investigation."

"But don't be silly, Khan. Investigation is no longer an issue. Investigation of what, by the way. You probably do not mean of these drawings and documents that came from Oslo?"

"Of course."

"But these Lavrov has seen already, so no time for this at all."

"But Lavrov does not know what I know!"

The general looked like a question mark. "What do you know?"

"That the whole thing is a construction. When the Norwegian prime minister kept his New Year speech, he talked much about this moon landing."

"Yes, and?"

"Yes, he was the whole time talking about CO2 purification plant that would be built. No rocket base! In other words, a pure metaphor."

"But who invented this with the rocket base?"

The general had become interested now and furious. Khan wanted to ask him to take care of his blood pressure but did not dare.

"Some idiots at the embassy in Oslo started it all, and then the snowball started rolling."

"But the drawings of the facilities then and the notes between the Minister of the State and the Foreign Minister?"

The general had raised himself now, swept the coffee cups to the side, and supported himself heavily against the desk. "We might need a vodka now, Major, but it's probably a little early. Let me hear the rest first."

"Fake everything. Produced by the courier's brother-in-law."

The vodka came on the table and the first glasses went straight down. But Khan did not say anything about some idiot in the United States administration. This guy had made his suggestion about just such a base at the North Pole, immediately after Stoltenberg's speech. No need to excite the general further, and perhaps it was a good idea to save some information until he himself could meet Little Father again.

"Can you prove this and take Donetski and SVR with you and preferably Lavrov in the same soup?"

Khan put a finger to his lips. "You can joke you, General. You meant Chernikov, of course."

"Did I say Lavrov? You must have heard wrong. Lavrov is the one who will clean up the chaos."

Khan blinked as a sign that everything was okay now. Certainly, the general's office was also monitored.

"Correct, General, but first, I must have your approval to an investigation here and in Norway and I must lead it. Then Lavrov must approve it all in writing."

"And what if Lavrov says no, again?"

"He does not, not this time. Now, we will examine the connection also between the Third Man and the CIA and the American colonel. We must also include in the mandate the investigation of the North Korean lady who was killed in Brasov."

"Was she North Korean? I thought she worked for SVR?"

"Maybe for them as well, but the key to it all is this brother-in-law of the Third Man."

"What if Lavrov would say no to another investigation?"

"Then you will say to him that in Russia's interest, you will go straight to Little Father."

"You put your head on the block now, Major, maybe mine too. And what about my pension?"

"Chernikov is still in Oslo. Call him on our special line and ask if he remembers one Bente who was going to take suicide after threats from Cobra and this Ivan. Ask him if Bente referred to this brother-in-law, Samuel. Tell him that his only chance to survive is that he shuts up to absolutely everyone except me. Then I eliminate him when I get over. You must call him privately, they are an hour behind us in time."

"As if I did not know that, Khan!"

The general was clearly uncomfortable with Khan's dictation. But at the same time, the gain could be enormous by an investigation. Take the rat on SVR before he got off.

"Chernikov?"

"Yes."

Khan followed on the extension.

"This is General Kuznevskov."

Khan more than knew that the wretch in the other hand imagined meeting up with a firing squad. Phone from the general in GRU at 6 in the morning.

"Go to the nearest kiosk. Get rid of anyone that might be there and call this number. Hang up immediately and I'll call you back. You have fifteen minutes on you."

"Satisfied now?" The general looked at Khan. "Let me do away paperwork while we wait, and we can have a car ready, so we go straight to the Foreign Ministry afterward."

"What should you write?"

"A statement that Lavrov signs. Top secret and with all judiciary rights bestowed on you."

"I hope you do not think it is too rude of me, but to save time, I have allowed myself to make a proposal."

They were interrupted by the phone. Kuznevskov noted and called the number in Norway.

"So, Chernikov, one word about this to anyone except Khan who comes over, then Siberia does not wait, there will be immediate execution."

They could hear Chernikov shrinking there in the kiosk. "Three questions: One, do you know the story of this Bente? Two, did she say that the brother-in-law of the Third Man had made all the drawings?"

"Do you mean the brother-in-law of this Tor?"

"Of course, you idiot. Tor was the Third Man. Three, is Bente dead now?"

"The answer is yes to all three questions, General. I swear."

"Okay! Go to work as usual. Khan will contact you in Oslo and remember what I said about your throat."

The general threw a glance at Khan.

"Do you have copies?"

"Yes, here in this envelope."

"Do you have an appointment?"

The secretary looked at them in horror. She had hardly heard of Khan, but General Kuznevskov was well-known. But she did not have to report them. The minister had realized that he had received guests. The office door was half open this early morning. A Secretary of State picked up speed on the way out. Khan was asked to wait in the anteroom.

"Are you sure about this, General?"

"One hundred percent. I've even had contacts in Oslo in this morning."

"With whom, then?"

"Mr. Foreign Minister, I'm managing my office as you do yours. Should I reveal my informants? Unprofessional and I think our boss would rather not like that we mix our roles. But what about SVR, this is really their table, is it not?"

"With all due respect, there are several reasons why we have two intelligence organizations, Comrade Foreign Minister. SVR must under no circumstances be informed, not until Putin himself gives the go-ahead."

The rivalry between the two was well-known. Was this a pure act of revenge?

"You know what happens to your upcoming retirement if this investigation is inconclusive general."

"It will not be inconclusive. Comrade Lavrov and I have not planned for Siberia. Are you expecting a visit from our president soon or are you going to him? Regardless, I would wait to involve him at the present time. Here's your pen if you will allow me. My man will catch a flight to Oslo as soon as we have your okay."

"You are stretching this far now, General Kuznevskov. Are you trying to tell me how to do my job?"

"No, of course not, Comrade Foreign Minister. I'm just trying to do things right to secure our country's interests."

Lavrov used his own pen.

97

It All Comes Together

Should he spend time at Chernikov's, or should he go straight to Trondheim?

And what about Ivan? He was not in Oslo. He had checked with the terrified Chernikov. No, not in Oslo. He was quite sure that he had travelled to Trondheim. Maybe he was in Gråkallen too. What about Igor? No, Chernikov did not think he was here anymore. But Khan was sure.

Imagine being able to take all four together.

Had to keep in mind extra batteries for the small tape recorder. Nothing was to go wrong now. Get the confessions on tape and then home to a new star.

Surprises paid off as a rule, so there was accommodation at Gardermoen Rica and then a taxi to Majorstuen at 4 in the morning. He did not bother to use the bell, but entered the front door of the apartment complex together with the newspaper delivery man. Chernikov lived in a small two-bedroom apartment with his wife. The children had long since moved home to Tula south of Moscow.

It took him an extra minute to remove the safety chain and then he was inside. The idiot had not set the alarm. He quickly cut the alarm cable for safety and then stood in the bedroom door. But Olga slept lightly and closed her eyes only when the chloroform found its way. Then she had to die too. The phone call to the Foreign Ministry in Moscow did not last long.

"Chernikov and his wife have said goodbye to this earth. Have them removed in silence. We do not want any trouble with the Norwegian Ministry of Foreign Affairs."

"Who are you?"

"Ask General Kuznevskov if you dare."

Too bad this with Chernikov. He hung up, cut the phone and then he was out. The gloves went in the trash at the next tram stop. An hour later, he checked in on the plane to Trondheim as Paulsen, a Norwegian businessman living in Stavanger. The moustache took off for the light Asian facial features.

He was waiting at Værnes. The agreement with the Cobra had been clear.

"No killing now, Major Khan. This is an order, and one day, I might be your boss in GRU. Would not love to be in your shoes if you invite to vendetta with Igor. By the way, how long do you think you will survive a walk without shoes in Eastern Siberia? You will meet with Captain Ivan at Værnes, and I have arranged for you that you are to meet Tor and Samuel, but I repeat, behave sensibly."

"What about Igor, is he also under your protection?"

"Everyone who works in SVR or for SVR is under my personal protection. Do you want the general to remind you of this? Take just one quick phone call, if you dare. I call first and warn him about that one former Major Khan comes to call."

The line went dead.

"Hello?" Khan tried again, but there was no one on the other end. This had to go deep. The general's words, "Do not touch the Cobra," still rang in Khan's ears. But accidents like Igor getting lost in the rugged terrain down from this Gråkallen? Well, maybe he could get this Captain Ivan on board. After all, he was subordinate. Then he could take care of Igor afterward.

The blue Volvo was standing there, but only one man was waiting, Igor, who greeted tightly. Idiot greeting out here in public.

"Where's the captain?"

Igor looked at him confused. "Captain? No captain here, I'm waiting for the degree, but have not received it yet."

A sour smile came over the lips of Khan.

"So are you waiting?"

Igor nodded.

"For the grade you mean?"

Igor nodded again.

"I repeat, where is the captain?"

Igor seemed completely confused.

"Sometimes I wonder how you got your grades, Igor. Shit in Ivan, let's drive to SINTEF and wait for Samuel."

"Does he know we're coming?"

"Do not be an idiot. We are waiting for him coming out of his office. We know where he's going, maybe you do not, but I know! And when all this is over, we go for a trip, just you and I. Do you have a gun? Bring it forward, he might try for a run."

"Who then?"

Igor was completely gone now. Meet Khan here?

The Cobra had only sent a slightly cryptic message: "You might get company up to Gråkallen."

Well, well, maybe Tor had taken his wife with him? After all, she and Samuel were siblings. He did not know where the two were now, but the agreement was to meet in Gråkallen at 17:00. It went quickly inwards toward Lade.

"No speeding now, Igor, we do not want any contact with the police, do we?"

Igor felt the dominant tone from the KGB school way back in time. Almost scornfully commanding, especially now, a degree above him.

"Turn left here!"

"Here?"

"Yes, stop by the hotdog kiosk."

Was Khan so damn locally informed? Had he been here before?

"Aerial photo, Igor." It was as if he could read his mind. "If there is anything else you want to know about this country, just say so. I did not need specialization in Norwegian."

The mockery washed over Igor.

"You're waiting here while I take care of the hot dog queue. Norwegians eat dogs and cats only when they come in sausage bread. But this you know, not true, Igor? You come from here."

Igor looked blankly at him, shook his head, and shut it.

"Take out the gun and check the fuse."

And then Khan was out.

Not strange that Igor is still waiting on his stars. As childish as he was at the recruiting school.

That was probably why the Cobra had taken with him this captain from Tokyo. Field name Ivan had this captain. The same as Igor?

Strange. Then it would be Ivan 1 and Ivan 2?

Little doubt about who was the number 2. Should have a three in front at best.

When he returned to Moscow, he had to get rid of this gay Victor. Could not take the chance of having a loose cannon going.

If someone in the brothel had a little too good a memory, then there was either cash or a hole in the forehead. Or maybe better with a silent cut of the throat

Oops, he checked the photo once more, because there he was, this Samuel. Typical engineer look, glasses, for sure design specialist, lying over PC and desk for a long time and made fake drawings or copied them?

98

The Reunion

Samuel looked forward to the settlement, new money on the account. Not least, he was glad that they had maintained the friendship throughout, he and Tor. Remembered to call Randi and say he had to work long hours. Officially, he was going out to buy dog and continue working. But he was utterly ready for Gråkallen to meet Tor and this Ivan who had insisted on being present. Just had to have this piece of dog before he got in the car. In the queue for the dog kiosk, he noticed a pressure on the back and a voice whispered in English, "I can shoot you with silencer now or we go both out of the queue and get yourself into my car here, the blue Volvo on the corner."

The English was perfect.

Should he cry out and risk to be killed on the spot or wait and see? Who was the man with the gun?

Eastern European, perhaps. Hopeless to figure out just by the voice. Could it be the major from GRU himself or a hired killer he had sent? It was the Cobra and Ivan who had won this game also over this GRU major or?

"I'm Khan."

Did he hear right? So was this the end or what? Khan had come himself. Did Ivan know anything about this? Hardly. But was he in the car?

"You are good, Samuel. Skilled professional."

They were on their way over to Volvo now, where one other man held a pistol. Ready to shoot if Khan would miss, something which in itself was unthinkable.

"We may not be as good as you are, or what do you think? But we are smarter, much smarter. You should have been paid long ago and fled to your friends in the United States with a new identity and then we perhaps had not found you. But now you're here and you know where we're going? Of course, you know that. We're going to Gråkallen and meet the Third Man, the man with the suitcase."

The man at his side said nothing. Put the gun back in the casing and then drove the backroad to Byåsen and Gråkallen. The man was clearly familiar with the area.

He was about to say something, but Khan cut him off. "Not any chatting before we come up. I want to have everything on tape to the general."

So next Skistua and they began on the little trip.

"Samuel, you can walk freely, but you have two pistols aimed at your back, so take it nicely."

Could he have warned Tor?

But Tor was probably waiting inside the hall.

Khan read his mind. "Give me your cell phone, Samuel. Maybe you have two?"

He took one quick review of the pockets, found just the one, and they pulled on up the path.

99

Entering Gråkallen, Again

"Are we taking the emergency exit or the main entrance, Samuel?"

Heck, he was well oriented this Khan.

They crawled past the rocks at the emergency exit and then they were inside. Tor had left the steel door open now. Had probably not imagined any visitors. The case was closed. Then he spotted the three down on the OPS floor. They had taken Samuel. It had to be Khan this, he would avenge himself on Igor. The Vendetta from old or? But what role did Igor play now?

The shout echoed in the hall.

"Who are you with, Ivan?"

Khan turned around. "What do you think, Tor, because you are Tor, right?"

Khan had drawn his pistol. Was this a trap and where was this Ivan? Had he hidden himself behind some dusty obstacles?

"Igor, take a round and check if there is anyone else here, come forward with your gun!"

It began to come clear to Igor. So Khan thought there was an Ivan here as well. Maybe he did not know that Igor's field name was Ivan?

Skilled Khan, with control of every detail, here he had missed. What about shooting him? How to get away with a so-called accident?

But one more time, Khan could read his mind.

"I don't trust you, Igor. Never have. You're not Russian, you know!" He was close to him now. "I'm taking your gun."

And it was over before Igor could react.

"For sure, I know that we are colleagues in one way, colleagues, Russian officers both. But you're fake and I'll explain why I had to disarm you. Up to the bridge now, both of you. You first, Ivan, for it is you that Igor. Smart to try to fool me! Well, it was here in Gråkallen that you cooked it all together."

Khan is very clear. Samuel fades.

"We have not cooked anything. The drawings from Oksebåsen are okay. The CO2 plant is okay. You can see my copies of the drawings here."

But Khan just swept it to the side.

"The moon landing, Samuel. Let's get to the point. It is the one we have asked for, it is the one that Tor had promised us and that you should deliver and get paid for. Have you forgotten that?"

"It was never a case invented by us. It is the prime minister who has launched this expression."

"But you led us to believe that it was about a rocket base at the North Pole!"

"It's what we were told."

"By whom then? By your foreign minister? George Bush?"

Sarcasm shone now, and Igor had become pale, well knowing about Khan's anger.

Khan had made it clear to him that he now was the boss. Lavrov had given him all the powers.

"It may be that someone has posted this as a blind alley for us."

"How much do you believe in this yourself then Samuel?"

"I do not know, have only seen the notes and principal sketches from the United States. You have received copies of it all."

Samuel felt he had managed quite well, but now things began to unravel.

"What do you say, Ivan, or should I say, Igor, it is you who know these people? That is, you have not met your father since you were two years old."

The trump card was played. Igor knew nothing, but Samuel knew all too well. This could be the end and what about Astrid, his big sister?

"What do you mean? My father? He is dead at sea, some thirty years ago. And you knew all about it, Khan, yes, it happened long, long ago."

"The Cobra sent this envelope to use in case we needed it. This is your father, Igor. But it may also be that your mother's stepfather is your father. The stepfather fucked Astrid from the time she was twelve or thirteen. So who knows? But you were in any case christened Lars, but thereafter you were thrown in the ocean, i.e., up in a dinghy. Not in a sack, tied on hands and feet according to Mongolian custom. You remember that? Was it revenge you wanted? Now you have the chance, we were all deceived by your fathers, as well as he who is married to your mother. He's standing there in the doorway and maybe your mother is not completely unaware of this arrangement, either."

Tor had trouble grasping Khan's information. This was the reason for the crying in the Christmas party? But now death could be imminent, and he had no possibility for getting away. He joined the small group. Best to be close to the center of events.

He regretted now that both the Glock and the Beretta had been thrown in the garbage at the old Borispol airport in Kiev.

Igor was the one who had the hardest time. Should he believe in Khan?

"Are you able to even read the letter, Lars? You've specialized in Norwegian so far as I know. Then you can see for yourself what your grandmother writes about the two siblings. That they lay and had sex with each other as young people and that you were the result and that you were dumped in a dinghy to die."

Obviously, Igor had to read. "Is this true, Samuel, and how much have you known about this, Tor?"

Khan had sat down, smoked a cigar, and seemed very pleased with the play, as he called it.

"Samuel has to answer for himself, Lars, because it's Lars you were baptized then probably. We have to believe that."

"All I know is that Astrid and Samuel have been talking about an envelope that should contain things from their childhood. Things that they wanted to hide and that I never, never have wanted to know anything about."

"Do you want to talk about this, Samuel, now?"

"Because you have to."

"Do you want to talk about how the drawings were made up, Tor, because you have to."

"For my part, I choose to shut up." Samuel walked over to the OBS bridge and looked out. "The only thing I want to say is that my American contacts were very excited about the rocket base."

"Is it you or I that shall squeeze the truth out your father, Igor?"

But Igor was half paralyzed.

"Then it will be the two of us then, Samuel." Khan went against him. "Igor is too much of a coward to kill his father, but I do not work in cowardly FSB anymore. Have never done it either, but in GRU, we know how to use what we are trained to."

"To kill, Khan?"

"Yes, just that, Tor, when and if we must. And, Samuel, I want to know the truth. Now I connect the tape recorder. General Kuznevskov smells blood."

The stranglehold on Samuel was not strong enough to take his breath right away and good luck or was it bad luck? They both fell backward against the aluminium railing that was bent outward already and then it was over. On the concrete floor twelve meters down, they both lie with an unnatural position on their necks. The cord of Khan's tape recorder had wrapped around his right arm, which also had a twisted position.

Tor almost fainted when he looked down to the floor. Should the killings never end? He thought he was done with all this now and Igor? Or should he say Lars?

But Igor stood motionless, looking down on the remains of his father and arch-enemy Mongol Khan. Tor finally pulled himself together. How much should he tell Astrid?

Just that her brother was killed in an accident.

A fall of twelve meters down from the gallery in the OPS room and a broken neck?

And what about Lars? The FSB and later the SVR man with the pseudos, Igor and Ivan. Would he try to kill his uncle?

Not a word was uttered from Lars. Only after Tor had spoken to him several times, then it came: "I want to meet my mother."

"Then come to dinner and tell me that you are a Ukrainian businessman. But the bodies, Lars?"

"We have to remove all tracks here on the bridge. Then I remove everything on Khan. You take the papers, and then you will then make one anonymous call from a kiosk telling that those two corpses are found inside Gråkallen."

"And the money Samuel should have?"

"Take care of his wife or do whatever you want with them. Let's get out of here. Go to your hotel and call Samuel's home and pretend you want to meet him. Then you are in the clear. Assume you got up here without anyone seeing you."

"And you?"

"I get unseen from here and later to Oslo."

"Talk to Astrid or whatever you want. But I would like to meet her."

There was only a small notice in the Adressa newspaper.

"The police reported that they have found bodies of two men at Gråkallen. Perhaps it was a gang shooting. One was a foreigner."

A few days later, it was announced that Samuel had passed away after a heart attack, probably occurred on a run. The funeral took place in silence.

"Do you have it all now, my Astrid?"

"Just about that everything is over?"

"That's it, and then we draw the line here, my girl. But I have one Ukrainian businessman coming on a visit. No, this is not something fishy. He wants to see a Norwegian home."

"We'll talk about it later, Tor. Now it is you I need."

100

Epilogue 1

"There was a lot of commotion about this moon landing case in Norway, Donetski. SVR lost people and so did GRU."

"But I heard that General Kuznevskov has retired and that the Cobra had gotten his job?"

"Is he not in the SVR then?"

"Yes, but he had a past from Berlin and the same does Putin."

Lavrov overheard the comment and went on.

"It was especially bad with this GRU major that Little Father had met. And then we lost one in the office here."

"Who are you thinking of?"

"Yes, the liaison officer from the FSB. This Victor."

"Did not know he belonged to the FSB. I thought he was one of yours, Donetski?"

"And I, Comrade Lavrov, thought he was one of yours. Then we were both tricked. Someone found him outside the door of an old, shaggy officers' brothel up by the river somewhere. They had not bothered to remove the ID or other papers, just taken the wallet and given him two."

"Two, what do you mean?"

"One in the forehead and one in the neck."

Lavrov pretended not to hear.

"Scandal if it turns out that you have had such a man walking around here, Donetski!"

He was forced to swallow it.

"But it helped a little that we got planted our flag on the North Pole then."

Lavrov looked at him. "Are you trying to joke it away?"

"No but look here. One of our people in Washington sent me this clip from the *Washington Post*."

Lavrov put on his glasses. "Not quite clear this message."

Perhaps he would not admit that American English was not his strongest point. Donetski took the hint.

"I took the trouble to have it translated into Russian by an expert. Look at the attachment if you prefer."

"Maybe American is not your strength, Donetski?"

"Fair enough. Perhaps someone else also will see the notice."

"Are you thinking of Little Father?"

"You must not offend him with questions about his language skills. I think that to him it is a matter of principle that everything should be in Russian."

Lavrov lingered for a while on the translation. "He sure knows his job, this guy."

"But what about the content, Lavrov, the rocket base?"

"You mean the one we got drawings from in the end?"

"Yes, look at the context. Here we have the name of the idiot who went all in for it."

The note was not long: "It is with great sadness I confirm that the corpse of my twin brother was found one English mile from the North Pole. He had frozen to death. My brother who was a rocket scientist was all his adult life obsessed with the idea of developing the polar regions, especially the North Pole. It is rumoured that he was paid by FOX Television to carry out this, which became his last expedition. Likewise, it was forces from the Republican Party in Alaska that also contributed financially, with regard to the construction of a rocket base at the pole itself.

I can clearly deny these allegations. My brother's expeditions, even the one that became his last, were paid for by our family's trust funds—Oscar Harzlig LtCol."

"Obviously he had to deny it. But we are sitting on the drawings or, correct me, the copies of the drawings of the plant, Donetski."

"But for sure, it must be someone who started all this with the moon landing, Comrade Lavrov?"

"Obviously, but now we are ready and as possible next move, it will be *our* Moon Landing, Donetski. Where did the Third Man go, anyway?"

"I hope he is at home in Oslo now. He lost someone close as well."

"What shall we say to Little Father?"

"Not us, but I, Donetski. I will show him the clip from the *Washington Post* as well as the log that shows our proud Russian flags now flying at 90 degrees north. In solid rock, depth 4,261 meters."

101

Epilogue 2

It was over now for Tor. But not quite for Astrid who had lost her only brother. Heart attack? Yes, maybe it was like that.

But Tor had talked about that they could finally take a long trip together now.

She could apply for leave, and they could travel to Colorado to this nice couple Tor had met in Brasov. An American colonel who soon was to finish his service in Europe and then was going home.

"Were we not invited to Colorado to new friends of yours?"

"Yes, with the very warmest invitations from both the two adults and the four daughters."

"Send a mail then and ask if they will receive us, so can we go for walks in the mountains there and get away from all that has happened here."

"Will do that, but Theodore was supposed to have contacted me when he came to Oslo a month ago and now it has been five weeks. Maybe he has been transferred."

Tor found the card; there was an e-mail address. Just tried it and it seemed okay. A few days passed. He felt he had to send another email to check if they had gotten the first one

No answer. *Strange. I will phone instead,* he thought. No answer? Then he called NATO Headquarters in Brussels and asked for Theodore.

"Who is calling? I do not know you. Who should you talk to? Nobody knows that name here."

"But could it be someone working with you previously, and with this name?"

Sorry, she could not provide information on possible officials.

"You can send us a letter if you want."

Tor thanked her and hung up. This was too much.

He looked in his passport. Well then, he had been to Romania. Had ticket from Dracula castle and it had come money into the account of his in London and Samuel?

Samuel was dead! Undisputedly dead.

Did they look at him as a dangerous agent, the Americans? Had he still been the target at the taxi in Brasov?

Maybe it was right as it was said that Dracula was on the move again?

102

Epilogue 3

"And Stoltenberg's own moon landing, how did it go with that one, Grandfather?"

"I do not know, my friend."

"What do you not know? Say it then!"

"I do not know if Stoltenberg may have forgotten all about it."

"But then he will not go to the moon either, Grandfather?"

"No, I do not think so, my sweet!"

103

Epilogue 4

The metaphor Stoltenberg would have liked to have been left unsaid, yes, it got its sting of mercy on September 20, 2013.

When it got to the media, then many engineers had known about it for several months already?

The facility for CO_2 capture at Mongstad was stopped after it was realized that the goal of 100 percent purification could not be reached.

And the bill?

Yes, it would not be quantified, but media had the revised the numbers to 20, maybe 30, billion. Nobody knew exactly, no politician wanted to know either. Maybe not the Office of the Auditor General either?

But Neil Armstrong, the man on the Moon! He spent five days in Valdres, Norway, before passing away.

Nobody talked to him about the Norwegian moon landing, or did anyone?

Obs 33, 44 45 should not be in fat blocks
Map sketch Trondheim and Bymarka
Map sketch Romania, Transylvania and Dracula castle
Explantations, FBI, CIA, SVR, etc.
Person and place references:

Some explanations of concepts:

- FBI: Federal Bureau of Investigation (American)
- CIA: Central Intelligence Agency (American)
- FSB: Russian Civil Intelligence
- Domestic KGB: Former Russian Intelligence
- SVR: Russian civilian Intelligence, abroad
- GRU: Russian military Intelligence
- POT: Norwegian Intelligence surveillance service
- MI5: British special unit, intelligence, national protection

Some personal and place references (follows the novel's page progression):

- Stoltenberg: Norwegian prime minister 2006
- Arne Treholt: Norwegian official convicted of espionage
- Sakharov: Russian Nobel laureate, writer, and dissident
- Solzhenitsyn: Russian author and dissident
- "Ja til EF" ("Yes to the EEC"): the organization that fought for getting Norway into the EU, lost narrowly the referendum in 1972
- Stay Behind: Norwegian (?) organization that had significant stockpiles of weapons and that took care of organizations from the war period 1940–45. Should be a kind of new home front if the Russians invaded Norway
- Securitate: Romanian domestic police, security forces
- Stasi: East German security police

- Commissioner Donetski: key figure in Russian UD (Ministry of Foreign Affairs)
- Spetznaz: elite division, USSR
- Gromyko: former Secretary of the Soviet Union
- Lavrov: Foreign Minister Russia, 2011
- Jagland: Norwegian politician and prime minister, 1996–1997
- Kennedy: president of the United States, 1962–63
- Bay of Pigs: American possession, Cuba 1963
- Hoover: FBI chief in 1963
- Datcha: country house for Russian politicians and the wealthy ones
- Putin: president and later prime minister, Russia, then reelected again, maybe for life
- Little Father: mention of Czar/Emperor, also Putin
- Dypfjorden: large fjord in Finnmark
- Participating class: designation for submarine class
- Murmansk: Russian border against Norway, naval base
- Aker: major Norwegian industrial company
- Condeep: concrete-based drilling rigs
- Chechenia: republic of the former Soviet Union
- Hannah Montana: film character, American
- SINTEF: Norwegian Research Institute, Trondheim
- NASA: American Institute of Space Research
- Omar: the contact in Romania
- Ibsen: world-renowned Norwegian author
- The Cobra: codename of Russian KGB colonel
- Furua: bus stop and kiosk at Vollen, Asker
- Sandspollen: popular exit point by boat west of Oslo
- Oksebåsen: satellite launch base, Andøya Northern Norway
- The bank square: at the Fortress Oslo
- Stansted: airport west of London
- Brasov: biggest city in Transylvania, Romania
- Pandora's box: from Greek mythology. The box must not be opened, full of worms

- Trade: Department of Commerce
- Sjølyst: old exhibition area
- Grotten: restaurant and bar, closed, by Slottsparken
- Haugstvedt: former Minister of Trade KRF
- Kvaerner: Norwegian industrial company, now part of AKER
- Kremlin: Russian state headquarters, but also frequently used term for Russian interrogation chamber
- Jens Evensen: former Norwegian Minister of Trade
- Youngstorget: Labor Party bastion
- Hovedøya: the largest island right by the port of Oslo
- Nansen / Amundsen: Norwegian polar scientists and explorers
- The grey zone: negotiation area with the Russians in the North / Barents Sea
- Azerbaijan: former Soviet Republic
- Nittedal: area northeast of Oslo
- Vnestorgreklama: Russian central unit for advertising and marketing, Moscow
- Grefsen: small railway station, on the Gjovik line
- Technical Museum: large Museum, Grefsen
- East Station: older name for Oslo Central Station
- Hakadal: east of Oslo
- Movatn: station on the train to Hakadal
- Vaksholm: island in the Stockholm archipelago
- Blågulan: back road, inner road to Strømstad via Halden
- Fiskartorpet: world famous restaurant in Helsinki
- Titov: colonel in the KGB
- Victoria Terrace: Norwegian Ministry of Foreign Affairs
- The Moscow trials: purge trials from 1936–1938
- Cluj: Cluj Napocha, university city in Transylvania, Romania
- Lillomarka: outdoor area, east of Oslo
- Sundvollen: small town north of Oslo
- Sandvika: city west of Oslo
- Disco Borsa: large disco in Cluj

- Redcoat: special airport service, assistance
- Sonderabteilung: special mission within the police
- Vettre: small village west of Oslo
- Kolbotn: town east of Oslo
- Teaterk: Theatercafeen, restaurant, Oslo
- Britannia: top hotel Trondheim
- Gråkallen: closed air radar station, Bymarka, Trondheim
- Byåsen Shopping Center: small shopping center, Byåsen, Trondheim
- Gresvig: sports retailer
- Nordre: Nordre gate, street, Trondheim
- Bærum: municipality west of Oslo
- St. Mary's Church: Catholic Church, Trondheim
- Cathedral: the Cathedral, Trondheim
- RBK: Rosenborg Ballklub, football club, Trondheim
- Lund: Helge Lund, former CEO of Statoil (currently Equinor)
- Cape Canaveral: renowned launch base, Amr. Space base
- The rocket shield: negotiation object for protection against rocket attacks from e.g., North Korea
- OPS Hall/PPP Hall: the large plot hall for aircraft movements, Gråkallen
- Nille: retail store
- Storheia: Bymarka, Trondheim
- Lian: café, Bymarka, Trondheim
- Mongstad: oil refinery, Western Norway
- Bellona: organization, environmentalists
- Bush: former American president
- Bergan's: Norwegian leisure equipment manufacturer
- Mr. Hong: Chinese restaurant, Oslo
- Værnes: airport, Trondheim
- Skistua, café in Bymarka, Trondheim
- Kuznevskov: colonel, GRU
- Thon Helsfyr: hotel in the Thon hotel chain
- Ås: small town to the south of Oslo
- Délite

- Leopards: Special Forces Soviet and parts of the Eastern bloc
- Wizz air: Hungarian low-cost airline
- Pyongyang: capital, North Korea
- Aro Palace: giant hotel from the communist era, Brasov
- Vladivostok: Russian border city
- Mossad: Israeli Intelligence
- Pentagon: US military headquarters
- Ceausescu: former dictator of Romania
- Tupolev: Russian aircraft type
- Mirage: French aircraft
- PHD: PhD (doctorate)
- Sighisoara: Transylvanian city
- Novaya Zemlya: Russian island, Northern Areas
- Casa Wagner: hotel in Sighisoara
- Tarantula: type of spider
- Sibiu: Transylvanian city
- Marburg: German city
- Satu Mare: village in Transylvania
- Sapânta: town with the world's only cemetery with blue-painted tombstones
- Sighetu Marmatiei: Transylvanian border
- E-14: secret Norwegian spy organization
- Andressa: the newspaper Adresseavisen, Trondheim
- Fox: Fox Television, conservative American broadcaster
- Denver, Colorado: American city

www.ingramcontent.com/pod-product-compliance
Lightning Source LLC
Chambersburg PA
CBHW030702190726

48286CB00001B/133